"YOU INTRIGUE ME, DEBA McCLOUD."

Deba heaved herself up and out of the pool. As she reached for a towel her mouth opened to retort when she caught the hot gaze roving her body. "And I'm not a piece of meat on a hook that you get to make a choice on, either."

"You're too slender, but you do have a wonderful body."

The heat from Wolf's words made the lake steam . . . or was that just her imagination? "I'll type, collate, take dictation . . . even make your coffee, but you get someone else to warm your bed."

"Sounds fair," he drawled, his eyes seeming to pierce the toweling material that she'd wrapped around herself. "I admire the *Mona Lisa,* Deba McCloud. I have never tried to take it home."

"They'd shoot you if you did," Deba muttered.

"Why do I get the feeling you'd be there with your gun?"

"Lucky guess?"

D1315195

Also by Helen Mittermeyer from Dell:

BRIEF ENCOUNTER

DIAMOND FIRE

◊

Helen Mittermeyer

A DELL BOOK

Published by
Dell Publishing
a division of
Bantam Doubleday Dell Publishing Group, Inc.
666 Fifth Avenue
New York, New York 10103

ISBN: 0-440-20260-4

Printed in the United States of America
Published simultaneously in Canada

April 1989

10 9 8 7 6 5 4 3 2 1

KRI

DIAMOND
FIRE

Wolf Clinton had had a long ride in the heat. Though the Mexican mesa was high and there was always a breeze, both horse and man glistened with sweat as they watched and listened to the cacophony of voices below the knoll near the front gate. Wolf and his horse were shaded and somewhat screened from the snakelike line of people who sought bit parts in the movie being filmed on his land.

Many times he'd regretted the decision to allow the movie company to film on his Rancho Lobo, though he'd taken various steps to see that his privacy wouldn't be violated.

But . . . right now, at that moment, the scenery was intriguing. His interest was more than piqued by the woman. Who was the leggy, lissome creature who stood head and shoulders over the other hopefuls? The blond, slightly curling hair and too slender body would not fit any of the parts being cast as he recalled the script. Too slim and too beautiful, a desert diamond that caught the eye. Not only her coloring set her apart. There was a sensuous, high-spirited aura that tinted her world. Did her eyes have a turquoise sparkle? It was too far to be certain.

He wanted her. The familiar thread of desire ran through his lower body. He was tempted to know more about her, to ask questions of Diego, who was producing the movie, but he held back. Years of safeguarding his privacy kept him still. But . . . she damn well excited him. Damn it! He was no randy, un-fledged boy.

Starving to death was not a viable alternative, and she'd already lost about ten pounds she couldn't afford. She was go-ing to get a job, come hell or high water.

It was hard to ignore the cold perspiration dampening her underarms. Hot sweat beaded her upper lip. What could he do? Kill her? Why shouldn't El Lobo have a crack at her? Others were trying. She was being fanciful. Maybe the heat was getting to her.

Would Aldebaran McCloud Beene, who had shortened her name to Deba, ever have taken the long shot of trying for a part had she not been stranded in Mexico? Maybe not, but there was no time to psychologize her actions now.

"Let the games begin," she murmured, blowing upward to see if she could cool her forehead and lift some of the strands of hair that clung there, limp and wet.

"Did you say something, senorita?" one of the women in front of her asked cautiously.

"I talk to myself," Deba explained in fairly fluent Spanish.

"Ahh." The woman moved closer to her friend, suspicion deepening on her face.

Deba was on the property of the man referred to, in the tabloids, as the Yankee Sultan, Wolfgang Clinton. Called Lobo by some, friend and foe, he lived on an estate that would have been considered a fiefdom in medieval Europe. "Doesn't the man accept the twentieth century?"

"Qué?"

"Ah, nothing. Just rambling."

The two women moved even further away from Deba.

"Rich bastard," Deba muttered, willing her body not to retreat, but to go steadily forward. She pressed her hand to her forehead, feeling a little dizzy.

The two women glanced askance at her, then scurried for-ward once more.

What was a cattle call like in Mexico? Was casting for a movie the same as in the United States? Deba wished she knew more about moviemaking, but as with many of the other jobs she'd had, she only had a surface knowledge of the business.

The line inched forward.

Some said Lobo Clinton's holdings in Mexico were the size of Rhode Island. Others said they were only the tip of the iceberg.

No one really knew how much property, money, and people he controlled. What did it matter? She only wanted a sliver of it, enough to keep food in her stomach and clothing on her back.

With a little luck he wouldn't kill her. After all, he did have the devil's own reputation. With heaven's grace she might even have a job by nightfall. Was that a contradiction in terms? Having a job with the devil with heaven's intervention? Lord, the sun was getting to her.

Lobo Clinton was a mystery. Let him stay that way. If she got a job, surely she would be dealing with his minions anyway, perhaps never even seeing him. Yes! Be confident. Put aside the negative. Rely on the positive.

The line inched forward. Damn! It was so hot. Wasn't anyone else bothered by the extreme heat?

Deba looked around her at the clusters of people looking for a job.

Mexico was a changed country, or so she was told by various inhabitants. Gone were the great vestiges of poverty and deprivation. Things were changing, there were more goods available, and more people were employed. Citizens worked and were unafraid.

Maybe that was so. Deba McCloud smiled and nodded when people said that to her, but she didn't accept it totally. She was in Mexico and she was certainly in the grip of poverty, with no money, no prospects, slim pickings. It would be great if that changed.

If you had money you could be independent and sightsee and buy anything you chose, but if you were an American and had been abandoned by a shoestring movie company in a foreign country, with just a few dollars in your pocket, it was a different story.

Maybe if she hadn't had to keep such a low profile she could've gone to the United States embassy with her hardship story . . . but she was wary of even the hint of publicity. She might still have to do that, but she was leaving it as a last resort. Being detained by anyone, even the United States government, was not something she sought. Anything that could focus attention on her was to be avoided. There was too much at stake to risk exposure. Even a preliminary investigation might uncover too much. That could be dangerous, and not only to her but to her beloved parents in the Witness Protection Program. Could the United States government protect them? Maybe.

"You're being silly, Aldebaran. The embassy will help you." Her Mexican friend, Maria Delgado, who was one of the few who used her full name or even knew it, had been adamant when they'd talked yesterday. "I'm sure they get wilder stories than yours, and from what I hear, they come through with help most of the time. I've had friends tell me that this was true."

Deba nodded at the friend she'd known since arriving in Mexico. The total rapport between them still amazed her, and it had happened almost at once. Maria was one of the few who knew anything at all about Deba . . . and she didn't know much.

Deba was fond of Maria, but not even the sweet, smiling young woman who'd taken her in knew the complete story of Aldebaran McCloud Beene, called Deba McCloud. "Maybe you're right." Deba's gaze slid away from Maria's. "I promise to look into it if all else fails." She would get out of the country fast before there was an investigation into Deba McCloud.

Maria frowned at her. "I think you're going about this the wrong way, Aldebaran. You're making foot bricks for yourself."

"Stumbling blocks," Deba corrected absently.

"That's what I said."

"I'm going to sift through my options before I decide on a course of action. I can't tell you how grateful I am that you let me stay here."

"That has been no trouble, Aldebaran," Maria answered testily. "It's just that you are going about all this in the wrong way."

Deba shrugged. "It won't be the first time. Tell me again about that job a friend described to you, Maria."

Maria shook her head. "Some of these things are pigs in the poke, as I used to say when I went to school in the States."

Deba smiled. Maria had been schooled in the United States, but some of the vernacular had escaped her completely.

Maria bit her lip. "But this is work in a movie being shot right here on Lobo Clinton's rancho outside Mexico City. This movie will be made by Mexicans and not Americans, so maybe you won't be stranded this time without pay or housing." Maria giggled.

"Very funny." Deba grinned at the woman who'd been a true friend to her when she'd been alone and without funds. Maria had been an extra on the same movie as Deba and had generously shared her one-room apartment and her food.

"Perhaps you should have stuck to your job in New York as editor on a magazine," Maria ventured.

Deba sighed. "I was hardly the editor. I was the lowest rung on the ladder, more like a gofer than anything else." And that was ten jobs ago, but she didn't tell Maria that. "I did manage to pick up a few tidbits about the writing business along the way. Very intriguing." She grinned at her friend. "I discovered that a good way to make money is to do a biography on someone important."

"Do you know anyone like that?" Maria stared at her.

"Just you."

"Now you are joking. But if it's a good way to make money . . ."

"It is, but I haven't the talent for it. What interests me is eating money for the present."

Maria shrugged, grimacing. "You should be able to get a very romantic job. Your name, Aldebaran, is so *muy buena,* especially after you told me what it means. Imagine being named for the brightest star in the constellation of Taurus. Your mother must have loved Byron. It sounds like a name he might use."

Deba laughed. "Why? Because I was born on April 29th under the sign of Taurus?" At the mention of her mother, Deba's insides twisted. Would she ever see her parents again? Sometimes it seemed as though she never would. "Actually, both my parents loved Byron." Deba bit her lip, trying not to think of the gentle people who'd nurtured her and who were now caught in a web of another's making.

"*Sí.* I knew that."

Deba smiled, tamping down the searing desire to talk to her mother and father. It was better to attempt little communication with them, safer for them . . . and for her. Japan was far enough away to keep in loose contact, and that's where her parents were at the moment. They never stayed in one place too long, ostensibly collecting data for a book. Actually, they traveled under the express directions of the Witness Protection Pro-

gram, which was safeguarding them. Deba often felt uneasy.
Hadn't there been cases where the people in the program were
discovered and killed? Imagining such a thing happening to her
parents made her blood freeze in her veins.

There were many days when Deba doubted the WPP.
She'd had a few close calls herself. Her parents were in constant
jeopardy; they had to be ever vigilant. And that was a particular
hell in her life.

"You are thinking of your mother and father, Aldebaran.
Are you not?"

Deba nodded.

"But you will not tell me about them?"

Deba shook her head, her throat clogged with tears.

"Then they do not know that you were in a movie here in
Mexico when the company folded?"

"Don't ask me any more, Maria. Please."

Maria had patted her arm and nodded.

Even now as she recalled that conversation with Maria, her
mind tumbled with thoughts of her parents.

God! It was so hot. The Mexican sun blistered down on
Deba's head even as she huddled into the small amount of
shade offered by a nearby dusty tree.

Mother and father! They had the credentials to be researching a book on the ancient Shinto religion and the people
who had inhabited the Japanese islands many centuries ago.
Her father and mother had been professors of paleontology, and
the research provided a good cover for them now that they
could no longer teach. Could the WPP protect them when the
people after them were cunning and persistent?

Deba couldn't contact them about her penury. It was too
small a reason to risk breaking cover. Though her parents had
told her to get in touch with them at any time, whenever she
needed them, she couldn't bring herself to put them at risk.

When her parents had gone into protective hiding, so had
she, leaving the university she loved in her junior year and
going to New York to look for work. Would her family ever be
free to be themselves?

Deba had taken her small savings and risked it on a job
chance in Manhattan. It had been fun to work on a magazine,
but when she'd been there less than a year, she'd been told by
her parents that she could be at risk. She'd left the job the same
week.

She'd worked her way to the West Coast doing odd jobs. It had been in Los Angeles that she'd tried out for a movie that had been casting and had been thrilled when she'd landed a part. The idea of going to Mexico had great appeal. No one knew her there. Her part called for a dark wig that made her unrecognizable. She had been so eager to go and in such a hurry to leave that she hadn't bothered to get her visa validated.

When the film company folded because the money source disappeared, she'd been left high and dry. Not that she was that anxious to get back to the United States. She wasn't, but she needed a job, something, anything, to support herself.

Now it was the day after her conversation with Maria. She'd risen early that morning and dressed in her last good outfit that hadn't been washed into rag softness.

Juan, Maria's cousin, had driven out to the rancho in his taxi. "The location for the film is right on the property," Juan had told her in hushed tones. "It is my first time on this rancho."

"Mine too," Deba had whispered back.

"*Sí*, you will like it. Good-bye."

Juan had departed in a whirl of dust and Deba took her place at the end of the serpentine of hopefuls. How many jobs were there? Who would be hired? All? Or none?

All strata of society were represented, all the women lovely, many downright beautiful. The men were young, dashing, and confident.

That had been two hours ago when she'd first gotten in line. Deba licked her lips, trying to find some moisture for her desert-dry mouth and throat as she moved slowly in the arid heat toward a wooden open-sided structure where several men sat talking to various aspirants.

Deba didn't know when she became aware of someone staring at her.

"Look, that is The Lobo himself. Wolf Clinton," the woman in front of Deba whispered to her companion. "It is his land that the movie will be made on, so there will be good food and nice places to sleep, I am sure. He is supposed to own a good deal of Mexico now. He's into drugs, I think."

The rapid dialectic Spanish was hard to understand, but Deba got the gist of it.

"And women, and jewels," the friend whispered back. "He is one bad hombre, I know this. My mama, she tell me . . ."

The voices faded.

Deba found herself staring at the man in question. It jarred her when he seemed to be staring back at her, but she couldn't be quite sure, since he wore reflecting sunglasses that hid his eyes. The huge bay horse under him whinnied and sidled, though the master had stayed still as a statue. He was a Titan, with hair the color of coal oil, heavy brows over . . . What color were those eyes? Devil black? He had to be tall—his long, sinewed legs hung low on the horse that had to be more than sixteen hands high. His chest was wide, but he wasn't burly. He looked strong, smoothly muscled. A lumberjack in designer sport clothes? Who was he?

Then in slow, sure moves, the large animal stepped lightly over the dusty, stony ground, heading in her direction.

Deba looked away but could tell, in her peripheral vision, that the horseman was going to pass very close to her.

The line moved another foot and she moved with it, out of the shade into the blistering sunshine. Not even the breeze ameliorated the stifling heat.

"Your fair coloring is not for this clime, senorita." The horseman manuvered the large bay into a position so that Aldebaran was somewhat shaded. He looked down at her like a leonine statue of old Rome, come to life.

"Thank you, senor. I'm fine." The huskiness in her voice surprised Deba. Dry, dry throat. She was well aware that the two women in line in front of her were straining to hear every word.

"Your Spanish is very good, but I sense it is not your first language, senorita."

"No, senor, I'm American, from . . . America." White teeth flashed in that tanned visage at her answer, and Deba caught her breath.

"There will be no part for you in this movie, senorita. I know the script and know what they're casting for quite well. I suggest that you get out of this hot line and . . ."

"No!" Deba waved a hand in front of her face, seeing hot spots in front of her eyes. The heat was like an unbearably heavy blanket. "I need this job, senor. I won't get out of line."

A large hand leaned down and took hold of her arm, steadying her. "Even if you faint? This weather is not for you, child. Come, step on my boot and swing up behind me. I'll take you to the hacienda, where you can get a cool drink."

Deba's protests died aborning as she felt her weight lifted upward. It was either swing up behind him or dangle at the side of the horse from that strong arm. "But if I get out of line . . ."

"Don't worry. If you need a job so desperately, talk to me. I'm Wolf Clinton."

If he hadn't been steadying her, Deba would have fallen off the horse. The women had said it was he, but she hadn't really believed it. His eyes would be devil black. Definitely!

Deba was reeling, and not just from the heat. Had Lobo Clinton offered her a job? Was she hallucinating? Probably. She had to swallow four times to moisten her mouth enough so that she could speak. "About work?" Her voice was almost hoarse.

"If you qualify I could have work for you, that's true, and that's the only work you'll get around here. Your coloring is all wrong for the parts they're casting." Wolf slanted a look over his shoulder. "You're very pale."

"Always have been," Deba said huskily, fighting a great fatigue all at once. "Tell me more about the job."

"My assistant left today. He returned to England to care for his aging mother, and when he returns to my employ he'll be staying in the London office to be close to her. Would you like to interview for that job?" Wolf Clinton asked over his shoulder as they trotted past the uneven line of upturned faces.

"If this is a come-on, it isn't too original," Deba muttered, reeling a little, then gripping his shirt tightly.

"What did you say?"

"Nothing." The heat hurt her head.

"*Madre de Dios,* that must be his new lady," someone in line observed sotto voce, the sound reaching Deba's ears.

"You're wrong about that." The words were little more than a croak, not even carrying to the line of hopefuls.

"Maybe you'd better be quiet until you've had a cool drink."

Deba wanted to tell him to go suck an egg, but she was too fatigued all at once. She put her forehead against his back and closed her eyes. Why was he offering her a job? What was in it for him? How much would he pay? Anything was better than nothing. If only she could salivate.

"Would you be interested in the job?"

His words vibrated through his back to her face.

Deba nodded once, hoping he could feel the action and interpret it.

"Good, it will pay far more than you would get on Diego's set. He is a very clever man, and his flicks make money or else I wouldn't back him, but he tends to be rather clutch-fisted with his employees."

Deba had already discovered a great many people with that affliction. She nodded again. Then she could feel Wolf Clinton's rumbling laugh through his back. He had understood.

All at once the horse jumped into a run and Deba's hands, which had been lightly gripping his shirt, clutched around his hard, spare middle.

"I will get you out of the sun as quickly as possible. It was foolish of you to tackle this project without a hat, senorita."

Deba formulated a tart reply in her brain, but her mouth didn't work, so she said nothing. After all, words did have a way of fading into the wind, especially since the horse had moved from an easy canter into a gallop. And her throat was so tight and dry it threatened to close completely. "I'm Deba McCloud," she managed hoarsely.

"Ah, a beautiful name. Is it your own?"

Deba nodded against his shirt back. Well, really, it was. She'd been christened Aldebaran McCloud Beene.

"Drop the Beene from your name, child. It will go easier for you." The gentle man who was her father had had a rock-hard look to him at the moment he'd told her that just before she'd parted from them. "Your mother and I insist on it, my dear."

"All right, Father." Deba had cried herself to sleep that night, after her folks had bid her adieu. She hadn't seen them since.

They reached a small knoll, pausing at the apex for a moment. Deba lifted her heavy head for a look and gasped. She'd never seen such a beautiful cluster of buildings, all of pale pink adobe with terrazzo roofs of a deeper hue, and forest green trimming the shutters.

The center of the widespread cluster was an oversized hacienda with a center court and closed gate. Deba licked her lips and swallowed twice. "Your home is lovely, Senor . . . Clinton."

"Thank you. I imagine I was described to you by those in

line as the greatest *bandido* in all Mexico?" He removed his sunglasses a moment.

"Certainly in the top five," Deba muttered, rocking on her perch when he turned to her and chuckled. His eyes weren't black! Where had he gotten those leonine eyes, the golden irises with coal black rims?

It was when Lobo Clinton urged his steed down the incline that she felt the nausea along with the dizziness. Deba tried to swallow again, but her tongue felt swollen, her throat dry. There was a ringing in her ears that increased until she couldn't make out what Clinton was saying.

When he dismounted from his horse in front of the hacienda, she squinted down at him, trying to read his lips. It was a relief to slide off the horse into his arms.

Sweeping her limp body high into his grasp, Clinton strode across the paved outer court, calling to his people. "Julia, come at once, and bring ice. Pablo, go to the kitchen and brew some of the special tea, bring it to my study. *Rápido.*"

Stalking down the wide center corridor floored in terra cotta tiles, Clinton kicked open a heavy oaken door, making the round brass decorative knockers jangle discordantly.

"What is it, senor? Heat stroke?" Julia bustled in behind him, placid and capable, carrying an ice bag. "I will take her up to a guest room and minister to her."

"Fine . . . later. Right now, put the ice on her head. Damn Pablo. Where is he? I want the tea."

"It will, how do you say, knock her out, senor," Julia observed calmly. "The special tea from the cocoa leaves is very strong."

"She's out of it now." Clinton laughed harshly. "But she needs the healing sleep the tea will give her. I think she's suffering from exhaustion and she's too damn thin. When she wakens sometime tomorrow I will be interviewing her for Crandall's job, Julia."

"No! *You* would have a woman around you? I don't think so," she announced with the ease of a valued employee.

"I love women around me, Julia," Wolf drawled, his eyes flashing toward the plump custodian of his house. "You're here."

"Ha! As if I were the kind of woman who would crawl up and down your vest, senor, like the light of loves you have in the city. I am not one of those long-legged creatures with an eye for gold and hands that fasten to a man until he gives it to them."

"You're more of a cynic than I, Julia. Ah, here's the tea. Put it there, Pablo, I will feed it to her." Clinton put an arm under Deba's head, the motion stirring her to her surroundings once more. "No, no, don't struggle, I want to give you something that will make you better. That's it, drink it down, all of it."

Julia lifted the limp hand and held her fingers on the pulse. *"Sí,* her pulse is slowing. Soon she will be asleep."

Wolf gave her the cup and waved her aside. Leaning down and lifting the woman on the couch as though she were weightless, he stared at his housekeeper. "I'm putting her in the Turquoise Suite."

"But that is next to your own, senor. It is not proper, and . . ."

"Julia, no more." The soft command lanced around the room like a velvet spear, silencing everyone and bringing Pablo to attention.

"You talk too much," Pablo said from the side of his mouth as he and Julia followed the master out to the hall again and watched him climb the curving stairway that hugged the wall of the foyer.

"Hush, fool. Isn't it better that I tell the senor that he should stay away from all women rather than risk his life with another Natasha?"

"Quiet! How dare you mention her name? You know it is not permitted. The senor has ordered it."

"Ah, bah." Julia stalked toward the kitchen. "I have soup to make for the senorita. When she wakens she'll be hungry."

Wolf Clinton placed his burden on the huge bed, slapping away the netting that was the same turquoise hue as the bedspread, and stared down at the woman. He was a fool for allowing her into his house. After years of privacy and having a close-kept household, he was stupid to let a stranger enter and reside. Why did he want to keep her near him? The question irritated and puzzled him, and he pushed it from his brain. Wasn't there room enough for her in one of the guest houses? She would be well taken care of, provided for just as carefully as she would be here. Besides, if she took the job he offered, wouldn't she be staying in a guest cottage anyway? Maybe she would not recall the job offer. With sour acceptance he realized he would make the offer again.

What the hell was the matter with him? Had the sun gotten to him, too? He'd spent years and a great deal of money trying to protect his privacy. Why would he jeopardize it now?

Deba's eyes flickered open and she stared at the man who loomed above her. His twisted smile seemed to stretch the skin on that hard-planed face as though it wasn't used to the exercise.

"Hello . . . Mr. Clinton. I never faint."

"And you didn't this time. You were just hazy and unsteady. Soon you'll sleep."

"There are two of you." Deba reached up a hand to touch his face. "It should feel like steel but it's soft . . . and hard. Foolish." Her words slurred and she laughed. "You're a sultan. The women in front of me in line called you that."

"Then this must be my seraglio."

Deba squinted at him. "Try anything with me and I'll deck you." Her hand fell to her side and she giggled. "Wouldn't that be something? Deba McCloud punches Wolf Clinton's lights out. That would be funny." Deba fell asleep so suddenly that her mouth was still open, laughing, as she slipped into unconsciousness.

"Have you issued a challenge to me, Deba McCloud? Intriguing." His heart thudded against his ribs. He felt an exhilaration that he thought had gone from his life; his body tingled with a need to know Deba McCloud.

2

Wolf Clinton straightened when he heard the unmistakable sound of Julia's crisp apron rustling toward them. Sighing, he turned to face her. Not surprised when he saw her scowl, he put his hand up, palm outward. "Don't lecture."

"You never bring your women here. You take them to the Casa Rojo," Julia stated firmly. "You did not tell me that anyone was coming today."

"Never mind that. She'll be staying . . . and working. Stop looking so offended."

"You do not hire people so quickly—"

"Julia!"

The peremptory tone brought Julia's lips together in a tight line. Though she frowned at him, she was silent. "And will she continue to use this suite?"

Clinton had had misgivings about putting Deba McCloud in the Turquoise Suite. Only his mother and stepfather—and Natasha—had ever stayed there. He'd never wanted or let anyone else get that close to him since he'd come to Mexico. After he lost his mother and stepfather, and since Natasha would never again come to Rancho Lobo, the Turquoise Suite had virtually become part of the master suite. He couldn't explain why he'd put Deba McCloud into it . . . not even to himself.

All the years he'd spent building up barriers, walls as shields, space between himself and the unfriendly world he'd left behind in Europe, Asia, and the United States, and now everything seemed to be trembling on the brink of destruction because of his gesture. Was the life of total privacy he'd fought for and struggled to keep to disintegrate now? No! He hadn't changed his mind about that. "I haven't made up my mind about that," he told Julia in answer to her query.

"Humph."

Her angry exhalation interrupted his grim reverie. "Well?" There was a lacing of irritation in his voice.

The housekeeper lifted her chin and stared straight at him. "I do not like you to be angry, senor, but I must remind you that you have said you were through with your Americano life. Many times you said it."

"Yes, yes, but—"

"You said those people were not for you, that they were cruel, nasty—"

"And boring. I said I would be brain dead if I continued, but I didn't say it to you, I said it to Crandall."

"Sí, I overheard you say it. No more spotlight, no more celebrity life—"

"Does this young woman look like a celebrity to you, Julia?"

"You understand me very well, senor," Julia said sternly, with the determination only a valued employee would dare.

"Julia, I don't want to hear any more."

"Sí, I know. But you are forty-one years old and do not need the other life. You have plenty of money. You are happy here," she pursued doggedly.

"All right, Julia, that's enough."

"Sí." Julia frowned at the bed, then flounced out of the room.

It was true he didn't want the other life. When he did travel to Europe or the United States he went incognito. His frantic search for plastic pleasure was done.

Wolf Clinton looked down at the too slender form on the bed and felt a familiar stirring of desire . . . and more. It baffled him. He wanted her, and that he understood. There had been more than one woman he'd wanted on sight. But . . . he'd never felt so protective about someone, except Natasha. Where had that feeling come from? Why with Deba McCloud?

He should put her in the guest wing.

Julia reentered with another tray, carrying ice and cold cloths. "I will put these on her forehead, senor. Shall I ready a guest room?"

Wolf shot a sharp look at his tight-lipped employee. "Let her sleep. When she wakens we will see to getting her things brought out here."

"Sí, señor." Julia turned stiffly and left the room.

Wolf returned upstairs after spending several hours working in his study. The study had become the heart of his empire, and from it he dictated the policy and procedure of his worldwide holdings. Yawning, he stripped the wrinkled cottons from his body, striding toward the shower.

It would be a solitary, late meal, but he had always showered and dressed for his evening repast, whether he had company or dined alone.

Earlier in the day he'd toyed with the idea of taking the helicopter to Casa Rojo, but he'd changed his mind. The need for a woman had blurred somewhat through the day.

Wolf Clinton treasured his privacy and enjoyed his solitude. After years in the public eye, he relished the times he could read a book, cogitate, meditate, or just plain relax.

His hand worried the scar that traveled from the corner of his left eye down to his chin. It had been years since it had happened, and the mark had faded. Yet, even now, remembering how he got it made his hands curl into fists.

When the door opened from the other suite, the habits of survival made him drop low and swing around, his hand fumbling in the drawer for the handgun he kept there.

"Oops." Deba blinked at the gun, then at the man in a crouched, threatening position. "My mouth feels like the bottom of a bird cage. What was in that damned tea you gave me?"

"I applaud your insouciance, Miss McCloud. Most people are alarmed at seeing a gun pointed at them."

"I hate the stupid things, but I've seen a great deal of them since coming to this country." She stared at him for a moment. "Stress makes that facial scar stand out white against your brown skin. Dramatic . . . but not unattractive."

"I'm quite sure there are more guns in your country." Wolf ignored her clinical study of his features.

"Maybe. But isn't the United States your country, Mr.

Clinton?" Seating herself on his bed, she curled one arm around
the Spanish-carved poster at the foot and stared at him. "I don't
know too much about you, it was before my time, but I'm sure I
recall that you're American."

"I was. I'm now a Mexican citizen."

"And I'll bet you haven't given up your American citizenship, either."

"Are you taking a survey, Miss McCloud?"

"That question must have stung. You have a touch of red
in your cheeks, and that scar is whiter than ever." Deba
yawned. "Thanks for the tea—I think—but I should go. What
was in that brew? Peyote?" She gave him a crooked smile.
"Never mind. I can see you're busy getting spiffed up. Hot
date?"

"Would you like to join me?" The woman was most irritating. He wasn't used to being quizzed about his dining compan-
ions, and she had a carefree attitude that puzzled him.

"Ah, I would love to, but I had better get back. I have a
friend who will be waiting for my call to come and pick me up."

Wolf shrugged. "Suit yourself, but I thought you were desperate for a job."

"I am, but I think I've pricked your skin more than once,
Mr. Clinton, and I have no desire to join a seraglio, even in
Mexico."

"What makes you think you'd be invited to join?"

The silky question wrapped around her like a whip and
Deba blinked, getting down from the bed and facing the man in
front of her with her hands clenched. "There is that, of course,"
she answered him quietly.

Wolf noted the wariness, the deeply indrawn breath. She
was going to stand her ground. Was it her courage that drew
him to her? "Why don't you call your friend, tell her you're
having dinner? If during dinner we both decide it would be
mutually beneficial for you to have the job, we'll go with it. If
not, at least you will have had one of Julia's dinners, which are
always exceptional." He watched the play of emotions over
those mobile features, sensing a desperation that she tried to
mask.

"Done. No problems and no come-ons. Agreed?" Chin
lifted, Deba challenged him.

Clinton was more than a little irked. The chit was dictating
policy in his home. "Done." He should have shown her the

door. When she put out her hand, he grasped it with his own, feeling the fragile bone structure but surprised by the strength of her grip. She was fey, unreal, but as earthy as any woman he'd ever met. And she was sensuous and exciting and aroused him unbelievably. Damn her! He could feel the muscles in his lower body harden just by looking at her. That irritated him.

Deba looked down at herself. "On second thought it might be better if I back out of the dinner. I'm pretty wrinkled, and . . ."

"Don't worry, Julia will have something for you. I'll call her."

"Keep a store, do you?"

"Something like that." The brat really got under his skin.

Julia's overt displeasure added to Deba's own certainty that she had made a mistake by agreeing to dine with Wolfgang Clinton, called Lobo by so many.

Funny! Wolfgang Clinton didn't refer to himself as Lobo. Maybe not so funny. Wolves were canny, secretive creatures.

As she sat on the bed in the Turquoise Suite she pondered her host. What did anyone know about Wolfgang Clinton? Wracking her brain, she tried to come up with the few scraps of information she had on him.

He made money quickly and easily in TV and cinema. He'd even starred in a few movies and directed many. He'd built up a cult of cinema followers until . . .

"Senorita, you will try on this dress, please." Julia had entered the room quietly. Now she held up a pale peach cotton dress, hand-embroidered. The dress had a square neckline that could be worn off the shoulder or on. Its skirt was tight at the waist, ruffled, and flaring at the ankles.

"Your eyes looked like the metal we mine in this area," Julia said gruffly, her mien having an affronted cast. She brushed Deba aside when she was about to pick up the hairbrush on the dresser. "I will fix your hair for you . . . swept high and off your neck. Even though this house is very cool, the heat can penetrate the body."

"Thank you, Julia."

"Nada." With a few quick twists she caught Deba's blond hair and twisted it into a thick bun at the crown of her head, leaving tendrils to fall about her face. "There. Now you will be cool." Julia shook her head. "You are beautiful."

The sad surprise in Julia's voice elicited a startled chortle from Deba. The laughter faded at Julia's dour look. "Thank you, Julia. You're very kind to help me. I'll just use the phone before I go downstairs."

"The senor told me that you would want to make a call. I will dial out of here so that you can make your call."

"You mean I can't just dial the number?"

Julia shook her head. "There is a central switchboard. All the calls go through it, except for the one private line of the senor's." Julia sniffed, then went to the phone, her back to Deba. She dialed, speaking softly into the phone.

Deba moved toward the housekeeper, who handed her the phone and then left the room. Deba could hear the whirr and crank as the call was put through. "Maria, please don't shout. No, no, there's nothing wrong. Yes, I know you and Juan must have been worried. But everything is fine . . . and with luck I may have a job. Really. I'll call you tomorrow. I promise."

Sometime later, Deba followed the directions Julia had given to the first floor before she'd left the bedroom. The solarium at the back of the house was her destination.

The house had many twists and turns, like a colorful maze, its adobe walls cool and painted the palest pink.

Finally, Deba found the room she sought.

Wolf Clinton was standing at a window wall watching the spectacular sunset. Deba coughed to get his attention.

He turned, drink in hand, his clothing looking aesthetically pristine against his darkened skin. "I have a glass of juice for you. Come over here and watch the sunset."

Deba approached him, gazing out the window at the lazily deepening kaleidoscope, the corals, oranges, blues, yellows stunning her eyes. Deba felt his eyes on her, not on the panorama in front of her.

Wolf handed her a tall glass of frosty papaya juice. "You're beautiful, like the wild spirit that is said to inhabit the desert area around here. Many of my Indian people are convinced that they have communicated with the spirit. Do you inhabit the desert at night?"

The whisper touched her like nettles, her skin quivering with a sensitized awareness of danger. Had he killed people? The people in Mexico seemed to feel that he would dare anything, that he had committed numerous crimes. Wolf Clinton

was a daring and mysterious legend to them. "I'm . . . not
. . . that . . . familiar with the desert."

"There's a quaver of fear in your voice, Miss Deba
McCloud. Because of me?"

"Yes."

"You fear me?" He went to the small bar in the corner and
freshened his own drink.

"Let's say I respect the power you have." Deba watched
him over the rim of her glass as he returned to her. The silk
shirt he wore was colored in shades of turquoise and coral. It
hung straight from his shoulders, loose, not quite reaching his
midsection. There was a tantalizing band of skin showing above
the black silk trousers, which were loose, tapering to a tight cuff
above the ankle. His feet were shod in black leather espadrilles.

"Why have you hidden yourself from the world?"

Her question stopped his motion toward her as though
he'd hit a wall.

"How to answer that question," he mused silkily, exhaling
aromatic cigar smoke into the air above his head.

"It was a stupid question. Consider it withdrawn." She
wrinkled her nose at the cigar odor. It wasn't unpleasant, but
she didn't care for it.

He moved then. His hand touched the tendrils of hair that
haloed her face. "You are a wild wood nymph, I think. Why are
you so silent now, Deba McCloud?"

"I have nothing to say." Deba jumped when he threw back
his head and laughed, loud and long. "Goodness, that was unexpected."

"Were you expecting barbs, Miss McCloud?"

"Maybe."

"Why do I hide from the world?" His abrupt repetition of
the question had Deba blinking. Wolf Clinton took hold of her
arm and led her back across the immense room with its tiled
floor and large woven Indian rugs dotting its surface. "I don't
accept that I do." He rolled the cigar around his mouth for a
moment, then put it in a receptacle near the door. "I noticed
you're not fond of cigars."

"And you haven't answered me," Deba riposted. Why was
she jousting with him? It was not the best way to get a job.

"Tart-tongued, aren't you?"

"Yes." Deba grimaced. There goes the job.

"I manage to spend enough time in the United States to

keep my franchise active, I meet the people I choose to meet and enjoy their company. Over the years I've developed a low threshold of boredom, so I ignore those who bring on attacks of that pernicious malady."

"Pompous." Deba looked down at the glass she was holding. She had always considered herself a wary and discreet person. Never would she have considered sparring with the gods. What goaded her now? It took great effort to look up at that stern face, those leonine eyes. "I'd better go, I'm sure you think I've overstepped the—"

"Don't try to read my mind, Miss McCloud. You are my dinner guest. Let me freshen your drink."

"No, thank you. I have enough juice and I don't drink that much alcohol. I've rarely touched tequila."

"Now who's being pompous?" Wolf Clinton lifted her glass and refilled it from a jug on the tile bar. "This punch is made of fresh papayas and mangos, with no alcohol. Very healthy."

"I like the fruit juice, Mr. Clinton, I just don't spike it with tequila."

"How prim and proper you sound. Shall we go into the dining room?" Once more he took her arm.

"I can walk by myself. There's no need to troll me like a hooked salmon," she told him sharply, stopping and taking a good-sized swallow of her drink. "Aaagh. My God."

"Oops. I am sorry. I poured from the wrong jug. It was an accident."

"Monster. Stop laughing." Deba coughed again as the hot liquor barely masked by the fruit juices coursed down her throat. "Battery . . . acid . . . couldn't . . . taste as lethal. And stop smacking me on the back, you could break something."

"Sorry." Wolf Clinton didn't sound sorry. Facing her, he took the drink from her hand and put it down on a carved oak table. "I'll get you some fresh juice. We can have a nice Chablis with dinner, so you don't have to finish this."

"The one thing they don't have in this country is good water. That's what I really want." Deba felt a little light-headed as they entered the dining room. Alcohol and the high-altitude "tea" she'd been given were reacting on her. "What are we having? Frijitas, frijoles?" Putting her index finger on her forehead, she squinted up at him when he seated her at a right angle to his own chair.

"I thought you might enjoy a little different fare this evening. So we are having *truite en couleur* with saffron rice, lemon herb Chinese cabbage for a salad, Julia's special wheat bread, and chocolate mousse for dessert."

"A little different? A cheeseburger with deep-fried onions on the side would be a welcome change at this point," Deba told him, feeling as though her eyes had fallen loose in their sockets. She had no headache, wonder of wonders, but the tequila had made her very woozy. "Alcohol is stupid," she muttered, glaring at Wolf Clinton. Was he laughing at her? Had his mouth just twitched?

"You haven't been eating the nouvelle cuisine of the United States then?" Wolf lifted a silver bell next to his plate.

"My cuisine consists of whatever I can get my hands on, nouvelle or no," Deba muttered.

Wolf stared at her. She was a firebrand—a hungry one at that—who'd done some hard traveling.

Deba lifted her chin and stared back.

One ring of the bell near Wolf's plate brought the doors swinging open from what Deba assumed was the kitchen. "Serve us now, Julia."

"Sí, señor." Julia looked searchingly at Deba when the younger woman glanced at her.

"I'm starving, Julia," Deba told her owlishly.

"Senor, I think that the senorita is . . ."

"Serve the food, Julia. I will take care of the senorita."

"As you say, senor." Julia flounced back the way she'd come.

"She thinks I'm blotto," Deba told Wolf solemnly. "Actually, I don't feel half bad. The rotten stuff usually gives me a headache as big as Pittsburgh."

"You'll be fine when you've eaten something." Wolf patted her hand.

"Don't kid yourself, buster. Alcohol is insis . . . insidiot . . . insisious . . . bad for you."

"I can see that," Wolf murmured, chuckling as he leaned toward her, not paying any attention to Julia, who was standing in the doorway, gesturing to her subordinates about the food.

"She calls you buster, senor?" Affronted, Julia stared at Deba.

"Julia, you will see to the food." Irritation laced Clinton's voice.

"Boy, you'd better watch it, Julia. This old boy could fit you for cement shoes if you bug him." Deba frowned. "They used to do that quite a bit in Chicago . . . or was it New York? Well, no matter." Deba beamed again at the aghast housewoman. "Get on with the serving."

"Julia, you may go. I will see to the food myself." Wolf bit his lip, watching until the sputtering woman and her helpers had disappeared.

"She's having a snit," Deba leaned toward him and whispered. "Very tetchy female."

Wolf was taken aback by the feelings that assailed him. It had been eons since he'd been so diverted, felt such amusement, such warmth. He was happy all at once, wanting to extend the meal for hours, keep the fantasy that made him so lighthearted. The tipsy Miss McCloud had a certain magic.

Deba McCloud was certainly not that flush with the world's goods, but she seemed damned unimpressed with his. That in itself was intriguing. Or was she a consummate actress? The hell with it. Why should he psychologize her behavior when he was enjoying himself?

He knew nothing about her, but he had let her get closer to him than most had been able to do these last ten years.

She made him laugh! There was a fey quality about her that drew him. Mirth coiled in him, as though waiting for what else she might say. Irritating she might be, but very amusing as well. It felt good to laugh.

Reason dictated that he should have a battery of detectives investigate her. That would happen tomorrow, with or without his orders. Julia would tell Lazarus and that would be enough to get the ball rolling. So what would it hurt if he had a brief interlude? How long had it been since a woman had held his attention for more than a day . . . or a night?

"Umm, this is good." Deba put her elbow on the table and gestured toward Clinton with her fork. "I would have had my hand slapped for putting my elbow on the table at the private school I attended. Etiquette and manners were very important at Columbia School. We wore white gloves on occasion." Deba tried to moisten her dry lips without success.

When Wolf Clinton placed a glass of mineral water in front of her, she gulped it thirstily. "I'm glad I'm not jaded. Enjoying food like this is a real high. It's a shame everything that can give joy seems blunted in you." Deba smiled at him.

"Isn't that assuming a great deal?" Irritation warred with humor as he leaned down and retrieved—for the third time—the linen napkin that had fallen from her lap.

"Not really. I'm very good at reading people. In grammar school I was the first one to realize that Jimmy Weller lied when he said our teacher had warts on her backside. It stands to reason that anyone with warts on his—or her, as in this case—bottom would not be able to slouch so comfortably in their chair."

"Very moving analogy. I can see your great mental capacities started at an early age."

"Told ya." When Wolf leaned toward her to replace her napkin once more, she carefully dabbed at her lips with the loosely hanging sleeve of his shirt. "Thank you. Can't figure out why Julia didn't give me a napkin."

"Here you are."

"Oh. Thanks." Deba broke the hunk of wheat bread she'd been given and slathered it with curl after curl of butter. "Actually, butter isn't that good for you, but it's a weakness of mine."

"I can see that."

Deba washed the bread down with several swallows of Chablis. "Whoops. I meant to drink the mineral water." She smiled when Wolf lifted the wineglass and placed it next to his glass. "About this job you might have for me—what is it exactly?"

Wolf looked at her for long minutes. It was foolish to allow her into the sanctum sanctorum of his life and mind.

Years had been invested in the training of Milo Crandall and he had finally become the efficient machine Wolf required at his side. Though the two men had never been very close, there had been an understanding between them, a tightly organized business relationship. That was what was needed to replace Milo, a well-oiled machine, not a slip of a girl.

Wolf hadn't rushed to fill Crandall's position right away because he figured he would just use the electronic secretaries he had. He could forget the human element until he was able to screen many well-qualified applicants, then choose the best.

Now here he was considering placing an untried girl in Crandall's place of importance. It was madness.

"Having second thoughts about hiring me?" Deba put her other elbow on the table, cupping her chin in her hand. "It's your choice, but I sure could use some kind of job, since you kiboshed my chance in the film."

"Did I do that? I thought I told you you wouldn't fit the casting of any of the parts."

"You did, but how do I know that's so?" Deba widened her eyes for a moment as though they were in danger of closing. "Actually, you did take me out of the sun. I'm just grousing. What did you say we were having for dessert?"

Wolf rang the silver bell again and Julia entered and silently passed out the mousse. Her audible sniff when serving the coffee was not lost on Wolf. He shot her a level look and inclined his head in dismissal.

"Umm, this is good. I have enjoyed my dinner, and I hope I remember it all; it might be the best one I'll have for a while." Putting her napkin next to her empty dish, Deba rose to her feet, all at once swaying. "Oh, oh, I think I'll have a headache soon."

"Are you bothered by the altitude change? We are rather high here." Wolf rose in indolent fashion and went around to her side, sliding a supporting arm around her waist. "And there's the alcohol, of course."

Deba nodded, holding her forehead. When she took a step away from him, the pain seemed to stab behind her eyes. "Did you poison my food?" she quizzed him, dazed and aching.

"Of course. I always treat my guests that way."

"What?" There was a buzzing in her ears and her head felt like a pulsating motor.

"Never mind. Come along, I'll take you back to your room and you can lie down. Then I'll have Julia bring you some tea."

"That awful narcotic stuff, I'll bet," Deba muttered, leaning on him.

"Yes. That awful stuff as you call it is not much different than you would get anywhere in this part of the world in high altitudes."

"I know all about the special brew that people drink when the *siroche* comes." Deba saw stars and planets in front of her eyes as they faced the curving stairway leading to the second floor. "I was in Peru and I've been to Machu Picchu. Oooh. I didn't think it would be good in conjunction with alcohol. I was right."

Wolf leaned down and swept her up into his arms. "Shh. Don't struggle. Just close your eyes and relax."

Doing what he instructed seemed her only viable course, since any movement sent pain stabbing behind her eyes and over her cheekbones. "Alcohol generally gives me a headache. I should go back to the United States. This climate is killing me."

"That's why you want a job—to be able to earn some money to do that?"

"Whazzat?"

"Never mind. Shh."

Deba was glad to let her mind slip away and didn't even realize that Wolf had to pry her fingers from his shirtfront when he put her into bed.

"Your invitation is very tempting, Deba McCloud, however unconscious it might be." Wolf pressed his cool hand against her hot forehead and decided to let her sleep rather than let Julia waken her so that she might take the tea that would alleviate her discomfort. And perhaps she might have an adverse reaction after drinking.

Angry at himself for having served wine with dinner, he stared down at her. He knew full well the multitude of reactions that people had when coming to the high-altitude rancho.

When he tried to rise from the bed, Deba moaned and turned toward him, mumbling as though delirious. Her dress slipped lower on her breasts, revealing a satiny expanse of rosy white skin.

Wolf's blood boiled to the surface, his body hardening in response. It had been years since he had been unable to control his feelings. Now it was as though they were wild horses—unbroken, galloping runaways. "You don't make it easy, my little one. Leaving you is going to be arduous." There was surprise and some irritation in his voice.

Deba moaned again and Wolf sat down on the bed, his cool hand pressed to her forehead. Her exhaled breath was relaxed, satisfied.

Not even stopping to question his reasons, he settled down on the bed. Curving her body close to his own, he pulled the coverlet over her. His heart thudded against his chest, need rose in him like a flood, but there was a serene acceptance with it. Would he ever understand Deba McCloud or his response to her?

With his one free hand he loosened his tie and unbuttoned his shirt. Amazed at the contentment that filled him, he cuddled her close to him and shut his eyes.

Deba woke feeling warm and relaxed. It trembled through her consciousness that something new was giving her a sense of security that she hadn't experienced in some time. The delight that assailed her pushed aside any desire to further delve into what was causing it. She was safe, instinctively she knew that. Sighing, she turned into the warmth, burrowing into the protection that she had lacked for so long.

At the sharp rapping on the door, Deba sat bolt upright, feeling a little woozy but not feeling the discomfort she'd had. "Yes? What is it?"

"I am looking for the *señor, señorita.*"

"Julia? Why would you—"

"I'm here, Julia. What is it?"

"There is a phone call for you . . . and your breakfast is ready." Reproach vibrated through the words.

"All right, I'll take the call in my suite."

Deba swiveled around, looking down at the man, fully clothed, lying next to her. "What do you think you're doing?"

Wolf stretched, smothering a yawn with one hand. "Trying to straighten out the kinks in my back. I don't usually sleep in my clothes or in this guest bed." Wolf glared at the quilt covering him and threw it back. "I'm getting a king-size bed for this room."

"Your clothes are a mess," Deba said inanely. What was he doing in her bed? Had he doctored the drinks last evening? At best she was an indifferent drinker because of the harsh aftereffects. Normally she preferred mineral waters to any alcohol, but the wine hadn't tasted tainted to her. Had he made love to her? God! And she'd forgotten. Anger and frustration warred in her.

Wolf watched the play of emotions over her face. "Thinking I drugged you and had my wicked way with you?"

"It's within the realm of possibility."

"I'm surprised you'd want to work for such a devious swine."

"Needs must when the devil drives."

"Have you lived in England?"

"I lived in Scotland and Ireland for a time."

Wolf noticed how her gaze slid away from his, how her attention had been caught by his question. Why the look? Were Scotland and Ireland off limits to her? What had occurred there to cause her to become instantly tense? "Your clothes are wrinkled too."

"Ah, yes, so they are."

"Your face is telegraphing all sorts of questions."

"Is it? And do you have the answers?"

"Oh, I think so. One, we didn't make love. I rarely do so dressed, liking the feel of silken skin against my own. Two, as much as I wanted to leave and seek the comfort of my own bed, you wouldn't let me."

His smile was much like the look of the beast for whom he'd been named—Lobo, the wolf. "Touching tale. Are you saying that I kept you here against your will?" Sarcasm laced her words.

"Not exactly against my will . . . but you were persuasive. You're a sexy morsel, Miss McCloud, but I prefer my women awake when I make love to them."

"What a purist you are, Mr. Clinton." Her breath was coming in short gasps. Angry and titillated at the same time, she felt as though her world had tilted and she was sliding off.

She'd spent the night in bed with Wolf Clinton. Even with clothes on, that had to be at the top of the list of the most stupid things she'd ever done. The man was a world-class woman eater. And she had set herself out for him like a . . . a canapé, for God's sake. She'd cast herself into a dangerous situation with a man she'd known less than twenty-four hours. "Insane" was the kindest epithet she could fling at herself!

"I'd like to stay and debate this with you, but I imagine that the call Julia mentioned was the one from Europe that I've been waiting for, Deba McCloud." Rising from the bed, he leaned over her, his long, strong fingers taking hold of her chin. "Perhaps another time we'll be more *déshabillés* when we go to bed together."

"Don't hang by your heels, buster," she snapped.

Laughter combed out behind him as he crossed the room to the door. Opening it, he turned, his large, well-muscled body framed by the oak trim. "By the way, the job of assistant to me is yours, if you want it. Let me know by noon today. Otherwise I'll see to it that you get transportation back to Mexico City."

"What . . . did . . . you . . . say?" Deba thought she was choking.

"You heard me."

"May I use the phone?" Deba hurried her words as the door was closing.

"Dial eight to get an outside line," he told her without

turning, then the door clicked shut. "Tell them I cleared it for you." His voice came through the heavy wood.

Hands shaking, Deba dialed and answered the peremptory Spanish query. Then the line was put through and the phone rang and rang. Finally Maria answered. In a voice trembling with joy and fear she told her friend about the job.

"What do you mean, you won't be coming back to the city?"

"The job is here at Rancho Lobo, Maria."

"You said that you didn't get a part in the movie."

"I didn't, but I met Wolfgang Clinton and he offered me a job as his assistant. I think I'm going to take it."

"*Madre de Dios!* What are you saying? Have you been eating those jalapeño peppers that Ruiz grows? You know they make you feverish."

"Maria, stop it. I'm serious."

"You're mad if you'd even consider being in the same hacienda as that man. He chews up women and expectorates them."

"Spits them out," Deba corrected absently.

"*Sí.* I said that." Maria sighed. "Listen to me, Aldebaran. He's had thousands of mistresses."

"Come on, Maria, he has to sleep now and then, and then there's the matter of making a living. According to you, the man's a business dynamo."

"He is."

"Then how does he manage to be in bed all the time and still make money? Besides, wouldn't you think he'd be more discriminating about his lovemaking with all the disease scares in the world?"

"That man gives trouble, he doesn't get it. Besides, his type buys the best and the cleanest. I'm sure he makes them all get a blood screening," Maria muttered defiantly.

"I vill drink your blood." Deba teasingly imitated the great Dracula.

"Very amusing. I still think it's crazy to be out there. The man's positively dangerous. Better you should cozy up to a *bandido* than Wolf Clinton."

"One and the same thing. Beggars can't be choosers. I need the job, and if I take it he'll be sending someone to pick up my things. Will you take care of the packing for me?"

"Yes, but I don't like you being there. Be careful, and call

me every day. I want a daily log of your activities. How much
dinero will you get for this great job?"

"I forgot to ask."

"Madre de Dios, you are lost."

"Maria, don't be silly. I'm fine." Wasn't she fine? What
would Maria say if she told her that Wolf Clinton spent the
night in her bed? Mind-boggling!

Deba replaced the receiver, smiling at the instrument for
long minutes. Maria was amusing. A daily log! Actually it
wasn't a bad idea. She'd always kept a journal in college. It had
helped with the papers she'd had to write. Maybe it wouldn't be
a bad idea to log the happenings in and around the Rancho
Lobo. An article about Wolf Clinton might support her for a
while when she had to return to the States.

Deba had no illusions that her job with Clinton would last
forever. But a few months as his assistant would change her
financial picture drastically.

Reaching into her purse, Deba brought out a travel diary
she'd been keeping and began adding notes to it referring to her
arrival at Rancho Lobo and what had ensued since then. She
left out the incident in her bed last night, even though she
couldn't get it out of her mind—what she knew of it, that is. Of
all the times to be non compos mentis.

Scribbling rapidly, she managed to fill three pages. Dating
them, she put the notebook away, feeling that somehow she had
vindicated her presence at the rancho by recording it.

Showering and shampooing took a great deal of time. It
had been so long since she'd had the luxury of all the hot water
she wanted.

Taking her time, she shaved her legs and creamed them,
rubbed a precious emollient over her entire body, then stepped
back with a sigh to regard herself in the full-length mirror.
Perhaps it was her imagination, but she not only felt better but
felt there was a marked improvement in her looks.

The thought of impending employment could do that to
anyone.

On the vanity top in her bathroom was a selection of skin
treatments and conditioners. On impulse she used them on her
face, cleansing and lubricating the skin that had been neglected
since her arrival in Mexico.

When she looked at her wrinkled clothes, she grimaced.

The thought of putting her clean fresh body in crumpled clothing didn't sit well.

When someone knocked at the bedroom door, she grabbed for the towel she'd been using, wrapped it around her, toga fashion, and walked out of the bathroom. Standing in the middle of the bedroom, she faced the door. "Yes?"

"Senorita Mac-Cloud, the senor has sent these clothes for you. I wish to put them in your room."

"Clothes?" Deba crossed the room and flung open the door. "I have my own duds, they'll be out here sometime today. Then I—"

"Very true, but until then the senor says you will need these." Julia's arms were full as she passed Deba, heading for the closets that took up one long wall.

Deba saw the stiff look the housekeeper gave her. "I'm only taking a job as his assistant, Julia."

"Sí, that is what you say." Sniffing audibly, she began arranging the garments on hangers.

Deba poked out her tongue at the woman's back. Nasty-minded harridan! Assuming that she'd been in Wolf's bed. Actually, he'd been in hers—fully clothed. It was all innocent. What would Julia make of that? "Ah, my own clothes might be here this afternoon and . . ."

"Sí. I will bring them up here. Will this do for now?" Julia held out a native dress, cream-colored, in woven cotton. It had an open square-cut neck and fell straight from the yoke to the calves of her legs. Very cool-looking.

"Yes, but at the moment I would like to take a swim if I may."

"Sí. We have a natural pool. It is carved out of rock and is very big. There is a bathing suit and jacket to match in this closet." Julia sniffed again, then waddled back across the room, her ample hips quivering. "There are towels in the cabana, and if you wish you may use the sailboat."

"Sailboat in a pool?"

"I have said that it is a large one. We even have a waterfall," Maria told her in lofty pride.

"Heavens." Deba stared at the door long after it had closed. "A real business magnate is our Mr. Clinton." Fumbling through the closet, she found a one-piece Lycra suit that weighed next to nothing and looked as if it would fit.

Slipping it on, she took the nylon cap that matched the

turquoise coloring of the suit and took one of the summer cotton sarongs and wrapped it around her middle.

Making her way through the large cavernous house was an exercise in ingenuity. The house had many levels and layers to it, but finally she was out of doors in the stifling air.

Deba was about to retreat into the coolness of the house again when she spotted a worker in the shade of a tree, slowly weeding a rockery.

Gardens were everywhere, flowers in profusion, paths of crushed stone winding around hillocks of blooms and terraces of lush growth.

"*Por favor?*" In her rather limited Spanish, Deba inquired the way to the water.

Barely pausing in his work, the man pointed down a wide, winding pathway.

"*Sí.* Gracias," Deba murmured, gazing around her. "I'm in fantasy land to be sure."

"Do you always talk to yourself?" Wolf Clinton steadied her when she turned too quickly and staggered.

"Do you jump out of every bush and startle your guests?"

"You're not a guest, you're an employee, Miss McCloud." He took her arm and steered her along next to him, since there was ample room on the path for them to walk side by side.

Electricity ran up his arm, broadcasting through his system. It both irked and intrigued him that the slip of a girl-woman at his side could engender such hot feelings in him. Wolf was no stranger to sensual sensation, but the torrid river that had erupted in him when he saw Deba McCloud in a bikini had a lacing of wildness that was alien to him. He was in control, always. Why wasn't he with Deba McCloud? She was a captivating gamine. Her long lissome body fired him, he wanted those legs wrapped around him, that pouting, rather full lower lip pressed to his, those sharp white teeth biting his skin. . . . Damn!

Deba stopped. His body had tightened, she could feel his tension. Anger with her? "True. I forgot. In that case perhaps I shouldn't be . . ."

"Don't be prickly, Deba. You're my assistant. I'll want you to join me for a swim now and then."

"Big of you," Deba muttered.

"What I said to you rankled a bit, didn't it?"

"No. . . . Yes, it did."

"I'm not trying to set your back up, you know."

"I don't think you need to try, Mr. Clinton," she answered acerbically. His shout of laughter made her jump again, but she could feel a smile struggling over her face. The man had a magnetic laugh. It was like the rest of him. He was lethal and should be registered with the police. "I shouldn't make comments like that," Deba murmured, feeling uncomfortable.

"No, you shouldn't, but I doubt you'll stop." He paused and pointed. "There it is. What do you think?"

"It is a bloody lake, island and all," Deba pronounced, awestricken by the body of water facing her, with a small island about a hundred feet toward the middle.

"You can even sail if you like." Wolf gestured toward the three Sunfishes resting on shore. "Do you like to sail?"

"I don't know, I never have. I've done most of my swimming in pools." And she'd been glad of the chance to swim in them. Swimming had been an escape for her, especially in the past years when she'd been on the run. Whenever she could find a pool she'd used it avidly until she'd had to move on again. The water activity had been a balm to her soul. It had also been an easy way to make friends when she moved to a new place. Such relationships were shallow and short, but they were all she had. Many times, without the closeness, love, and nurturing of her dear parents, the existence of a real home, her life might have been unbearable. Swimming had been a way to sand those rough edges. "It's very clean."

"Yes, and deep and cool. It's very refreshing to swim here. Geologists tell me that it's an underground lake that provides this with innumerable springs. Some of the springs are siphoned into pipelines that provide water for the truck farms." Wolf smiled down at her. "You let me see things through your eyes and your focus provides a new luster, Deba McCloud."

Deba was nonplussed and speechless at his observation. Joy flooded through her, putting her off balance and making her a little uneasy. It was ridiculous! She barely knew the man.

Deba fitted the earplugs into her ears and donned her cap and goggles. Obeying a long-taught dictum, she didn't dive into the rock-edged pool. Instead she lowered herself into the crispy water, gasping but feeling deliciously cooled after the oppressive heat.

With a strong kick she was soon in deep water. Plunging

down, she reveled in the silky bath of freshness that coursed over her skin.

With strong strokes she thrust herself into the middle of the small lake, delighted to see a cross-section of fish swimming around her.

Lungs bursting for air, she broke the surface and saw Wolf Clinton next to her. Yanking off her goggles, she smiled at him. "It's wonderful. So refreshing, just as you said."

"Yes. You swim well. Most women would be hugging the edge, afraid to venture into the middle."

"Maybe the women you know. Most American women are venturesome."

"I'm an American, Deba. Did you forget?"

"No. But I also remember you said you're a Mexican national."

"I have dual citizenship, but I prefer residing in Mexico. The living is more relaxed."

"You have a very tight look to you. Are you on the run?"

"Are you?"

The breath caught in Deba's throat. She was on quicksand. "I suppose we all are in one way or another."

"True. Shall we confide in each other?"

Deba swallowed water. "Um, let's not spoil the mystique."

"Fine." His strong legs treading water, Wolf reached for her. "You intrigue me, Deba McCloud."

"It's the same for me." Why was her blood heating? Boiling? What sort of inner power did Wolfgang Clinton have?

"You don't bore me."

"Not yet anyway."

"True."

Her body had turned to gelatin, the power of her limbs had dissipated. Breathing was impeded. Oxygen was being displaced by Wolf Clinton's own special phosphorus.

When she slowly sank into the water, strong hands at her waist stopped her, suspending her easily in the deep water. "There's a lot about you I don't know."

She smiled at him weakly. "The water isn't salty."

"No, it's not, but you are. Are you interviewing me for your job, Miss McCloud?"

"No, but it's not a bad idea. If I believe half the rags in the States, you're one bad dude, Mr. Clinton . . . sir."

"Some of it's true, some of it's half-truths, most of it's a pack of lies." Irritation slashed his features. "Why am I explaining to you?"

Deba noted how his features changed, like steel bending. "I'll bet the truth's more interesting."

With a sudden jerk, Wolf pulled her down into the water, his mouth moving onto hers with surging force, the water swirling around them in a mini vortex.

Deba struggled against what she was sure would be violence. The gentleness paralyzed her, turned her tension to pliancy.

Never had anyone brought her to such a fiery level in the depths of rather chilly water. The paradox was frightening and exciting. More of Wolf Clinton's power!

When Wolf felt her surprise and sudden laxness, his heart thudded against his chest bone in alien awareness. Never had a woman made him feel unsure. He didn't like the feeling.

Moving his mouth over hers, he intended to dominate her. Instead he felt a yielding in himself. Why would he want to protect her?

Air gave out and he breathed the last of his oxygen into her mouth even as he shot to the surface, still holding her. Deba was stunned.

"Do . . . you . . . give . . . all your employees . . . this treatment?"

"Not the men." His voice was even but his heartbeat wasn't. He had the strange sensation of truly understanding what fibrillation meant. "Shall we swim?"

"Are there any *other* sharks in these waters?"

Wolf gave her a tight smile. "You noticed there was no salt, Deba McCloud."

"True." Deba struck out hard, using the smooth crawl that had earned her a berth on the varsity swim team, in another lifetime, as natural to her as walking.

Wolf wasn't used to women keeping up with his stroke, and it piqued his interest that the half-fed waif from the north was a very good athlete.

Wolf had done his level best to beat her when they were returning to shore.

Deba was just as determined that he wouldn't.

Wolf had to really exert himself to win. It annoyed and titillated him that she could bear down with such strength when she was just a slip of a girl.

When they reached the quay where they'd first entered the water, Wolf paused, treading water and breathing hard. "You were well trained."

"So . . . were . . . you." Air rasped from her lungs.

"Are there any other facets of your personality that would interest me?"

"Well, I'm a cop killer, a bank robber, and on weekends I knock down little old ladies for their purses."

"Amusing." With a powerful push of his arms, he heaved up on the dock and grabbed for a towel that was draped on a wooden bench there.

Deba leaned her forearms on the quay and looked up at him. "I guess I don't fit in with your image of an assistant."

Wolf looked over the edge of the towel, down at her. "No, you don't."

"I need the work."

"So you said."

"Would you prefer me to keep my mouth shut and mask all my thoughts? I need the money."

"I could never expect you to do the impossible."

"You can be pretty caustic yourself."

"I'm not the one throwing the bricks."

Deba heaved herself up and out of the pool. As she reached for a towel her mouth opened to retort when she caught the hot gaze roving her body. "And I'm not a piece of meat on a hook that you get to make a choice on, either."

"You're too slender, but you do have a wonderful body."

The heat from his words made the lake steam . . . or was that just her imagination. "I'll type, collate, take dictation . . . even make your coffee, but you get someone else to warm your bed."

"Sounds fair," he drawled, his eyes seeming to pierce the toweling material that she'd wrapped around herself. "I admire the *Mona Lisa,* Deba McCloud. I have never tried to take it home."

"They'd shoot you if you did," Deba muttered. The man was deadly.

"Why do I get the feeling you'd be there with your gun?"

"Lucky guess?" Damn the man! It was like dueling a shark.

Wolf closed his eyes for a moment as though in pain. "Why am I doing this to myself?"

"Good spiritual exercise." Deba patted him on the forearm, then pulled back her hand as though stung.

"I wasn't going to hit you."

"No?" Then what had caused that electric shock up her arm? Was he wired to lightning? No wonder he stayed out of the United States—they probably considered him a land-to-air missile.

"Would you like something to drink?"

Deba nodded. "Nonalcoholic if you please. I don't want any more headaches."

"How about fresh orange juice, mineral water, and lime?"

"A sunburst. Umm, I like them."

He watched the way her tongue ran along the edge of her upper lip and he had the sensation of his veins widening, of blood flowing faster. Wolf wanted that tongue in his mouth. "Good." He picked up the cellular phone on a table and spoke Spanish into it.

In short order a drink cart was being rolled toward them. A young man in white cotton slacks and loose shirt made the drinks, left the cart, and disappeared.

"You certainly get action." Deba took a chair in the shade of the umbrella.

"Yes."

"Does anyone ever thwart you?"

"Not until you," Wolf answered silkily, and was rewarded with a startled look, quickly masked.

"Pardon me for being skeptical."

Wolf shrugged.

They sat there as the sun moved higher.

More than once, Deba opened her mouth to say that she was returning to the house, but each time she closed it without saying anything.

Like a hypnotic light, the sun mesmerized them and kept them still as it began its daily ritual of throwing the kaleidoscope of oranges and yellows into the spectrum of sky, giving a copperish cast to the blue.

With a burst of rays that rainbowed the heavens, the sun climbed toward its zenith. Mauve, violet, coral, were aureoled around the hot orb.

"Shall we go?" Wolf whispered. "Work to do."

"Yes."

Was it his breath that touched her neck or had he kissed her?

Then he touched her hand. "One more quick, cooling swim and we'll leave."

"Yes," Deba answered him dazedly.

3

The first days were chaotic. Deba made horrendous mistakes on the computer.

Wolf cursed in long, low fluid tones.

Deba expected her dismissal at any time.

"It's a vicious animal that eats things," she told Wolf one afternoon when he'd found her with her head on her arms at her desk.

"What have you lost?"

She pointed to a folder that she had been using to fill a file. When Deba looked up and saw his mouth go slack, she groaned. "What was it?"

"I think you may have wiped out the stats on a deal I was working on, Deba. Move over and let me see if I can call up a backup file."

"Oh, God! I hate these monsters."

It had taken two sweaty hours to bring up most of the lost file.

"Maybe you should work on the typewriter instead."

Deba lifted her head and fixed bleary eyes on him. "No. Unless you order me away from this bête noire, I am going to master it."

"Then try not to lose any more of my files, will you?"

"Yessir."

After a few days she began to tame the electronic marvel that enjoyed writing DISK ERROR on the screen. Little by little she gained confidence that she could ride the wild mustang of a word processor. She knew it still hated her, but she had become adept at using a figurative whip and a gun. Soon *she* would be master, not the machine.

She had been there two weeks when she began, in her spare time, to fill a blank disk of her own, jotting down many things about the elusive and largely unknown Wolf Clinton. Deba titled her disk JOUR for journal. She kept the disk in the locked bottom drawer of her desk so that it wouldn't get mixed up with the others. Each day she would add to it, either statistics or minutiae, mostly about Wolf Clinton, or another fact about the many businesses that he dabbled in, from China to London. Her own ethics made her careful not to add any business knowledge she might have gleaned that could undermine Wolf Clinton's financial empire. Wolf Clinton fascinated her. She had to know more.

The picture that began to emerge for Deba was one of a ruthless, indomitable businessman who played a hard but honest game, who preferred anonymity to glaring publicity, but who'd had his share of screaming headlines. Someday she must search out Wolf Clinton's past. Could that be done? Or was it too deeply buried?

There was a "morgue" of sorts in the disk files that interested her. It had been hidden away—by Wolf, she supposed—in the back of the drawer, perhaps forgotten, perhaps stashed. Much of the file seemed to detail the happenings of Wolf's life back through his university and prep school days.

It was similar to her journal of events, except that it was more detailed.

She found out that as a child he'd been the focal point of a custody battle waged by acrimonious parents. What happened to those parents wasn't disclosed.

Then there was another custody battle among those anxious to get the Clinton money, or at least that's the way the newspaper clippings slanted it.

Step by step she went through the file, then put it away with the JOUR disk she'd already begun filling.

She didn't know when it occurred to her that writing a biography of such a man as Wolf Clinton might make a great book, but gradually she incorporated all the headlines and notes on him into a file of her own.

While working on the word processor one day, she found a secret drawer in the desk. That secret drawer, activated when a small brass handle on the bottom drawer of the desk was pushed, had revealed itself unexpectedly when the bottom drawer had stuck and she had yanked and pushed on it, accidentally activating the release.

Momentarily diverted from the agony of losing another file because she had hit the wrong button on the computer, she realized at once that the drawer had probably remained a secret from other users. It had a new-wood smell to it, and some of the shavings were still there. What woodmaker had had such a sense of humor that he'd made a drawer that few persons would be able to find? It was not a new piece of furniture, so the secret must have been kept a long time.

Then and there she'd decided that the drawer was a good hiding place for her journal . . . and for the disk with so much personal data on Wolf Clinton.

One afternoon when she'd been working for Wolf Clinton for a month he ambled into the office, frowning.

"Yes, Mr. Clinton? Was there a mistake on the letters again?"

Wolf shook his head, still frowning.

"Something's wrong."

"I just had an argument with the man whose place you're taking. He'd prefer coming back here when his mother is well."

"Oh. Maybe he liked being your assistant."

"Crandall and I got along well enough."

"There you are."

Wolf stared at her for a moment. "I wondered if you might like to take an hour out of your day and go riding."

Deba wrinkled her nose. "I don't think so. I'm really not that good with horses. Riding is not a skill I've mastered."

Wolf leaned over her shoulder and put her machine on hold. "There. Now close it up. You've been laboring over this thing for long hours every day and you've made good progress. Now you need to relax."

"I do relax. We swim every evening together, then enjoy our meal and listen to music." Deba shrugged. "That's plenty of stress-free time." Any more and she wouldn't be able to

control the uneven pulse beats she'd experienced at any hour of
the day when she might see him.

Fighting to control her feelings for a man was a new wrinkle for her. She'd always had the reins of her life securely in her
hands as far as men were concerned.

Now Wolf Clinton had put her out of stride.

It disgusted her that she was developing a schoolgirl crush
on the great Wolfgang Clinton. Didn't he have enough women
in reserve without adding her to his coup stick? Maybe it was
because she was somewhat cloistered here that his charm
seemed so magnified.

Deba needed to see Maria and her other friends. That
would bring her back to earth. That would dispel the awful rosy
aura she'd misplaced Wolf Clinton in . . . along with herself.

"Come on, please me. I'm the boss."

"Yes, that's true." Deba glared at him. When he smiled,
his face softened and lightened, yet there was a hard magnetism
to it that pulled her, drawing her into his force field. It titillated
and repelled her at the same time. Was Lobo Clinton the Satan
that Milton wrote of so eloquently? He certainly had the same
persuasive ways.

No wonder he had such a fierce reputation. Wolf Clinton
had too much power, he sucked people into his aura as if it were
a giant whirlpool . . . down, down into the vortex.

"Planning my death? Your face is like a video, with lights,
action, and fanfare included."

"I'd rather be open than devious," she told him tautly.
"Besides, orchestrating your demise would take an army of field
strategists, Mr. Clinton," Deba said in lemony observation. She
felt the color rise in her face at his continued scrutiny. "But I
suppose I shouldn't be so blunt with my employer."

"It would be a shame to reverse your field or change your
tactics now, Deba McCloud." He closed his eyes for a moment
as though he'd had a sudden headache. "I can't for the life of
me figure why I put up with you."

"I don't toady to you, which, no doubt, is a new experience."

"That tart tongue of yours will be dealt with one day." His
smile touched her from eyebrow to ankle. "I might enjoy doing
it myself."

His silky chuckle sent steel shivers over her skin. "You
sound like Dracula when you talk that way."

"Deba, I would never drink your blood . . . though biting your neck has great possibilities," he drawled. He reached out a strong index finger and scored it down her throat, pressing one spot. "Right here, on your pulse point. Feel the rhythm of life."

"Vampire," she told him faintly, her voice ending in a croak. "I studied the martial arts." It was true. She'd taken a course at a local YMCA in Chicago.

"Admirable. Get changed. We're going riding."

Had she read that he was a black belt? Damn! That had a familiar ring to it. Was he laughing at her? Like an automaton Deba left the good-sized study and went up the stairs to her room, changing into jeans and short-sleeved shirt. She didn't have regular riding clothes. "I should refuse. He doesn't own me," she told her mirror, mutinously. Then why are you going? "Mind your own business," Deba told the mirror.

She wasn't quite sure of her way going down the back stairs but she tried them anyway, assuming she would come out near the kitchen. Which she did.

When Julia turned from the kitchen sink where she was washing some lethal-looking yellow peppers, her black eyebrows rose. As usual she sniffed when she saw Deba.

Ignoring the housekeeper's tight-lipped displeasure, Deba asked the way to the stables.

"The señor has your horse out there." Julia pointed with a long sharp knife toward a back door.

"Thank you." Deba resisted the urge to again poke her tongue at Julia's ample back.

Deba sucked in her breath at the blast of heat after the air-conditioning. She stayed still for a few minutes to adjust to it, wondering how horses could stand the heat. Without the constant breeze across the high mesa it would be stifling.

Horses had always been part of another world to her. Not that she disliked them, she didn't. It was that she'd never taken the time to get comfortable with them. The only horses she'd ever ridden had been livery stable horses that were near the campus where she'd gone to school. The few times she'd gone riding had not made her eager to try it again, but she was not afraid of the beasts.

At first she didn't see Wolf Clinton, then he came around the side of a long low building, leading one horse, with another following on its own . . . the black beast named Diablo.

She didn't take her eyes off the smaller dapple gray, knowing that one would be for her. The black Diablo was Wolf's. "Look, I really don't have to go riding with you, even if you are my boss."

"True." He inclined his head. "Has no one ever tried to gag you?"

Deba opened up her mouth to retort. All at once she couldn't stem the humor that bubbled up in her, doubling her over. "Once Delta Kappa fraternity rolled me in an oriental rug and deposited me on the dean's front porch because I said in our campus newsletter that they were consummately boring. My sorority sisters saved me."

"You must have the luck of the Irish to have escaped death up until now." When he saw the arrested look on her face, he tried to figure what it was in their exchange that had caused her to withdraw from him. Why the sudden putty cast to her skin? Why had she turned away from him?

Deba's memory jarred painfully. The time in Dublin when someone had almost hit her with a car. Deba hadn't known if it was deliberate, but she'd left Ireland as soon as possible. "Ah, well, yes, I'll go horseback riding . . . I suppose."

"Good thinking. Let me give you a leg up."

"Ah, no, I'd like to use the mounting block, please."

Wolf shrugged and walked with her over to the rectangle of cement imbedded in the ground.

Deba was uncomfortably aware that several of the army of groundskeepers that Wolf employed had paused in their work to watch her. "I didn't sign on as the comic relief."

"What are you muttering about?"

"Nothing."

The stables were a distance away from the house along wide terrazzo walks edged in desert shrubs and cacti. Row upon row of fragrant blooms gave a kaleidoscopic effect that was at once exciting and soothing, their colors so vibrant as to hurt the eye. Deba would have preferred to continue strolling along the curving walks, rather than try to throw herself onto a horse's back.

She stared at the long, low buildings that housed the equines. "Good Lord, how many horses do you have?"

"Some of these were brought down from Kentucky for the winter," Wolf answered her noncommittally.

"I see." But Deba didn't see. Why would Clinton keep such large equine accommodations? "Do you breed horses?"

"Some." Again the answer was veiled.

Instead of mounting the horse that had been brought to the block for her, Deba was drawn to the stable. "Some of it is air-conditioned, isn't it?"

"Yes." Wolf handed the dapple gray's reins to a stable hand who had come running at their approach. Diablo stayed behind Wolf.

Deba paused near a corral where two young horses were frolicking. "They're beautiful."

"They should be, they come from prize Arabian and Thoroughbred stock. On Lobo we've tried to develop a new breed of strong, fast horses with good nature and intelligence. We've made pretty good progress."

"That's why you're so secretive? You think I might mention what you're doing to someone?"

"I don't consider myself secretive, Deba McCloud. And I don't think you'll discuss my life here or what I do, because the clause in the contract you signed stipulates that you don't talk about me until you've been out of my employ for five years."

Deba thought a moment then nodded slowly. "I forgot about that."

"Don't." The twisted hardness of his face softened when she looked up at him, then stepped back. "You're not frightened of me, Deba, so why did you move away?"

"Caution. You looked ready to chew rocks. I'm not afraid of dogs either, but I'm leery of ones that growl."

"Very wise." Wolf waved to a man on the corral fence, who climbed down and ambled toward them. "Juan, you will find the senorita another horse. She doesn't seem drawn to Juanita." The smile twisted his face when she glared up at him. "Angry with me?"

"You're assuming a great deal. Actually I thought the dapple gray was pretty."

"Perverse creature." Wolf leaned down and nipped at her ear with strong white teeth.

"Ouch!" It hadn't hurt, but it had sent such a charge of electricity through her that it had caused sweet pain. "How would you like me to dust your nose with my knuckles?" Why had she said that? She didn't talk to people that way . . . unless it was necessary. Wolf Clinton drove her crazy.

"I think you shocked Juan," Wolf murmured, leaning over her and chuckling.

"If he works for you he must be fireproof."

Juan, who seemed to understand English, stared at her openmouthed.

"He would never think of speaking to his patron in such a fashion." Wolf Clinton's arm circled her waist, tightening.

Deba opened her mouth and shut it again, feeling the warning in that hand.

"Perhaps Nina would be good—eh, Juan?" Wolf spoke in unaccented Spanish.

"Sí. She is very fresh and needs to exercise. That is good." Juan smiled at Deba and doffed his high-crowned hat with a brim that was almost the size of an umbrella.

"I hope she isn't as fresh as that." Deba stared at a black stallion that two men wrestled out of the stall. "You aren't going to ride that one, are you? Because if you are, I'm not going with you," Deba managed faintly over the angry screams of the stallion.

"I won't ride him today. He's too interested in the mares at this time of year, and I wouldn't want to mar his hide with spurs."

"Really? If he's that wild, I think you should shoot him." Deba saw the shocked look that Juan threw her way.

"No, he has no real malice, just a liking for the ladies."

"And you can empathize with that." Deba bit her lip, her gaze sliding away from the slack-jawed Juan, who was suddenly immobilized, his eyes glassy. "Oops, sorry. Talking out of turn again."

"When don't you?"

Deba shot him a sharp look, but he was watching a beautiful Arabian mare being led out of a stall, her mincing step and swaying neck like a ballerina's movements. Juan went to her, speaking softly, crooning to her.

Nuzzling him several times, the mare followed him to another mounting block.

"I will ride Diablo and you can ride that one." He pointed to the mare, who was not more than fourteen hands high and was sidling playfully, the gentle toss of her head telegraphing her good nature.

"Oh." Deba approached the animal, and though she nickered and pushed her face into her hand, Deba didn't feel super-confident.

Stepping to the block, she mounted clumsily, clutching the reins in her hands.

"Relax. She is very gentle and has a very smooth gait."

"Uh-huh." Deba didn't look up at Wolf as they moved slowly away from the stables and down a path, toward a hilly area strewn with rocks. "Why don't you go on ahead?" Deba suggested, without lifting her head.

"I'm fine." Wolf moved easily next to her.

They rode in silence for some distance.

Up, down, her body unbalanced most of the time, Deba fought to get the syncopation that would come with proper "posting," the ability of horse and rider to gain a rhythm.

They paused as they breasted a ridge, and suddenly an arid, boulder-strewn valley lay before them.

Deba shifted her weight, feeling a slight chafing from her jeans. "It's almost primeval, isn't it?" Deba didn't know why she whispered.

"Mexico is an amalgam, that's why I love it here. It's primitive and sophisticated, sleek and rough, raw and gentle." There was a placid sound to Wolf's voice, but when Deba looked at him she thought there was a haunted look to his eyes.

"Can you not go home again? Will you ever live in the United States?"

Wolf bared his teeth. "That damned tongue of yours should be plucked out, Deba McCloud." Then he kneed Diablo hard.

The horse jumped into a wind-raising gallop, scampering headlong down the hillside like a catapult in heedless aim to destruction as though he would tumble his rider and himself.

"Oh, dear, I hope you don't intend to do that, Nina. I'd pull out your mane in chunks no doubt," Deba murmured to the gentle animal as she sidled to the edge, then began a zigzag descent. "Besides, if I'm going to lose my job, I would like two healthy legs to walk out of Rancho Lobo."

Gritting her teeth and leaning as far back as she could, Deba struggled to keep from sliding off. The mare was being cautious and moving slowly. Deba was aware of that and grateful, but hanging on was still a perilous task as the mare eased down the steep slope.

At the bottom of the incline, Deba took a deep breath and

tapped the back of her hand at the beadings of moisture on her upper lip. "Good horsey."

"Her name is Nina."

"Aaagh." Nearly jumping out of her skin Deba struggled to turn around and face the man who'd startled her. "I thought you'd be at the Pacific Ocean by now."

The abrupt turning put her body out of balance. As she fought to regain her seat, the horse sidled. Though the action was gentle, it was enough to unseat her. In helpless fascination Deba felt she was watching the scenario from outside herself, that she could view her own fall in slow motion as she began to slide from the back of the mare.

Strong arms caught her up and lifted her free of the horse, plopping her not too gently onto the front of Wolf's western saddle.

"For corn sake, you rattled every tooth in my head." Deba blinked and tried to sit forward but couldn't.

"Would you rather have tumbled to the ground?"

"Let me think about it," Deba muttered. "I'll get down now. This horse is very high."

"So they tell me." Wolf kneed Diablo once more and the horse jumped forward.

"Good . . . Lord . . . stop . . . this thing." Deba's head slammed back against his chest. Her backside felt as though it was getting an old-fashioned paddling, and once more her teeth cracked together.

"No."

"Huh? What did you say? Slow down, will you? Heavens, you're not going to jump that dry bed. Yes, you are. You're a madman," Deba announced, eyes closed, as they flew through the air.

Somehow when they landed her posterior did not take the beating she was expecting. Wolf's strong thighs cushioned her as he held her close to his body.

Some minutes later, as they cantered along a dusty trail, Deba was finally able to find a comfortable position as she sat in the crook of his arm. "This can't be easy on the horse or you."

"No, but I have discovered a way to keep that tongue of yours in check. Jump a dry bed." Wolf's silvery chuckle ran over her skin, goosebumping the surface it touched.

"Is that so?"

"Original conversational riposte."

"Snob."

"You're nonplussed and angry with me because I can use two syllable words?"

"And you're pompous and . . . unlikable." Deba craned her neck. "Where's Nina?"

"On her way home, I suppose. She's quite able to take care of herself, unlike the person that rode her."

Deba squirmed around to stare up at him. "I told you that I wasn't a horsewoman."

"You were right."

"Then why drag me along with you?"

"Umm, I suppose I can answer that question."

"Do try," Deba said sarcastically, irked and sore.

"You arouse me, Deba McCloud, sexually and intellectually."

"Baloney," Deba said faintly. "You are trying to shock me."

"Shock you? Modern women are shockproof, aren't they?"

"Yes, so you should keep your observations to yourself."

"Does that make sense?"

"To me it does."

"Why doesn't that surprise me."

When he pulled back on the reins and the horse slightly reared, then stopped, she stared between the animal's ears, the hard body under hers causing her ears to ring. "He's an awfully strong beast, isn't he?"

"Yes. He would never have been gelded if he hadn't come down with an ailment that required the procedure. His stock is of the best."

"Is he Lobo stock too?"

"Yes." Wolf slid from the back of the horse, leaving her alone and sidesaddle on the mount. Looking up at her, he lifted his arms, then clasped her waist with his hands. "I like good stock. Are you good stock, Deba McCloud?"

"The best." Deba ignored the feathery sensation in her stomach. How was he able to make her skin goosebump that way? No doubt he subscribed to voodoo.

"I agree. If only there was a way to tame that wayward tongue of yours."

"Very funny." She tried to be scathing. It soothed her insides to strike back at Wolf Clinton. Sometimes it even made the fluttering sensation subside and made her feel that she hadn't lost control.

He squeezed her waist. "We could be good together. You're a modern lady. I have twentieth-century attitudes toward liaisons myself."

"Are you offering yourself as my lover, Mr. Clinton?"

"You could phrase it that way."

"If I say no, does my job disappear?"

"No."

"Then the answer is no." Deba took a deep, shuddering breath. "We don't know each other well enough for anything more than a one-night stand. I'm not into those."

Grasping her tightly, he lifted her off the motionless horse and stood her in front of him. "I think it might be more than one night, maybe two or three."

"That horse is very well trained, isn't he. He doesn't even need a hobble."

"Your voice is shaking. It's either fear or anger. I don't think you're afraid."

"Oh, but I am. If you say one more word I'm *afraid* that I might pop you one right in the snout. I am not a prostitute."

"I wasn't offering you money for sex."

"The inference was there . . . or is it implication? Well, either way it was there."

"Because I think we might suit each other sexually does not mean that I think you're a prostitute."

"And I think that making that offer dead out of the blue is insulting." She was taken aback by his slow smile. "What are you thinking?"

"It wasn't dead out of the blue. I've been thinking about getting you into my bed since I first saw you in that casting line."

"What about safe sex? Have you thought about that? A person can't be too careful these days." Her lips felt like melting wax.

"Are you referring to me or you?"

"Me."

"Do you have a dangerous sexual disease?"

"Certainly not!" Deba glared at him.

"Well, we're all set. My physical last month checked me out as very healthy."

"Umm, a lot can happen in a month." Deba smiled at him

weakly when his one eyebrow arched. "Besides, the list of people you've had sex with in the last ten years might fill the Manhattan telephone book."

"Someone is going to kill you and put your tongue in formaldehyde."

"How could we be good together—sexually—if I always irritate you so?"

"You infuriate, not irritate. A gag is not a bad idea. There are other . . . enchanting places to kiss a woman other than her mouth."

"It's disgusting. Imagine a woman in your bed with a gag in her mouth and there you are . . . with her . . ."

"Yes? It's very good so far, and I don't think the gag would detract at all."

"It's repulsive, and I refuse to consider it."

"I can't shut my mind down that easily."

"Do it."

"How about without the gag and I keep my mouth . . ."

"Discussion closed." She knew he was baiting her . . . and enjoying it. Damn him!

Wolf pulled her close, his mouth locking over hers, the explosion immediate and compelling. Electrocution couldn't have rocked him more. When he felt her body tremor, his hold tightened, his tongue touching hers, fire flowing in his veins at the wonderful moistness.

Deba wrenched free, staring up at him stupefied.

Wolf shook his head. "I don't think so."

"Just because I work for you does not mean that I need to share your bed." Deba quelled a shiver at the sudden Satan's smile on his face. It took all her strength to stem the quaking of her body.

"That's a twentieth-century female opinion. Don't be too out of step, Deba McCloud. This is Mexico. The feminist movement hasn't struck here with any measure of success."

"You just said that we were both modern," she ventured weakly.

"So I did . . . but I have my feudal moments."

"Does that mean that you intend to coerce me into your bed?"

"No, but I will tell you I mean to continue trying to persuade you."

"You haven't a prayer."

"Where did you get that tongue? Did a viper die and bequeath it to you?"

"Very amusing."

"And it's not funny to impugn my ability as a courtin' man."

"That's not what has you so steely-eyed. I dented your ego when I implied you were chauvinist."

"Is that right?"

"Yes."

When Diablo whinnied, Wolf looked behind him. "Well, I was wrong. Nina has followed us." Wolf crooned to her in Spanish and the mare approached him eagerly.

Deba couldn't quite mask her relief. Riding on Diablo in front of Wolf all the way back to the hacienda could have totally unraveled her. Wolf Clinton had gotten under her guard.

"Shall we get back? I have an appointment with my masseuse." He'd seen her palpable relief at the appearance of the mare.

"Trust you to have a woman."

"Helga would be insulted that you are trying to denigrate her art by implying sexual activity along with the treatment. She considers herself an artist in her field." Wolf hefted her into the saddle, noting the infinitesimal wince when her derriere hit the smooth saddle leather. "You might need a soak in the hot tub." Wolf didn't try to mask the amusement in his voice.

Deba glared at him. "Don't tell me what I need, and I don't want to hear a diary of your sexual acrobatics."

"How you talk, Deba McCloud." His voice was like jagged rusty iron.

"You're angry again."

"It would seem I've been that way since our first meeting." Mounting his horse quickly, he gave her a hard smile. "And Helga is a true artisan. Some women are proud of their prowess with the human body."

"Twaddle. You're just hitting out at me because I turned you down, Mr. Wolf Clinton."

"Do you have a death wish, little witch?"

Startled, Deba pulled back on the reins, making the mare rear slightly. Deba's backside slewed sideways.

"Watch it. Use your knees." Clinton's arm circled her waist, steadying her.

"Don't you push me." Deba glared at him as she fought to keep from falling off again.

"Damned little bitch. I wasn't doing that, and you know it."

"You bring out the worst in me," she blurted.

"You seem to do well all on your own."

Deba glared, choosing to ignore him. Besides, she had to concentrate on staying on the horse. Why didn't she leave Rancho Lobo?

Why didn't he get rid of her? Wolf shook his head, too many answers surfacing that he didn't like.

The talk between them was desultory as they rode back to the ranch proper.

When they reached the stable area, Deba was slightly ahead of Wolf. Dismounting clumsily but quickly, Deba hurried away from Wolf Clinton, breaking into a run when she rounded the corner of the stables.

By the time she reached the house, perspiration coated her face and body.

Catapulting herself into the kitchen earned a sharp-eyed frown from Julia. Ignoring it, Deba swept by her and up the kitchen stairs to her own suite of rooms, where she locked the door behind her.

Stripping off her clothes and throwing them every which way, she strode to the bathroom and stepped under the shower. "Damn him, damn him!" Why had her body turned to flame when he'd propositioned her? She was no tart. How dare he make such an offer? What would it be like to make love to him? God! Ooo, her back hurt.

Thinking of Wolf and herself on a bed, their bodies entwined with the rhythm of the ages upon them, made her body flush as though she'd just been put through a heatwave. Had he put a spell on her? He was a magnet that pulled her blood into a wild rhythm. Wanting a man wasn't so unusual. Women did that all the time. She closed her eyes. But not her. Now she hungered for a man's body.

Wolf Clinton was a monster, a throwback to the Neanderthal, she thought, trying to dismiss his effect on her. Clad in a bath sheet she reentered her room, gravitating to the small desk where she kept a journal. Often when she was away from her word processor, she brought the journal to her room so that she could made entries in it.

Now she scribbled her tangled emotions on paper, Wolf Clinton like a bull's-eye in her brain.

The notebook was filling fast. When she went back to the beginning and read her initial observations, they seemed alien to what she was writing now. Was there another person writing now? What had happened to that cool perspective?

The first entries were removed, objective. The last few entries in the journal were sniping, satiric. Desperate?

Putting down her pen, she locked the journal away in her desk, her hand shaking. Wolf Clinton was a very upsetting person. She smothered the voice deep inside her that said he was more than that.

Tired and disgruntled, she threw herself down on the bed, pulling the one towel from around her head and cushioning her face on her upraised arms. Deba knew she should brush out her hair. That was her last thought before sleep took her.

Wolf Clinton stared into his mirror as he shaved. He hadn't even enjoyed his massage. Damn Deba McCloud! Intimating that he was a chauvinist. The very word was archaic. "Ouch." He looked at the tiny nick in his chin. Why should he try to explicate his position on the planet to an urchin of a woman with a past? And Deba McCloud had a past. What was it? When he'd mentioned luck of the Irish, she'd actually blanched. Had something happened to her in Ireland? Was that it? Or was she entangled with an Irishman? Hot blood bubbled in his veins. Who the hell was the Irishman in her life?

Wiping his face of the last vestiges of shaving cream, and dabbing atringent on the nick, he donned beige cotton slacks and a matching peasant shirt that hung loose, barely touching his belt line.

Glancing at his watch, he cursed. He should get right to his office. There would be a conference call in another forty-five minutes, and he wanted the material on the desk in front of him.

Why was he letting Deba McCloud into his mind?

"Damn her!" He would ask her about the Irishman.

Clinton left his bedroom, slamming the door behind him. He went down the short hall to the suite adjacent to his.

When he reached Deba McCloud's rooms, he grasped the handle, then paused. No doubt he'd get a tongue-lashing for entering her rooms. What the hell! She was always doing that to him anyway.

Taking a deep breath, he knocked . . . once . . . twice. Then he turned the handle. Locked! Damn her. He was about to turn away, when he noticed the door to her sitting room. Striding to it he grasped the handle, turned it, and pushed into the room.

Frowning, he stared at the closed bedroom door. He should leave. Why the hell let her get under his skin?

Like an automaton he walked down the short hall between the bathroom, sauna, and steam room, crossed to the bedroom door, and opened it.

Wolf saw her at once, sprawled facedown on the bed. The towel that had been wrapped around her body had loosened, her hair was flyaway and not quite dry.

As he watched, she wriggled on the bed, burrowing her face deeper into the pillow, mumbling something and moving the towel completely off her.

Wolf sucked in a breath. His body hardened to readiness at once. Blood pulsated through him, bubbling into a sensuous response that was far beyond anything he expected. His body tingled with want and building desire. It was all he could do to hold back, not to climb into bed with her. Deba McCloud pulled him like a magnet, he wanted her body wrapped around him, he wanted to plunge into her and make her his. Tremors shook his body as he gazed at her.

When last had a woman captured his fantasy, his imagination, turned him on in a flash flood of need? Had any woman ever washed him in passion as Deba was doing? And she was even asleep!

She was exquisite. The shoulders were broad for her too slender frame, tapering down to lovely back and beautifully rounded buttocks. The legs were wonderfully muscled, long, slim right to the trim ankles and narrow feet.

His hands itched to touch that velvet skin, his lips needed to feather over it from neck to the sole of her beautiful foot. Wolf's skin was torrid, his flesh turning liquid with need. His breath was a pant, his nostrils flared with an attempt to get more oxygen into his brain. His hands curved as though they already held her in his grasp. Perspiration beaded his body as his eyes went over her. Never had he shivered with such need, quivered with such want. Damn her!

His want was a familiar throb in his being, but his desire to care and nurture her was new. Wolf liked women and he respected them, the give and take of passion being an integral part of his life. But the women who inhabited that sphere with him had no illusions about the future, nor did he. Now he wanted time to discover all the facets of the lovely Deba McCloud, past, present . . . and future.

Amused, irked, and baffled by his response, he moved closer.

Even as he did, Deba reared up and thrashed around, the mutterings unintelligible but with a lacing of panic, fear.

"Shh, darling, it's all right."

When he sat down on the bed and leaned toward her, trying to soothe her, she turned to him, as though seeking haven, clutching at him.

"Deba, easy." Wolf's libido galloped wildly as he held her. As aroused as he'd ever been, he fought down the urges that had never been tamped before, that had never required the chilling he was forcing from his brain.

For long moments he held her tightly, taking deep breaths, wondering how he was going to free himself from her. Whatever had troubled her sleep was enough for her to bear. He didn't want her to waken and see him beside her. Deba McCloud had enough fear in her life already.

As though on some signal, her body went slack and he was able to place her under the duvet that had been folded at the bottom of the bed.

Wolf left the room, pausing once to look back at her. There was an electricity there that couldn't be denied, and the charge that had come from her could burn him to a cinder.

When Deba awoke, bleary-eyed and dry-mouthed, she knew she'd had the nightmare again. It was always about the time she and her parents had nearly been discovered by the men seeking them. Running down a dark tunnel was the main theme of the dream, though they had not been in any tunnel. They had hidden in a farmer's potato cellar for two days, until her father had deemed it safe. It was two days later that the car had almost hit Deba in Dublin. After that they'd left Ireland. Not long after that she had separated from her parents, her father deeming it safer for her to be on her own.

She went back to the shower and stood under it for many

minutes, trying to wash the blackness away. Thoughts surfaced like tiny bubbles breaking the water. When had she pulled the duvet over her? Had she done it in her sleep? She must have.

That evening when she was dressing for dinner she decided to wear a Guatemalan dress that she'd purchased when she'd first arrived in Mexico. It was of soft cotton and hung baglike over her body, just touching her knees. It was cool and very casual, and the pale turquoise color was a match for the chunky Mexican jewelry she wore, which she had purchased before the movie set had shut down, permanently.

Her friend Maria had steered her to the Mexican Indian who was an artist with turquoise, and she'd been pleased at the price and the style. Touching it was, somehow, sustaining, comforting.

No doubt she would be eating alone that evening. If Wolf Clinton had had a masseuse come from Mexico City, no doubt he would be dining out with one of his many women. She ignored the shaft of pain that such a thought brought to her.

Maybe she could eat in the kitchen, Deba mused as she made her way to the first floor down the front staircase. Her woven leather huaraches slapped the terra-cotta as she ambled toward the back of the house.

"Where are you going?"

Wolf Clinton's soft query spun her around to face him. "Don't you know you could scare someone witless doing that?"

"With you it might be an improvement." He lounged against the door frame, his tall muscular body at ease in his peasant shirt and trousers, both in beige. On his feet he wore satin zapatos, a dressy shoe favored by some Mexican Indians.

"Very amusing. I thought you would be going out after getting loosened up by your masseuse."

As Wolf shoved his way to a standing position, his mouth curled up at one corner. "I should get a whip and chair to control that tongue of yours."

"I think your constant references to my . . . tongue, as you call it, are tedious and . . . and impolite."

"Oh, I see. You fire your bullets but I'm the one who's discourteous."

She hated that twisted smile. "I was going to eat in the kitchen." Looking down at herself and then up at him, she shrugged. "I'm not dressed for formal dining."

He lifted one shoulder in imitation of her. "I'm dressed

informally." Taking her arm, he moved back to the dining room. "Besides, you might insult Julia. I couldn't allow that, since a good cook is a treasure."

"Baloney."

"How have you lived this long?" Hard amusement laced his voice.

"Being selective of my acquaintances," Deba shot back, irked by his remark and annoyed with herself for speaking before thinking.

"What's more amazing is that I keep you here." Wolf seemed to speak more to himself than to her.

"Masochist?"

"I must be." He seated her at a right angle to himself. "So tell me what you thought of the small part of the ranch you saw today. That might be a safe topic for us."

"Don't count on it," Deba mumbled, then smiled weakly when his eyebrow rose again. "Sorry. Ah, I thought it was a lonely, raw place, but with a serenity that was very appealing."

Wolf put his elbows on the table, his chin on his hands, leaning toward her. "Well, there is a meeting of minds here. I see the area the same way. I'm well able to get to an airport if necessary, but I can be totally secluded from so-called civilization."

"You have a helipad; that should make it easier to get to an airport." Deba looked at him over the top of her water glass, seeing an infinitesimal drawing back. "Wasn't I supposed to have noticed it?"

"Many people don't take note of what they see."

"And you count on that."

"Yes."

"I am sorry that I notice things, but you do make it sound so mysterious that you whet a person's curiosity."

"I'll have to remember that. And do you have a great many questions about me?"

"Yes. Can I ask them?"

"If I can ask the same number to you." Wolf didn't miss how she stiffened in her chair

"Actually, I'm not that interesting, so it wouldn't be fair. We'll cancel the questions."

"Interesting." Wolf smiled blandly when she shot him a sharp look. "What do you think you know about me?"

"Not an awful lot," Deba answered carefully. It would be

foolish to fall into the trap of quizzing him; then he would begin his own inquisition and that she couldn't have. Though she now wished she had listened to Maria more carefully when her friend was expounding on Wolfgang Clinton. "I know the tabloids discuss you from time to time."

Wolf's hard laugh pulled an answering smile from her. "More often than I care to recall."

"There was something about a murder . . ." Deba knew at once that she'd stepped over the line. His face drew in on itself, turning to chipped ice in front of her, his eyes slitting and narrowing in rejection of her.

When Julia pushed open the swinging door, the swishing sound it made was like the crack of a whip in the silence.

"Senor, it is your favorite. Cold papaya and passion fruit soup to start and lobster fresh from Grenada." Julia's beaming smile wavered and she looked accusingly at Deba. "I hope you have not been putting the senor off his food with silliness."

"The opposite is true, I think," Deba murmured, lifting her spoon and letting it hover over the pink confection in the Waterford bowl. He could put a person off food for life.

"We will take our time with this, Julia. Bring the lobsters in in a little while." Wolf spoke quietly, but his eyes glittered and the hand holding the spoon had whitened.

The housekeeper glared at Deba, then flounced from the room.

"She'll be poisoning my food," Deba ventured.

"Unless I strangle you first."

"Angry, are you? Sorry about that, but I did read something about a murder in connection with you."

"That is long past, and most of what you read was fiction."

"Is that one of the reasons you don't travel freely in your own country?"

"You're pushing your luck, Deba McCloud."

"So I am. This is very good cold soup."

"Yes."

Deba sucked in a deep breath and worked her way through the cold soup, then she sat with her hands in her lap, looking around the room at everything and anything except her employer.

When Julia returned some time later, there had been no further conversation between them. "Senor, you didn't finish your soup. Shall I leave it?"

"No, Julia, take it away . . . and bring a bottle of tequila."

"Tequila, senor? You don't touch it anymore."

"Julia!"

"*Sí*, I will do it, but it will not go with the lobsters."

Deba looked at him then. "I am sorry. You're face looks as though it's been hammered from a rock. I had no intention of disturbing you in such a fashion."

"Didn't you? Why don't I believe that?"

Deba was prevented from answering by Julia's return.

The housekeeper held a bottle in front of her as though it were a coiled snake.

"None for me, thank you," Deba whispered to a glowering Julia, who twisted her hands in her apron when she put down the bottle.

"Senor, you will eat my lobsters, *por favor*?"

Wolf nodded without answering, his eyes on the bottle in front of him.

When the lobsters were served, steaming and bright red, Deba began cracking hers, but Wolf opened the bottle and drank from it, eschewing a glass.

"You promised Julia," Deba whispered, disturbed by the flat, hellish look to those golden eyes.

"So I did." Wolf didn't look at her as he cracked the lobster and systematically devoured it as though the taste and flavor had eluded him.

"The vegetable crepes are good." Deba offered him the platter after he'd taken another swig of the fiery liquid in front of him.

"They usually are." Wolf swallowed more of the tequila.

"Try the bread."

Wolf shook his head and lifted the bottle to his lips.

"Whatever it was I said that triggered this, I regret it. Surely you don't need to—"

"Surely I do." Wolf looked at her for long moments. "Shut up for once, Deba McCloud."

"Don't tell me to shut up." Bristling, she straightened in her chair, throwing her napkin onto the table.

"If that were a gauntlet, I'd pick it up and you'd rue the day you crossed me, Deba."

Staring into those opaque gold eyes made her shiver. It was

like raising the shade on Hades. "Excuse me, I'll go to my room."

"Do that." Wolf upended the bottle into his mouth.

Stalking out of the room, Deba was consumed by fury and a teary regret. If she'd said nothing, they would still be at the table, dining à deux. Remembering that smile when they'd first been seated made her skin coat with goosebumps. One hot, regretful tear coursed down her cheek.

No! It was just as well that they weren't on speaking terms. She still had to deal with his declaration of intent about getting her to bed. No way was she going to set herself up like that. The man was a positive sultan. How many times had she read things about him and women. . . . But why had she brought up the subject of the murder? It had brought hell to his eyes. Regret was like a lemony lump in her chest.

As Deba passed his study, she paused. That strong fascination that had drawn her to Wolf from the first, drew her to his study. It was Wolf Clinton's sanctum sanctorum. She rarely entered it and only when invited. Pushing at the door was an impulse, and the fact that it opened shocked her for a moment. Without considering the possibilities, she entered and closed it behind her. Hearing the click of the latch with mixed emotions, she leaned back and looked around her.

The book-lined room was a miniature library with novels, texts, classics, and research materials filling every available space.

The desk was like a magnet, drawing her to it.

That it was also unlocked was a similar shock. Opening the top drawer, she stared at the minutiae that seemed to be standard fare for a desk drawer. All the others were the same except the bottom right drawer, which yielded a notebook, eight by ten, thick and bulging with pictures, with strips of paper columns, underlined and notated. The name on the front of the book was Natasha Damon. The name rang a tiny bell but Deba couldn't fit it to a memory.

On the flyleaf of the book was an inscription:

TO WOLF, THIS IS SO MUCH OF WHAT YOU WANTED TO FORGET, DARLING, I THOUGHT I WOULD COLLECT IT ALL FOR YOU AND YOU COULD HAVE THE JOY OF BURNING IT. I DON'T THINK I MISSED A THING. XXX N.

Flipping the pagers slowly, Deba gasped at the font of information about her employer.

When she saw the word *murder,* she paused and read the article that looked to have been cut from a tabloid.

WOLF CLINTON CHARGED WITH DEATH OF FRIEND.
Natasha Sharansky, world-famous ballerina defected
from Russia, was the third in the triangle of murder
that took the life of Willard C. Temple. Wolf Clinton
directed the great Natasha in two movies, *Witchcraft*
and *Witch Hazel.* Reliable sources have revealed that
it was at this time that they became lovers.

Deba stared at the article. How hard must it be for him to live with himself, knowing that he killed his friend and took the woman that had been involved with both of them.

It would be no wonder he drank. Surcease from pain? To ease his conscience? And what had happened to Natasha Sharansky, who had used her maiden name professionally? What a great prima ballerina she'd been. Tiny, vibrant, quicksilver on the stage. The world had been at her feet.

Deba was no great follower of ballet, though she liked the dance, but she didn't recall that Natasha Sharansky danced anymore. What had happened to the black-haired, dark-eyed beauty who had electrified millions?

Had Wolf killed her as well? Deba shivered.

When she heard a noise she looked up from the notebook. The prospect of being caught in this room by Wolf Clinton made her blood chug through her veins painfully. Still, there was a need to know more of what was in the notebook. Dare she take it with her? The drawer had stuck and seemed not to be used much. The notebook had been the only thing in it. Would it be possible to copy the contents and return it? She had to try.

Grasping the notebook firmly, she went to the door and turned the handle. The door opened smoothly and quietly.

When she looked out into the wide corridor it was empty. Getting to her room without being seen would be a trick, though. There was always someone moving about the place.

Dry-mouthed, she stepped into the hall and closed the door behind her. Not looking left or right, she made for the stairs, praying that no servant would see her. There had been no place to hide the notebook on her person, so she carried it in her hand.

One day she would have to leave Wolf, she had to keep on the move, but at least if she had notes on him she would have something of him to look at, study, and remember.

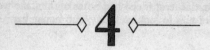

Deba fought the breathlessness that assailed her.

What had she done? Stolen! No way to gild it, she'd taken something that her employer considered important . . . and private. Just because she was nosy, she risked losing her job . . . maybe even an arm or a leg? Insanity wasn't a viral disease. So why had she just come down with it? Hadn't she signed a contract stating that she would never write anything about him for at least five years after she left his employ? Then she couldn't use what she took, even if she wanted to, which she didn't. Why the insatiable curiosity about a man who had been involved in crime? Didn't she have enough trouble in her life without courting more? So what if he was almost a fugitive? So was she. Wolf Clinton had been cleared by the courts, but many people still thought him guilty of first-degree murder. Did that make him "almost a fugitive"? No matter. She had no right to his private papers. Maybe not, but she needed to have something of him.

Damn, damn, damn. Why was she magnetized by Wolf-gang Clinton?

If Wolf Clinton ever discovered her perfidy he'd pull her apart and scatter the pieces. Why had she done it? She could not write an exposé on Wolf Clinton. It would be illegal, she'd signed a contract. But there were other reasons. Not just because it had been done a hundred times, but because he was dangerous . . . and maybe vengeful. More trouble like that she didn't need. It had been stupid to take the scrapbook. What if he decided to investigate her? What would happen to her parents? She'd been stupid to take it. Returning it quickly was the thing to do.

Besides, she had the distinct feeling what it would tell her would be just the tip of the iceberg. Wolf Clinton would not have had anything really important in an open desk drawer.

Deba knew she should put it back at once. But . . . ! As long as she had it she might as well take the time to look it over before returning it. Damnable, out-of-control curiosity!

Looking around her room, she tried to imagine a place where no one would look for what she'd taken. Going to her closet, she looked up at her battered suitcase. That would be it. It had been emptied. Now it was just stored in her closet. No one would give it a second glance.

The cleaning staff, consisting of local girls in their late teens, would never look inside the case even if they worked in the closet. They had been sternly trained by Julia.

Even as she reached to pull the case down, her hand stopped and she looked at the notebook. It was so tempting to study it further, to find out more about the lovely Natasha and what she meant to Wolf. Her fingers curled into her palm as she pictured them together. Better not put it away. Now was the time to study the material. Do it! A knife turned inside her as she pictured Wolf caressing the dainty ballerina.

Maybe at some other time she could make copies of the parts she didn't get to read. Why not put it all on the word processor? No, that would take time . . . but maybe little by little she could print or copy the material, then she could look at it at her leisure. There was a doomsday morbidity to her curiosity. Her imagination drew colorful enough pictures of Wolf and Natasha. Was it necessary to have those feelings reinforced? Resolutely she smothered the cautioning voice that told her to return the material unopened.

Why the sudden feeling of being a traitor, ungrateful? That was silly. She wasn't going to do anything with the information. Hadn't she already decided that? So? No problem. It was just that her curiosity had been sorely piqued. She needed to know about the boss man.

Hesitation still ran through her. Somehow it was more than just fear of being discovered by Wolf, perhaps even fired, if he saw her with the notebook. Deba didn't want to see that opaque look of distrust, the flat, emotionless acceptance of her betrayal. Her skin prickled with a shivery guilt and pain.

From the small amount she'd been able to read in his study, the chronological writings and clippings read like an adventure novel, a piece of fiction, not the happenings of a personal life of one Wolfgang Clinton.

Backing across the bedroom, the notebook clutched in her hand, she sat down on the bed, then kicked off her shoes.

Deba turned the pages slowly, speed-reading the contents as she moved through it. More than once she paused and shut the offending notebook. It wasn't usually her nature to be a snooper, and that's what she was at the moment.

He had been referred to as "Lobo" in many of the articles that were taped into the folder. The tongue-in-cheek attacks on him often bordered on libel. Had Clinton ever sued? Was this why he was a pariah in his own country? Had the many charges against him ever proved true?

Deba reopened the notebook as though her hands had a life of their own. Flipping through the front sections that she had already scanned, she began reading at about a third of the way through the notebook.

Page after page was devoted to his work in cinema, and it began to evolve, from the credits and reviews, that Wolfgang Clinton was considered somewhat of a genius in his field, even by his peers. Deba nodded. She had known that, remembering how enthralled she'd been when she'd seen *Witchcraft*, the movie that had garnered several Oscars and many plaudits. Natasha had been the leading lady, the one and only time she had danced on screen. Her dancing had been electric, her body a tuning fork that had picked up the vibrations of the universe and translated them into rhythmic motion.

Deba skipped to another section of the well-organized notebook.

In the business world he was another kind of success, rebuilding tottering financial empires, amalgamating them into his own business structure or reselling them at huge profits after putting them on their feet. Wolf Clinton had the Midas touch.

His team of business whizzes were coached by him, according to *Business Week* and *Forbes* magazine. Deba was impressed with the many articles clipped from business periodicals eulogizing his business acumen. There were just as many who called him charlatan.

Wolfgang Clinton, the Wall Street Lobo, the movie-making mogul, could do no wrong. Everything he touched turned to money. Success was his.

Yet another vignette began to appear from the comprehensive notebook. Wolf Clinton had beautiful, successful women, but there seemed to be constant trouble in his personal life.

The accounts of the murder of Willard C. Temple were garish and graphic. Much of it was one-sided. Willard Temple had been a close associate of Clinton's, some said an intimate friend. The gossip columns screamed with the travesty of justice, that a murderer could walk out of the courts a free man after deliberately killing his friend. Lobo Clinton, the alleged murderer, was guilty of cold-bloodedly killing the hapless Willard Temple . . . before he even had a trial. Then at his trial there had been numerous bits of circumstantial evidence that painted the defendant even blacker. And a man would of course look guilty when doing very little to defend himself.

There were batteries of lawyers who wove a defense for Lobo Clinton. The tabloids said that money had been the decisive factor. Clinton had bought his innocence. Justice was blind . . . and dumb!

There was no record of Lobo Clinton fighting the charges that mounted against him. The fact that he killed a long-time acquaintance and friend so that he could have the woman, Natasha, that both men wanted, was stated over and over in the periodicals. His guilt was a fait accompli.

Natasha was cleared of all charges; she wasn't even called to testify. She'd gone into seclusion. Heartbroken? Devastated? Her career would be irreparably damaged, the tabloids screamed.

Time seemed to prove the yellow journalists to be right. Deba had seen very little mention of the world-famous prima ballerina in the last few years. Was she dead?

Articles, raggedly cut and pasted in the book, spoke clearly and cruelly of her eventual entrance into a home for the mentally ill. Then came a marriage with a person named Marle Damon.

Halfway through the bulging portfolio, Deba put it down and inhaled shakily. What a book it would make! But it could

never be written. It would be too cruel to the lovers, to Natasha
. . . to Wolf.

Perhaps someday a fictional account with fictional names
could be done. In play or novel form the story would be powerful! Wolf Clinton should do it himself, the catharsis might be a
boon to his spirit.

Deba brought her knees up to her chin, the notebook sand-
wiched between her face and thigh. Wolf!

Wolf Clinton would sue anyone who wrote anything that
would approximate the truth. He loved Natasha. Why hadn't
they married? They had been silent all through their predica-
ment. Why had they chosen to be sacrificial lambs? Natasha
must have wanted to marry Wolf. Their love had been so great.
What agony it was to dwell on that!

Deba decided if she ever wrote of Wolf, it would be a novel,
not a biography. Wolf was too explosive, too volatile to be real.
It couldn't be brought out as the straight truth. Fictionalized
truth. Would that exorcise some of her own ghosts, the ghosts
that dogged her parents and her? Probably not. Hers were too
real . . . and wanted to kill her and her parents.

Even now she was too complacent. Had Wolf wrought the
change, caused her to let down her guard? She should run from
Wolf, not just to protect herself, but him as well . . . but he
pulled her like a magnet.

Maybe one day when she was alone she would write Wolf's
story, if for nothing more than to keep him close to her. Life in
his company was so vibrant, zinging with zest.

What if she wrote the novel just as it came to her, with the
facts, feelings, all intact . . . just put it down, no more, no less,
not trying to inject any literary touches. Taking the story of the
notebook and transcribing it to manuscript could be a tonic.

Weaving a tale of Wolf could bring her close to him, even
when she would be a world away.

Someday, in the not-too-distant future, she would be away
from Rancho Lobo, alone as always, looking for a way to survive, trying to keep in contact with her parents without putting
them in peril. Would fashioning a book on Wolf be solace?

Be practical! A book, well written, with the rich research
material provided by the notebook, could give her the edge she
needed, a freedom that could come from financial indepen-
dence.

Deba had signed a contract eschewing such action. She

couldn't do it just to keep her own "wolf" from the door. If she did it, it would be to keep Wolf alive for her.

Shaking her head, Deba clutched the notebook. Only in a dire emergency would she market the story of Wolfgang Clinton. Nothing so bad had occurred yet that would make that happen. Why should the future be any different? No! She would never sell his story no matter how much she missed him, or needed the money.

Envisioning the time when she would be away from Wolf Clinton was an awesome pain that had her gasping. She could go home to the United States, forget him. Ha! If not forget him, at least she might be able to stop dreaming about him, seeing him behind her eyelids the moment she closed them.

Wearily she rose and went to her closet and put the notebook in the battered suitcase.

Brushing her teeth and washing was an effort, and when she climbed between the sheets, sleep came at once . . . and so did the dreams.

Deba was running through a field, air coming in painful gasps from her throat, looking over her shoulder constantly and trying to increase her speed. What was chasing her? It was terrible, frightening, awesome. But what was it? If only the tunnel wasn't so dark she would be able to see who was after her.

Deba woke in a tangle of sheets, perspiration rolling down her face, out of breath, out of sorts, frightened. She pressed her damp face into her hands. It was morning. Thank God!

Shivering, she got out of bed and hurried to the bathroom. Standing, faceup, under the pulsating shower, she tried to wash away memories of the painful night.

Dressing in a pair of cotton jeans and lemony-toned shirt, she brushed her hair into a twist atop her head.

Going downstairs, she approached the breakfast room with some trepidation. Since "Lobo" Clinton hadn't summoned her to go riding with him, she had to assume that he was sleeping the morning away. That wouldn't be surprising considering the way he'd swilled down tequila at the dinner table.

Deba stopped in her tracks. He could have discovered that the notebook was missing from his study!

Cold perspiration dampened her underarms, though she'd just come from a shower and shampoo.

Taking a deep breath, she stepped into the morning room.

Julia turned, tight-lipped, cocking her head. "The senor is not here. He had to go into the city."

Deba assumed that Julia meant Mexico City, and she sighed with relief. Her appetite came back with a vengeance. "I think I would like eggs over medium and muffins this morning, Julia, with those wonderful peppers you fix, not the hot ones. And maybe coffee . . . and some papaya juice, I think." Deba took her seat and smiled at the housekeeper, who was watching her narrow-eyed. "Is something wrong, Julia?"

"You have a good appetite, Senorita Mac-Cloud." Julia shrugged. "You are too skinny."

"I'm hungry today."

"*Sí,* I will bring the food. Then you will take a nice sunbath today, eh?"

Deba thought of the notebook. "Ah, no, I have some things of Mr. Clinton's I should work on this morning, Julia." That was no lie, but it wasn't the total truth either.

After a very satisfying breakfast in which she'd had to struggle against the disappointment of not going riding with Wolf Clinton, she rose from the table annoyed with herself. Stupid, stupid! She didn't even like riding all that well, she generally was sore afterwards . . . yet she'd yearned for those moments together now.

Wolf Clinton was insidious and well named. Lobo. He was working his way into her bloodstream . . . devouring her. It angered her mightily that she seemed to be caught in his jaws.

One moment he could make her more skittish than the colt one of the hands had been trying to gentle. At other times she felt teary and confused around him. Soon she wouldn't be able to recognize herself. She was becoming dependent on him. That couldn't happen. If she was to save herself, protect her parents, she had to be vigilant, on her own, trusting only herself.

How long had she been on Rancho Lobo? Years? Or mere days?

Maybe it was time to leave Rancho Lobo, leave Mexico, escape the influence of Clinton. Where would she go this time?

Tamping down the spurt of grief that rose in her, she put future plans on hold and returned to her bedroom to retrieve the notebook. Then she went downstairs again to her office.

Entering the room, Deba did something she'd never done, she locked the door behind her. Then she went to the windows and opened them but fastened and locked the grilles.

Turning to the copier, she checked for ink and paper. Then glancing once over her shoulder at the locked door, she switched on the machine.

Separating the sheets took longer than expected. Though it was a three-ring-type portfolio with the kind of sheets that were normally easy to remove, this was not the case. The age of the material had made some of the sheets subject to tearing, so she had to go slowly.

At last all the pages were free, and then she began copying. First one side, then the other.

Time flew as she fed the copier.

A rap at the door and shaking of the doorknob made her freeze in place. "Yes?"

"Senorita Mac-Cloud, it's Julia. You have locked the door. How can I bring you coffee?"

Deba took a deep breath, put the cover back on the copier so that it covered the sheets as well. "Coming." Opening the door, she smiled brightly at the housekeeper, who frowned at her, glancing from her face to the door, then around her shoulder. "Umm, the coffee smells wonderful. Did you make the turnovers too?"

"Of course." Julia looked affronted, glancing around the room as though she suspected something might be missing.

"I must have pressed the lock by mistake. Thank you for the coffee and pastries, Julia. I should get back to work."

"*Sí.*" Julia looked puzzled, but she obligingly left.

Deba's hand hovered over the lock, but she resisted the temptation. Julia could be right outside the door.

Moving more rapidly now, she ignored the coffee and fed the copier with the material as fast as she could.

It was almost noon when she finished, the coffee untouched, the Mexican fruit tournedos ignored.

Shutting down the copier, she went to the window and opened the grilles, then went out to the terrace and poured the cold coffee into the yucca plant there.

Once back in the room, she tidied the place, checking twice to see that she had the copies and the masters.

Then, packing the materials and uneaten tournedos in a tote bag, she left the office.

Hurrying to her room, she put the originals back into the portfolio, and then that into the battered suitcase, which she replaced on the top of her closet.

Putting the copies together as carefully as possible took time. By the time she'd assembled and stapled it, a full hour had passed. She put the sheets into a folder and then she put them in the suitcase in the closet, removing the portfolio.

With luck she could replace it before Wolf returned from Mexico City. What if his study was locked? It made sense that it would be, since Wolf wasn't in residence. Deba blocked that from her mind.

Taking deep breaths to calm herself, Deba put the portfolio in the tote she'd brought from her office, and opened her bedroom door.

There was no one in the downstairs hall. Why did her footsteps sound so loud all at once? The house had an empty feeling. Maybe she was fooling herself. Coast clear! No one was near Wolf's study.

Would Julia come looking for her? Lunch was usually served between twelve and two.

Trying the door to the study, she had a heart-stopping moment. Was it locked? It wasn't!

Glancing quickly up and down the wide main corridor of the house, she plunged into the study, shutting the door behind her and leaning against it, eyes closed. Her heart thudded like a trip hammer.

Rushing to the desk, she pulled open the center drawer that released the bottom one and replaced the portfolio in relatively the same position as she'd found it.

Returning to the door, her perspiring hand slipping on the doorknob, she turned the handle and opened it. Counting to three she checked the hall. No one! Moisture beaded her upper lip.

Crossing the hall to the stairs, she had put her foot on the first one.

"Hello. Been working? Julia says you haven't had lunch."

Angst needled her spine, her skin prickled with goosebumps. Turning in measured movements, she tried to smile at her employer. Had he seen her come from his study?

Swallowing twice to clear the tightness in her throat, she stared at him. Had he grown a foot? Were there horns growing through that chestnut hair? Did he have cloven hooves or feet? "Ah, Julia told me you were out for the day, that you'd gone to the city."

Wolf nodded. "I did. Los Angeles was crowded and noisy."

"Los Angeles! I thought you'd gone to Mexico City. How did you get back so quickly?"

"I can see you missed me." The harsh laugh was like a gunshot in the quiet house. Damn! He was being defensive with her again.

Deba swallowed. "I managed to get a little work done." They were sparring like a couple of wary dogs. Was he going to fire her?

"I wasn't censuring you." He wanted to start anew with her, be back on an easy footing. Easy? Was anything easy with Deba McCloud?

Why did she feel guilty? "Ah, maybe you'd like to work now?" He had given her a job. She wasn't starving, so she had no reason to lash out at him.

"No. I'd rather grab some fruit and go swimming. Would you like that too?"

"Ah, yes, I like swimming . . . and the fruit sounds good." She had missed lunch. Deba felt giddy with relief that he hadn't spotted her coming out of his study.

"Good." He hadn't even realized he was holding his breath until she gave him a positive answer. When he was on the plane he'd planned what they'd do to make up for the miserable dinner the night before, but he'd had no great hopes she'd go along with it. He felt positively gleeful. "Get some things together. We'll be dining away from home this evening."

"Aren't we swimming in the pool?" Deba called after him as he passed her and went up the stairs two at a time.

"No. Get moving, Deba McCloud."

His smile was easy, his drawl the same, but Deba felt uneasy, shivering as though someone had walked on her grave.

"Don't forget the fruit."

"You and your appetite, Deba McCloud." His laugh curled out behind him, wrapping around Deba, holding her.

Before she could ask him where they would be swimming he'd disappeared into his wing of the house.

Getting her things together in her room, her eyes kept going to the closet and the piece of luggage on the shelf. Even while she packed a garment bag that had mysteriously appeared on her bed, her eyes and mind traveled to the closet. It would be all right there. No one would interfere with her things.

Releasing a shuddering sigh, she fastened the case and

looked around her, lifting it and slinging her shoulder bag into place. Where was she going? Why hadn't she protested?

Going down the stairs, she had the sensation of going to her own hanging.

"Good, you're ready. Shall we go?" Wolf saw the uncertainty in her eyes, the way they probed his face, studied it.

Had he seen her come from his study? Deba still wasn't sure.

Women! They always had to pry, to dig, to ruffle the surface of things with their curiosity. He didn't know what she'd been up to, but he would bet she'd been nosing around some. He shrugged off his suspicions. "Shall we go?"

"Ah, where are we going?"

"Wouldn't it be nice to have the afternoon off, to have a holiday?"

"Your Socratic answers tell me nothing," she responded tartly.

"Aren't we all secretive at times?"

Why did his mild question set her back up, cause her to shiver? "I suppose."

Once out-of-doors, they went to the four-wheel-drive vehicle that had been parked in front of the hacienda.

As an attendant approached the jeep, Wolf waved him away. "Have someone pick it up at the helipad, José."

Deba was able to translate the rapidly spoken Spanish and she gave a start of surprise. She paused, but before she could say anything she was all but lifted into the jeep, and then Wolf was around the front and behind the wheel.

With a roar and a jerk the vehicle spat stones on its exit down the curving driveway, dust pluming out behind it.

Gripping the seat and the roll bar above her head, Deba was sure her garment bag had been tossed out of the vehicle by his erratic driving. "You're a maniac," she shouted at him.

"In a hurry," Wolf answered tersely, gripping the wheel and going over the high ground.

"Can't we use the road?" Deba raised her voice to be heard, every tooth in her head rattling, in danger of biting her tongue.

"Relax."

With Wolfgang Clinton? That was one thing she couldn't do.

The helicopter ride had been a sensational experience for Deba. Rising almost straight up in the air, seeing the wonderful high, flat, sometimes rolling, often mountainous countryside had been an unforgettable sensation. It almost made her forget her trepidation, almost but not quite.

"You're very silent, Deba McCloud." Wolf turned to look at her as they sat behind the pilot.

"It's my first helicopter ride. I like it."

"I can see that." When she turned quickly to look at him, he caught the vulnerable, defensive expression on her face, which she quickly masked. What made him lean down and take her lips, he'd never know. The sudden unexpected racing of his heart shook him. He was too used to being in command of his emotions, so he was shocked at the way his blood raced. When her hand came up and touched his cheek, he saw stars and planets behind his closed eyes.

Deba felt his body shudder, and an answering tremor went through her frame. His body shifted so that he could lift her closer to him. Lights flashed in her head as though a very personal fireworks display had begun. "Pilot," she gasped, her mouth centimeters from his.

"He's busy with his instruments." Wolf let his mouth course up and down her neck.

"Do you fly?"

A smile of awareness snaked across that tough mouth. It touched Deba like a velvet whip, filling her with warmth, vibrating her skin with a spirit quake that shocked her.

"Putting me off, darling?"

"Trying. I'm your employee."

"So you are." Wolf kissed her again, gently, searchingly. "And you are much more than that." There was a lacing of surprise in his voice and in his glance. His fingers feathered over her arm.

"Tell me where we're going." Deba leaned away from him, her gaze touching the pilot's back.

Wolf looked at her a moment longer, then leaned back in his own seat, threading his fingers through hers. "We're going to a place I own where the diving is very good. It's a beautiful lagoon. I thought you'd enjoy that."

"I will." Deba thought her hand throbbed with new life because Wolf was holding it. "Ah, does this helicopter go faster than most or is it my imagination?"

"It's not your imagination. The newest technology, pretty lady. In some ways it's as powerful as a jet. It is certainly more useful to me, since it takes far less space for landing."

Deba nodded, trying hard to concentrate on what he was saying. Her body pulsated in a new rhythm because he was touching her. Wolf Clinton had raised her consciousness to a sensual awareness that she had never thought existed. "And can you fly it?"

"Yes, I often do, but not this time." His fingers tightened on hers.

How long they sat there, hands clasped, Wolf wasn't sure, but when he looked over and found that she was asleep, he felt a rush of protectiveness. She had fallen asleep very fast. Was she ill? Overtired? Concern filled him. Only with Natasha had he ever felt such a desire to shield. Natasha! How was she really doing? Sometimes it seemed when he saw her she was putting on a facade, that she was hiding her real self from him.

Pressing the button on the seat, he let it move back, and the action caused Deba to slide his way. He caught her close and shut his eyes. A feeling of ineffable peace invaded him.

There were no constants on the unfriendly planet where he dwelled, but for now, there was Deba McCloud.

The helicopter was setting down when Wolf woke, looking down at the woman who was cuddled close to him. Kissing her hair, he placed her back in her seat and went forward to sit next to the pilot.

"I'll call you when I want you to come and get us."

"Right, sir."

Wolf returned to Deba, waking her with a gentle searching kiss. "Hi. We're here."

"Ah, good." Deba's heart thudded to her shoes and back again when he kissed her gently.

"I'll be right back." Wolf returned to the cockpit, telling the pilot what frequency he'd be using when he radioed him.

They deplaned quickly, Wolf and the pilot loading the small amount of supplies and luggage in the back of a jeep.

When they returned to the helicopter for more sundries, Deba was in the doorway, rubbing her eyes.

Wolf moved quickly around the pilot, lifting her to the ground and carrying her to the jeep before she could say anything.

In minutes the job was done and the pilot was closing the doors.

A sleepy-eyed Deba watched the helicopter leave from the passenger seat of the vehicle that had been waiting for them, and then she and Wolf were racing over the rough ground. The prime thing was to hang on and not be flung out of the jeep. Now the ride seemed exciting, not dangerous. "Why are we going so fast?"

"Frightened?" Wolf laughed out loud.

"No! I must be crazy too. I'm beginning to like it." Deba laughed too.

Wolf braked as they came in sight of the water, stopping on a knoll. "Well?"

"I remember a lagoon like this at Xalha. We took a motor trip one weekend when . . . when the movie was still on and we had some time off," Deba whispered, looking around her at the expanse of jungle that surrounded the lagoon, the clearing with the small cottage on it seeming to be the only bare space for miles. "It's very isolated."

"Very." Wolf smiled at her, trying to mask the tension that

was building in him. "There's another helicopter here, plus there are vehicles that can take us overland."

Deba stared at him. "So you're giving me an out."

"If you want it."

She should tell him that she did. "I'd like to stay." She smiled when he exhaled.

"I'm glad." Putting the jeep in gear, he drove to the parking space next to the cottage. Taking the few pieces of luggage that were all they had with them, he gestured for her to precede him. "The door's open. Only the cleaning staff comes here." Once inside he put down the two bags and looked at her. "What do you think?"

Deba looked around her and smiled. "It's nice. I like it."

Crossing the room to her side, he bent down and kissed her, worrying her lips apart so that his tongue could touch hers. "That makes me happy . . . but somehow I knew you would like it." Again there was a thread of surprise in his voice. "This is one of my favorite places. Usually I come here alone." His mouth met hers once more. "I'll get the rest of the supplies. Be right back. Miss me." He touched the tip of her nose with his index finger.

What was happening? Who speeded up the planet? Why should Wolf's telling her to miss him make her so inordinately happy? Wolf Clinton lived a zany life, but he'd brought a measure of serenity into her nomadic existence. Maybe she couldn't let her guard down, but she could savor the time with him. Such precious moments shouldn't be wasted. There had been so few warm, wonderful times in her life the last few years. She yearned to be held by this man, cared for by him. He had magnetized her from their first meeting. Even if the feelings he engendered were bogus, she meant to treasure them. Soon she would have to leave him. Why not have a little ecstasy?

When Wolf returned with the stores, setting them in the small kitchen, Deba approached him. "Hi."

He turned toward her and smiled. "Hi," he said huskily.

Heart pounding, she twined her arms around his neck. Whatever warnings were going off in her head, none penetrated the heated aura of being held by Wolf, of being alone with him. Her mouth opened on his so naturally.

When he pulled back from her, he was out of breath and frowning.

"Did I do something wrong?" Deba felt such a chill of rejection.

Wolf kissed her forehead. "No, darling, I'm just baffled by the power you have. Never have I been in such a force field," he told her ruefully.

Sheer relief was in her laugh. "Then I won't feel bad if I tell you that I've had the same sensation."

Wolf tightened his hold, leaning over her, his mouth barely touching hers. "We generate a great deal of electricity, Deba McCloud."

"Do you think it's safe for us to enter the lagoon? I'd hate to set up a charge that burned us."

"Too late. I'm already in flames."

His purring voice went over her skin like poured satin.

Wolf felt her body tremble and held her tighter.

"We should get our suits on before the day is gone." Deba felt a wrenching regret, her hand feathering over his cheek before it dropped to her side.

"Yes." Wolf kissed her hard. "I'll race you across the lagoon, Deba, love, so hurry and change."

The endearment was like a bubble in her blood, it interfered with her breathing, her limbs were melting wax. "You're on," she told him breathlessly, then looked around her. "Which room is mine?"

Wolf pointed, watching until she disappeared. His body tingled and stung as though he'd just come out of a long sleep, as though he'd just come alive. Maybe he had. Deba did that to him.

Leaping up into the air, he slapped the ceiling with the palm of his hand.

Deba's door opened and she poked out her head. "What was that?"

"I slammed the ceiling with my hand."

She grinned. "Macho man." Then she shut the door again.

"Yeah!" He grinned at the door. "Damn her," he muttered out loud. "She's got a tongue that could slice through wood, but she's the most feminine creature I've ever known." He sprinted for the other bedroom and tossed his duffel on the bed. He had ample clothing stashed at the cottage, so he rarely brought anything with him but toiletries.

He grabbed a pair of riviera briefs and donned them quickly.

In minutes he was out of the room again, noting that Deba's door was open. He saw her when he looked out the floor-to-ceiling window. She was running toward the lagoon.

Right at her heels he slowed his pace when he saw her pause at the water's edge. "Looking for unfriendly fish life?"

She turned, smiling. "Are there any?"

He shook his head, pointing toward the ocean and moving closer. "There's a reef that manages to keep out the dangerous underwater life." He touched her chin with one hand. "You're lovely, darling."

It was like being hit in the chest when he used an endearment. If she looked behind her, Deba was sure she would see her bridges burning. Not all the warning voices in the world would make a difference. Wolf Clinton had taken hold of her. She reacted to his touch and turned toward him, smiling.

"Let me." He removed the toweling shirt she wore and dropped it onto a rock that edged the lagoon. His eyes roved her from shoulder to foot. "You have a lovely, lissome body. Why are you so slender? Do you diet?"

Yes, if you could call being on the run and too frightened to eat, dieting. "I suppose I just burn more calories than most," Deba said lamely.

A light went off in his brain. Deba had lied to him. Why? It was the same sort of withdrawal that he'd experienced from her when he'd mentioned Ireland. He had an urge to know what had caused her to be secretive. Wolf stemmed the questions. There were too many hidden areas in his life not to understand a need for secrecy. But if someone was frightening her, he would discover who it was and he would take care of that. "Shall we swim?"

"How about the depth?"

"Very good for swimming and diving."

Deba grinned, then back-tracking a few feet, she ran for the ledge on the lagoon. Flinging herself into the air in a powerful racing dive, she hit the water, stroking hard at the moment of contact.

"Damned little devil." Wolf laughed out loud, running toward the water, his body knifing through the air in full pursuit.

Deba reckoned that the lagoon was roughly half a mile across at the narrowest part, to an outcropping on the other shore. She aimed herself at that point. Wolf would be right at her heels. Bearing down, she pushed herself to the limit.

With a burst of strength Wolf pulled even with her, his body zinging with good feeling. Zest! That had been missing from his life for a long time.

Pulling past Deba as they neared the far side, Wolf could sense that she had turned on a new burst of speed. Far from backing down, she was giving it everything she had.

Reaching the outcropping, Wolf flip-turned and caught Deba as she approached the point, full steam. "Darling, you could have cracked your head coming in that fast." Wolf couched her form with his, catching a blow to his elbow when the force of her body pushed it back against the ledge rock.

"You're . . . barely . . . breathing hard," Deba told him, panting.

"You almost won." Wolf kissed her, wincing when his arm hit the rock again.

"Oh. That hurt, didn't it?" Concerned, Deba reached for his arm.

"Actually I'm fine, but you're welcome to baby me for a while."

"No." She smiled up at him, feeling his strong legs moving against her in the gentle movement of the water.

"Kiss me, Deba. I need that."

Lifting her face blindly, like a flower to the sun, she welcomed his mouth.

The kiss went on, binding them, making them malleable as it fired them. Arms around each other, they sank below the surface.

Oxygen gone, Wolf blew the last of his into her mouth and rose from the depths like a dolphin.

Turning to look at him, water rivering down her face, Deba knew that the desire on his face was mirrored in her own.

"Come here, love, I want to show you something."

Unquestioning, Deba swam closer to Wolf as he moved toward the shore.

"Wait here." Wolf climbed out of the water and went to a shed that sat back from the shore. Bringing back two masks and some flippers, he slipped into the water again.

"Oh, dear, I'll have to get out to put on my flippers. I can't put them on in the water."

"I'll do it for you." Without waiting for her reply, Wolf dove down near her feet, fitting first one, then the other of the

swimming aids to her feet. Then he surfaced, taking a deep
breath.

"Was your mother a dolphin? You have terrific lung
power." Deba felt shy with him all at once.

"Thank you." Wolf felt helium-light and pleased with himself because Deba had complimented him. It was all new to
him, the reactions brought on by Deba McCloud. "Shall I fit
your mask for you?"

Deba shook her head. "I can do that. I've done a fair
amount of snorkeling . . . and I love it."

"Good, I have something to show you." He donned his
own equipment, then turned to her. Taking her hand, he pulled
her gently out into the lagoon, treading water easily, and supporting her. "Follow me."

Anywhere! That was the thought that went through her
mind. Adjusting the mask, Deba nodded, putting her face down
into the water and breathing through the tube.

Wolf kept her hand until they neared the entrance of the
underwater cave. Then he signaled her to stay with him and
dived downward, finding the opening easily. Kicking hard as he
moved his body through the curving underground tunnel, he
thrust powerfully to get through the narrow opening that led to
the underwater cave.

Surfacing, he blew his tube, turning at once to find Deba.
Almost at once she broke the water and blew her tube. He took
off his mask and moved close to her. Her smile was wide when
she took off her mask, then he saw her eyes dilate, her features
seeming to draw in on themselves, contract as though dry ice
had been sprayed on her features. "Darling! What is it?"

Fear tremored her body, shuddering through her blood until every part of her was in the grip of panic. "I . . . can't . . .
stay." Her speech had changed, it was like the words of an
automaton.

Wolf saw how her eyes darted around the enclosed area.
"You fear being shut in? Are you claustrophobic?" His voice
didn't penetrate her fear aura. He wasn't reaching her. Panic
had shut her down. "Deba, look at me, look in my eyes." He
took her face in his hands and forced her concentration his way.
"Listen to me, put on your mask and breathe through your
tube. I'm taking you out of here. I want you to keep your eyes
closed and breathe normally. Do you understand?"

Deba put on her mask and felt a little better. The cave

closeness was obscured now, not so threatening. It didn't remind her so much of the well she'd fallen into when she'd been a child.

Her father had been a professor at Southern Methodist University in Dallas. They had lived outside the city on a very small ranch. She'd been walking with her mother and a friend one day when she'd fallen into the well. It had taken a whole day to get her out. Deba had been unhurt, but her brain had refused to allow her to enter any closed areas again. It had taken years for her to sleep without the lights on after that time.

Wolf prayed that he could get her through the narrow exit of the cave. It would be close, because he would have to go first.

Taking a deep breath, he dived, pulling her with him, not releasing her when he went through the opening. Difficulty! He almost stuck because he wasn't able to turn sideways and hold on to her. Through! Kicking hard, he felt her resistance.

Tightening his hold, Wolf kicked harder, her resistance increasing when their bodies bumped the ceiling of the water tunnel.

With lungs bursting, he pulled her along, ignoring the thrashing of her body, the pulling back from him, the building of panic that was destroying her control. Did she have any oxygen left in her lungs? Was she taking water?

With a powerful lunge he made it through the last opening, bursting through the surface of the water like an angry shark.

Twisting his body toward her, he tore off her mask, holding her afloat while she coughed, wheezed, and sputtered.

He ripped off his own mask, supporting both their bodies with a powerful, steady kick. "Darling, I'm sorry, I didn't know. Forgive me."

"Not . . . your . . . fault." Deba clung to him, her chest spasming as she tried to control the coughing.

"Yes, it is. I should have explained to you about the cave."

Deba shook her head. "No, no, I'm trying to get over it. Really I am." Deba took in gulps of air, reaction shuddering through her. "I . . . have . . . to . . . deal . . . with the nightmare." In slow stages her breathing quieted.

Quite naturally she put her head on his shoulder as though Wolf's body was a comfort. "Funny. I've never really discussed this with anyone, never wanted to, though my parents urged me to talk it out with them after it happened." Deba inhaled as though she'd been without oxygen for a long time. There was a rawness in her throat and chest. Their bodies swayed against one another in the calm water of the lagoon.

"We lived in Texas," Deba told him after a time. "I fell into an old dry well. When they tried to get me out, the sides kept giving way." She closed her eyes for a moment. "The wooden shoring formed a tent over me, protecting me somewhat, but there was still a heavy fall of sand. I was down there for over twenty-four hours, immobilized from the waist down by the soil that was constantly caving in around me."

Wolf pulled her close, there in the water, his strong legs keeping them afloat easily. He was both horrified and elated. What an ordeal for a child! Yet it was the first time Deba had talked about it, and it was to him! She had really opened up, talked about a painful secret. He wanted to know everything! Every second of the time she had lived before they met had become something he must know. Shaken by the depth of reaction he was experiencing, he leaned back from her, noting the glassy fatigue in her eyes. "Enough swimming for today. Let's go in, darling."

"Yes."

When Deba would have pushed back from him, he held on to her and shook his head. "I'm taking you in, love. Turn on your back."

"But I can swim."

"You swim well, but you're exhausted now." Slipping an arm across her breast when she complied, he maneuvered her through the water.

Deba couldn't believe the strength of Wolf as he propelled them rapidly across the lagoon to the cottage side. In minutes they were touching ledge rock.

He didn't let Deba stand. Instead he swept her up into his arms, carrying her out of the water, the heat of the sun drying them almost at once.

"I can walk."

"Put your arms around my neck. That's better." It made his flesh chill when he recalled the abject fear in her eyes when they'd been in the underwater cave. He hurried, carrying her easily, high and close to his body.

Once in the cottage, Wolf kicked the door shut behind him and carried her through to his bedroom. "You need the hot tub."

"On a day like this?" Deba laughed shakily. What would

he think if he knew that she wanted to be in his bedroom . . . his bed?

"You've had a shock." Wolf put his shoulder to the door leading into the large bathroom. Beyond the bathroom was the separate area with hot tub and sauna.

Placing her on her feet, he leaned down and twisted the spigots.

Deba was about to step down with her suit on, but Wolf stopped her. When she felt his hands on her, she pushed at them. "No." Her voice sounded reedy, weak; she felt the same way.

"Yes." Carefully, slowly, gently, he removed her suit.

Her skin goosebumped from toes to eyebrow. Deba felt weak and like Wonder Woman all at the same time. She wanted to hide . . . and thrust out her chest, embrace him, yet escape. In all her life she'd never been so alive, so quivering with awareness. It was as though at long last she was privy to the secrets of life, that the scales had fallen from her eyes and she stepped into a new dimension. Wolf Clinton had created a new planet and invited her to inhabit it with him. Fight him! She put out her hand to him.

Taking her hand, he helped her down the two steps into the tub.

"This is quite a tub for a cottage." Why didn't she feel embarrassed? Deba had never been into heavy sexual relationships. Not only had her background kept her from it, for being on the run wasn't conducive to commitment, but there was an innate fastidiousness that made her choosy. Deba had always felt that there could be someone special for her, one day. That had made her careful. Sleeping around seemed an exercise in futility to her. Besides, it could be dangerous to one's health.

She'd once loved someone for an entire year at university. At the end of her senior year they'd parted amicably, neither having regrets. Since then, Deba had had friends, but no one had been close enough to her to love.

In minutes Wolf Clinton had changed all that. He had taken her barriers down, brick by brick, cutting a swath through which he had moved easily into her life. She wanted him there.

"I want you, Deba McCloud." Wolf stood back from her, his hands at his sides, only his eyes holding her. Why was he getting involved with this fey witch?

Deba stared at him, then nodded slowly. "I want you . . . and that is a surprise." She watched the smile twist those hard lips upward. "Do you understand the way I mean it?"

"Are you saying that you had no intention of getting involved with anyone?"

Deba nodded.

"I had the same plan. You blew it apart, Deba mine."

Reaching upward, she placed her hands on either side of the face leaning over her, her eyes searching each feature as though she would imprint it on her mind. "It's strange, isn't it? I should run from you. You should shun me."

"Never."

"We're wrong for each other. But we're drawn together. Bizarre." She smiled at the hard chuckle that escaped him.

"I feel connected to you," Wolf murmured. He freed himself from her for an instant, stripping off his briefs and tossing them into the corner of the room. Then he moved back to her, his fingers grazing her cheekbones. "You're blushing. Embarrassed?"

"Yes." And so turned on to Wolf Clinton that her body was on fire.

"Hold me. I like it very much."

"Me too." Her hands touched his forearms, sliding up to his shoulders. Fingers pressed there. "Lots of muscles. I like that." Deba giggled, surprising herself, her hand flying to her lips. "I feel as though I've taken on another personality."

"I feel a little alien myself," Wolf told her huskily. "I want you very much, but I've never been more comfortable with anyone in my life." He stepped down into the hot bubbling water. "Yet I feel weak as a kitten, as though I could topple over at any moment."

Deba moved closer so that her breasts were just touching his chest. He was one step lower than she in the swirling water. Moving her body back and forth once, brushing skin against skin, made the breath catch in her throat.

Electricity crackled in the air. Deba felt it enter her and become a torrent of want and need. Alien and a little frightening, it filled her.

Feathering her hands over him, it was as though she needed that quest of him to find her way. She touched those strong male nipples, feeling her own harden in response when Wolf groaned. It was as though, like some wonderful osmosis, he entered her being through her pores. Fiercely she wanted him all at once, and that took her aback. Control and wariness deserted her, and she was shaken.

None of the negative things she could dredge up about Wolf Clinton mattered a whit. Whether he was kind or cruel was immaterial, Deba wanted him with a basic desperation that knew no bonds or bounds, that crashed through any barriers. Now!

Deba kissed his throat, those masculine nipples. Aroused delight was a flood in her.

"Jee-zus," Wolf whispered through his teeth.

"What?" Deba asked dazedly.

"I'm getting less comfortable by the minute," he told her huskily.

"A little tension in places?" Deba's hand feathered down his chest and stopped on his abdomen.

"You could say that. Don't stop there, darling. Feel free to explore." Dazed, Wolf put his hands at her waist.

"All right." Had she ever been so brazen? It felt so right to touch his aroused body. Her being surged with a passion it had never known.

Curses escaped his mouth in low, rhythmic flow. His hands gripped her, his mouth going down to hers.

Had there ever been such a kiss? Deba flew apart, all the pieces grafting to Wolf. She'd expected roughness, she got ineffable gentleness that fragmented her, aroused her as nothing had ever done.

"Wolf." The name was exhaled like a caressing sigh. Deba's eyelids were lead, her body like soft plastic, yet she'd never been so energized, so alive, so potent.

"Deba, my sweet."

They sank together into the depths, her body atop his.

Deba had the feeling they'd made love a million times before, maybe in another life. When his hands went over her, there was a sensation of coming home. Deba shut her eyes as waves of delight coursed through her. It was brand-new, but oh so familiar. Had she known Wolf for a thousand years?

Digging her hands into his neck, she moved over him, wanting him.

When he surged to his feet, her eyes flew open. "What is it?"

"Nothing, darling," he told her huskily. "I want to see all

of you when we make love. I don't want even water to obscure you from me."

Laughter catching on a sob, she let him lead her out of the tub, taking a towel to dry him as he was drying her.

Putting his index finger to her lips, he bent toward her when she was dry. "Wait, love, I want to protect you."

In seconds he was back at her side, his smile widening at the languorous look to her. "Aphrodite . . . you should have been called that."

"That's my new name." Deba leaned toward him in voluptuous seduction. "I'm practicing my wiles. Is it working?"

"Oh, yes," Wolf told her, leaning toward her and kissing her. "You're beautiful, sensuous, and you are driving me wild, Deba McCloud," he told her slowly.

"Good. I didn't want to be the only one going out of my mind."

Arms around each other, they entered the bedroom.

They sank down on the bed together, body to body, hands entwined.

"Wolf . . . Wolf . . ." Deba was out of breath as she felt his mouth move slowly down her body, taking her, loving her. Each pulse point was touched until passion was a flash flood that tossed her willy-nilly in its power. She was helpless, potent, fearful, unafraid, out of control, more capable than she'd ever been.

Wolf was in awe, clumsy, stricken with her beauty. Had he ever loved anyone before? Was the cataclysmic delight new, real? Never before had he felt so wild, so free, so new.

"Goodness, I like this," Deba said breathily.

"So do I," Wolf whispered roughly.

Wolf turned her over gently, his tongue laving her slender back. He kissed each toe, then worked his way back up her body, loving it, her body shaking as he kissed her behind the knee.

"Wonderful," Deba said, her voice slurred, her body languorous but electric. "Don't leave me," she murmured, urgent and excited, just a thread of fear in her voice.

"I'm here, darling, where I'll always be." There was a hot, feverish quality to his voice.

Then his tongue intruded into her body in the most intimate way . . . and she was taken by Wolf . . . for all time.

Deba thought she was exploding. Was love so dynamic?

She was no longer whole, but in pieces flying into Wolf's aura, magnetized to him, rebuilt as part of him. Never could she be free of him again. It was a truth that throbbed through her.

The slow exploration back up her body had both of them shuddering against one another, desire like a hot wire entangling them.

In one smooth stroke he took her, their bodies arcing as passion took them, need erupting in them, tossing them away on a sea of love so great, they could only gasp.

Deba gripped him and instigated a rhythm she'd never known, pulsating in a sensation so new, yet so elemental. Body glued to body, they entered the far spaces, the special place that was theirs alone, where no other could go. Feverish touching of hands, limbs locking to limbs, souls quivering with a need to give, they found the answer of the ages, the mystery meant only for true lovers, the cup of love.

"Deba, Deba, my love."

"Wolf, Wolf, my darling."

"Love me, Deba, take me away and keep me."

In the throes of passion there was a dart of pain as she thought of the time when their "forever" would be over and she would have to leave him. That surety didn't mask the realization that Wolfgang Clinton was her true love, and the only one she would ever want.

Wolf was going to keep her. He would never let her go. Never, never would he release her, give her up. She was his now.

In one cataclysmic release, they came together and sank down from the moon back to earth, slowly, exquisitely. Passion burst from them in joyous cries of fulfillment. They could never be single entities again; now they were double, but as one.

"Deba? Was it good for you, love?"

"Amazing," she answered him with her eyes closed. "Yes."

Languidly Deba ran her fingers over his chest. "I don't think it can always be that wonderful. Can it?"

Wolf kept his eyes closed, his hands caressing her possessively. "It's a first for me. Your skin is satin to me, do you know that?" He opened his eyes slowly, smiled, then closed them again. "Yes, it can always be that way, with us, darling."

"Ummm, it's very special. Do you think we should patent it?"

"Good idea." Wolf pulled her close to him, drawing a silk sheet over them. "I love holding you."

They slept in one another's arms.

When Deba awoke, she thought she was still in a dream. There was no feeling of fear, and fear had been a constant companion for some time. If she was awake she had to be wary, fearful. Why wasn't she? Wolf!

Turning her head, she looked at him, his mouth slightly parted in sleep. For this moment, now, he was hers.

Feeling daring, she leaned closer and pressed her lips to his, feeling the instant contraction of that strong mouth, then the loving pressure of recognition.

Knowing he was awake now, too, she leaned over him, suspended over his chest. "You're a great lover. Is that why you've made all the tabloids for years?"

"Right the first time," he told her in silky irony. "I've even come to love that rapier tongue of yours."

Fingers played with the chestnut hair on his chest. "There are secrets between us."

"Yes."

"Can we have a relationship with those secrets?"

"I intend to have a relationship with you, Deba McCloud, even if you're carrying state secrets in your head."

Relieved, she grinned at him. "Nothing so lofty."

"It wouldn't matter." Wolf pulled her close to him. "I have a hankering to love you."

"We just did that," Deba answered him, delighted.

"No, we just slept." He pushed the hair back from her face, bringing a few strands to his mouth where he sucked them. "Are you going to refuse me, darling?"

"Never." Deba shook her head, relaxed and confident. "I want you so much. In fact I was going to suggest it." She grinned.

Wolf's chest heaved as he laughed out loud. "Making love is fun with you, lady."

"You're right about that."

Still smiling, he turned her on her back. "You also happen to be incredibly beautiful, but that's just an afterthought," he told her wryly, amusement in his eyes.

Mouth agape, she stared at him. "But I'm not. I'm too tall and leggy."

"And your breasts drive me mad with those sweet pink

nipples, your legs are luscious and I want them wrapped around me always. Your height is perfect for me. Your turquoise eyes must have been mined here in Mexico and they bewitch me. Tie me up in your blond hair, love." He smiled down at her arrested gaze. "You're gorgeous . . . and I love you." He kissed her open mouth, letting his tongue intrude there. "And I have never, never wanted to make love to a woman as much."

"Me either . . . You know what I mean."

"Yes, I do." He saw her face change. "What is it?"

"I suppose I should tell you the truth."

"If you like." He smiled at her lazily.

"Love is an elusive commodity that only belongs to a special few that are free to give it. I'm not in that number."

His heart banged against his chest wall. "Is that agony I hear in your voice?"

Deba swallowed. "Even if I could, I don't know if I'd want to love you."

"I promise I won't take advantage of you."

Deba touched his face, running her fingers down his cheek. "Your face is tight and angry."

"But I still want you."

"And I want you," Deba sighed.

"That's enough for now."

"It could make us very vulnerable."

"I'll risk it. How about you?"

Slowly she nodded.

"Good. We settled that. Now, can I make love to you?"

"Please."

Slowly he let his mouth course over her face, loving the little cat sounds she made. But Deba wasn't passive. She mapped his body with her fingers, kissing any part of him that came close to her mouth. Was there ever such a fantasy? To love a man totally and have him love her back? The world was theirs! They had built it.

Wolf's body tingled with a new life when she touched him. All of his being was involved with Deba; all of him wanted her. Rubbing his toes next to hers sent his libido through the roof. He could have made love to her toes and it would have blown him apart.

Again the kaleidoscope rise to passion, their reckless love catapulting them to new heights of sensation. Love exploded through them, time after time.

Fear lanced Wolf. He was at the apex of happiness. He had it all. What could happen at the top? The bottom of hell would be being away from her. He pushed away the morbid vision and pressed his mouth to her breasts.

The last barrier had dropped away. Though there were secrets between them, that was accepted. But there was no other impediment to hot feeling as they gave and took from one another in consummate joining.

In supreme giving Deba became the aggressor, moving down his body to caress and kiss him. When she heard the shocked hiss of response, felt the shudder in his body as she caressed his aroused form, a joy of giving was born in her that she had never hoped to know.

In throbbing ascent they took each other to the stars.

Minutes or hours later they lay close together, their bodies still connected and slippery with love dew. They were nose to nose, mouth to mouth.

"Wonderful," Deba breathed.

"Very."

"I'm hungry."

Wolf embraced her, laughing. "All that exercise give you an appetite?"

"Yes." She grinned at him, kissing him again, scoring a finger down the scar on his face.

The emotional planet they'd created whisked them away in throbbing wonder, clinging to each other, never wanting it to end.

"God, I'll be dead in a month." Wolf grinned happily. "One kiss and you fire me again."

There was no finis to the emotion that claimed them.

Long moments they watched each other, as though the answer to their sweet passion would be written on one another's features.

"Wonderful."

"It was more than that, Deba mine."

Deba smothered a yawn with the back of her hand. "I have never, never been so relaxed in my life."

Wolf tightened his hold. "Some of the nightmare gone, love?"

"All of it." She kissed his chin. Well, it was. . . . For a while. "Thank you."

"I want to take away all your bad times, Deba." He saw the shadows in her eyes.

"Can't be done." She kissed his mouth. "I would like to do that for you. Is it possible?"

Wolf's lips tightened. "I doubt it."

"See. We have to take what we can, and put the rest on the shelf."

"Is this Deba McCloud wisdom?"

"Maybe not wisdom, but certainly knowledge gleaned along the way. Happiness can be so damned elusive, so short-lived."

"Darling, you're going to be happy a long time." Wolf kissed her tenderly. "How would you like a barbecue of lobsters?" He loved the way her eyes widened in pleasure, her tongue coming out to run over her lips. "God, don't do that." Wolf closed his eyes. "I won't ever get out of this bed if you stay so sexy."

"Can't help it. You do it to me."

"And you sure as hell do it to me." With one surge, Wolf lifted the two of them out of bed. "Come on, get dressed. You're going to help."

Laughter dotted their every action. When their bodies touched, they would turn and kiss. They managed to reach out to each other constantly.

Wolf was sure he could lose himself forever in her eyes.

Deba could feel him watching her. It made her preen. Her being glowed as though she'd just been sanitized, in and out, the love renewal complete with Wolf.

Wolf knew when her eyes were on him, his skin prickled with her laser touch. It shook him that each time he felt weak as a kitten . . . and like Superman.

Once when Deba passed him, he hooked an arm around her. "We're going to travel, darling. First I'm going to show you Mexico, then the United States and Canada. Europe and Asia with you will be a brand new sighting, I know it."

Deba turned in his arms, her hands coming up to clasp his face. "Don't plan too far ahead. We're a day-to-day twosome. Did you forget?" Deba smoothed the crease of a frown from his forehead. "I would like to travel anywhere with you, but we can't project too far in the future."

"All right. We'll do it one day at a time, but whenever I do leave the ranch you'll be with me."

Deba smiled ruefully. "I'm not sure about my passport." She explained about her hurry in getting to Mexico and failure to get a proper working card.

Wolf shrugged. "Don't worry. I'll take care of that."

"Big man." Deba kissed his mouth.

"Yeah. Let's eat, woman, I'm hungry . . . and not just for you."

They stayed at the cottage only three days, but it was paradise for them.

Swimming, sailing, diving, all took on new meanings for both of them. They were never apart for more than a few moments.

"I would like to try the underwater cave again," Deba told him at one point, moisture beading her upper lip at the thought.

Wolf shook his head. "Not that one. There are other ones, more easily attainable with air pockets along the way. We'll try those first and see how you do."

"Thank you. I would like to get over that terror of being enclosed."

"Claustrophobia is pretty awful and a great many people have it to some degree, love." Wolf kissed her, his mouth lingering on hers. "Maybe we can deal with it, one step at a time." Wolf held her close. "But I won't ever let you be that fearful again."

On the morning of the day they were to leave, they were lying on the beach after diving. They had gone down to one of the smaller caves and Deba had muddled through it. She'd had to fight the fear, but she'd successfully traversed the underwater tunnel in and out again without panicking.

"You were wonderful," Wolf told her as he cradled her in the water afterwards, feeling the thud of her heart against his chest. "I'm proud of you."

"I'm proud of me too," Deba told him shakily, smiling. "I couldn't have done it without a very special man by the name of Wolf Clinton." She pressed her open mouth to his, welcoming his tongue.

Wolf stared down at her. "Do you mean that? Am I special to you?"

She nodded, her finger scoring lazily down his cheek.

"We're two parts of a whole." Wolf kissed her lingeringly. They sank down in the water, only surfacing when they needed air.

Swimming to the shore in easy strokes, they got out on the ledge and dried each other in slow, loving motions.

They would be leaving in the afternoon, but for now they had time to relax and look at the water. Deba was under an umbrella, Wolf was lying in the sun.

"You're restless, darling. What is it?" Wolf turned over on his stomach.

"I don't want to leave." She tried to smile but felt as though her face were collapsing.

"Don't look like that. We'll be coming back all the time now. What do you say if we return each weekend?"

"But don't you have meetings and . . ."

"To hell with that, I work hard enough during the week. We'll come here on Friday mornings and return on Monday mornings from now on, love. How does that sound?"

"Wonderful." Deba opened up her arms, delighted at how speedily he was beside her, holding her. "We'll be spoiled."

"Never. We work very hard. I've noticed you've been taking more and more on yourself since you've gotten the hang of the computer."

Deba nodded. "It's less and less of a monster." She thought of the journal she was keeping and the disks. No need to keep them, she had Wolf. He was hers.

Wolf stroked her body. "Now you don't have to feel bad about leaving, do you?"

Deba looked around her, at the lagoon, the jungle that was so close, the beauty, the wonderful isolation that allowed them to learn about each other, to love. "I'll never forget this place if I live to be a thousand. This is Eden."

"Yes, it is. And I hope I live right along with you for those thousand years." Wolf muttered into her breast. "I know we said we might as well swim without suits as long as it's just the two of us here . . . but . . ."

"But what?"

"You drive me crazy each time I look at you. I want to make love to you all the time."

"Don't let me stop you."

"Darling!"

They rolled together across the beach mattress that Deba was lying on, laughing, loving, passion building through the humor, so that their coming together was an explosion of joy.

When they returned to Rancho Lobo, it looked different.

"What is it, love?"

"Everything has a strange cast, as though it had changed radically. Colors, textures, all different."

Wolf kissed her neck. "We've changed. Love does that."

Deba looked at him and smiled tremulously. What would it be like to have his child? A shining pain lanced through her. It wasn't good to think of those things. And yet? Had they taken precautions while they'd been at the cottage? The first time Wolf had . . . but . . .

"Daydreaming? About me, I hope."

"It was. Very nice, provocative thoughts." Deba threaded her hand through his. Why worry about something that probably wouldn't happen? She couldn't stop the vision of a little chestnut-crested child with golden eyes and dark-edged irises, from dancing around her head.

They landed on the helipad in a whirl of dust, their bags taken by workers as the doors were opened.

Wolf smiled at her and touched her constantly in the short jeep ride to the house.

Wolf accompanied her up to her room.

Deba faced him, smiling. "You must have a hundred calls to make."

"About that. But I have to ask you something important first."

Deba cocked her head. "And what might that be?"

"Which room do you prefer? This one or mine? Now, my suite is larger and has more accoutrements. There's an extra bedroom with huge closets for your clothes . . ."

Deba grinned. "I don't need that much space."

"You will when I take you to Paris for the spring showings."

Deba straightened. "I don't want anything. . . ."

Wolf crossed to her side quickly. "Don't take it wrong, darling. I know you. Just let me indulge myself a little and buy you a few things. No shower of jewels or furs, I promise you that. Don't look so suspicious. Don't you trust me?"

"With my life, but—"

"Then don't worry about the unimportant. I won't. Now, which room? I won't be separated from you."

"Well, your suite, I suppose, because of the space. But what if we fight and you wish me in North Podunk?"

"That won't happen. If we have a disagreement, we'll do

what other people do, we'll settle it, talk about it, come to an agreement, but we won't part."

"Your place, I guess." Deba grinned at the happy surprise on his face. "You're too big for mine."

"Yeah." He breathed into her neck. "I'll have Julia move your things." He felt her wriggle against him. "That would embarrass you?"

Deba nodded reluctantly. "She'll be aware that I'm in your suite at once . . . but . . ."

"All right." Wolf grinned. "We'll do it, after I make some calls. Suit you?"

"Yes. I want to call Maria anyway. She'll think I've disappeared."

Wolf nodded. "Your messages will be on your office desk, darling, if there are any."

"I'll take a shower then go down there."

Wolf kissed her hard. "I'll hurry. I'll miss you too much as it is."

When he left her on the run, Deba felt totally bereft, as though they'd really separated.

Shaking herself from her black mood, she took a quick shower and shampooed her hair.

Drying it quickly, she twisted it on top of her head and donned a pair of unwashed cotton safari shorts and shirt, leather espadrilles on her bare feet. Hurrying downstairs, she met Julia in the foyer.

The tight-lipped maîtresse d' looked her up and down, inclining her head in stiff salutation. "The senor says that you will be ordering the dinner."

"Me? Ah, well, ah, why don't you surprise me. Your cooking is always so good."

Julia unbent a fraction. "You have messages in your office."

"Thank you." Deba smiled, hurrying past Julia down the hall and into her office, closing the door behind her thankfully. Julia would never approve of her.

Spying the small sheaf of notes on her desk, she sat down and went through them slowly. Smiling, she pressed for an outside line and dialed Maria's home. "Hello, friend."

"Aldebaran! I've been so worried."

"Will you call me Deba, please?"

"I forgot. I don't like Deba as well as Aldebaran. How are

you? Where were you? I thought you'd been whisked to a monastery in Tibet."

"Your parents should never have sent you to the United States to be educated. Your imagination was fine-tuned there."

"It was." Maria gave a short laugh.

"Was that a sigh I heard? What's up?"

"Oh, the job is drying up and I'll be let go soon. I think I'll go back to the States. Making a living isn't easy there, but it will be better than Mexico."

"When will you go?"

"I think I'll be let go in a few weeks, a month at most."

"Oh, I'm sorry, Maria. I wish I could do something for you."

"Write to me. I'll be lonely in California. But never mind about me. Let's talk about you. So what have you been doing?"

"Working, but this past weekend we went on vacation."

"We? Tell me more."

Deba proceeded to sketch the bare bones of the weekend while going through the other messages. Most were from business persons, but the last one, taken on Friday, as the others were, froze her in her chair.

"Deba? Deba, what is it? Tell me. Aldebaran, say something."

"What? Ah, it's nothing. I'm sorry, I didn't mean to alarm you, Maria. I was just looking at my messages."

There was a short silence.

"Is this like the mysterious ones you got at my apartment from a Mr. Dryden?"

"Maria! Don't ask questions, please."

"I won't, but I hope you know I'm there for you if you need me."

"I know that, and I don't mean to be short with you, but . . . it isn't safe for you to know some things. Trust me?"

"I do. Call me again soon. Will you?"

"Tomorrow or the next day."

After she hung up the phone, Deba stared at the message, then looked at the clock. Two fifteen. She could make the call at two thirty. One or the other of them would be at the number. What was the emergency? Had something happened to either of them?

Deba rose to her feet and went to her office door and shut it, returning to her seat and taking a deep breath.

Watching the clock made her crazy, but she didn't dare immerse herself in something unless the half hour went by and she didn't make the call. She wouldn't be able to make another until eight thirty in the evening. That was the system she'd set up with her parents when they'd gone into hiding.

On the stroke of two thirty she buzzed for an outside line and dialed the new number that had been given to her a month ago. "Mr. Dryden, please."

"Speaking."

"How are you?" Deba had to steady her voice. How she missed her mother and father. Did her father sound older? Would she ever get to see either one of them again?

"Fine. How are you?"

"The same." How she ached to tell them how much she loved them, but it had been agreed from the beginning that the messages would be as short and ambiguous as possible.

"Ah, there is word from our friend that pressure has escalated. We feel that you should dig your hole deeper."

"Will do. Best to Mrs. Dryden."

"Best to you."

Click! The connection was broken. Deba held the phone away from her and stared at it, smothering the sob that rose in her throat. She swiped at the single tear that coursed down her cheek.

The friend her father referred to in his cryptic message was Chatsworth Brown, his literary agent, who acted as go-between for her father and the WPP, Witness Protection Program.

Many years before, when her father was a well-known paleontologist, he had published books on the subject that were used in universities throughout the world. Unfortunately the great wisdom and knowledge that had made him highly esteemed and renowned worked against him when he'd had to hide out.

The people who were after her father had stepped up their search for him. That's what the message said. As her parents' only child she was in as much danger as they.

It had seemed such a small thing when her father had agreed to testify.

Deba shook her head. To think that her very gentle, honest parents had had to go into hiding while criminals traveled freely everywhere. The notion that her father could be openly stalked by killers who had no fear of legal intervention was painful to

accept. The laws of a free state were meant to protect the innocent, and not the criminal, as they often did. What a macabre
effect when blind justice was an enemy of the innocent!

Should she move from where she was? It didn't seem necessary, since few persons were allowed on the Rancho Lobo. It
was as good a haven as any, so she would stay for the time
being. How could she face leaving Wolf anyway? Yet she would
go at once if there was any chance that he would be threatened
by the men who hunted her family.

Days moved into weeks, and if anything, Wolf and Deba
became closer. Happiness bound them and they clung to one
another, reveling in the aura that gave them joy.

Even Julia glanced approvingly at Deba now and then because she had seen how relaxed and happy her employer was.
"It is good for you to enjoy life, Senor Clinton."

"Thank you, Julia. I'm glad you approve." His hearty
laugh brought a reluctant smile to his housekeeper's face.

"It is good to have you happy again, senor." Julia
shrugged and went back to her work.

Deba had laughed when Wolf told her of the conversation.

"What are you thinking?" Deba looked up into Wolf's
eyes.

It was shortly after dawn and as usual they awoke with the
sun to make love and to converse before the start of the day.

"I was thinking how empty my existence was until you
came into it."

"The world does seem more wonderful," Deba murmured,
bringing his face down to her so that she could nip his chin.

"Ouch, don't do that. You know I love it when you bite
me. It makes me so damned horny."

"Everything makes you horny."

"Giggling again? You never did that when you first came
to the rancho."

"I never did it, period, until I met you. It's so stupid."

"I love the sound of it."

"That's good, because I can't seem to stop doing it. Childish regression, do you suppose?"

"Love does it, darling. You're warm, relaxed, and confident because you know how much I love you."

"And I love you." Deba had fought making such a declaration, but soon after their return to the rancho she'd begun
telling him. She hadn't been able to hold back with Wolf.

Once more they held each other in serene passion, letting the emotion roll over them, take them, fling them around, grip them forever.

By the time they rose to dress, their eyes had a slumbrous look as though the passion hadn't died but was only minimally sated.

Wolf stretched his naked body, looking sleek and powerful. "I have never felt so good, so . . . so damned healthy. Stop laughing. You look sleek as a seal yourself, lady love. When you came here you had so damned many fences around you, so defensive and brittle I would have needed a battering ram to get to you." Wolf grinned. "Not anymore."

Deba picked up one of the many pillows on their bed and flung it at him, smiling when he caught it easily, his smile staying the same. "Conceited."

"Yes. I even like it when we fight, when your face gets red and your eyes glitter like fresh-mined gems."

"You're getting poetic."

"I know. I like it."

Deba shook her head. "What am I going to do with you? Your head will soon be too large to get through the door."

"You'll always manage to get me into any room where you are, darling."

"Well, if you don't get dressed, I'll . . . I'll fire you." Deba laughed out loud and sprinted for the bathroom, knowing that Wolf was right on her heels.

Day followed day and they became even closer. Love was their spur, their peace, their glue.

Often Wolf would come into her office, lift her up and kiss her, then go back to work.

Her intention to destroy the journal and the disks she'd been keeping on him disappeared. Deba couldn't bring herself to destroy any of it. She'd keep it all . . . and then on a special occasion she would show it to Wolf, make a gift of it to him. It was a relief to know she could keep all she'd garnered about the man she loved.

She called Maria several times, feeling progressively saddened that her good friend would soon be leaving Mexico. Actually Maria was her link to the outside world. Maybe that's why she never discussed Maria with Wolf. It was like letting the alien world outside the Rancho Lobo intrude.

One day when she'd called Maria, her friend had made firm plans to leave.

"So I think I'll be going to the States next week. A friend is going to take me on his cargo plane."

"Make sure it isn't connected with the drug trade."

"Deba! How you talk. This is a food-and-clothing lift, supplied by churches. He's going to pick up some more in the Los Angeles area."

"Good. Stay as far away from drug traffickers as you can."

"Don't worry, I will. Deba, what is it? You're so intense."

"Nothing, friend. I'll be talking to you before you leave."

"Right."

That night when they were dressing for dinner, Deba caught Wolf smiling at her all the time. He usually did that, but tonight his glances were more intense, caressing. She wasn't a bit embarrassed dressing in front of him because they were always together, but her skin prickled with a new awareness.

Turning, she faced him. "What is it? You've been watching me like a hawk. And that grin on your face is downright naughty."

Wolf shook his head. "It's a secret. Hurry up."

"Why the hurry?" Deba glared at him. "Stop that. I hate it when you're mysterious. What are you planning?"

"Are you ready?"

"Wolf!" Her plaintive cry widened his grin.

Striding to her side, he leaned down and kissed her. "I love that sarong on you. You take my breath away." He kissed the shell of her ear. "We're having a very special dinner tonight in the gazebo out by the lake."

"We are?" Delighted, Deba looked up at him. It was beautiful by the lake in the evening.

"Yes. Are you ready?"

Before she barely had time to nod, he was whisking her out the door and down the stairs.

"Wolf, I'm flying!" But she was laughing and as exhilarated as he was. It was that way all the time with them. One could spark the other one, easily and quickly.

He kept his arm around her as they made their way down the winding path to the lake.

Deba caught her breath at the diffused light in the screened gazebo, the soft music and the night sounds a serene orchestra for their entertainment. "It's wonderful."

They dined on the large lobsters flown from Grenada that both of them favored.

"Dom Pérignon champagne. It must be an occasion." Deba smiled at him as he seated himself next to her on the wicker settee.

Conversation between them was hushed and sporadic all at once, as though the magic of the evening had consumed them.

Neither wanted a dessert, contenting themselves with a cheese and fruit board.

Then the staff of waiters melted away and they were alone.

Deba turned around and Wolf's face was very close, so she kissed him.

"Hold out your hand, darling," Wolf whispered huskily.

Deba hesitated.

"I told you I wouldn't overwhelm you with jewels and furs and I won't," he told her gently. "This is different."

When Deba saw the emerald that he slipped on her finger and almost touched her middle knuckle, tears sprang to her eyes. "Wolf?"

He lifted her from the chair. "I want you to be my wife, the mother of my children. I love you, Deba McCloud. Will you take me and make me forever happy?"

When Wolf gathered her into his arms, she looked over his shoulder at the exquisite emerald, her eyes moist.

Now she would have to run. Away from Wolf! The thought cut her like a knife. There was no way she could stay. If they married it would get out one way or another. The newspapers would pick it up. Her name in bold type along with Wolf's. The Cosentinos would come gunning. Wolf could be killed because of her, because he would do his utmost to protect her and the Cosentinos would let nothing stand in their way. A hellish Mexican standoff! How ironic.

Clutching him to her, she closed her eyes. "I love you, Wolf, with all my heart."

The beautiful emerald would not stay on her finger too long. It would be left behind when she departed Rancho Lobo.

6

It had been harrowing getting away from Rancho Lobo. There'd been so many gaps. Not wanting to go, loving the man, finding a blinding happiness when she'd only looked for a measure of serenity. The list was bittersweet and lengthening. With Maria's help and by tricking Wolf, she'd managed it.

When he'd gone into Mexico City on business, she'd pleaded a sick headache. He had almost ruined the plan by saying he wouldn't go if she was ill. It had taken a great deal of persuading to convince him to go.

"No! No, don't break your appointment. I'll just keep a cool cloth on my head and stay in the bedroom with the drapes drawn. By the time you return, I'll be fine."

"All right, if you insist, but you have the number. If your headache doesn't get better, have Julia phone me."

Julia had been told to let her alone, that she would sleep in a darkened room.

Instead, leaving behind the emerald and all else that Wolf had given her along with a short note, she'd taken the disks and the journal, all she had of him, and left. Taking the equivalent of two weeks severance pay was necessary for travel expenses. If her hand trembled and tears fell, it didn't matter. There was no one to witness her grief.

Getting transportation hadn't been hard because she knew where the keys were to all the vehicles. Wolf had been so open with her, wanting her to use all he had. She must stop crying!

Waiting in the gloom of the garage until all the ranch hands had departed for their chores, she'd gone to a station wagon with tinted windows. Starting it, she drove from the moderately cool shelter into the blistering sun of the high plata.

Getting off the rancho unseen was probably impossible, since Wolf's workers were everywhere and he employed an army of them. Her one solace was that they would not be able to see who drove the big car because of the tinted windows.

Tears clogged her throat and stung her eyes as she tried to maneuver the car through the winding narrow roads that would take her to the highway toward Mexico City.

At a prearranged destination she spotted Maria, lowered the window, and waved. Then her friend changed cars with her.

Deba followed in the battered car while Maria drove the large ranch wagon into town and parked it at the bus station, leaving the keys under the front seat and locking it. Deba knew that there was another set of keys for it at the ranch. Maria then walked back a block and joined her in the rattletrap of a car belonging to Juan.

From there the two women drove to the private air field.

Flying back to the United States in an empty cargo plane might have seemed strange if she'd been able to feel anything at all. But Deba was numb. Not in all the times she'd been on the run had she felt so bereft, so lost. It was as though Wolf still had the integral part of her and only a shell was flying north.

When they'd landed in a private field outside Los Angeles, she and Maria were picked up by a family friend of Maria's.

"I won't be staying here long, Maria. I'm heading east."

"I'm coming with you, then."

"No! I'm on the run. Believe me when I tell you I'm not a criminal, but some pretty dangerous people want my hide. You can't come with me."

"I can and I will. And we'll travel cross-country by train. You'll wear a wig and dress in baggy clothes, maybe even wear a mustache."

"You are a total nut." Deba laughed, but tears mixed with the laughter. Not even to herself had she ever admitted how lonely she'd often been, how cut off from other people. Having

Maria with her would be an unexpected boon. Deba should have argued her down, but she couldn't.

"I won't leave you, Aldebaran, I mean it. We'll do all right, you'll see."

Deba cried then, great gulping sobs, as her friend held her. "I . . . don't . . . want . . . to . . . endanger you."

"You won't." Maria hugged her, patting her on the back.

Deba was too emotionally hollow to fight with her energetic friend. Wolf had drained her. Maria had taken the last vestige of control with her generosity.

Deciding on taking the bus as far as Nevada, they then took a milk-run commercial flight to Chicago. From Chicago they took the train.

"This is a wonderful country, Aldebaran," Maria murmured to her, face pressed against the window of the fast-moving ground traveler. "I'm glad my mother was American. It made it so easy to come here or live in Mexico." Maria turned around when she didn't get any response and saw that her friend was busy writing in a notebook. "Are you working on that journal still?"

"Yes." Deba looked up, a rather vague smile on her face.

"And you have a full disk too?"

"Actually, I filled seven disks when I worked for Wolf," Deba told her, smiling weakly. "It surprised me too . . . but there was so much to say about him."

"I could write a book about him myself, just using the newspapers of a few years back."

Deba didn't return her smile. "We never talked about the Natasha Sharansky thing, but I know that he is an honest business man. I saw the records." Deba bit her lip. "Wolf is a man of honor, Maria."

"Then why don't you write the truth about him?" Maria shrugged. "Write a damned book. We have to travel, then we have to find jobs. In the meantime you'll be doing something that keeps you close to the man you love."

Deba smiled, blinking hard. "Believe it or not it helps to do this."

"So?" Maria's Latin shrug was more expressive than words. "Do a book on the big man."

"It might be therapy," Deba mumbled. It was as though he was there beside her, bigger than life, enclosing her.

Maria reached over and kissed Deba's cheek. "Do it. It will help."

"Maybe I'll do something like that."

"Good. We'll be pessimistic."

"Optimistic," Deba said absently. A book on Wolf, a story of the man she loved. Deba shook her head slowly. "Maria, I can't write a book on Wolf. I signed a contract that prohibits me from doing anything like that for five years after leaving his employ."

Maria's shrug was pure Latina. "Oh? Then, I guess I'd better write it."

Deba laughed.

"What kind of job will you look for? You once were in publishing. Will you try that?"

"Huh? Ah. No. I thought I'd try domestic service this time."

"What? Have you ever done it?"

"No, and that's why I'm going for it."

"But, Aldebaran, it's so hard." Maria stared at her, mouth agape.

"And I can be so invisible. I have to keep low for a while. Those people are looking for me . . . and Wolf might look for me, too, for a time. After I've been a domestic for a while, I could try something else."

"If you survive," Maria muttered, looking at her friend from the corner of her eyes. "I can't help remembering those tacos you made, or what you did to that white blouse you bought."

"Minor details."

"Setting a kitchen on fire is not minor, nor is turning a white blouse yellow."

"Trust you to remember all the bad things." Deba lifted her chin.

"Hah! With you in the kitchen an entire family could be at risk. This I know." Maria's slight accent became more pronounced when she was excited.

"Will you stop that! I'll be fine. Tell me what you're going to do."

"I think I'll look for office work, but in Manhattan it might be touch and go." Maria looked doubtful.

"I think you should. You helped the screen writer on that

movie we were on, more than once. I wish my typing was as good."

"At least you know how to handle a computer. I've never done that."

"I could show you." Deba looked thoughtful. "In fact, when we reach New York, I'll call Chatsworth Brown. He has a literary agency. If he can't use you, he might be able to recommend someone to us. It won't hurt to try. He's been my father's —" Deba paused and bit her lip.

"Don't be afraid to tell me things, Deba. I would never say anything."

Deba smiled at her friend. "That doesn't worry me; your safety does. The less you know about me, the less threatened you can be, Maria."

Maria hooked her arm through her friend's. "Tell me about your father."

Deba looked at her friend a long time, then sighed. It would be so good to talk to someone about her beloved parents. "He's a paleontologist, as is my mother. Father is rather famous in his field. He's written several books on the subject. His lectures are always crowded, and he's been invited to speak at the most prestigious universities. Chatsworth Brown is his agent." Deba felt as though she'd dropped a hundred pounds. She had carried the burden of silence for so long. "My mother and father are kind, gentle people. You'd like them," she finished gently.

Maria smiled at her. "We're going to fool them all by doing so well that no one will find us. I'm going to use the name Tobles. That's my mother's name. What name will you take?"

"What do you think of the name Alde Baran?"

Maria chuckled. "Al-da Bar-on. Very theatrical." Then she frowned. "How could you stand it? Being on the run, I mean."

"It's not been easy, but you learn to cope. I have discovered that I have a finely honed desire to survive . . . and to see . . ." Deba smothered a sob, taking a deep shuddering breath. "I want to see my family again." She looked out the dirt-smudged window, at the blurry landscape. Wolf's face was there.

"And Wolfgang Clinton," Maria said softly.

Deba looked down at her hands. "Yes, but that isn't meant to be."

Maria squeezed her hand. "You love him."

"Oh, yes, much more than I ever thought it possible to love anyone." Deba smiled shakily. "Trust me to find the right man in the wrong place at a bad time."

"You do have a knack," Maria said huskily, squeezing her hand again.

The two girls ate a small lunch, since the food was not too appealing, and then they napped.

They opened their eyes at the flurry of activity.

"New York?" Maria asked.

"I think so."

Both girls had traveled as light as they could, but there were still bulky pieces of luggage to haul onto the platform.

"I'm risking the money for a redcap. I'll get two jobs if I have to," Deba muttered. "It's cheaper than a broken back." She gestured to a man with a dolly.

"Right." Maria looked around her. "So this is Grand Central Station. It's got beautiful workmanship in the ceiling and walls, and look at the center."

"It's also a nuthouse of activity." Deba paused and followed the direction of the other girl's gaze toward some homeless persons sitting on the steps leading up and out of the station. "It's not just Mexico that has destitute people. New York has too many of them."

"What are you doing, Deba?"

Deba didn't answer her but approached a homeless woman who had a child at her side. "Madam, I think you dropped this five-dollar bill. You should be more careful with your money," Deba told her, pressing the money into her hand.

"I will be. Thank you." The woman's rather dirty face cracked into a smile. The child's didn't change expression.

"Let's go, Maria."

Maria blinked. "I hate to see people that way. It hurts to know how scared and lost they must feel."

Deba nodded. "We're going to Chatsworth's office. Maybe he can suggest a place where we can crash cheaply."

"Come on, friend. Our redcap is in a hurry." Once on the street, Deba paid the redcap and signaled for a taxi. It was an unseasonably cold, rainy day for August in Manhattan, and all the passing cabs seemed busy.

Maria hunched down in her coat, shivering. "My blood isn't ready for this. If this is summer, what will winter be?"

"Wait inside the station until I get a cab, Maria. Go on,

hurry. I'm used to weather like this." Deba fought down a
shudder of cold as she watched her friend disappear inside the
door. She'd been in Mexico too long. As she turned back to the
street, her glance touched the Gran Hyatt, just a stone's throw
away.

On one of their many trips to New York, before they went
into hiding, she and her parents had stayed there. Deba could
almost taste the fresh-squeezed orange juice she'd ordered every
morning. "Taxi!"

The vehicle cruised to the curb.

A man went to step in front of her and take the cab. Deba
threw her shoulder at him, knocking him off balance so that he
slid into the mud puddle at the curb and went down to his
knees. "Sorry! Hope you didn't get wet." Deba gave him her
best crocodile smile as the man struggled to his feet, brushing
ineffectually at his wet trousers. "It's a tough world, isn't it?"
She'd learned to fight back or die.

"Bitch," the man muttered, shaking one foot that had been
encased in the dirty water.

"Bastard," Deba whispered back. "No doubt you do better
with old ladies or the handicapped." Deba lifted her chin and
stared back at him.

"Get in the cab, Deba," Maria murmured behind her,
laughter threading her voice. "Have you ever considered trying
out for the L.A. Raiders?"

"The jerk, I should have decked him."

"You did," Maria giggled.

The cabdriver stared over his shoulder, cracking his gum
over and over. "Nice block, lady. Now if you're ready, we could
get going here. I gotta schedule, ya know." The gum cracked
loudly.

"Let's go." Deba got into the back with a still chuckling
Maria.

"Youse from up north?"

"Right." Deba tried to smile at the cabdriver, who shot a
questioning look over his shoulder.

"Yeah? From Yonkers?"

Deba searched her mind for an upstate city other than
Rochester, where her father had taught for a time. "Syracuse."

"Yeah? That far, huh? They get lots of snow up there.
Right?" The driver creamed through the honking traffic at a
ridiculous speed.

"We could get killed today, and then those sinister friends of yours would stop chasing us. Lord, it's cold," Maria muttered. "Eeek. We almost hit that bus."

"Close your eyes. Only a block to go."

"If we make it." Maria let out a whush of relief when the car slid to the curb, scrambling to get out to the relative safety of the sidewalk.

It took several minutes to unload the bags.

Glaring after the driver, who'd set their bags down at the curb in front of the Madison Avenue building, then scooted back to his warm, dry taxi, Maria began loading up. "We shouldn't have tipped him. He could have given us more help with these."

"This is the big city, kid." Deba grimaced at the weight of her carry-on bag. "Let's get inside, Maria. That wind is like a knife."

They struggled into the building, hauling their belongings. Under the watchful eye of security they staggered into an elevator and punched the buttons for the twenty-fifth floor.

"I hope he doesn't throw us out." Maria leaned against the wall of the elevator, out of breath, her face red. "We cart those bags around much more and I'm going to collapse."

"Chin up, here we go." Deba grabbed one of the big bags and put a smaller one under her arm so that she could take a medium-sized one in her other hand. Head down, she thrust out of the elevator, propping the door open with her shoulder so that Maria could bring her load.

"God! This is insane," Maria muttered as she accompanied Deba down the short hall, dragging the luggage.

Putting down her bags, Deba managed to open the door to a spacious office. She ignored the aghast receptionist, who rose to her feet, protesting. "Mr. Brown, please."

"Do you have an appointment?" The frosty gaze of the receptionist fixed on a perspiring Maria, who was now sitting on the larger piece of luggage she'd managed to lug into the office.

"Tell him Mr. Dryden's daughter is here." Deba stared back at the receptionist until the woman seated herself again.

The receptionist was disapproving. "I'll speak to his secretary and . . ."

Deba leaned across the the phone console, glaring at the

blonde with the curvy body and manicured nails. "You'll call Chatsworth and give him my message."

"Very well, but I don't think he'll like it."

Maria closed her eyes. "I don't know where we have to go with these, but I have to have a cold drink. I'm thirsty."

The office door was flung open. "Aldebaran!" Chatsworth Brown stormed through the opening, stopping abruptly as he took in the tableau in front of him. "Good God, where's the kitchen sink?" His medium build, medium coloring, were enhanced by a warm, welcoming smile. It lightened his features and put sparkle in his blue eyes.

"In the hall," Maria said wearily, smothering a yawn.

Chatsworth looked her way, then crossed the room and lifted her to her feet, his hands on her upper arms. "And who are you? Black hair, black eyes, creamy skin. Are you my dream come true?"

"Good Lord," Deba said, her eyes widening in amusement, when Maria straightened, fatigue forgotten. "Chatsworth, must we stand here, guarding our luggage?"

"Don't be silly. Miss Garson will watch it, won't you, Lena?"

"Yessir," Lena answered tightly.

"Come this way, ladies," Chatsworth invited, taking Maria's arm.

Once the door was closed, he faced Deba unsmilingly. "What in hell are you thinking of, Aldebaran?"

"I had to run," Deba said tautly, turning away to the window. "Accept that."

When he would have retorted, Maria put a hand on his arm, eliciting a sudden smile from him. Maria shook her head.

Chatsworth stared down at the diminutive brunette and nodded slowly. "Where are you staying?"

"On the street at the moment." Deba still hadn't turned away from the window. "I was hoping you might point Maria toward a job and both of us to good, cheap lodging."

"Easy. Stay with me and Maria can come here and work. I need an . . . assistant."

Deba whirled around, a satirical smile on her face. "That will answer for tonight." Noting that he hadn't looked at her, she coughed. "Chatsworth, are you leering at Maria?"

Reddening to the roots of his hair, he slanted an irritated glance Deba's way. "Maria will be as safe with me as . . ."

"Sounds dull." Deba grinned, feeling the first real relief since leaving Wolf.

"Still have that tongue that could cut steel, have you?" There was raillery in his tone, but when he saw Deba whiten, he went to her at once. "Hey, it was just a joke."

"What? Oh, I know." Deba couldn't tell Chatsworth that Wolf had one day made a similar observation, and that remembering his voice, his intonations, was anguish for her.

Chatsworth looked back at Maria when Deba looked away from him. Then he moved toward the other woman. "Why did that hurt her?"

"She's in love with a very complex man, as complex as she is."

"And you empathize with her?" Chatsworth touched Maria's arm.

"Aldebaran is very special."

Chatsworth nodded, smiling at Maria. "So, it's settled. You'll stay at my brownstone. I rattle around in the thing anyway. Most times I wonder why I don't sell it."

Deba turned around, fatigue etching her smile. "Because your aunt Brunhilde would come back from the grave and smite you."

"Well, there is that reason. Come along, ladies. I'll call my housekeeper, and she'll have a lunch ready for us and you can settle into your rooms. Tomorrow, Maria, you can take some time to come into the office and I'll show you what the drill is."

"You mean it about the job?"

"Oh, yes, I think you'll fit in admirably."

"So do I," Deba murmured, but the other two were looking at each other and not noticing her.

Maria and Deba both sighed with relief when a member of the building maintenance staff arrived and put their luggage on a dolly, taking it to the basement parking garage.

Lena Garson was even a shade warmer to them as they were leaving with Chatsworth.

"Tell me about yourself, Maria."

Deba caught the caressing note in Chatsworth's voice, then her eyes closed. Sleeping for a year did not seem outlandish.

"I don't care what it takes. Find her."

"We are doing our best, sir."

"Do more." Wolf slammed down the receiver and leaned

back in the leather chair behind his study desk. Where the hell had Deba gone? Why did she leave without telling him? Because he wouldn't have let her leave if she'd told him!

When the phone rang again, he glared at it, not wanting to speak to anyone. But . . . it might be about Deba McCloud. "Hello."

"Mr. Clinton? It's Crandall, sir. How are you?"

"Ah, I honestly don't have time to chat, Crandall." It seemed a million years ago that Crandall had been his assistant. Now it was hard to imagine anyone near him except Deba.

"No, sir, of course not. I wanted to tell you that my mother is fine and I'm ready to come back to Mexico."

"Oh. Well, I think I'm going to utilize your knowledge in the L.A. office, Crandall. I've talked to the people up there and they seem to think you could make a difference too. So if you're set to come back to America, make plans to go there. It will be the usual arrangement as far as money and accommodations."

"But, sir, I was hoping to rejoin you . . ."

"As it happens, I don't need an assistant at this time. I would like you to stay with the organization, but if you feel that you can't . . ."

"Los Angeles will be a disappointment, sir, but I'm sure I can handle it. I'll arrange to leave here at the end of the week."

"Good-bye. Keep in touch."

Wolf couldn't even remember what he and Crandall had said once the connection was cut. Deba was on his mind! Where did she go? Why had she skipped right after he'd proposed marriage to her? That was a question that made him move his shoulders as though there was a pain between them that went from front to back, and made his breathing ragged.

Putting his hand into his trouser pocket, he fingered Deba's emerald ring, which he carried with him all the time.

All at once he surged to his feet. He was damned well going to find her . . . and he was going to get some answers. Who the hell did she think she was jerking around?

Grief turned to blistering anger. He would do some jerking around of his own!

When the phone rang again he hoisted the receiver on the first ring. "What?" Fury riddled his query.

"Ah, sir, Mr. Clinton, this is Lazarus, sir. I think I have discovered a trail. If I have this right, there were two women who left Los Angeles two weeks ago, on a Thursday."

"That would be the day after she left here," Wolf muttered. "Two women? I don't think that's right. She didn't know anyone around here." All at once a moment from the past flashed into his mind. The day she had told him she would call her friend Maria. "Wait a minute. Who was the other one?"

"Well, that was how I got my lead." Lazarus laughed softly. "I have been many times back and forth from the United States, senor."

"Go on."

Wolf's harsh command dried up Lazarus's humor. "I discovered that a friend of Miss McCloud's, Maria Delgado, had left the area. I talked to a cousin of . . ."

"Maria. Yes, yes, that's the name. Go on."

"He told me that his cousin and her friend were going to Los Angeles . . . but that they might not be staying there. They could be going east." There was a rattle of paper. "I traced them as far as Chicago and . . ."

"Chicago?" Wolf's shock echoed in his voice.

"Yessir, but I haven't been able to pick up anything since."

"Get on it, at once, Lazarus. Good work. I want her found, and soon. Put every man you can muster on this, unlimited funds."

"Yessir, I have done that. I think I will hear more at the end of the day."

"Good. I want to know the minute you hear anything. I'll be waiting." Wolf hung up the phone and looked around him. He had begun to hate his haven. Rancho Lobo had become a jail that echoed voices. Whenever he was in his bedroom, he would hear the laughter that had been between them at all times. When had he ever been so carefree? And damn her, she'd been happy too. Why the hell had she thrown it over? He'd find her!

The house resounded with Deba's whispers. When he was out riding, sometimes the kiss of the wind was like her caress. It was driving him crazy. Rancho Lobo was a prison!

Cursing all women, he stormed out of his study, then almost at a run as he left the rancho for the stables. He had to get away!

The stablehands scattered, letting Wolf saddle Diablo by himself. The patron had been a madman for days now. What devil drove him?

Riding had always been a form of therapy for him. Man

and horse racing across the plata. Now it annoyed and frustrated him.

Pulling the horse up hard, man and beast out of breath, Wolf patted the equine neck. "It isn't you, old fellow, it's Deba. Let's get back, you need a cool bath and drink and I need . . . Damn it, what I need, I'm getting back."

The pace back to the stables was less frantic but still speedy, and man and horse were sweating when the stableboys went to the head of the high-spirited animal.

"Get him cooled down and watered." Wolf swiped at his face with his damp sleeve and strode away.

The stablehand shivered. The patron was in a murderous mood.

When Wolf left the stables, he went right to the lake. Swimming hard up and down the length of the good-sized body of water should have sanded down some of the raw edges, the prickling, gnawing sensation under his skin. It didn't.

When he took out his snorkeling equipment so that he could search the bottom, Deba's face was there, staring at him. Her terror in the water cave at the cottage was something he would never forget. Even now when his temper fulminated, when he hated her, his protective instinct rose in him like a flood. Who was caring for her now? Was she afraid?

Rising out of the water, he yanked the mask off his face, slapping at the water with it. "Damn you, Deba McCloud. I'll find you." Wolf shook his fist at the heavens.

◇ 7 ◇

Time rolled through a Manhattan autumn, then the city decked itself out for the holidays before working its way through the cold winter months into spring.

Not a day went by without Deba's thinking of Wolf. Missing him was a rusty tear in her heart . . . but in a small way she was adjusting to the pain.

Smoothing an infinitesimal wrinkle from her maid's uniform, she left her bedroom in Chatsworth's house, smothering the sigh of regret.

Deba went down the short hall to Maria's room, knocked, then entered when she heard the muffled welcome. Maria was looking at herself in the mirror.

"What's keeping you? Chatsworth is downstairs."

"I can't eat breakfast," Maria muttered. "I never feel as beautiful as that receptionist of his."

Deba chuckled. They had been living at Chatsworth's for quite awhile, and Maria generally made a similar comment each day. "What you mean is that you don't want any lovely creatures near your man."

"Aldebaran! That's not true. Besides, Chatsworth isn't my man, he's my employer."

"Hah! The games you play. Hurry, will you. I have to get back to Casa Winsome, *tout de suite.*" Deba grimaced.

"It sounds awful out there on Long Island. Are you sure you're not the caretaker of Bedlam? Those three kids sound crazy and the mother should be certified."

Deba shrugged. "Little Robbie, Beth, and Belinda are darlings . . . sometimes." Deba winced. "But not yesterday. They put sugar in the saltshaker and Mr. W., who's liberal with the salt, spread a coating of sugar over his overdone steak and french fries."

Maria shuddered. "A health-food freak, I see. It's a wonder you weren't fired. Of course that wouldn't be too bad there."

"Beggars can't be choosers. I was lucky to get this job, and I wouldn't have it if the Winsomes were able to hire anyone on a first-class level. Their unruly children cancel that out, according to the senior Mrs. Winsome."

"At least you can come home every night." Maria turned to look at her friend, wincing at the crisp black-and-white maid's uniform. "That color combination is all wrong for you. Something in cream and coral would be better."

Deba laughed. "I'll mention your suggestion to Mrs. Winsome. I'm sure she'll get right on it. Come on, let's get some breakfast. Incidentally, you look terrific. That deep red is your color. Watch out for Chatsworth, he's liable to corner you near the filing cabinet today."

"I wish he would," Maria murmured, then reddened when Deba raised her eyebrows. "Isn't he just the sweetest man you've ever met, Aldebaran? But he's so shy."

"No doubt there are a few hundred editors who would gladly hand you his head in a basket. I understand he's one sharp dude in the negotiation department."

"That's just shrewd business and has nothing to do with his basic goodness," Maria told her loftily, raising her chin when her friend scoffed. "Come on, we're holding up Chatsworth."

"La-di-da." Deba smiled when her friend passed her. She leaned forward. "You've got it bad for your boss, lady."

"You should know what that's like." Maria skidded to a stop and grimaced. "I'm sorry. I wasn't referring to Wolfgang Clinton. It was just a joke, Aldebaran."

"I know, but you're right." Deba threaded her arm

through Maria's. "My life would have been far less complicated if I hadn't fallen for Wolf Clinton."

"I think it's beyond anything believable that you even got to see him, then got employed by him. Having him fall in love with you had to be a kick." Maria looked dreamy-eyed for a moment. "It's so romantic. I read all about him in the trades and you and Natasha Sharansky are the only women he's ever been serious about. Of course, I'm sure there was the odd mistress now and then."

Deba glared at her. "Odd being the operative word. You needn't catalogue his women for me. I know all about them too."

Maria looked chastened. "No, you didn't, you're just saying that so I won't see how hurt you are. I'm sorry, Aldebaran, I seem to be so damn gauche at times."

Deba gave her a twisted smile. "I'm too touchy, and you're a good friend." Deba squeezed her arm. "Let's face it, Maria, there really is nothing to say about Wolf that wouldn't hurt in some way. It's not your fault, it's mine," Deba told her as they left the room and wandered down from the third floor of the brownstone, where their bedrooms were, to the foyer.

"Hey, it's about time. I was going to send a search party." Chatsworth had come out of the high-ceilinged dining room into the center hall that bisected the downstairs. His voice trailed. "Wow. My office has never looked as good as it has these last several months." His low-voiced observation was followed by a foot-to-eyebrow inspection of Maria.

"No doubt you're referring to me." Deba inclined her head at the two persons so absorbed in each other.

"What? Oh, yes, Aldebaran, you look lovely in that outfit. Right color for you. Is it new?" Chatsworth smiled blindly. Then he took Maria's arm and led her toward the dining room.

"Fool," Deba said softly, smiling at the backs of her two friends. She remembered how close she'd been to Wolf, how unaware they were of anyone else when they were together. Inhaling painfully, she tried to smother the aching rock in her chest. Wolf! What was he doing now?

As usual, breakfast for the three friends was an animated time. It seemed there was always much to discuss, and if it was politics they often argued.

Although Deba knew that Maria had discussed Wolf with Chatsworth, Deba never brought up the subject of the man who occupied her thoughts twenty hours of the day. Sometimes she slept and never thought of him at all. Still, Chatsworth's words caught her by surprise.

"Deba, Maria tells me that you have the makings of a fine novel, that your notes on Wolf Clinton are broad-based and in depth. Easy does it." Chatsworth caught the spoon that threatened to tumble from Maria's hand.

"Chatsworth!"

"Maria!"

Maria and Deba spoke at the same time, their eyes on the persons they called.

"Aldebaran, I'm sorry, but I can't stand to see you doing such menial tasks. If you were good at it, it would be one thing, but you're a terrible housekeeper. Even you said you're a rank amateur." Maria shuddered. The pancake-shaped soufflé, the lumpy sauces, the overdone vegetables. Cooking was not for Alde Baran.

"With emphasis on the word *rank,*" Deba observed wryly. "Never mind about my abilities. It's a good cover, and I'll be safer out there than I would be working in Manhattan."

"Deba's right there," Chatsworth said slowly, patting Maria's hand when he looked crestfallen. "But I think if Maria's half right about those notes and the work on the disks, you should let me look at them."

"No." Deba shook her head. "It's personal . . . very personal. No one should be looking at the disks; I'm sure Wolf would say not even me." She waved a hand in front of her face as though to wipe away a memory. "I really can't go into it." Deba stood. "Actually I should get going. I'm going out on the early train. Mrs. W. wants me to clean the library today." Deba went around the table to kiss Maria's cheek, then when Chatsworth stood, she kissed him as well.

"Why don't you take my car, Deba? It would be so much simpler for you. Maria and I can grab a cab." He followed her out of the morning room.

"You're a darling, Chatsworth, but I don't think I want to do that. A Mercedes Sport is a little rich for my blood." Deba held up her hand, palm outward. "Please don't suggest I drive Aunt Brunhilde's Rolls-Royce, which is in your garage. Mr. Winsome would choke on his prunes if he ever saw that."

Chatsworth grimaced. "I suppose it would seem a bit strange."

"A tad. See you."

"Don't work too hard." Chatsworth went back into the dining room, looking directly at Maria. "There's still time to tell her. She's upstairs brushing her teeth."

Maria shook her head. "I know it's risky, but it's worth it."

Chatsworth went around to her chair and knelt down next to it when he saw the sheen of tears in her eyes. "You're a good friend to Aldebaran, but she might consider this a great invasion of privacy, Maria."

Maria nodded, biting her lip. "I know, but when I think how frightening it's been for her, how scary to be on the run for such a long time . . ." Maria shook her head. "Wolf Clinton loved her, he would want her to have some protection." She turned her head and looked at him. "This book could be her lifelong security blanket. I want you to read what I've managed to print out. The journal is upstairs. I'll get it when she's gone."

Chatsworth stood so that she could rise from her chair. When she would have moved away from him, he put his arm around her waist, leaning down to kiss her ear. "You're a very special lady, and not just because you're a good friend to Aldebaran."

"No?" Maria looked up into his warm eyes, her hand lifting to his chin as though it had a life of its own. "You're not bad yourself."

Chuckling, Chatsworth lowered his mouth to hers.

The kiss deepened while their hearts pounded and the world spun.

Pushing back from him, Maria stared up at him, blinking. "I . . . I'll be late for work."

"I'll talk to your boss." Chatsworth's head lowered.

Maria laughed, her hands firm on his chest. "Promise me you'll read the journal."

Chatsworth closed his eyes. "You're a hard-hearted woman. I'm in the mood for love, not reading."

"Please."

"I'll read it, I'll read it, but put a bookmark where we were, please. We're taking up where we left off very soon."

"Suits me," Maria told him cheekily, almost skipping from the room.

* * *

Days tumbled into weeks. Deba went to her maid's job every day. Maria went to the office with Chatsworth. Each day began like the one before it, but like all of life there were subtle changes.

Spring was being assertive. Crocuses and daffodils appeared in Manhattan. Heads were up to the sun, not down into the wind. Day was pushing back the night, shortening it.

Deba looked at the Winsome home as she walked up the drive that would take her to the back door. It was a lovely house overlooking the sound, but the precise, almost plastic groupings in the landscaping detracted from the richness of the brick-and-stone frame. "Nouveau riche landscaping," Deba muttered, for the hundredth time.

The back door opened before she reached it. "Hi, Alde. Come in."

"Hi, Belinda," Deba said cautiously.

"Bumper threw up in the morning room, then Mom lost her breakfast. You shoulda been here. Wild."

"Wonderful," Deba muttered.

"And Robbie got whipped last night."

"Why?" Deba didn't approve of the way Mr. Winsome's mother encouraged her son to cane his son at every infraction. The cane had been provided by Mrs. Winsome, proud that her father had never needed to use it on her. It didn't seem to do any good, and more than once the young boy had been hurt.

Deba bit her lip hard the last time she'd seen a bruise on the boy's arm, but she didn't intend to look away next time. Job or no job, she wasn't going to be a silent partner to child beatings.

"He drove Daddy's car down the driveway and hit a tree." Belinda beamed.

"Good Lord." Deba closed her eyes, torn between running back to the train station and going into the house. It was almost as though Robbie courted such disasters. Since it was two miles back to the station, she went into the house.

Minding her own business had become a dictum since she'd been on the run, and it was a good course to follow. Why didn't she get out of the Winsome household, then? Why stay in a place where her own temperament might launch her into a full-scale war with her employer. She didn't need the complications that such a confrontation could bring.

Pausing in the small entryway leading to the kitchen, Deba heard sounds coming from the front part of the house and sighed.

The door leading to the kitchen opened and a slack-jawed Mrs. Winsome leaned against the jamb. "My mother-in-law is having one of her hissy fits again," she mentioned weakly. "And I have my bridge club today."

"Tell the old toad to go to Florida," Alde told the fortyish woman, who must have been pretty when younger. Now she was harried and flighty.

Mrs. Winsome blinked. "Do you think I could? No, no, that's silly. Wilfred wouldn't allow it." Tipping the scales in her marriage could lose her the husband she loved. For all Wilfred's faults, he was basically good, and she wanted to remain his wife.

"Then do it on your own. She only has the rights in your home that you allow her. Boot her out if she causes trouble. She's in good shape physically and financially. For heaven's sake, she's only in her early sixties. Let her fend for herself."

"Oh, dear, wouldn't it be wonderful if I had the guts." Mrs. Winsome closed her eyes and sighed, stepping back so that Deba could move past her.

Deba entered the kitchen and gasped. Chaos!

Dishes and silverware were everywhere. Cooled coffee with cream congealing on the top was in the cups, crusted egg, soggy bacon, and bits of toast were on plates, crumbs on the floor. "Give me strength," Deba whispered, wishing for the umpteenth time that a good fairy would light on her shoulder and whisk the work away. She was a deplorable housekeeper, but the Winsomes were worse.

Her sense of organization had been on a high level when she worked with Wolf in his office. She was totally disorganized doing housework, especially in such a big house. Her admiration for Julia, Wolf's housekeeper, increased daily by leaps and bounds. Wolf! Again he was in her mind. Was there never going to be an hour in the day when he wasn't? Would her thoughts be colored by him forever?

"We cleared the table after the . . . the incident," Mrs. Winsome said faintly. "My mother-in-law says we have to put the dog down, but I don't know how I can do that. The children love Bumper and . . . oh, no, Bumper. How did you get in the house again?"

"He was cold outside, and he's my friend." Robbie Winsome put his arms around the neck of the bumbling mixed-breed, whose wet tongue washed any face within reach and whose paws, the size of fry pans, were leaving muddy marks on the oak floor.

Alde studied the boy and saw the angry spots high on his face, the bruise on his arm. Damn Wilfred Winsome! Didn't he see how destructive it was to punish the boy the way he did?

The dog had become very important to all the Winsome children, but especially to the oldest, Robbie. He seemed to be the boy's anchor.

"Make sure he doesn't do any more antisocial parlor tricks. Okay?"

"Okay, Alde. Will you watch him while I'm in school? Nanna says he's going to the pound today."

"He's staying with me today, Robbie. Don't worry about that." When relief colored his features, determination to protect the canine hardened in Deba.

"Thanks." The boy looked around the kitchen, resiliency changing his focus. "Boy, I wouldn't wanna be you today, Alde. What a mess!"

"Tell me about it," Deba muttered, running soapy water into the sink. She would have to soak everything before she could put it in the dishwasher.

"And she'll probably break some of the dishes while she's doing them. She usually does." Beth, the middle child, wore glasses that gave her face an owl-like appearance. "Has anyone seen my math book? The school bus will be here in five minutes."

"Beth, you're a zero," her brother said scathingly.

"Mo-thhherrr, talk to him."

"Robbie," Mrs. Winsome whispered, touching a messy plate and shaking her head. "Do you think you'll have things ready in time for the bridge club, Alde?"

Deba shrugged. "I'll give it my best shot. Why don't you go upstairs and lie down? I'll get the children off to school," Alde told the dazed woman soothingly. "I ordered kuchen from the bakery yesterday. They'll be delivered this morning. The deli will send out the sandwiches and I'll make the coffee. We'll be fine." Deba crossed her fingers.

"Thank you, Alde," Mrs. Winsome gulped. "What did I ever do before you came?"

"Well, you had a lot more dishes," Beth remarked thoughtfully, finding her math book in the dog's dish. "Bumper's put tooth marks in my book," she added conversationally. "Maybe we should change his diet."

"We could feed the delivery man to him," Alde interjected sweetly.

"Is he still coming on to you, Alde?" Robbie asked, his question bringing around the heads of the other two children, their eyes snapping in curiosity.

Alde watched Mrs. Winsome totter from the kitchen. No need for Mrs. Winsome to get involved in another problem. She had too many as it was. "It's nothing I can't handle, Robbie."

"You should deck him, Alde," Belinda offered.

"Or shove your knee in his whatsis." Beth looked pensive. "That should cool him."

"Beth's right, Alde. Don't take any crap from Reggie. He's not tough." Robbie curled his fingers into fists. "We can take him."

But he was burly and six feet tall. Deba mentally shrugged. She could always bean him with a fry pan. "Let's go, gang. School bus in five minutes, and you have to get down the driveway."

Deba ushered them to the front door, found Belinda's book bag when she couldn't find it, and then stood in the front door waving. It was February and cold, and she shivered.

"Don't forget to be careful of what Bumper eats, Alde. He barfs, you know," Belinda caroled just before the trio disappeared around a curve in the drive.

"Lucky me." Sighing, Deba went back to the kitchen, trying not to look at the mess. Putting her head down, she began cleaning up the dishes.

Sometime later, when she felt a cold nose on her, she looked down at Bumper. "Hi. You've been good. Want to go out for a while?"

Deba knew from experience that she had to go with the dog or he would wander off. The last time he'd done that he'd rooted out an entire hedge that one of the neighbors had prized. Bumper had to be watched. Deba put on her coat and followed the canine out of doors.

Bumper took his time, sniffing, pausing, looking, but finally he was ready to return to the house, just as the delivery truck from the deli pulled up to the back door.

"Hi, baby, waiting for me?" Reggie took his deliveries from the back and carried them to the door.

"Go suck an egg, Reggie." Deba held the door until he passed through with his parcels. "Is that all?"

"Yep." Reggie frowned. "I don't like it when girls talk to me like that."

Deba opened the door again. "Leave."

As Reggie went by her, his one hand feathered over her breast.

Without thinking Deba lifted her foot and planted it on his backside as he passed her.

Reggie stumbled down the steps and fell. Getting to his feet, he clenched his fists and moved toward her. "Nobody does that to me."

Deba looked around for a weapon. Why hadn't she picked up the rolling pin that was in the utensil container on the counter?

When she heard the growl, she looked down at easygoing Bumper and blinked. Bumper was a mixed-breed, but mostly Newfoundland, and was of a very good size.

Reggie stopped his forward motion. "Hey, I don't have to put up with no vicious dogs."

"And I don't have to put up with you. You tried to assault me. Mr. Wiener won't keep you on at the deli when I tell him that."

Reggie stared from Deba to the stiff-stanced dog, then went to his truck. "I was trying to have a little fun, Alde, that's all."

"Don't try it again."

When the truck had disappeared around the house, Deba closed the door and leaned down to the dog. "You're a darling, Bumper, and you are not going to the pound."

The dog's wet tongue lapped her from chin to eyebrow.

"Aaagh. Don't do that." Deba went to the small bathroom off the butler's pantry and washed her face, then returned to her chores, the dog at her heels.

Deba was still talking to herself about the noxious Reggie as she put the last touches on the card tables that had been set up in the large living room. "Damn him anyway."

"What are you talking about, Alde? I don't like people muttering, and I don't like the tables. The flowers are limp."

Deba turned about to face the senior Mrs. Winsome.

"You're free to change them or fix them yourself, Mrs. Winsome."

"You're not paid to be insolent, Alde."

"There's the doorbell." Deba ground her teeth. She was inches from telling the old harridan what she thought of her.

Mrs. Winsome sniffed. "The guests are arriving and my daughter-in-law isn't here to greet them. She's a deplorable hostess."

"Aren't you going out this morning, Mrs. Winsome?" Deba asked, moving toward the door.

"No, I think I'll stay here today, perhaps watch." The older woman, tall, spare, silver-haired, with a perpetual frown on her face, let a small smile cross her features.

Cause trouble and interfere, that's what she'd do. Deba hurried to the door and let in the morning bridge club.

Deba was busy getting out the munchies for the ladies and pouring tea, but it didn't take her many trips from the kitchen to the living room to see that Mrs. Winsome senior was doing a job on her daughter-in-law.

Deba wished Mrs. W. junior would shoot back, but the younger woman sat shrinking in her chair. "Ahem, Mrs. Winsome." Deba smiled at the older woman, who sat near her daughter-in-law in an overstuffed chair, commenting on the play.

"What is it, Alde?" Mrs. W. senior looked irritated at the interruption of her caustic monologue.

Deba shot a quick glance at Mrs. Morgan, one of Mrs. W. junior's friends and an active member of the ASPCA. "You did want to put the dog down today, and I was wondering what I would tell the man who comes to put him in the truck. Bumper's such a gentle dog, so sweet." Deba sighed. "It will break the children's heart to lose such a friend, but as you say, that's not important, so what shall I tell the man when he comes?"

"I don't want to discuss it now."

Cards were put on the table as heads swerved toward Mrs. Winsome senior.

Mrs. Winsome junior straightened in her chair, a tart smile flitting around her mouth as she looked at her maid. "Yes, do tell us what to tell the man when he comes to destroy our dog." Mrs. Winsome junior placed her cards facedown on the table.

"Get on with your game, Silvia. That will all be handled

later today." Mrs. Winsome turned toward Deba. "Alde, you have too much to say. Now leave the room."

"Don't talk like that to her." Silvia Winsome rose to her feet, her hands fluttering nervously, color high. "This is my home and Alde is my maid and I like the way she handles things . . . and . . . and when the dogcatcher comes, he'll be sent packing—by me."

"Hurray for you, Silvie! about time." Mrs. Morgan picked up her tea, grimaced at its tepidness, then smiled at Deba. "I'd love some hot. Is there some?"

"Coming right up, Mrs. Morgan."

Deba noticed from the corner of her eye that the senior Mrs. Winsome was livid, if mute.

When Deba returned to the living room, Bumper followed her through, reaching up to the table to get a cookie from Mrs. Winsome's plate.

"Oh, no, you don't." Deba put down the tea, and grabbed his collar. "He's very sneaky." She smiled when the women chuckled and commented on the animal. "And very brave. This morning he protected me when I was . . . having problems."

Mrs. Winsome junior looked sharp-eyed at Deba for a moment. "Was it Reggie? The children said that he had made you uncomfortable."

"He won't anymore. Bumper told him where to head in."

The women oohed and aahed about the brave, brave doggy. Bumper looked soulful and suitably humble.

Mrs. Winsome senior sat ramrod straight, her eyes darting from one to the other before settling balefully on the canine.

"Ham," Deba muttered to the dog before going back to the kitchen for more sandwiches.

The rest of the afternoon went fairly well for Deba, except for burning a tablecloth she was ironing, breaking a casserole dish, and spilling cold tea on some of the hand-crocheted napkins.

The children came in after three, and talked to her about their day while she and Mrs. Winsome tried to clean up the broken casserole pieces.

"Only one dish today, Alde? You're getting better," Beth pronounced generously.

"You're a zip, Beth," her brother said.

"Motherrrrr, talk to Robbie."

"Robbie," Mrs. W. said tiredly.

At six Mr. W. came into the kitchen, his face stern, his mother at his side. "I must talk to you, Alde."

"All right."

The door to the dining room burst open and the children and Silvie came through.

"I won't let you fire Alde, no matter what your mother says, Wilfred. I need Alde here. If you won't let me keep her, the children and I are leaving."

Both Deba's and Wilfred's mouths fell open.

"Let them leave, Wilfred."

Well, she'd been three months on the job, that was better than most. Deba lifted her chin and stared at her employer.

Wilfred Winsome's mouth snapped shut and he whirled to stare at his mother. "Let my family leave?"

"Of course. What good are they? They . . ."

"I love my wife, and my children." Wilfred's glasses slid down his nose. "I want them with me." For long moments he stared at his mother. Then he turned to look at his wife, then at his son. "I've been wrong. It's been making me sick to see how my son turns away from me." His hand went out to his oldest, then dropped to his side. Then he looked at his wife. "To see your eyes slide away when I want to talk to you, beloved, is more pain than I ever hoped to have. Silvie, I love you. What do you want me to do?"

His mother made a strangling sound. "Wilfred, you have money. You don't need her. Your father would be ashamed to see you grovel."

Wilfred looked at his mother, then he inhaled deeply. "Maybe you should go and live near Aunt Grace in Phoenix. I've let you come between me and my family, Mother. That was wrong. I hurt my son when I knew it wasn't right, and that won't happen again."

"Discipline is good for children." Mrs. Winsome senior's voice rose, crackling with animosity when she glanced fleetingly at her daughter-in-law.

"Not with a cane. That's punishment, and it's stupid," Deba blurted, her face reddening when her employer stared at her. "I'm sorry, sir, I spoke out of turn."

"Do you see what I mean, Wilfred? You don't want such a woman in your house. Fire her. Maybe that will help you to manage your family better."

"No." Wilfred spoke quietly, removing his glasses to wipe

them with a clean handkerchief he'd taken from his breast pocket. "Leave, Mother. Leave while we're still friends. We won't be close at all if you stay. You've been making my family suffer, and that's my fault because I knew what you were doing, though it was easier to pretend I didn't. I'll help you pack if you like."

"You're a fool." A tiny bubble of spittle appeared at the corner of Mrs. Winsome senior's mouth.

"Don't you say that about Wilfred." Tears stood in Silvie's eyes. "It's my fault it's gone this far. I should have tossed you out on your backside like Alde said. This is my home and I'll run it and my children my way . . . our way." Her wobbly smile touched her husband, who nodded encouragingly. "As my husband's mother you are welcome to visit at holiday time, but only for a week, and you will never interfere with this household again. Ever."

"Bravo," Deba muttered, earning a glare from the elder woman, who stared at them all, sniffed, and turned, speaking over her shoulder. "I'll get my own things together and send for the rest, but you'll be running to me, Wilfred, begging me to come back. This family of yours is not good for your image of a successful businessman. Mark my words, you'll regret this." Mrs. Winsome senior flounced down the hallway leading to the front foyer.

Silence.

"Ah, Silvie, I think we should talk in private."

"All right, dearest, I'd like that." Silvia's smile had a tinge more confidence and a lacing of shyness. It widened when her spouse smiled back.

Mr. Winsome looked across the room at his eldest. "Robbie, I'd like to ask your forgiveness. That cane will be tossed out."

The boy stepped forward, redfaced. "I'd like to break it."

"We'll break it together, my son."

The girls whooped and laughed.

"And Bumper and Alde are going to stay with us." Wilfred put his left hand on his son's shoulder and put the other out to his maid. "Thank you for championing my son."

Deba shook hands with Wilfred Winsome, her opinion of him doing a one-hundred-and-eighty-degree turn. "Ah, I should get back to work."

"Did you know that Alde only broke one casserole dish today, Daddy?"

"You're a wimp, Beth."

"Motherrrr, speak to Robbie."

"Robbie," Mrs. Winsome junior said softly, moving close to her husband. Then she straightened, her hand going to cover her mouth. "Oh, dear, I forgot to tell Alde that we're having last-minute guests for dinner tonight."

"You mean Thursday evening, don't you, Mrs. Winsome?" Deba prayed.

Mrs. Winsome nodded slowly. "Then too, but tonight we'll be entertaining two of the members of the United Way committee that Wilfred and I will be chairing. Will you be able to stay, Alde? They won't be coming until seven."

"An hour?" Deba swallowed a groan and nodded. "Maybe we'd better make it simple. I'll put some of the frozen beef bourguignon from last week into the microwave. I have a good crusty French bread. With a spinach salad and a hot dressing, it should go." Deba looked around her messy kitchen, then glanced at the children, who were leaving. "Hold it. I need help and you're elected." Deba held up her hand, palm outward. "Before you complain, may I remind you that I saved Bumper's backside today."

"I'll vacuum. I can do that." Beth looked determined. "Belinda, you can help me dust."

The youngest nodded reluctantly.

Robbie grinned at her. "I'll set the table, Alde. I'll bet I don't break any dishes either." He left on the run.

"I can mix a mean salad," Wilfred ventured, smiling at his surprised wife. "Have you forgotten all those dinners we made together when we were still at university?"

"Let's go," Silvie answered, then looked at her husband when he crossed the kitchen to the door. "Where are you going?"

"Calling mother a cab. I'll be back to do the salad."

"I don't care if you poison the guests tonight, Alde. I'm too happy to be upset by anything," Silvia breathed ecstatically, then hurried from the kitchen.

"Thanks," Deba said dryly, going to the freezer and removing the frozen meat that would become the main course . . . with a little luck.

Deba didn't feel as confident two days after the dinner

party, when she had to plan another. The still radiant Mrs. Winsome junior was offhand about what Deba considered an abject failure.

"Don't be silly. Mrs. Earhart wasn't too put out by Bumper crashing into the dining room."

"He toppled her salad over into her beef bourguignon. I don't how he got in there, Mrs. Winsome."

"No matter," Silvia Winsome said airily, her eyes sparkling with happiness.

It would seem that the entire Winsome household had a different aura with the departure of the grandmother, and the glitches in their lives seemed to be taken in stride.

Silvie was lighthearted and carefree, even if her employee was not. "Wilfred wasn't even one bit upset when you spilled the soup, Alde." Silvia looked pensive. "Though I must say the Earharts were taken aback when he assured them that you were the best help he's ever had and that he wouldn't take a king's ransom for you."

"He exaggerates," Deba said weakly, still shaking her head about the Spode tureen that had smashed on the dining-room floor. "I wish you would take the cost of the dish out of my salary. Please."

"Do you plan on being with us for fifty years?" Silvie grinned at her agape mouth. "It was one of a kind and dated, but I don't care and neither does Wilfred. Don't be silly, Alde; take your face out of your hands. It's not the end of the world."

"No? Don't bet your check on it. Tonight we have another dinner," Deba pronounced in a doomsday voice.

"We'll do better," Silvie said briskly. "Hurry, I want to make sure the shrimp are just right. Wilfred says that Mr. Sharan is a most influential man. He's in television and is dealing through Wilfred's bank for the backing for a new made-for-television movie. Isn't that exciting?"

"Terrific," Deba responded heavily. "Have you considered the merits of a catered affair?"

Silvia waggled her index finger playfully at Deba. "How you joke, when you know we have those beautiful crab legs to broil." She beamed at Deba. "Saffron rice will be a nice touch. Everything will go well, you'll see. I'll just set the table myself."

Deba shrugged. She'd been with the Winsomes for several months now and was very comfortable with them, but her housekeeping skills were at best marginal. Ah, well, if Silvie and

Wilfred could stand her, she supposed she shouldn't look for trouble. Would she ever get the hang of being an organized housekeeper?

That evening as she put the last touches on the dinner, Deba was more calm. Things were working out: her cooking had improved, even if the housekeeping hadn't.

Everything was ready.

Returning to the soup that would precede the entrée and follow the shrimp cocktail, she took a deep breath. Time to serve.

Deba balanced the tray with the first course and walked to the swinging door leading to the dining room, pushing it open with her hip while carefully balancing a tray of shrimp cocktails. Everything looked luscious.

Deba turned to look at her employers, who were watching her closely, though they had smiles on their faces. Deba smiled back. Then she glanced at the guest, gurgled in protest, the tray slipping and bobbling dangerously. The world danced and tipped, black spots whirling in front of her eyes.

"Oh, dear, she's dropped the shrimp," Silvie breathed, just as Deba sank to the floor, facedown in a bowl of the delectable shellfish, out cold.

◇ 8 ◇

"Did you think you'd ever sell it, let alone have it burst through the roof?" Maria stood in the circle of Chatsworth's arm, staring at some of the copies of the book *Exclusive Rights,* by Aldebaran McCloud. "She certainly has a great many names, doesn't she? Alde, Aldebaran, Deba. Such a choice." The smile wobbled off her face as she stared up at Chatsworth. "I have to tell her tonight. I can't put it off any longer."

Chatsworth nodded. "The book is doing so well in its first week she's liable to see it in a store somewhere. We should have told her at the outset, Maria."

"I should have. I was the one who pushed for its early publication when you sold it so fast."

Chatsworth shrugged. "Nothing about Wolfgang Clinton would be hard to sell." He leaned down and kissed her gently. "Not that I want her to come home that much. It's been wonderful being alone with you. Shall we tell her that we're marrying in a month's time?"

Maria nodded her head against his chest. "It all happened so fast, yet I feel as though I've known you a century."

"Me too." Chatsworth lifted her left hand to kiss the ring that he'd given her only last night. "I don't know if I want to wait a month."

Maria laughed. "Me either. But I want to wait until we can have time to fly to Mexico. I want you to meet my family."

"I know, but it seems a long time. Come along, love, let's go home. We'll take these copies with us and show them to Aldebaran."

"I'm not looking forward to telling her. Losing her friendship would be a terrible blow."

"You won't lose it. Aldebaran is very fond of you."

"Was fond, you mean."

"Don't sound so morose. I love you, so does Aldebaran."

The ride home was managed in silence. It was as though both had to arm themselves for the evening ahead.

Maria was upstairs in front of her dressing table when Aldebaran staggered into the room. "What on earth happened? Were you hit by a truck?"

"Yes," Deba answered weakly, sinking down to sprawl on her friend's bed, closing her eyes. "And the truck's name was Wolfgang Clinton." She gulped back a sob. "He was the guest named Sharan."

"What?" Maria sank into a chair. "You saw the book. That tears it," she muttered.

"Tears what?" Deba didn't open her eyes. "I know he'll find me here."

"You didn't read the . . . What did you say? Do you mean Wolf Clinton's here?"

"Yes." Deba yawned. "What did you mean?"

"How did he find you at the Winsomes'?" Maria ignored the previous question.

"How do I know?" Her eyes flashed open. "Do you know I passed out? I never do that. Lord, the man's eyes are probably deadly lasers. No doubt he's killing me with looks."

Maria put her hand on her friend's arm. "Stop that. Your voice is reedy and funny. You sound like you're on the edge of hysterics."

"I am." Deba closed her eyes again. "He and Mr. Winsome carried me up to my room. I pretended to be too sick to talk, I told them I needed a doctor. Then, when I was alone, I went down the back stairs and got the gardener to give me a ride in his truck to the station. Here I am. I have to get out of the country. Nicaragua would be nice this time of year." Deba opened her eyes and yawned again, then frowned at her friend. "Why are you calling Chatsworth on the intercom?"

"You'll know in a minute." Maria faced her friend, biting her lip, her eyes flying to the door, then back to Deba. "Forget Nicaragua, it's under siege."

"So is Long Island." Deba focused on her friend. "Maria, what is it? You're pale." Deba struggled to a sitting position. "Has there been word about my parents?"

"It's nothing like that," Chatsworth said from the doorway. "Maria felt she needed my support to tell you about something." Chatsworth smiled, went over to Maria and kissed her, then approached Deba. "Maria and I will be marrying in a month's time, Aldebaran."

Deba felt a surge of good feeling. "It's about time you two realized you were made for each other." Her puzzled glance went from Maria to Chatsworth. "But that isn't the important thing you have to tell me, is it? You said there was nothing wrong with my parents." She swallowed. "Is it about Wolf?"

"Yes," Maria answered hurriedly. "Don't hate me, Aldebaran."

Deba felt a curl of panic, but she gave her friend a genuine smile. "That I couldn't do, and you know it. What's wrong?"

Chatsworth moved away from Maria, approaching the bed. He hesitated, then put the book down on the bed. "This is the skeleton in the closet, and I'm as guilty as Maria."

Deba lifted the book, stared at the title and author's name. For long moments nothing was said as she opened the book and skimmed it, studied the jacket and the short description. "This is my journal and the disks? It's been made into a book?"

Maria nodded, tears in her eyes. "I did it, not Chatsworth. I wanted you to have something so that you didn't have to do housework, which you don't do well."

"Don't rub it in," Deba mused.

"Aldebaran, the first editor that Chatsworth showed it to loved it, and ultimately bought it. They hurried it right through because they said the writing was good and the content . . ."

"Dynamite, no doubt."

"Yes," Maria answered moistly.

Deba stared at her friend, seeing her obvious distress. She smiled wryly. "Did anyone ever tell you that you're too determined?"

"You have," Maria gulped. "Don't hate me, Aldebaran."

"Dopey." Deba rose from the bed and embraced her friend. "But now I'm really in the suds."

"What do you mean?" Chatsworth moved close to the two women.

"Wolfgang Clinton was at the Winsome home for dinner tonight," Deba said resignedly. "The man is spooky."

"Good Lord. No wonder you looked so shaky when I walked in here."

"It's awful," Maria said shakily.

"The end of the world . . . maybe." Deba tried to smile.

"It won't touch this house. I'll see to that." Chatsworth's chin came out, his eyes glinting in militant fashion.

Deba shook her head. "Oh, no, Chatsworth, you're not going to battle the Titan. I'm leaving."

"Deba," Maria wailed. "I want you to be my attendant when I marry."

"And I want you there." Chatsworth looked stubborn.

"How did he find me?" Deba's face crumpled. Then she shook her head. "It doesn't matter, I have to leave here tonight."

"Damn!" Chatsworth smacked his palm with his fist.

"I have to go with her, Chatsworth. We can postpone our wedding."

"No!" Both Deba and Chatsworth spoke at the same time.

Deba looked from Maria to Chatsworth, then she smiled. "I knew something good had to happen today. You two discovering how much you loved one another is the best thing to happen in a long time. I suspected the first day you met."

"Know-it-all." Chatsworth kissed her cheek, then leaned down to kiss Maria. "We'll work something out, love. Don't worry." He lifted his fiancée from the chair. "Come along, ladies, let's eat. We'll settle our problems over the Scotch broth that Mrs. Dale made."

Dinner wasn't exactly festive, but the three managed to relax enough to discuss the wedding and work their way through the Scotch broth. They were on the sole amandine when the door chime sounded.

Maria dropped her fork.

Deba stiffened.

Chatsworth frowned, then rose and went to the sideboard to get another utensil for Maria.

Maria stared at Chatsworth, clutching his hand when he set the fork at her place.

"It's all right, darling." He soothed his fiancée, but a crease of concern was on his face when he faced the door leading to the central hall. "I'll get it. The housekeeper's gone for the day." He paused, glancing from one to the other of the women. "Stop looking that way. I often get deliveries of manuscripts here and at this time of evening . . . sometimes even later too."

Chatsworth inhaled deeply and paused at the door to the airlock, the space between the foyer door and the outside door. He could see through to the outside shallow porch, though the person outside couldn't see in because of the way the glass was frosted. Chatsworth noted how the large person was outlined in the beveled glass of the door to the brownstone.

Caution dictating action, he opened the door on the chain. He had seen too many pictures of Wolfgang Clinton not to recognize him. "Yes?"

"I'm Wolfgang Clinton. This is the address given me by the Winsomes for a Miss Alde Baran. I would like to see her."

"I'm sorry but that's not . . ."

"I think you know why I'm here. Either open it or I'll kick in your beveled-glass door."

"I'll have you arrested."

"You have until the count of three."

"You can't intimidate me, not in my own home. I don't give a damn who you are."

"Stop! Chatsworth, I'll talk to him. Keep the chain on the door."

"No!" Wolf raised his voice. "I won't talk to you through a door, Deba, or should I say Alde. Open the door, or as God is my witness I will smash it."

Hands shaking, Deba went past Chatsworth and fumbled with the chain.

Chatsworth reached around her and released it. Then he put his arm around Deba and backed into the larger foyer. "Say what you have to say, then leave, Mr. Clinton."

"Don't you dare try to intimidate them."

Three pairs of eyes looked at Maria, who stood with the fireplace poker poised over her shoulder, her chin up, her stance bellicose.

Wolf stepped from the airlock, staring at the warlike woman. "You must be Maria, Deba's friend."

"And she's also my fiancée." Chatsworth moved slightly so that he was confronting Wolf and shielding the two women.

"Don't hit him, Wolf," Deba blurted, her chin rising when that gold stare fixed on her, the eyebrows slightly elevated.

"Maybe I should concentrate on you," he told her silkily.

"Don't . . . don't you use that tone with me." Deba swallowed, wondering whether she should run, smack him, or find a hole, jump in, and hide for a century.

"No one is going to intimidate anyone here," Chatsworth said firmly, calculating that he would last about ten seconds in a free-for-all with Wolf Clinton. He was even bigger than his pictures showed him. Weren't people supposed to look smaller in real life?

"There will be no trouble if I get to talk to Deba," Wolf said quietly. "But I will do that no matter what it takes."

"Did you show him the book?" Maria quavered.

Deba closed her eyes, ignoring Wolf's sharp query. "No." Turning, she went to her friend and took her arm. "Let's have some tea and dessert."

"Dessert? We aren't having dessert. Are we? Oh, I don't like any of this. Is Chatsworth behind us? I won't let Wolfgang Clinton hurt him, you know. Am I chattering, Aldebaran?"

"Yes."

"Aldebaran?" Wolf asked conversationally as he followed the others and took a chair at the table. "I wouldn't mind some tea."

"We have leftover Scotch broth." Maria wrung her hands. At his nod she went to the sideboard, where the tureen sat on a warming unit. "We don't let Aldebaran near this. She broke one at the Winsomes' that was priceless," Maria told Wolf as she set a steaming bowl in front of him. "I don't suppose that interests you, but I can't concentrate on anything but minutiae for the moment. My usually quick brain is dysfunctioning, you see."

"Sit down, darling." Chatsworth pulled her chair closer to his when Maria returned to her place.

"Thank you," Maria said faintly, reaching for his hand. Then she looked back at Wolf. "I know you have a great deal of power. I lived on Plata Verde."

"A neighbor, in fact," Wolf said silkily.

Maria shivered and rolled her eyes. Wolf Clinton would hate the book.

Chatsworth kissed her shoulder.

Maria looked at him gratefully, then glanced back at Wolf. "I won't let you hurt her, even if you don't like the book."

"Book? That's the second time you've alluded to it. Should I know what you mean?" Wolf quizzed, after he'd taken several spoonfuls of the thick soup. "This is good."

Chatsworth rolled his eyes toward Deba when she made a strangled sound in her throat.

Wolf looked at Deba, his spoon poised between mouth and plate, his eyes assessing. "Not going to faint, are you? You did that last time you made that noise."

Maria lifted the book that had been near Chatsworth's plate and pushed it toward Wolf.

Wolf glanced at the book, then lifted it, staring at the cover, then opening it to read the flyleaf, his eyebrows snapping together over his nose, his soup forgotten. "Jee-zus Christ!"

"Oh, Lord, he's going to murder us," Maria murmured, grabbing her dessert fork.

"Shh, darling. Maybe you shouldn't have shown it to him until he'd finished his soup," Chatsworth ventured mildly.

"Do you think he wouldn't have killed us on a full stomach?"

"Maybe."

Wolf fixed Deba with a hard stare. "You signed a contract."

"So? I changed my mind. Sue me."

"Damned if I won't!"

The air between them crackled as though a live wire had whirled through the room.

"I did it," Maria said in a small voice.

"Maria!" Deba glared at her friend. "He gets no explanations from us."

"What does she mean?" Wolf's voice sucked up the oxygen around the table.

"She means nothing," Deba attacked. "It's none of your business."

"How the hell do you figure that?" Wolf waved the book in the air. "This is my life that's been put in the spotlight. All the years I've spent keeping the lid on have just blown up in my face. Who the hell's business is it if it isn't mine?"

"So? It's about time you climbed down off your own private planet and faced life. Other people do it," Deba lashed out.

"Faced life?" Wolf's low roar rattled windows in the near vicinity. "Who the hell are you to judge me?"

"Oh, Lord," Chatsworth muttered, edging Maria's chair

closer to him. "I think that we should take the coffee into the lounge and . . ."

Deba scowled at Wolf. "Somebody should have the guts to speak up to you, Wolfgang Clinton."

Neither seemed to have heard Chatsworth's polite interjection.

Wolf glared at Deba. "When did you ever hold back? That tongue of yours is like a scythe." He leaned across the table, his soup ignored. "And what is more to the point, I have been facing life. You damn well don't know enough about me to make your lofty judgments."

"Then we could all sit quietly and talk. Doesn't that sound . . ." Chatsworth struggled mightily.

"Lofty? My judgments are lofty? This coming from *l'empereur* of Rancho Lobo? What a joke!"

"They're not listening, Chatsworth," Maria murmured, looking from one to the other. "Their eyes are snapping as fast as their mouths."

"You sound awed, my love. Don't be. Titans often war on this level," Chatsworth said wryly, rising to his feet and urging Maria to hers. Then he handed her a tray with cups, saucers, sugar, and creamer. "Go along to the lounge. I'll try to arbitrate this battle. Stop looking worried. We'll be right along with you."

"I'm afraid to leave you with them."

"Not to worry." Chatsworth watched her leave the room. Then, taking a deep breath, he went around to Deba's chair and lifted her bodily from it.

"What are you doing?" Wolf's voice dropped a few decibels, his large frame rising in his chair, muscles bunching in angry reaction.

"We're having coffee in the lounge." Chatsworth put his finger to Deba's lips. "Aldebaran, we're going to talk this out, and we'll do it in the living room, where it's comfortable."

"Aldebaran," Wolf said slowly. "Is that your real name?" Wolf picked up the book. "Aldebaran McCloud."

Deba coughed, feeling shaky, though Chatsworth hadn't released her arm. "My name is Aldebaran McCloud Beene." Before Wolf could respond, she turned blindly and left the room.

Wolf exhaled heavily, his glance swinging to Chatsworth. "Damn her, she's led me a chase these last months."

Chatsworth nodded. "Let me tell you, here and now, that if you try to hurt her, I'll do everything in my power to stop you, even if I die trying. She's suffered enough."

"And haven't I?"

"What drove you to Mexico is your business. If you were in pain you had only to reach out to the media to have it smoothed out for you. Despite your exile you exerted great power over communications and you know that too. Maybe the people who were around you paid lip service to friendship, I don't know, but the fact remains you could reach out to a host of helping hands had you chosen that course."

"Wish it were as simple as you paint it, Mr. . . . Brown, isn't it?"

"Yes, Chatsworth Brown."

"You're angry." Wolfgang settled back in his chair and watched the run of blood up the other man's face.

"Frustrated, furious, and ready to fight describes it better. Aldebaran McCloud Beene has had a hell of a hand dealt to her, Mr. Clinton. She's been on the run, trying to hide when she's done nothing, skulking like a fugitive when she's been involved in nothing; she's committed no crime, caused no harm, yet scuttles from place to place like an escaped criminal."

Wolf hadn't moved, but there was a sudden air of tension in the room. He stared at Chatsworth narrow-eyed. "Go on."

"I shouldn't be telling you this." Chatsworth resumed his seat and looked down at his hands as they rested on the table. "I'm sworn to secrecy, but damn it, because of you she'll have to run again—and you should know that." Chatsworth's fingers curled into fists. "I could kill the lot of you."

"The lot? Meaning?"

"All of you damned, self-righteous bastards who think the world was created just for you," Chatsworth burst out angrily. "She wouldn't be running if a borderline criminal, whose cohorts and henchmen have broken every rule of decent behavior, hadn't threatened her and her parents. Good people are on the run while that pernicious aberration of mankind goes on his merry way, attending church like the good person he isn't, and having the freedom that should belong to Aldebaran and her family. Why should she hide when she's innocent of wrongdoing? Why does the dope peddler threaten her and still walk in society with impunity?" Chatsworth paused, breathing heavily, his color heightened.

"That's why she was in Mexico?"

"In Europe, Asia, Africa, you name it," Chatsworth said, his voice hard. "She's crossed a few continents, alone. I'm up to here with it all, and I'm prepared to go to the wall on this if you try to hassle her in any way, Clinton." Chatsworth swallowed. "I don't care what it costs me."

"Is that right?" Wolf leaned against the dining-room table, his voice mild. "She means that much to you?"

"Aldebaran is the sister I never had," Chatsworth said simply.

"Go on."

"I'm not sure just where her parents are at the moment, but she hasn't seen them in a year," Chatsworth said huskily. "Maybe she'll never see them. Damn the fates!"

"Who's after them?"

"The Cosentino family," Chatworth answered gloomily.

Wolf was quiet for a moment, as though a computer in his brain was sifting the information through a memory bank. He nodded. "I remember now. The heir apparent to the mob throne got nailed in Turkey. He's doing hard time there."

Chatsworth nodded glumly. "So the old man vowed to make Aldebaran's family pay because her father caught him trying to smuggle opium over the mountains. Professor Beene informed the police and the rest you know." Chatsworth inhaled shakily. "Her father, Horace Beene, is a world-renowned paleontologist and one of the gentlest men I've ever known. I doubt whether he'd ever had a parking ticket, but the scum, Cosimo Cosentino, has broken every statute on the books and is an affront to the natural laws, but he walks free. Margaret McCloud Beene, Aldebaran's mother, is a lovely, truly sweet woman." Chatsworth paused, shaking his head. "At least they've had each other. Aldebaran has been alone."

"Tough situation to be in," Wolf said softly.

"Tough is a mild word for it. The parents and the child hiding out but separated, to make it harder for the mob to spot them."

Wolf hefted the book and was about to speak when Deba appeared in the doorway. "Hello, Aldebaran, looking for us?"

Deba bit her lip, then nodded. "I thought you might have killed Chatsworth."

"Not yet," Wolf answered sweetly, bringing the agent's suspicious glance to him. "Relax, I'm just baiting Deba." Wolf ran a hot look over her. "She's irresistible . . . when it comes to baiting."

"Very amusing." Deba bristled at once. "Why are you still in here?"

"We're coming right now." Wolf rose and stepped to her side in swift, fluid motions. With a hard smile he noted her sudden step backward.

"Yes, yes, that's right, Aldebaran. We were just coming."

"Maria is a nervous wreck waiting for you." Deba stared hard at Wolf, though she spoke to Chatsworth.

"Lord, of course she would be," Chatsworth said, hurrying past Deba.

When Deba swung around to follow the hurrying Chatsworth, she felt a hand slide around her waist and tighten there. "Release me," she told him grittily.

"Why didn't you come to me if you had a problem?"

"You had plenty of your own."

"True, but I would have made time for yours."

"Terrific."

"Why the cynical undertone? Do you have any reason to doubt my veracity?"

"What's to doubt? You? A man in hiding for years, who slips back and forth, in and out of his own country like a spy?"

"When was I ever underhanded or less than honest with you?"

"This is a fruitless conversation."

"Damn you, Deba, I'm the one who's the subject of an unauthorized book. If anyone should have an injured air, it should be me."

Deba felt his breath stir the hair at her nape. "Sue me."

"The squeaky voice is still with you, I see."

"Shall we go into the living room?"

"Explain to me about the book."

"No. I'm going to have coffee with Chatsworth and Maria."

"Just understand that I'm not leaving your side until I get a few answers . . . nor are you escaping me, Aldebaran McCloud Beene, author of an exposé on Wolfgang Clinton." He noted her flinch. *"Comprende?"*

"Sí, jefe, comprendo. But you're wrong about keeping me on a leash. This is America, not Mexico. You don't run things here, and I'm not your peon."

"You're not exactly a free-wheeling Yankee, either. If the Cosentino family dictates your movements, causes you to run, jump, and hide, you're not much more than a slave." When he saw her wince, he could have cut out his impulsive tongue, called back the words that caused her anguish. When she turned to face him, he swallowed, his chest heaving painfully. His hands reached out to her but she stepped back.

"Chatsworth told you too much. That still doesn't make you my proctor, so stay out of my face, Wolfgang Clinton." Her turquoise eyes had turned metallic.

"You're so tough, Aldebaran McCloud Beene."

"Yes, I am. Believe this. I will be out of here tonight, destination unknown, still in control of my own life." Did he own her just because he filled her thoughts twenty hours out of twenty-four? At that moment she could have torn at him with her nails, scratched, kicked, bitten, anything to hurt him. The emotional bonds that tied her to him would inhibit her, cripple her, maybe kill her. She had to break them, learn to hate the man she loved so desperately.

"If that's the case, I'll be right on your heels. You're not free of me until we have it all out in the open, lady."

"No way! It was all settled when I left Rancho Lobo. You have no place in my life, and I don't want to be in yours. We're quits." She whirled away from him.

"Not by a damn sight." Wolf's arm moved around her, brandishing the book titled *Exclusive Rights* in her face. "This puts a new facet on everything, Aldebaran."

"I won't discuss it," Deba muttered.

"Aldebaran, brightest star in the constellation Taurus, all questions will be answered. As sure as the sun rises and sets, I'll know everything."

"Don't try to threaten me, Wolfgang Clinton." Deba strove to keep the tremor from her voice.

"Is that what I was doing?"

"Chatsworth and Maria will think you've murdered me."

"The thought crossed my mind a time or two in the last weeks and months since you disappeared."

"How did you find me? I covered my tracks."

"So you did. And that made it more difficult. But you should have expected me. We've been apart many months, many, many nights, but no longer. Let's go." Wolf pressed his hand to the middle of her back, urging her toward the living room.

He hadn't answered her question.

Maria jumped to her feet, relief washing through her face in a red flood. "Oh, you're here."

"There are too many witnesses for me to get . . . innovative," Wolf said smoothly, handing Deba into a chair.

"Pay no attention to his phony machismo, Maria," Deba said bitingly when her friend blanched. "He can't scare us."

"He hasn't read the book yet," Chatsworth murmured, earning a sharp glance from his fiancée and a glare from his friend.

"Maybe I could do that now." Wolf lowered himself to the floor in front of Deba's chair, his head resting near her knee. He glanced up, his teeth showing in a feral smile. "Comfortable?"

"Perfectly," Deba said between her teeth. The heat from that chestnut hair permeating through to her leg sent her libido into chaos. "Wouldn't you be more so in a chair?"

"I'm fine. I like the feel of your leg on my neck. It brings back memories."

Maria and Deba gasped, one in shock, the other in anger.

"Damn, it's like being in the Circus Maximus," Chatsworth muttered, pouring the coffee as Maria sat transfixed.

In minutes Wolf was absorbed, his hand flipping the pages quickly as he speed-read.

Deba wanted to speak, but words were like logs in her throat. The man was lethal, he caused casual after-dinner conversation to dry up and blow away.

"Well, tell us, Aldebaran, what did you break at the Winsomes' today?" Maria asked brightly, her eyes glazed.

"A set of crystal plates with fresh prawns on them. The prawns were delectable-looking, but of course they had to be discarded. I understand the dishes belonged to Mr. Winsome's mother," Wolf said easily, then went on reading.

"Be quiet," Deba blurted at the edge of her control.

"Shh, I'm concentrating," Wolf murmured.

"Don't start anything, Deba," Maria begged.

"Don't let him intimidate you, Maria. He's nothing."

Chatsworth patted her hand and held his brandy snifter to her lips. "Take a little of this. It will help."

"If I become a drunkard, my mother will be displeased." One large tear stood in the corner of Maria's eye.

"Look how upset you've made her." Deba pushed at Wolf's head. "Maria was never nervous before you arrived."

Wolf lifted his eyes from the book for a fraction of a second. "Don't fret, Maria. It's Aldebaran who's the culprit. She's the one going to the guillotine. Ah, figuratively speaking, that is." He went back to reading, flipping the pages.

"See." Chatsworth smiled at his bride-to-be. "He'll remove Aldebaran's head, not yours." He leaned across the settee and kissed her gently.

Deba stared at her friend. "What a sweetheart you are, Chatsworth."

"I don't feel that much better." Maria sighed. "I wish we could get married tomorrow."

"I'll arrange it. Don't change your mind."

"But what about my mother?"

"I'll be her son-in-law when I see her. That's a position of greater strength than just a son-in-law-to-be. And there won't be a question of where I should sleep."

"In the barn with the rest of the hogs, you mean?" Deba quizzed tartly. Damn Wolf Clinton! She was becoming a shrew.

"Aldebaran!" Maria stared at her friend, then smiled up at Chatsworth. "She didn't mean it."

"I did." Deba sighed. "Sorry."

Chatsworth smiled. "And you're going to be a witness to our wedding. Shame on you."

"Bull," Deba said.

"Charming, isn't she?" Wolf put in, still turning pages. "Her vocabulary is so innovative."

Deba's fingers curled into fists. "Stick to what you're doing and stay out of this conversation." She could smack him right on the top of the head and . . .

"I was thinking of asking him to be my best man," Chatsworth mused.

"Oh, dear." Maria sank against the back of the settee.

"What? It's a contradiction in terms," Deba riposted.

"Nasty little thing, isn't she? I accept the position of best man, Chatsworth."

"Oh, dear," Maria sighed. "It will be chaos. My wedding will be a no-man's-land."

Contrite, Deba made a move to rise from her chair and go to her friend. Wolf pressed his head against her legs. "Do you mind?"

"I like having you behind my head."

"I would like to talk to my friend."

"Feel free."

"Has anyone ever told you that you're a . . . an interloper?"

"Your vocabulary is improving. Now be quiet, you're interrupting me."

Deba fulminated. Her eyes searched the room for a weapon.

"And don't try to bash in my skull, Aldebaran, or I might just take you across my knees, pull down your skivvies, and redden your bottom."

"In the living room?" Maria was aghast.

Chatsworth grinned at Deba. "I'd like to see that."

"Boor." Deba envisioned a hundred ways to kill Wolf. To think that she'd considered Chatsworth Brown her friend at one time! Dragging Wolf behind a Manhattan taxi had great appeal. "Where did the name Sharan come from?" The question thrust out into the room unbidden. For a moment Deba wasn't even sure she'd asked it.

"Family name," Wolf murmured.

"Oh? And all this time I thought you'd been dug up in Mexico."

"Cat," Wolf murmured, continuing to read.

"What kind of name is Sharan?" Chatsworth ignored both women who were trying to get his attention.

"Jewish."

"I didn't know you were Jewish."

Both women leaned forward as though waiting for Wolf's response.

"I'm not. My stepfather, who raised me, was and I often use his name when I travel."

Chatsworth frowned. "I've never seen anything like that in any of the bios that have been done on you, and there have been plenty."

"Yes, there have." Wolf hadn't paused in his reading nor had he raised his head.

"Were you close to your stepfather?"

"Very. I considered him my father."

"But . . . but I was sure I recalled . . ." Chatsworth's voice trailed. "Wasn't there something about your own father being in aircraft or something?"

All at once the air in the livingroom was filled with an electric charge.

Chatsworth settled back next to Maria and said no more.

Wolf put the book down for the first time. "I don't discuss my father." His voice was neutral but the point was clear. "The facts that have been written in the various periodicals and books have a semblance of truth. That's all I'm willing to say."

"Sorry. I didn't mean to be intrusive."

"I know that." Wolf went back to reading.

"And you have the gall to question me—and Chatsworth —about my background?" Anger made Deba's voice quaver.

"The situation is different."

"How? You're so curious about me, you ask so many questions, but you baldly state that you're not going to talk about your past."

"That's true. If you want those rights, that information, you'll have to marry me to get them. *Comprende*?" Wolf didn't look up from his reading.

"You're insane." Deba sat back. "Just because I wanted to know about your father . . ."

"I don't discuss him," Wolf said abruptly.

Deba sat transfixed. Her mind whirled with what she'd just heard. Did he still want to marry her? Who was Wolf's father? Why the secrecy about him? Was there more than one mystery about Wolfgang Clinton? And had he mentioned marriage?

Maria was threading her fingers together. "I think I'll go and make more coffee."

"I'll come with you, darling."

Deba didn't want them to leave. When she tried to rise to join them, she felt the pressure on her legs again.

"Uncomfortable?"

"Yes, let me go."

"No. Sit there until I finish. It will only be a few minutes more."

Wolf felt her relax slightly, but there was still great tension radiating from her.

Page after page he turned. When he came to the end he sighed. "Damned well written." He turned his head and looked up at her. "You have talent."

"How do I know that? I haven't read the finished copy. Maybe an editor did all the work."

"Maybe. You'll have to read it and see."

"So sue me!" Deba blurted.

Wolf put the book on the coffee table in front of him, then turned to look up at her. Because he was so large, he didn't have to look up far. Because he was so broad, he seemed to fill the space in front of her.

"You look more like a wrestler than a man of the world."

"I wrestled in university, and crewed, and swam." His smile twisted.

"You told me that as though the information had been pulled from you under torture. There's a great deal written about you, I could have found that out in the library."

"Most of what's written about me is false."

"Then why not come out with a book of your own and straighten everyone out."

"I can't do that."

The staccato reply ripped around the room.

"What could be so terrible that would corkscrew your life the way it's done, turn you upside down, make you bitter?" Deba's quiet query was mostly said to herself, not to him.

Wolf took her hand, and kissed the palm. "My wife will be privy to . . . most of my secrets."

"But not to all?"

"Some are better left buried . . . under tons of rock if possible."

His hard voice sent shivers up her spine. "This is about the murder you . . . were involved in, isn't it?"

"There are murders . . . and murders."

"That's a riddle."

"Yes." Wolf moved closer, his mouth centimeters from hers. "I have missed those lips on mine, that tongue in my mouth driving me wild. May I have it again?"

Deba was going to blister him with negatives. Instead, she leaned down the short distance and placed her open mouth over his. There was a hazy certainty that Wolf didn't want her talking of his father or his past, that his past was even blacker than hers, and then all thought left her. She was thrown backward in time into the vortex of passion they'd shared over and over again, minute by minute, hour to hour, day after day. The moments shared with Wolf in Mexico were as fresh in her mind as though they'd happened an hour ago, not weeks and months. At last! She was alive again.

Wolf's blood throbbed into his head, threatening to blow

the top off it. Memory was a hot, liquid emotion that pulled at him, demanding that he take her, love her, make her his. He wanted all of Aldebaran McCloud Beene wrapped around him, her mind, her spirit, not just her long, sensuous body. His arm moved up to encircle her waist, pulling her closer. Her tongue touched his gently, and his libido went to the moon. Had it been a lifetime since he'd kissed her? Why was kissing Deba more erotic and satisfying than the most intimate sexual experiences with other women? Her kisses made him feel sexier than the most graphic love play of anyone else . . . yet he had a desire to protect her, even from himself. Deba put him in an untenable and alien position. Wolf was vulnerable, fragmented, angry, and passionate, but at the same time warm, whole, complete. Damn her!

His hand moved down her spine to cup her backside, wanting her with a blind fever, needing her.

Deba heard the footsteps and murmurs of her friend through the roaring in her ears and pulled back. "Chatsworth . . . and Maria."

"Who?" Wolf stared at her, his eyes molten gold, his mouth slack and sensuous. "Let's go to my hotel."

"No." She had to leave. If she went near a bed with Wolf, she wouldn't leave that evening, she wouldn't be able to part from him. She'd stay in the bed for years! God! The thought was sweetly destroying.

Go she would, because she must. Finding another temporary haven was imperative, if only for a short while. It wasn't only her skin on the line this time. If the Cosentinos found her, they could use her as leverage to smoke her father out of hiding. Then . . . no, it did no good to dwell on that.

"Yes." Wolf's face re-formed itself into the tough lines and planes that gave it a flintlike appearance.

"I said no, and that's what I mean," Deba told him firmly, though her insides were jelly and her mind and heart were reaching out to him, embracing him, entwining with him.

"Damn you, Aldebaran McCloud Beene, and all your devious ways."

"Compared to you, I'm the original straight arrow."

"Don't try to thwart me, Aldebaran. Trickier folks than you have tried."

"Don't call me tricky," Deba said through her teeth.

Maria stepped into the room, hesitantly. "Hot coffee," she

said brightly, though her eyes flashed worriedly between Deba and Wolf, who were now approximately back in their original positions.

Following behind was Chatsworth, who was carrying the tray with cups, saucers, and utensils.

"There was a nice New York cheddar cheese and grapes, so I brought those," Maria said hopefully.

"There was rat poison under the sink that would have done as well," Chatsworth murmured, earning a hard look from his intended.

"It might have been just the thing," Wolf drawled. When Maria's startled gaze fixed on him, he relented and smiled slowly. "The cheese and grapes sound very good."

"Really?" Maria looked disbelieving. "Have you been hurting Aldebaran? She looks grim."

"I would have to say that the shoe is on the other foot."

"Crap," Deba said inelegantly.

"Something's wrong." Maria looked at Chatsworth from the corners of her eyes.

"Everything's fine, love. It's just that mating tigers often generate an excess of energy, some of it rather nasty," Chatsworth said kindly.

"Chatsworth," Maria said faintly.

"Gorgon," Deba said scathingly.

"You have a knack for going for the throat," Wolf observed. "You must be a hell of an agent. Watch your backside, somebody might blow it off."

"And it might be me," Deba interjected darkly.

"Thanks for the warning . . . from both of you."

Maria moved closer to her love, her hand finding his buns and staying there.

Chatsworth looked down at her. "I don't care what they say as long as you keep your hand there."

Maria looked up at him. "Tomorrow we'll be married," she told him dreamily. "Wonderful."

"Yes."

"Oh, come on, Maria," Deba said straightly.

"Spoiler," Wolf drawled.

"I couldn't agree more," Chatsworth responded, wrinkling his nose at Deba.

"Rat." Deba tried not to smile at the agent, but they'd

been through so much and he had been so very caring of her parents. "What time tomorrow will you be tying the knot?"

"Noon."

"Noon?" Deba straightened in her chair. "But that will be hard. I have to work . . ." Deba shut her mouth abruptly.

"Changing your mind about leaving?" Wolf quizzed softly.

"Ah . . ."

"Deba! You wouldn't leave without being my attendant. You couldn't. I'm counting on you."

Deba was going to disabuse her of that notion, but when she saw the tears standing in her friend's eyes, she nodded limply. "I'm going to be your attendant." Rising from her chair, she smiled at Maria. "I should call the Winsomes and let them know I won't be working for them."

Wolf stood too. "You have no reason to believe you've been discovered by the people searching for you. My people haven't picked up any ripples of that. And I assure you they would. I'll keep them on the job and they'll know if anyone is getting close. Why not finish out the month?"

Deba hesitated, starting to shake her head.

"I assure you the people I had searching for you are very discreet . . . and thorough. They'll put an invisible wall around you. You won't even know they're doing it . . . and no one will get through it." Wolf's satirical smile touched her like a sexy brand. "In fact . . . they were the ones who told me that you were on the run." Wolf gave a mirthless laugh. "I assumed someone was trying to murder you in order to close that mouth of yours."

"Very funny," Deba said, staring at him. "I hope you don't think your snoopers are any more efficient than the ones who work for the Cosentinos."

"I assure you they are, or they wouldn't be in my employ."

Deba faced him angrily. "You know that, do you? Even without knowing the whole story, you assume that you have the answers."

"Yes," Wolf said abruptly.

Deba's hands flexed into fists. "You . . . don't . . . know . . . them."

"And you don't know me, if you think I can't handle this."

"Here we go again." Chatsworth grinned when Deba's baleful stare touched him.

"I don't see any future for you two," Maria said morosely.

"And Deba said that you had such a wonderful time at the rancho, that you were so close. What a plumper that is! I had a feeling, from what Deba said, that there was so much warmth between you, such giving." She sighed and stared at Chatsworth, seeming not hear Deba's gasp. "Aldebaran doesn't usually make up stories."

"Maria!" Deba's anger faded in the woebegone expression of her friend. "Forget it. I'll be there at your side tomorrow."

Maria moved across the room to embrace her friend, tearfully. "I knew you wouldn't fail me. I wish you would be happy, like me and Chatsworth."

"Let's not worry about that." Deba hugged her back. "Shouldn't we look out a dress for you to wear tomorrow?"

Maria's mouth dropped. "I forgot. Lord!"

"You go ahead up to your room. I'll make a call to the Winsomes, then come up and help you."

Maria nodded hurriedly, then looked at Chatsworth wildly. "I have to find something to wear."

"Don't worry, love, a skirt and blouse will do."

Maria looked at him askance. "For my wedding?"

Deba scowled at her friend. "Plebeian," she said, and left the room. Was it stupid to hang around when all her instincts dictated escape? That had been the saving factor so far. Run when you felt that prickly feeling, disappear when a sixth sense said now was the time.

Deba didn't realize she'd had her fists clenched until she made her way down the short main hall that bisected the brownstone. The library was off the hall.

Chatsworth's library was small but very cozy. Deba settled herself in Chatsworth's chair and dialed her employer's number. "Yes. Robbie, it's Alde. May I speak with your mother or father? What? Oh, yes, I'm fine now. No, I'm not pregnant, and if I were I wouldn't be giving birth to Damien. Would you please stop watching those funky movies? Yes, mother or father." Deba waited for a few moments before another voice came on the line. "Hello, Mrs. Winsome, it's Alde. A friend of mine is being married tomorrow and she wanted me to be her attendant . . . oh, that's very kind of you. Thank you. Ah, the next day. Yes, I'll be in then, but I do have to talk to you. Yes, thank you again. Good-bye." Deba hung up the phone, swiveling the chair around so that she could look out the window into the darkened garden. It would be hard to leave the Winsomes.

She hadn't improved in housekeeping capabilities, but she had become fond of the family.

Wolf! He was back in her life. How could that be? What did he really want? Had he really mentioned marriage?

Deba pressed her fingertips to her forehead, trying to drive away the confusion. What was the right move?

◆ 9 ◆

"Ah, I think the book on Wolfgang Clinton is very good, sir. Ah, may I ask to whom I'm speaking? Dillon. Yes, Mr. Dillon. I don't see where this conversation is heading, since . . ."

"The book on Wolfgang Clinton was interesting but not complete. I have the complete background on the murder he committed some years ago."

"What? Now, look, Mr. Dillon, this is a reputable firm. We don't deal in phoney exposés or innuendoes, nor are we comfortable with . . ."

"If you don't want to see my proposal, then I'll send it elsewhere."

Silence.

"Mr. Dillon, do you have an agent?"

"No."

"I see. May I ask how you knew to call me?"

"I asked for Aldebaran McCloud's editor and they put me through to you."

"If this is a ploy to meet the author I must tell you that I have no knowledge of the author, but work through an agent."

"I am interested in my own book."

"Perhaps you might send me the proposal, with maybe an outline and some sample chapters."

"I'll send you the completed manuscript, Mrs. Horwitz."

"You have that?"

"I see I've surprised you."

"You have." Rena Horwitz stared at the phone for a moment. "All right, I'd like to see it. I assume you're in New York."

"I am."

"Good, why don't you bring the manuscript over sometime tomorrow. Then I'll read it and get back to you."

"I'll send it by messenger. I'll leave a number where I can be contacted."

"Very well, if that's what you want."

"It is."

Rena Horwitz looked at the phone for long moments after the connection was broken. Damn! What was going on here? Who was the elusive Mr. Dillon who didn't want a personal meeting with an editor? What the hell had made her say that she would look at the work? It was probably a damn poor copy of *Exclusive Rights*.

Maria was taking deep breaths all the way to the chapel where Chatsworth had arranged the wedding to take place. "I don't know how you got a priest so fast," Maria said faintly. "He isn't defrocked or anything, is he?"

"He's in good order," Chatsworth soothed.

"Was that a pun?"

"Aldebaran, don't joke," Maria said weakly. "This is a big moment."

"Of course it is." Deba kissed her friend on the cheek.

Wolf watched from his position on the jump seat of the limousine.

"This is my first time in a Rolls-Royce," Maria confided to Wolf. "I'm glad it's for my wedding. Thank you."

"No doubt he has a fleet of them," Deba murmured.

"Really?" Maria's eyes widened.

"I don't have a fleet of them." Wolf's irritation was wiped away in an instant, but Deba had glimpsed it. She had discovered in her short but close relationship with him that he didn't like ostentation and was more apt to eschew any sort of pomp.

It was one sure way to jab at him, and she needed that. He seemed to get under her guard so easily.

It gave her a measure of satisfaction, somehow tipping the scales in her favor, if only a tad and for only a moment.

Wolfgang Clinton had become used to too much control. Shaking him out of that surety was a distinct pleasure.

"Here we are." Chatsworth didn't wait for the chauffeur to come around to the door but opened it himself and clambered out to the sidewalk.

Deba was out before Maria. "You never did say how you got the license so fast, chum."

"That was easy. I got that the second day I met her."

Deba chuckled. "Why you old romantic! And I thought it was business that drove you."

"It was until that day." Chatsworth grinned. "I called your mother and father last night and told them. They've come to mean so much to me, sometimes I feel as though they're my parents."

"They feel the same way about you." Deba kissed his cheek and turned around to catch Wolf's hard smile. The color in his face had turned putty-hued. "Have a headache?"

"You could say that. Why don't we get inside? We don't want to be late."

"Never." Chatsworth turned to help his intended from the limousine.

"I'm not nervous anymore." Maria stared at the sign in front of the building that said ST. FRANCIS OF ASSISI PARISH. "I never hoped to see such a beautiful old church in Manhattan. It's like a touch of home."

In a courtly gesture, Chatsworth took the boxes that had been on the front seat near the driver. "These are your flowers, darling. I thought you would like white roses. With that rose-colored suit they'll be beautiful."

"Shall we follow, Aldebaran?" Wolf took her arm, none too gently, moving behind the intended bride and groom.

"Stop trolling me like a damned trout," Deba told Wolf acidly. "I want to put on my flowers."

"Here, let me." Wolf took the box from her fingers. "Let's go inside. The wind has a bite to it." Ushering her through the heavy oak doors, Wolf stopped her in the foyer.

Deba felt as though her pulse was coming through her skin as Wolf leaned over her. "I . . . I can do it."

"No problem." His hand brushed the skin of her throat as he attempted to pin the flowers to her suit. "That turquoise color in your suit makes your eyes look even a deeper hue . . . so large, lovely." Wolf bent toward her and kissed her on the lips.

For a moment she wasn't even sure it was a kiss that had feathered over her mouth, the contact had been so light. Only the blood thundering through her veins gave any clue. Would there ever be a time in the next millennium when she wouldn't react to the man?

"Do you like your roses? I thought the cream roses would complement your blouse."

"How . . . how did you know about my blouse?" Deba was dry-mouthed.

"I asked Maria, darling."

"I'm not your darling," Deba said faintly.

"You're not anyone else's," Wolf told her smoothly, his voice steel-edged.

"Wedding."

"I know. Do you want a church wedding?"

"Irrelevant. Not marrying." Deba was finding it difficult to deal with the lack of oxygen.

"Don't you like church ceremonies?"

"Love 'em."

"Good. I like them myself. Something permanent about it."

"How many times have you been married in a church?"

"Very amusing, Aldebaran. Why are you wheezing?"

"Not."

"Are you asthmatic?"

"No. Have to find Maria."

"I'll go with you."

"Lord." Deba closed her eyes for a minute, then moved toward the church proper.

"See." Wolf leaned down and whispered to her as he followed her, his breath raising the hair on her neck. "You've kept everyone waiting."

"Have not." Deba tried to increase her speed. Wolf stayed with her.

The aisle was long, their footsteps echoing up into the gothic structure.

The three people at the end of the aisle in front of the sanctuary seemed to grow in stature as they moved forward.

"We thought you'd gotten lost." Chatsworth's low-voiced remark was like a clarion call in the cavernous building.

"Shh." Maria smiled nervously at the priest, who smiled back.

"Shall we begin?" Father Deimont urged everyone into a sort of semicircle.

The sacred words of the age-old ceremony reverberated upward, touching the saintly statues, bouncing from the mosaic stations of the cross, curling upward into the cathedral ceiling.

Deba felt the sting of tears behind her eyes.

Wolf's throat tightened. Had he ever really listened to the formal words of commitment, the binding between a man and woman that gave them new life as one? He wanted that all at once, with an aching need.

The call from Wolf Clinton had been succinct and to the point. There was no margin for not understanding. The directions had been in clear, one-syllable declarative sentences.

Lazarus spoke to his people. "The bossman wants her wrapped up in cotton batting."

"Maybe it's too late."

"What do you mean, Cajun?"

"There's been some unfriendlies in the area, we know that. I don't have the feeling we have a complete handle on this."

A couple of the men smiled at each other. Caj kept to himself but he was well liked . . . and he had a finely honed sense of danger that rarely failed him.

"That Indian intuition again?" Lazarus didn't smile. Caj was about as scary as could be when it came to sensing what was in the wind. Lazarus was damn sure he could read minds.

Cajun nodded. "The girl has more than one set of enemies."

"Scatter 'em."

Caj looked at the man who'd spoken, and shrugged. "We'd have to know who they were first."

"We'd better do that . . . fast. Mr. Clinton is fond of the woman."

Cajun nodded.

Lazarus looked around at some of the men who watched him silently. "Listen up, all of you. The woman is first priority, though I agree with Caj. We don't have the full story. I think Cajun's onto something, and we'd better work harder and get this cleared up or we could lose the woman. We have a fair picture of what we're dealing with and what we have to do to take care of her." Lazarus paused. "Why aren't you nodding like the others, Petey?"

Petey shrugged. He was a shy, taciturn man, preferring the work of the shadow to being seen. The spotlight wasn't for him, but there wasn't much he missed. "I'm getting some mixed signals out there . . . like Cajun says. How do we handle it if we find that we have two mob families after her?"

"Meaning?"

"Are we in the middle of a war?"

Lazarus shook his head. "I wouldn't like to think that."

"It might be better to play as though we were. Even then they could use outside talent to take this woman down, but at least we would have our armor up and would be more protection to her."

"Petey's right," Cajun said shortly.

"All right, then we get some more people and we start collecting names, dates, and areas. If anyone at all has been in the same vicinity as the woman, we work 'em. Hard." Lazarus looked grim.

Petey shrugged. "I'll ask around, I still have a few contacts in the families. They might not want to tell me anything, but I can usually tell when they're lying. So . . ." Petey shrugged again.

"It will come down to the questions you ask then, Petey." Lazarus laughed harshly.

"Cajun, you know some people." Petey spoke as though all the words were hurting his throat. He, like Cajun, kept to himself, talking only when necessary.

"Yeah. A few."

Lazarus looked worried. "We can't afford glitches on this. The Man wants the lady protected."

"I'll check it out . . . but what if there is some outside talent in this?"

"Then we'll handle it." Lazarus looked angry.

Petey looked thoughtful. "It wouldn't be a bad idea, actually. Using outside talent would be a good way to take her out. Nothing could be traced back to the Cosentinos or any other family involved."

One of the men spat tobacco juice on the cement floor of the warehouse, one of the meeting places Lazarus's people used.

Lazarus looked at Cajun. "Spearhead this—you and Petey."

Cajun nodded.

Maria stared up at the early spring sky when they left the church. "I'm married." She smiled blindly at Deba, still clutching her new husband's arm. "I like it."

"How would you know? You've only been married about thirty minutes." Deba grinned at her ecstatic friend.

"I know. But I'll feel this way when we've been married fifty years. Won't I, Chatsworth?"

"Yes, my darling, you will. And I know I will." Chatsworth gave his wife a long, slow kiss.

"The car's here and you're gathering a crowd," Wolf said, amusement in his voice.

Chatsworth lifted his head an inch. "In Manhattan? Never. Besides, I don't care." He kissed his wife again.

Wolf's smile widened. "We have reservations at the Primrose."

"The Primrose?" Chatsworth whirled around to stare at Wolf. "I was going to take them to Papillon."

"I thought you might like this. It's my gift to you." Wolf smiled when Maria kissed him.

"It'll cost the earth," Chatsworth whispered to Deba from the corner of his mouth.

"Is it a club?"

Chatsworth nodded. "With a list of members that includes the first families of the area, heads of state, and business tycoons. A little above my touch. Nice of him, wasn't it?"

"Always in control, that's our Wolf," Deba responded grimly, bending low to get into the limousine.

Wolf managed to move between Maria and Chatsworth, his hand feathering over Deba's backside. "I heard that, sweetheart."

"Don't call me that." Deba's jaw ached from keeping her teeth together.

In minutes they were wheeling uptown through Manhattan toward the ornate and elegant building that housed the Primrose.

On the sidewalk in front of the club, Maria stood, lips

slightly parted, looking at the facade. "It's edged in gold, Deba. The building I mean."

"It is pretty." Deba saw that it was a large structure, Italianate Victorian in brick, cheek by jowl with two of the elegant apartment houses that abounded in the Central Park area. "It's not real gold," she muttered, trying to keep on keel.

"Close enough for me," Maria said dreamily, leaning on her husband when he put his arm around her. "I love you, Chatsworth."

◇ **10** ◇

"You are Mr. Dillon." Chatsworth rose to his feet when the other man entered Rena Horwitz's office. "I'm Chatsworth Brown. I'm sorry I wasn't able to see you sooner but I've been out of the country." Though it was a dull day, the man called Dillon wore sunglasses . . . and his mustache was decidedly fake. What kind of fiasco was this? Was Rena jerking his chain? Chatsworth felt a rush of annoyance. Damn it! He had a week's worth of work on his desk. He didn't need this.

"Yes, so I understand. Camper Rayton and I wrote the book on Wolfgang Clinton."

Chatsworth stared at the man, trying to see behind the glasses and mustache. "I've read this." Chatsworth tapped the manuscript in front of him. "You realize that you come very close to plagiarism in your book, Mr. Dillon," Chatsworth said smoothly, seating himself again.

"I don't think so. *Exclusive Rights* does not deal in any way with the secret life of Natasha Sharansky and Wolfgang Clinton. They were lovers for years and he killed the man who tried to take her away from her. I have inside information on that killing and I put it in my book. There's nothing in my work that overlaps Aldebaran McCloud's work, whoever he is."

Chatsworth stared at his steepled hands. Who was this shit digging into Wolf's life?

Rena coughed. "I had our legals look at this, Chatsworth. They tend to agree with him."

Chatsworth shot Rena a sharp look. "So you're going to publish it."

Rena shrugged, her eyes sliding away from Chatsworth to touch on Dall Dillon. "Could be. There are certain things to consider before we commit ourselves, but Mr. Dillon and Mr. Rayton seem to have documented their facts. And let's face it, the elusive, mysterious Wolfgang Clinton has been newsworthy since his teenage days. Any story about him should sell well. *Exclusive Rights* is running wild."

"My point exactly. Why would you want to water down the sales by following it up with this?" This time Chatsworth tapped the work a little harder.

"My people think it will work," Rena said firmly.

"Then you won't mind if I have our lawyers scan this, Rena." Chatsworth rose to his feet. "Nice meeting you, Mr. Dillon. Sorry to rush off, but I do have an appointment."

"Nice meeting you." Dall Dillon rose to his feet, his hand outstretched.

Chatsworth shook it once and left the room, Rena in his wake.

"Don't be angry, Chatsworth, it's only business. If we don't take it, someone else will."

Chatsworth wheeled around to face her in the outer office. "It's too damned pat. You might get taken for a ride on this. Where the hell did they get the information on Sharansky when no one has been able to pin down anything about her for years? This has a smell to it, Rena. I'd be careful if I were you."

"I felt that way, too, when I first saw it, but I can't see anything that smacks of plagiarism in it." Rena caught his sardonic look. "Close, maybe, but still not illegal. And it could be a nice follow-up to *Exclusive Rights.*"

"I doubt whether Wolf would agree with you."

"Oh? Do you know Clinton?" Disbelief and curiosity warred in her face.

"In a way." Chatsworth frowned. "How the hell did this Dillon hit upon so many pertinent facts on the murder? They were hushed up." Chatsworth cocked an eyebrow. "If this guy is pulling a fast one, you could lose your shirt, Rena."

Rena frowned. "We have research people, too, Chatsworth." But her frown deepened. "I'll have our people look into it in more depth."

"Not a bad idea." Chatsworth chewed his lower lip. "There's something about that Dillon fellow—"

"Because he isn't your client, no doubt."

"Rena, you know better than that."

"I think we'll be going forward on this, Chatsworth," Rena told him firmly.

"I assumed you were, but I'm going over the piece with a fine-tooth comb."

"Understood." Rena smiled suddenly. "I hear congratulations are in order."

Chatsworth grinned. "She's wonderful. We've been married three weeks, but it feels like she's been part of me forever."

"You've got it bad."

"Very."

Wolf Clinton was walking in New York. He had been in Manhattan for six weeks and felt very comfortable in the open air, walking free. The air itself was brisk, but the sky was a pale sapphire, the clouds like giant, uneven pearls, with the sun a central glittering topaz touching all. It was a jewel of a day and he inhaled deeply. Manhattan was a joy to visit. No city on earth allowed such a wonderful anonymity. Celebrities moved more freely there than anywhere. If the wish was to be invisible it could be accomplished easily.

Wolf flexed his shoulders as though to shift any confinement to his body. The barriers had broken, the tight rein he'd been keeping had released itself. He'd found Deba McCloud. And unlike what he'd almost hoped would happen, she didn't bore him the moment he saw her again. If anything, he was more firmly bound to her than ever. She was so real to him that even when he wasn't with her, he felt manacled to her. Damn her hide! Why had she run from him?

Irritation furrowed his spirit at how easily she was conjured up in front of him. Damn her for the power she had over him! She was like a jackhammer in his mind, yet she was so offhand with him, tossing him away like yesterday's news. She wasn't going to get away with it.

It had given him black satisfaction to know that it upset her when Chatsworth had invited him to stay at the brownstone. That had been the spur that had him accepting the invitation and moving from his place overlooking Central Park.

Reading people and situations had always been his strength, but with Aldebaran McCloud Beene he was often adrift in uncertainty. That angered him more than the cool attitude she'd had toward him since he more or less coerced her into staying in Manhattan.

Running was what Aldebaran did well. But no more. He was going to see to that. He should kidnap her back to the cottage on the lagoon, then force her to talk to him, to tell him everything.

When a woman raised a lazy eyebrow at him, Wolf was sure he'd spoken aloud. Typical of New York, others took no notice.

From street sweeper to show producer there was an easy sophistication that made space for all. Wolf Clinton felt totally at ease as he continued walking.

When he looked in the shop windows along Fifth Avenue he felt gleeful as a boy. He had never admitted to himself how lost he'd been at times, being an expatriate. And New York was U.S.A. in the grandest yet most basic way. Though he'd never resided there, he felt at home.

He had time to spare before he drove out to Long Island to pick up Aldebaran. He had come to use her full name so easily. He didn't usually call her Deba now . . . unless he was angry with her, which still happened often. Damn her! She could be so stubborn. But at least there was an uneasy truce about her leaving New York. Now if he could talk her into leaving the Winsomes and living with him . . .

The bookstore was large and caught his eye. He decided to buy the new mystery by a top writer that was touted so highly.

Moving into the large, bustling store, his eye was caught by a dump of books prominently displayed. *Exclusive Rights*. His eyes ran quickly over the cover, then to the publicity above it. The full story of Wolf—

The indrawn breath was painful as his eyes went to the publicity photo of him just to one side of *Exclusive Rights*. Coming soon! That's what the publicity said. A book dealing with the hidden part of Wolfgang Clinton, the follow-up to *Exclusive Rights*.

Clawlike, his hand reached toward the man-size publicity cardboard, then drew back. His picture was on the cover, not a recent one but the older publicity picture used in *Exclusive Rights*. It had been made when he'd been working in Hollywood.

What the hell was going on? No way would he let this happen. One unauthorized bio was enough.

The authors of the new one were different. C. Rayton and D. Dillon. Who the hell were they? More important, what could they know?

Cold perspiration coated his body as he recalled the secrets that could never surface.

What was this about? He checked the publishing firm. The same one that had published *Exclusive Rights*. Betrayal was a sour taste in his mouth. Had Chatsworth helped Aldebaran do this to him?

The new highly touted mystery was forgotten. He was damn well going to find out what was going on, and today.

"Have you read that?" A young girl who was stacking books near him smiled. "You'd like that one, sir. We've had very good feedback from our readers."

"Thank you." Wolf saw her smile falter for a moment as though there'd been a flash of recognition.

All at once the Manhattan anonymity was not so complete and he was glad for his dark glasses.

He left the store and hailed a cab, giving the address of the Central Park area where he owned a building. He still kept his car there, since Chatsworth had only one garage.

Driving out to Long Island now would make him a little early, but the action of driving the car was what he needed. Then he was going to face Aldebaran McCloud Beene with this new fiasco. Sinking back against the cracked upholstery of the cab, he closed his eyes.

It was choking, smothering, to see the reviews of the book *Exclusive Rights*! It was selling, climbing the charts week after week.

Vinegar of the soul eroded his good feelings. Just when he thought he had overcome the obstacles, someone like Aldebaran McCloud had sailed under his guard and come out with a story about Wolf Clinton. Who the hell was Aldebaran McCloud? Rena Horwitz didn't have a clue, though he'd told her to ask around, to probe, to question Chatsworth Brown.

Beene's agent had been hot under the collar about the book that would be coming out the following year.

But it didn't come close to the anger he felt. He'd waited so long, garnered his material from his sources so slowly, so carefully. It had taken kid gloves to search out Wolfgang Clinton's life, since many of his friends in the United States and elsewhere were leery of giving out information about him. But he'd managed. And now he'd been outmaneuvered by the unknown Aldebaran McCloud.

Damn! There were a few cloudy issues about some of those years of Clinton's that no amount of digging had clarified, but he'd learned a great deal. So much had to be taken from the tabloids of that time. If only he'd been able to get more lurid details about the murder, even . . . but then again, he had enough to fill in the chinks.

Damn! If only his book could have been first. He owed Aldebaran McCloud one for that.

And he hated the name Dall Dillon. It galled him not to use his own. Wouldn't that have surprised Mr. Wolfgang Clinton?

All during the drive out to Long Island, Wolf went over and over the scant information that had been on the publicity board in the store. A NEW FACET ON THE WOLFGANG CLINTON LIFE—THE STORY GOES ON.

He struck the steering wheel with his fist. Damn it! He would get some answers.

Because he ran into unexpected traffic, the trip took over a half hour longer than it should have, but he still had another twenty minutes to wait before Aldebaran was through for the day.

Idly watching the children play in the yard with the dog, he noted a black panel truck driving past slowly. It was too far away to read the plates from where he was parked under a tree, but he was aware it was a brand-new model. It was unusual to see a car other than his own, since the road was only used by five families.

Then his attention was taken by the tableau on the lawn as Aldebaran joined the children with something on a tray. When the dog came charging across the clipped lawn and launched himself at her, he saw her mouth open in rejection. Then she was flying through the air with the contents of the tray.

Wolf was about to get out of the car when he saw her jump to her feet, shaking her fist at the dog. Sinking back against the upholstery, he chuckled.

Sometime later he watched her come down the driveway in street clothes with the children and the dog cavorting around her, Reeboks on her feet. She was going to walk to the train station. Sometimes he met her there. No matter how many times he'd told her to wait until he arrived to pick her up, she still started walking each day. Damn stubborn woman.

Putting the car in gear he approached the driveway entrance, seeing the four heads turn his way. He waited while Aldebaran said good-bye to the children, kissing each one and patting the dog. Then she approached the car, her expression quizzical.

Getting into the car, she looked at him as he turned the car around to drive back to the main road. "You're early."

"Yes. I was in a bookstore on Fifth Avenue today and I saw a publicity feature about a . . . a new book on Wolfgang Clinton."

Deba turned in the seat and looked at him blinking. "Is this a joke?"

"Not to me, Aldebaran."

"You're angry."

"Yes."

"Is there really another book?"

"There will be several months from now, but the ad campaign has begun, so they must think it's going to be a big seller."

Deba shook her head. "It's ridiculous. Maria wouldn't . . . that is, we don't have any more information about you. It was all put into *Exclusive Rights.*"

"So you don't know anything about another book?"

Deba hesitated.

"Tell me." Wolf forced the words from his throat.

"I heard Chatsworth tell Maria that someone else was writing a book on you, but that he was trying to stop it." Deba frowned. "To tell the truth I didn't give it much credence, since it seemed like such a foolish venture."

"But you didn't think I needed to know that."

"Don't bark at me. I'm not your employee."

"But you were when you kept a dossier on me so that you could write a book. A gross breach of contract."

"It wasn't like that," Deba burst out.

"Then tell me how it was."

"No." Deba faced front, staring out the windshield. "You can let me off at the station and—"

"Stuff it, Aldebaran McCloud Beene."

"Don't shout at me, buster."

"You'd make a saint scream."

"And you're no saint."

"Remember that."

"How can I forget? Your picture is in every bookstore window." Deba bit her lip.

"Thanks to you and Maria."

"*Exclusive Rights* is selling well, Mr. Clinton. Or did you know?"

"So Chatsworth says, and the woman in the bookstore where I saw the advertising for the new book," Wolf mused, glancing into his rearview mirror. Was that the black panel truck he'd seen near the Winsomes'?

"What's the new book about?"

"How in hell would I know that?" Anger lent an edge to his voice. None of that information could come out, not after being buried so long and so well! Damn. It could be the end of everything.

"Stop shouting."

A movement in the sideview mirror caught Wolf's eye. The black vehicle was closing on them fast. The semiprivate road was narrow and winding, not conducive to passing.

Another quick glance in the rearview mirror showed the truck far too close.

Wolf increased his speed.

The other vehicle stayed with him. It damn well looked like the same one parked not far from the Winsome home.

Even as his eyes went back to the road he sensed that the other vehicle had picked up speed and was drawing even closer. Too fast!

Wolf took the ninety-degree turn that brought the road close to the water too sharply, the powerful car rocking dangerously.

With the ocean on one side and high, grassy, tree-topped bank on the other, it was a potentially lethal stretch of road. It would imperil both vehicles if one tried to pass the other.

Wolf depressed the accelerator, shooting the car forward.

"What is it?" Deba's head swiveled toward him, saw the way he stiffened, how he gripped the wheel tighter.

"I'm not sure. Seat belt fastened?"

"Yes, but . . ." Deba looked over her shoulder just as the other vehicle started to pass. "Good Lord, Wolf . . ."

"I know." Wolf floored the accelerator, the car leaping ahead wildly in the narrow winding road.

The other vehicle kept pace, then began pulling ahead.

Gritting his teeth, Wolf kept his eyes glued to the road. When he felt the first bang on the side of the car, he realized that it was no macabre highway game the driver of the truck was playing. Bang! The car slewed under Wolf's strong hands. No, it was a deadly serious intent to drive them off the highway.

Deba clung to the danger bar over the door, her eyes swiveling from Wolf to the road. "The worst curve is coming up," she whispered.

"Right."

Again the car was hit, almost causing it to hydroplane, the sound reverberating from door to door.

Gripping the wheel tightly, Wolf calculated the moment when his adversary would mount a fresh attack.

At the narrowest portion of the road, right on the curve, he turned his own car sharply into the other, clutching the wheel as the car bucked under his hands.

Then the other car was past them in the inside and careening down the highway.

Wolf couldn't get control at first and the car seemed to arrow toward the metal barrier between them and the ocean. Straining the wheel around caused the car to swing sharply, then they were across the road and up the bank.

They were thrust forward and back by the rocketing car as it plowed up the steep incline, furrowing the ground before skidding and rocking to a stop against a windblown sapling.

Deba's head snapped back and forth, the seat belt biting into her middle.

"Aldebaran! Are you all right?" Wolf's hands tore off her seat belt, lifting her into his arms. "Talk to me."

"You're a hell of a driver." Deba's face was pressed into his neck as he held her. "If I had been injured you probably should have left me in my seat." Hysteria guided the reedy sound of her laughter.

"Are you hurt?"

"No, I don't think so. Shaken, maybe." Deba lifted her head, her eyes even with his. "That was some driving . . . but I'm not hurt."

"I couldn't bear that."

Wolf's breath feathered over her features like a sensuous shiver before his mouth fastened to hers.

The kiss went on and on, as though it were a sustenance to both of them, as though life depended on it.

Deba's body and mind tingled and sprang into life. Her arms had their own direction as they encircled him, pressing him.

Wolf would never let her go. His hands quested up and down her spine, the feel of her a familiar aching need.

Deba pulled back, her mouth inches from his, out of breath and out of sync. "Are . . . you . . . all . . . right, Wolf?"

Wolf stared at her, kissing her gently again and again. "No, I'm damned mad. I'm going to find out who the hell did this."

"I know. Now do you see why I should have run weeks ago, before this could happen?"

"The Cosentinos?"

"Yes."

"I won't let you go without me."

"Wolf, no. Don't you see that it's better if I go alone."

"No, I don't see that. When do you want to leave?"

"At once."

"Fine. I'm going with you." Wolf kissed her hard. "It's not over, Aldebaran. You know it. So do I."

"Natasha, why are you brooding?"

"I'm not, Marle. I'm just thinking."

"Of Wolfgang?"

There was a noticeable pause, then a slight affirmative nod. She reached up and clasped his hand, bringing it to her cheek. "You are so understanding. I don't deserve you."

Marle leaned down to kiss her gently. "Why don't you call him?"

"I have, but he's not there."

"But you didn't talk to his housekeeper? Only used his private line?"

Natasha nodded, her slender neck seeming almost incapable of holding her head. "I can't risk talking to anyone else."

"Can you tell me what bothers you, Natasha?"

The woman on the chaise longue was far too thin, too languid, for real health, but there was an ethereal beauty that not even illness could disguise. She shook her head. "You know I would tell you if I could . . . but it's that nebulous foreboding that I've had at other times." She shrugged. "Why I feel it I don't know."

"You have always been bound to him in that special way. And now you fear for him."

"Yes."

"And you grieve for him."

"Yes." She looked up at the gray-haired man who was bending over her. "But I love you."

"I know that." When he smiled there was a boyish youthfulness that was hidden in repose.

"Will it ever be ended, Marle?"

"Yes, my love, it will."

"How do you know she's still in New York?"

"Guido, I pay people to do nothing but search for that family. They discovered her there."

"I know this, uncle, but I have had no word of the rest of the Beene family. Monsters that they are."

"They are indeed, but we will have our vengeance, Guido. I promise you that."

"I must have vengeance, uncle. Aldo was . . . is my cousin."

"There, you've done it again. Spoken of my son as though he were dead. Does that not prove how awful it must be for him to be buried in a dungeon in a foreign country?"

"Of course, uncle, and we'll get him out."

"How? Nothing has worked so far."

"I know, but somehow—"

"Ah, bah, what do you know of a father's pain?"

Guido backed away and bowed his head, leaving the old man to his painful broodings.

The plane circled over San Francisco airport.

Deba turned to Wolf. "Wouldn't it be better for you to return to Mexico?"

Wolf's gaze touched her hotly. "Yes. Shall we go there?"

"Ah, no. Actually, I think I'm going to Hong Kong." That idea had burst on her last night. Perhaps there would be some way to see her parents—if they were still in Japan when she reached the Orient.

Wolf's gaze widened fractionally.

"Do you think it's crazy?"

"I like Hong Kong. And . . . I have access to a place there. A friend of mine owns a beautiful home overlooking the bay." He chuckled softly when he saw irritation flash across her features. "Did I pull your cork again?"

"Know-it-all." Deba could feel the smile stretch her face, though she fought it. Traveling with Wolf was such fun! She'd been so relaxed since they'd left New York. He was a very exciting man, and at the same time as comfortable as a warm blanket in a cold wind. All would be right with the world if she weren't on the run . . . if she could always be with Wolf.

"You're frowning. Are you missing Maria and Chatsworth?"

Deba nodded, sinking back against the cushioned seat of the private jet. Not to mention how she longed to see her parents. "In the short time I've known her she has become the dearest friend anyone could ever have." Her head swiveled toward Wolf. "Will I see them again?" Why was she asking him? She was in charge of her fate. Maybe.

Wolf nodded. "If we can't shake the Cosentinos, we'll invite Maria and Chatsworth to meet us somewhere in the Orient. How would that suit you?"

Sudden tears stung her eyes and she could only nod.

"And at the same time we'll get in touch with your folks so that they can meet with their daughter. Would you like that?"

Tears puddled out of her eyes in a deluge she couldn't stem. "Don't . . . be . . . so . . . nice . . . to . . . me, please," Deba hiccuped.

"Too late, darling. I love doing things for you. And I want to meet your parents. We'll travel with them if you like."

Panic iced through her. "No big plans. I can't endanger them."

"I promise that every precaution will be taken." Wolf threaded his fingers through hers.

Uncertainty rippled through him. Years of avoiding people, entanglements, commitments, keeping his focus narrowed, were now fragmenting. His insides turmoiled with the flood of feeling toward Aldebaran, caused by the irrevocable steps he would be taking. Still, he wanted nothing more than to begin again, wipe the slate clean—with Aldebaran. What he was about to embark on was a total departure from anything he'd done. Aldebaran McCloud Beene would really know him and everything about him. Maybe he was a fool, but it didn't matter. "Aldebaran."

"Yes."

"I'm taking you to meet someone."

"Who?"

"Someone very special."

"Ah, that's nice, but Wolf, I think I should get out of the country as fast as possible."

"No one is going to trace you here to San Francisco. I own the airline that flies this private jet we're on, and no word will get out on either of us. My people are handpicked. They understand blackmail and how to deal with it."

Deba sank back in her seat again, realizing that she wasn't going to budge him. "And who is it we'll be seeing?"

"Natasha Sharansky."

Deba was about to sip her tea, but her start of surprise tipped the scalding liquid into her lap.

"Careful! Wait, let me." Wolf grasped a napkin and dabbed at her clothes. "Are you burned?" He took ice cubes from a glass and pressed them to her lap. "I want you to get out of those clothes at once." Wolf signaled to an attendant. "Get Miss McCloud's bag and put it into the back cabin for her." Wolf lifted her, cradling her close to him as he led her back to the cabin.

"I'm all right. I can walk by myself."

Wolf glared at her. "I want to look at your thighs and see for myself that there's no damage."

Deba saw the attendant's sidelong glance and made faces at Wolf.

"What? Are you in pain? What's wrong?" He all but lifted her through the door of the cabin, kicking the door shut behind him.

"Did you have to make a scene?" Deba said grittily.

"Why are you whispering? Sit down. No, wait. Stand still. It might be easier this way."

"Did you see the look . . . Ah, what are you doing? It stings, but it's not that bad." Before Deba could do more than gasp, Wolf had unfastened her tailored slacks and was easing them off her hips. The sudden brush of air across her thighs had them smarting anew, but she barely noticed. Wolf's head was there at her middle. She sucked in a shaken breath when she felt his mouth at the top of her thighs, first one leg, then the other. "I'm . . . I'm fine."

"I'm not," he responded, his voice husky. "You have slight burns. I'm going to fix them."

"Not necessary. See. No damage." Oxygen left her body, Deba gasped with the touch of the man she'd loved so quickly and so well.

Wolf's mouth scored gently over the red areas, pausing infinitesimally at the apex of her legs.

"Goodness." Deba felt dizzy all at once.

"It's been too long, love."

"Burns," Deba managed weakly.

"Your legs or me?" Wolf kissed her thighs again tenderly, then rose to his feet, staring at her for a moment, then going to a cabinet and removing first-aid ointment from it.

"I can do it."

"No, I will." Going down on his knees again, he patted the emollient onto her skin. "They don't look bad." He kissed each leg. "The ointment tastes awful but it will do the job. Do they sting?"

All of her stung, vibrated, sang, in response to that strong mouth on her body. "No."

He pulled the cotton material fully off her before rising to his feet, his smile twisted. "I could tend to your legs for a lifetime."

"What about Natasha Sharansky?" Deba noticed the minute stiffening, the pulling back, and regretted that she had been the one to destroy the warm, sweet aura of the moment. "I'll get some other clothes," she muttered.

"Natasha has a part of my life that has nothing to do with us, Aldebaran."

Jealousy was a hot spear that choked her. Deba stepped back from him. "I see."

"No, you don't," Wolf told her roughly. "But you will . . . one day."

"I'd better change." She looked pointedly at her case.

"All right."

"I'll be along as soon as I'm dressed. We should be landing soon, according to the captain." Deba turned away from him.

"I won't let there be barriers between us, Aldebaran."

She gestured to the door blindly. "Thank you for the ointment."

"The pleasure was all mine, my sweet," he whispered.

Tears still clouded her eyes like a fog as she made her way to her seat some moments later. How was she to face the woman the magazines and papers had described as one of the "world's great beauties" and the "great love of Wolfgang Clinton's life"?

They landed at a private field not far from San Francisco International and were met by a stretch limousine with darkened windows.

"Does Natasha Sharansky live in San Francisco?" Deba quizzed stiffly from her corner of the wide seat. Asking questions about the great dancer was like inflicting stab wounds on herself.

"No, she lives on a ranch in the Napa Valley area. We'll go there tomorrow. Tonight I thought you might like to dine in the city and stroll on Ghirardelli Square."

Deba's gloomy mood moved out of the way. "And ride the cable cars on Powell Street?"

"All the way to the bay. We'll be staying on Lombard Street, so we'll be very close to the line."

Deba straightened. "It's a very pretty city, isn't it?"

"One of my favorites."

Deba heard the odd note in his voice and looked at him. "And there are memories here?"

"Oh, yes, there are those."

California was putting on her best face. The sun shone over San Francisco, turning the water to diamonds, the clouds to pearls, and the sky to blue jade.

◆ 11 ◆

It hadn't been that hard to trace the whereabouts of Alde-baran McCloud Beene. That he could get money for the infor-mation was an extra boon. What a stroke of luck it had been to see the notice in that mercenary magazine calling for a "liquida-tion project in need of an engineer" with the name of the target in bold print. It hadn't been too difficult to put two and two together and realize that Aldebaran McCloud, author of *Exclu-sive Rights*, and Aldebaran McCloud Beene were one and the same.

"What did you say your name was?"

"I didn't say, Mr. Cosentino. It's better for me to remain anonymous."

"I don't do business that way. Good-bye."

"Wait! Wait, listen to me, Mr. Cosentino. One minute, please." He held his breath until he was sure he was still con-nected. "I have a way to keep in constant touch with Aldebaran McCloud Beene . . . and through her with her family."

"I'm listening."

"I won't go into detail, but I will be able to give you the complete itinerary of Aldebaran." He took a deep breath. "When you decide on the coup de grâce, you will have your target, but in the meantime you will be privy to all her movements."

Silence.

He swallowed hard. "Mr. Cosentino, I . . ."

"I will think about what you say and then we talk. What is your number?"

"I will call you tomorrow at the same time."

"I do not like these mysteries."

"It's necessary that I remain invisible . . . and since it will cost you nothing if I don't succeed in what I say . . ."

"And if you do succeed?"

"I'll want the reward money that you've posted throughout the world."

"How do you know about that?"

"I'm good at what I do."

"But you are not a professional."

"Not a hitman, no, but I do know how to keep an objective in sight, and I'm patient."

"I am not patient with failure."

"I understand that. Do we have a deal?"

"Yes, but don't disappoint me. I don't like that." The harsh wheezing breath was a threat in itself. "And where is Aldebaran McCloud Beene now?"

"She is in California."

San Francisco was wonderful in the daytime. After the intermittent gray days in New York, the sunshine was welcome. But the crisp, star-filled nights were even better.

Through the window of the bedroom she'd been given, Deba stared at the lamplit garden spectacle of the "crookedest street in the world." She had a funny bereft feeling all mixed up with the relief she'd experienced when she had been given a separate room from Wolf. It would have been impossible to share a room with him with all that was unresolved between them, but it hurt that he hadn't suggested they stay together. "Stupid, stupid. What did you expect?" Nothing. Everything.

She still wanted him with a raw hunger that ate at her, but she couldn't have let him love her. There were walls of problems between them, and very few doors. There was danger, there was the gray, looming unseen monster of the Cosentinos. What a mess.

* * *

Wolf nicked himself shaving, noting the dot of blood with a mixture of anger and resignation. Aldebaran was across the bridge of the house in the master suite . . . and he wanted to be there. Naked on the bed, mouth to mouth, body to body, he desired her. His need of her had only increased, not dissipated. Maybe deep down he'd known that his feelings for her wouldn't disappear once she was back in his company. It had worked with other women. But right from the start it had been different with Aldebaran. Hot, warm, sensuous, caring, involvement, delight. All the words that had seemed to be erased from his vocabulary had come back with a vengeance when she'd entered his life. Now he couldn't dig her out if he chose to . . . and he didn't.

Wolf had been off balance since their first meeting, and it was still unsettling.

He glared at the man in the mirror. How the hell had it happened? One minute he'd been in charge of it all—life, future, feelings, passions—and the next he was tumbling down a new set of stairs, banging his head on every step.

What would Aldebaran say if he told her that Natasha Sharansky had given him the house on Lombard Street, that years ago he and Natasha had met there to be alone and talk . . . before hell had broken loose in their lives.

Shaking his head to clear it of the cobwebby memories that were better forgotten, he stared at his image in the mirror, noting the muscle that jumped at the side of his mouth. Natasha would say that his nerves were breaking loose.

He wanted Aldebaran McCloud Beene in his life . . . badly. How to accomplish that was going to be monumental, yet she was only a room away from him.

Perhaps it would have been better if he hadn't brought her here, if he'd let sleeping dogs lie. His skin prickled with a familiar resentment as he pondered the dark secrets of his life. Not even Aldebaran McCloud Beene should be privy to those. They were buried, let them stay that way. What good would it do anyone to resurrect the specters of the past? Only poison and pain would be the result.

Yet . . . he needed to be open with her, to have a new, clean slate, to love her, make her his wife. . . .

This time the razor took more than a nick.

Had she told him everything? Hell, no. Even now he was

sure she was keeping something from him, though he didn't
know what the hell it could be. It had to be something, though,
because she was anxious to be shuck of him. Getting away from
him seemed her prime objective.

Cosentinos! They were a force to be handled. Why hadn't
he heard from his people in a while? As the question surfaced,
he reached for the phone on the first ring. "Yes, it's Clinton.
What's up?"

"Actually, sir, there isn't even a glimmer of activity with
the family. It would seem the Cosentinos have gone to ground."

"Do you believe that?"

"Ah, no, I don't, because they are a particularly vindictive
group, and they usually pay their debts."

"What, then? Outsiders doing the job for them?"

"There are outsiders doing groundwork for them, but
they've backed off too. I don't know what's going on, but I
think we should keep a close watch on Miss Beene."

"I agree. We'll be going out this evening, perhaps walking
down to the wharf."

"All right, sir, we'll be on you."

"Good."

When Deba went downstairs later she could hear the chink
of ice hitting a glass and went directly into the living room.

Wolf turned at once, smiling. "Come here and look. The
setting sun is turning the garden to bronze."

Deba wanted to preen under his openly admiring glance.
Her tummy tucked itself, she was inches taller, her stroll to him
more sinuous.

"You're too lovely. That color makes your skin bloom
pearly peach."

"Poetry," Deba said huskily, moving naturally into the
curve of his arm. Then, as she turned to follow his gaze, she
gasped at the apricot-tinted fire of the sun that touched the
garden, bronzing it. "It's wonderful."

"Isn't it? Would you like to walk before we dine so that
you can see the area?"

"Yes." When he pulled back from her, Deba looked at him
inquiringly. "Where are you going?"

"To get you some walking shoes. Those slippers you're
wearing won't do."

"I can't wear sneakers with this gown." Deba laughed at

Wolf's aloof smile. "Oh, I see. With you I can wear anything." Her breath caught at the sudden boyishness of his look.

Minutes later they were out on Lombard Street, making their way down the brick pavement of the road, then back up again.

"It's prettier than the pictures I've seen." Deba was loath to return to the house. "Your home is lovely."

"Thank you." He leaned down and kissed her. "Should we get ready and catch the next cable car to the wharf? I think you'll like the place I've chosen. It's not a tourist trap."

Deba nodded eagerly. She felt like a child. It had been ages since she'd had such fun.

Back in the house she took hold of her slippers and was about to change.

"No. Keep on the Reeboks. They'll help you jump on and off the trolley."

Deba laughed out loud. "Will we be doing that?"

"This is San Francisco. Everyone does that. Put your dress shoes in a tote and we'll carry them." Wolf's lip curled in amusement. "What's so funny?"

"I don't know. I just felt like laughing." Never had she felt so free. "Can we go now?"

"Of course." Wolf spoke softly, his eyes going over her. "You look especially beautiful, Aldebaran."

"Do I? I'll put my shoes in a carry bag." Hurrying up the stairs to her room, Deba felt like a rosebud opening in the sunlight. She was almost running when she returned to Wolf. "Let's go."

"Right." It pleased him to see her so carefree. Not even when they were first together had the shadows been out of her eyes. Even now they were there. But she didn't have that wary, stiff stance that had once been such a part of her.

They strolled up the world-famous zigzag street hand in hand. Then they had to run to catch the trolley that arrived, bell ringing, as they approached the corner.

Hopping on ahead of Wolf, who'd helped her aboard, she took a seat on the outside and turned to smile at him.

It had been amusing to watch Aldebaran McCloud Beene jump on board the trolley with Wolf Clinton at her heels. Neither of them noticed any of the other passengers, and that was an advantage.

With a bit of luck many of the troubles brought down on his head by Aldebaran McCloud Beene would soon be over. That would be a plus!

Touching the unfamiliar mustache and the wig that covered his head gave a measure of confidence. Disguises had their uses, especially if there was work to be done. Getting away clean was paramount and he knew how to do that.

Checking to see that the others on the cable car were not watching took a few minutes. Timing was everything. Wait! When the trolley was on the downward path toward the wharf would be the best time. Many of the persons on board would be watching the motorman. Excitement would be high, people would chatter, comment. Some would even scream at the steep decline. All the better.

The cable car crested the hill. With a noisy changing of gears, the motorman pulled on the mammoth gear lever and the trolley began its descent down the hill toward the wharf.

As the motorman shifted the large sticklike gear that drove the conveyance, many of the tourists oohed and aahed in delight as the forty-five-degree angle of the hill pitched them out of balance.

Waiting until Aldebaran McCloud Beene had leaned forward to see one of the sights pointed out by Wolf Clinton, who was momentarily turned away from her, was the ideal opportunity. He took it.

With a strength born of purpose he thrust at Deba's back hard enough to unseat her and cast her forward.

Passengers screamed. Wolf turned, hurling his body outward to catch her, then they were both on the brick pavement rolling away from the trolley.

The motorman flung himself on the gear, intent on stopping the trolley.

"Watch out for the car." The passenger's voice was shrill. "They'll be hurt!"

The motorman clanged his bell over and over again.

No one noticed the lithe figure getting off on the far side of the cable car and disappearing down a side street.

"I'm all right. Really." Deba had insisted on getting back on the cable car, assuring everyone that she was fine.

"I'll get a cab and take you home. You must have hurt yourself in the fall."

Deba's laugh was shaky. "I think we're both a little worse for wear, but unless you want to go back, I'd rather walk along the wharf for a while, then go to Ghirardelli Square."

Wolf nodded, tight-lipped.

Deba answered the many solicitous comments made to her, her hand curling into Wolf's. She could feel his resistance. He wanted to take her home. "Really, I'm fine."

Wolf turned his head and pressed his mouth on her forehead. "You have a dirt smudge right there."

"We both look a little messy . . . but we're not hurt."

"That's true."

"You took the brunt of it. You caught me when I fell."

"Are you really not hurt?" Wolf wiped her smudged hands with his pristine handkerchief, noting a small scrape, which he kissed gently.

"Honestly, I'm fine. We were fortunate."

"You could say that," Wolf said thoughtfully, looking around at the other passengers.

When they were getting off, the motorman leaned toward Deba. "You were lucky. I can't say I've ever had anyone fall off my cable car, but I know it can be dangerous." He frowned. "I didn't even see it. Did you lean too far out?"

"Ah . . . I guess that was it."

They moved away in the crowd of people getting off, gravitating to the wharf, where an old-time sailing ship was anchored.

"Shall we go there first?" Deba looked up at him, blinking when she noticed the putty hue of his face. "What's wrong? Aren't you feeling well?"

"Tell me why you hesitated when the motorman asked whether you'd leaned out too far?"

Trust Wolf Clinton to notice her hesitation. Deba put her hand through the crook of his arm and urged him down the wharf, where a handful of persons were embarking. "Shall we look at the ship?"

"If you like," Wolf said absently. "Answer my question, Aldebaran."

Deba didn't look at him. "I will."

Wolf followed her up the gangway. But though he followed her into the hold and walked to the bow and stern, he didn't take his eyes off her.

"That man swam right past that seal. Aren't there sharks

in San Francisco Bay? And aren't seals the main food of the
Great White?"

"You're babbling, Deba. Answer me."

"Watching the seal."

"You're frightened."

"Yes."

Wolf sent sharp looks around him, scanning the many persons who came on board, the people on the wharf. Was the
crowd growing? He put his arm around her and pulled her tight
to his body.

His warmth seeped into her, and though it was a mild day
with the falling sun shining, she cuddled to him as though for
heat. When his lips touched her hair, she closed her eyes and
swallowed hard.

"Are you crying, darling?"

"Don't cry."

"Of course not. But you are upset."

Deba nodded, pushing her face into his chest.

Wolf's body tented hers for a moment. When a group of
schoolchildren ran around the corner of the main cabin, then
stopped to stare at them curiously, he turned her and led her
from the ship.

Still not speaking, he hurried along the wharf.

"Where are we going in such a rush?" Deba felt as though
her feet touched the ground at every third step.

"I'm buying you a hot fudge sundae at Ghirardelli's. See."
Wolf pointed to the large sign that announced in big letters
GHIRARDELLI SQUARE. "We can eat dinner later. It's dessert
time, I think."

Down the street and up the steps to the square, Wolf didn't
lessen speed until he'd seated her at one of the round tables in
the famous chocolate factory and ice cream shop.

Returning to her with large elegant ice cream delights, two
pots of hot tea, and cups, Wolf handed her a spoon. "Now eat
. . . and talk."

Deba spooned the gooey confection into her mouth, then
more, and more. "I'm beginning to feel better."

"Some say sugar is good for shock," Wolf murmured, scanning her.

"Maybe it was imagination."

"What?" The harsh interrogative turned some heads toward them.

"I . . . I thought I was pushed."

Wolf inhaled slowly and deeply, putting down his spoon in deliberate fashion, not taking his eyes from her. "I thought it might be that."

"Maybe I'm wrong." Deba rushed her words. "I could be."

"But you don't believe that, and neither do I. It happened when I was turned away from you, urging you to look my way. What a perfect moment to assault you." Wolf's hands gripped the table in front of him. "Tell me exactly what happened."

"Let's eat our ice cream first. It's so good."

Wolf's features softened a fraction, but his eyes had an Antarctic hue, frosted gold. "All right, but I know you're hedging, Aldebaran." He finished his sundae quickly, then watched her savor hers. "You're like a little girl."

"You don't rush Ghirardelli treats. Places like this and Rumpelmayer's in New York are shrines to the chocoholic."

"And you're that."

"Yes." Deba caught her breath when she saw the dimple appear at the corner of his mouth. The only other times she'd seen that was when they'd been making love. She shivered with delight.

"Don't, darling." Wolf leaned toward her, his arms going around her, his mouth pressing hers in an urgent kiss.

Shock held her immobile, even as his touch fired through her. A titter of laughter from the table next to them was the spur that made her pull back from him. "Wolf!" Air became trapped in her lungs and she inhaled heavily to quell the feeling of choking.

"You shivered in fear."

Deba blushed. "Not in fear."

His eyes fixed on her, he read her as though she were a report he perused, then his slow smile went over her like a caress. "Remembering when we were together?"

"No," she told him abruptly, taking too hearty a sip of the hot tea she'd had with the ice cream.

"Liar. I like recalling that, too, Aldebaran, but right now I'm more interested in what happened on the cable car."

"People are staring at us because . . ."

"Aldebaran!"

"All right." Swallowing, she pulled the napkin through her fingers. "I wasn't leaning that far forward when you were showing me things along the route, I didn't have to, because I could see so clearly."

"And it did occur when I was leaning forward, not looking at you."

"Yes. I was looking past your shoulder, not really bent over too far."

"That's when it happened?"

"I felt hands on me, lifting and thrusting me out of the seat. There was no way to get my balance. It was like lightning."

Wolf felt the blood in his body plummet to his shoes. "I felt your body move suddenly, alarming me. That's why I was able to catch you."

"And fall to the ground with me on top of you. It's a wonder you didn't break something, Wolf."

"Or maybe go under the wheels of a car," Wolf said casually, but his eyes glittered. "It was no accident."

"It could have been my imagination."

"Neither of us believes that." Wolf pushed his empty dish away from him.

Deba saw the far-off look in his eyes. "What planet are you on?"

Blinking, Wolf looked at her, then grimaced. "Not a new one for me, but no less repulsive."

"Repulsive?" Deba's spoon clattered on the plate as she set it down and looked at him quizzically. "What do you mean?"

"Some years ago before I settled in Mexico . . . after the trouble occurred here . . ."

"The murder of your friend."

"Yes," Wolf said tersely, his lips twisting. He inhaled deeply. "The same sort of things began happening to me. I received crank calls. A few times I was jostled in a crowd by people who openly challenged me. It was gruesome and very uncomfortable."

"And you think this is one of those incidents?" Deba swallowed. "I think it was the Cosentinos."

Wolf gripped her hands. "Listen to me. I have people watching them. I would know if they were in the area."

"A Mafia family has many arms, Wolf, you know that," Deba said sadly. "They have unlimited funds, workers and vindictiveness. Very hard to fight."

"Yes. But we are fighting them, Aldebaran. And I win when I fight."

"So do they."

It was infuriating, but it wasn't wise to give way to emotion.

Aldebaran McCloud Beene had gotten away . . . again. There would be other times.

And getting rid of Wolf Clinton might become necessary. He was very protective of the girl.

Damn! It could have worked.

He was damned sick of obstacles. There had been too many. It was time to great rid of all of them, starting with Aldebaran McCloud Beene. Besides, there was a nice bounty on her head. The underworld grapevine had mentioned a really interesting figure if the whole family was destroyed. Now that he'd talked to old man Cosentino he had every intention of collecting the bounty.

What a shock to find that it had been a woman who'd foiled him! All he had to do was dwell on that and his being turned to lava. Damn her! He'd been so sure that Aldebaran McCloud Beene would be a man. What difference did it make? A woman! Damn her eyes. How dare she take his story, the one he'd sweated over, suffered humiliation on humiliation to get. He could dismember her for that.

Not until he'd put together the information gleaned in New York and ferreted around the Clinton house on Lombard Street had he been able to discover that the author of *Exclusive Rights* was not only a woman but Clinton's special lady. How ironic! How had the great Wolfgang Clinton felt when he'd discovered that she'd written a forbidden book? And he was sure the book had not been sanctioned by Wolf Clinton. The man worshiped privacy. Had he been furious? Had he forgiven her because she was beautiful? Or was he waiting for the right moment to level her? Wolf Clinton had a long memory and was dangerous when crossed. Was he even now setting a trap for the woman who shared his time and bed?

But no matter the cost, he was going to clear the decks so that his life could proceed the way he'd always dreamed. Not Wolfgang Clinton, Aldebaran McCloud Beene, or any persons like them would be allowed to interfere with his goals again. He deserved the comfort and ease he'd always craved, and he would get it.

Success! It had always eluded him. Now, when he had the prime opportunity for it, he would let nothing stand in his way.

Deba and Wolf strolled along the wharf after dining. The food had been fresh-caught and excellent.

"You called someone just before we dined." Deba looked up at him.

"Yes. I called the man who coordinated the search for you and has been in charge of watching the Cosentinos."

"Oh."

"I told him what happened on the cable car."

"And?"

"He says that it could have been a free-lancer hired by the Cosentinos," Wolf told her slowly.

"You don't have to walk around it, Wolf. I know that there's a bounty on my family and me . . . and that's more reason why you shouldn't be with me."

"Forget that, Aldebaran. Tomorrow we drive into the hills overlooking the Napa Valley. After that we go to Hong Kong."

"And you can just travel at will? You don't have a business to run?"

"I do, and I have spent a great deal of time and money building it into the conglomerate it is today, but if I were to die tomorrow the company would go on smoothly. I have excellent people."

"You sound like King Tut," Deba muttered.

"And you would know exactly how he sounded."

"That is a childish remark."

"It's a childish conversation. So let's talk about something else. Are you tired?"

"No. It's so nice here and the breeze off the bay is very refreshing."

"All right, we'll walk for awhile."

Deba noticed that despite Wolf's relaxed demeanor, he scanned the people around them, looked over his shoulder and around them at all times. "It wouldn't happen twice in one day. Would it?"

Wolf looked down at her. Could he be sure that her enemies would be predictable? "Let's go home." He hailed a cab, ignoring the waiting cable cars.

They didn't say much to each other, but Deba held tight to his hand. She needed him. No matter how much she resented her own admission, there was no sense in trying to fool herself. Wolf had woven himself into the fabric of her life. To get him out now would take major surgery of the brain, the heart, the blood stream, the . . . oh, what the hell, the man was a Svengali. Deba had to admit her need and want of him; the other elusive emotion that poked at her she wouldn't even try to identify.

"Why are you glaring at me?" Wolf asked her as he followed her out of the cab that had let them out on Powell Street at Wolf's request. They would walk the short distance down the corkscrew street and up the steep steps to the front door of the house on Lombard Street.

Deba preceded him in the door to the airlock, then beyond to the foyer, where she turned to face him. "You are not running my life, nor can you dictate where I go."

"I thought that's what you were doing to my life." He shut the door behind them. "I want you with me, Aldebaran, wherever I go. Do you want that?"

"I . . . I . . ."

"Yes?"

"I won't answer."

He clenched his fists. "You know I want to marry you. And I know it isn't fair to ask you to take on me and my troubles. But I want that, even if it can't be right away. There's so much I can't explain to you."

"Who mentioned marriage? Not me." But she wanted that! A life with Wolf would be the wildest joy. The pain that lanced her made her gasp.

"I did, and you damn well know it." He wanted her as his wife, more than he'd ever thought possible. Having her with him day and night would be an unlooked-for delight, a happiness that he'd never even pondered before meeting her.

"Well, I don't want marriage either." A life with him, bearing his children. What a wondrous fantasy!

"Stop talking nonsense. We both want it, and maybe some day we'll have it. Will you stay with me?"

Deba fully intended to tell him to go to hell. "How long?"

"Always."

"That's a commitment . . . more than involvement."

"Yes."

"Too much like marriage . . . yet I wouldn't be privy to your secrets. Right?"

"Not yet. There may come a time when you can know everything, my sweet one."

"You're being ambiguous and opaque."

"I would like you as my wife, I admit that . . ."

"But what?" It was like swallowing red-hot coals to press him. Was she masochistic?

Wolf shook his head. "It isn't fair to pull you into my life with its black corners. If we were to marry, the tabloids would run all those stories again and . . ."

"*Exclusive Rights* was an exposé. Didn't that rake everything up?" Deba watched Wolf's face tighten, close. "Wolf?"

His eyes focused on her, then he nodded. "Yes, I suppose it did."

Deba had felt his hesitation. Was he keeping back the darkest of the corners?

His golden eyes warmed her. "And will you stay with me?"

"Let me think about it. How do you know I don't have a husband somewhere?"

"And do you?"

The harsh question cracked the air like a whip. "Ah, no, not at present."

"That's a foolish answer, since you won't be seeing other men."

"How do you know that? I could fall in love with a skycap at the airport when we're on our way to Hong Kong."

"Well, there is that possibility."

"Are you scoffing? Don't you dare. Stranger things have happened."

"And to you, I've no doubt." Wolf crossed the room to her side in quick strides, sweeping her into his arms, his mouth going down to hers like a homing device. He lifted his mouth after a time, his body throbbing with want. "I want to keep you forever, Aldebaran McCloud Beene."

"Things . . . change," Deba whispered, hanging onto him for fear she would fall, her feet dangling above the floor. Her being had turned to jelly.

"That won't."

"I watched a lifetime of things change in a week's time."

Her fingers convulsed on him. "You tire of women easily according to the rags."

"Trust me." Wolf kissed her again. "Don't forget to pack your riding clothes, love." Wolf smiled when she looked up horrified. "We're going to a ranch."

"Horses don't like me. You know that."

"Yes, they do. You'll be surprised at how much better you'll be this time. Riding is a skill that improves with practice."

"I'll be amazed if I don't tumble on my head," Deba muttered, not really caring what she said. Being in Wolf's arms was so comforting, so right. Falling out of a plane wouldn't panic her if he had hold of her.

"There are several gentle mares on the ranch that will suit you."

"Are they yours?"

"Yes."

Jealousy nicked through her, chipping at veins and arteries until she was sure she was dripping blood from a thousand cuts. "So why should I go when you have Natasha Sharansky at your fingertips?"

"I want you to meet her. I thought you liked ballet and admired her."

"I did . . . I do. But I don't want to be a third wheel."

"There will be four of us. You, Natasha, me, and Natasha's husband."

Deba inhaled deeply. "That's right. She's married. And will he be there the entire time?"

"He rarely leaves her side."

Deba opened her mouth to respond when she noted how his face had pulled in on itself as though his inmost thoughts had taken a body blow. She said no more. No matter how she tried she couldn't quite smother her trepidation.

◇ 12 ◇

The ride through the Napa Valley was intriguing, but Deba saw little. Her mind was a spinning top that flung things away from it and clung to nothing. Thoughts couldn't hold or jell.

"Are you sure you wouldn't like to stop at one of the wineries? They abound along this road. We could sample the wares."

"No, thanks, I'm swearing off." Deba tried to picture what Natasha Sharansky would look like now. The woman was in her middle to late thirties now, so she would be somewhat different from the tiny, electric person, barely twenty, who'd flown across the stage of the New York City Ballet at Lincoln Center and captivated the world. But . . . most beautiful women were lovelier in their thirties. What then? Wolf hadn't tried to make love to her last night. Why would she have expected that? Was he thinking of Natasha Sharansky?

"You've sworn off drinking wine? To my knowledge you drink very little of it anyway. Why swear off?"

"Huh? Oh. Ah, alcoholism is rampant, I don't want to be a statistic."

"Really?" Wolf shot a quick look at her. Myriad emotions were chasing themselves across her features. What pyramid was Aldebaran building now?

Deba couldn't stop thinking of the great prima ballerina. How the world had loved her! London had been at her feet. Paris had cheered and cried. When the great Sharansky had danced with the Bolshoi in Moscow, the Russians cheered her as their own, even though she'd been an American. After all, weren't her antecedents from Mother Russia? But it had been her talent that had gripped them. In the country where the dance was king, she had wrested the throne from the natives.

"Aldebaran!"

"What?" Deba jumped and turned in her seat to glare at him.

"Stop. You're building fences you don't need." Wolf took one hand off the wheel and gripped hers, which were threaded tightly together. "You will love Natasha. She's sweet and very kind."

"Of course. Is she still beautiful?"

"Incredibly so." Wolf paused. "She was sick for many years, as you know, and is still too slender. And there are some limits in her life. But she is on the mend and is happy."

Deba's head whipped toward him. There was a pathos . . . an anger in his voice that puzzled her. "What is it?"

Wolf shook his head. Then he turned to look at her. "There's a great deal I can't tell you, Aldebaran. If I could I would insist that we marry . . . at once."

"You're not the only one who decides on marriage, and I say marriage is out," Deba said briskly, quite sure she heard a cracking in her chest region. Can the heart weep?

"I know, I know. Don't belabor it."

What would Wolf say if she told him that she wanted to be his wife more than anything in the world, that she wanted his children, that she wanted to grow old with the reclusive "Lobo" of Rancho Lobo, Mexico?

"There it is." Wolf drove up a hill, rounded a curve, and stopped before a gate.

Trees and brush abounded. Only the tall iron gate signaled that there might be people behind it.

Deba noted that he took an electronic activator from the glove compartment to open the gate.

"It's like a wilderness."

"Yes, they keep it that way. The ranch house is back from the road about a mile, and the gullies, trees, and wild growth discourage visitors."

"Does she never leave here?"

"Now she does, but not for any great length of time. Natasha is happy here, and that's what I want for her . . . peace and quiet joy."

Again Deba heard the thread of fury in his voice, a primal anger, barely controlled, that vibrated like a live thing in the car.

Her attention was drawn by the way the vegetation seemed to coil into itself everywhere, providing great depths of walls for the winding road.

Abruptly they came out into a clearing that sloped upward to the house, an adobe one-story structure that clung to the ground like a golden dog, sprawled and comfortable.

Deba straightened in her seat. "It's lovely."

"Yes, I think it's one of the most beautiful places in all of California." Wolf pulled into the circular courtyard and parked.

"It's like something out of early Mexico with the center fountain and the walled courtyard." She turned to smile at him. "It reminds me of Rancho Lobo."

"You're perceptive, beautiful lady." Wolf leaned toward her, kissing her searchingly, slowly.

Deba pulled back from him, out of breath. Would she ever get used to the power of the man? "Wolf . . . ?"

"Yes, darling."

"Ah, tell me about the house."

Wolf inhaled a shaky breath, his crooked smile touching her. "All right, we'll cool down a little . . . but only because I don't want to make love to you in the car." He stared at her for long moments, his index finger trailing over her lips. "Bite me, darling. That would excite me more than a night of love with any other woman. Owww, not that hard."

"I don't suppose you've catalogued the number of women."

"Now, Deba, that's all before I met you." He grinned at her. "About the house. It is modeled after Rancho Lobo. And there's an inner courtyard as well. Interesting? Ah, there's our host." Wolf squeezed her thigh gently, then unfolded himself from the seat of the sports car, smiling. "How are you, Marle?"

"Better for seeing you."

Deba thought the bass voice fitted the rather burly build of the man who approached the car. He looked more like a teamster than the professor of literature that Wolf had described.

The two men embraced and Deba saw the real affection between them in the smiles they shared.

"How is she?"

"Anxious to see you, as always."

Wolf laughed out loud, leaning around the other man to look into the house. Then he looked back at Deba and went around to open her door. "Marle, this is Aldebaran McCloud Beene."

Marle Damon's lips parted in a gasp. "This is the person who wrote *Exclusive Rights*?"

"Yes, though she had no desire to publish it. A mutual friend did that."

"You're taking it well." Marle looked at Wolf with narrowed eyes. "Unless of course you plan to murder her here. That won't do. I won't have bodies buried at Stella Ranch." Marle moved forward with his hand outthrust. "If Wolf trusts you, so must I."

"Thanks . . . I think." Deba smiled when the other man laughed, putting her hand into his. His clasp was warm and sure. "Miguel here"—he indicated a young man who was approaching from the house— "will take care of the car and your things. Come inside."

"How are you, Miguel?"

"Fine, senor. How is my *tía*?"

"Tough as ever." Wolf turned to Deba. "Julia is his *tía*."

"I can testify to the toughness." Deba smiled at the young man, who nodded briefly before moving off to take care of the car. "How is it that you and Natasha have servants from the same family?" Deba asked as she and Wolf started walking toward the house. "Coincidence?"

Deba stared up at Wolf. It was clear he didn't want her to question him. When he leaned down to kiss her, she touched his chin, keeping his mouth on hers.

"Keep that thought for later," he told her huskily.

"Shall I leave you alone with . . . with Aldebaran?"

"We're coming, Marle." Wolf grinned at the other man.

Marle moved to Deba's side when she walked through to the inner courtyard. "That is a very unusual and beautiful name."

"Yes, it is."

"A beautiful name for a beautiful woman." Marle smiled

down at her. "I never thought he'd bring anyone here. I'm glad he brought you."

Some of the tension that had built in Deba during the drive from San Francisco eased. She smiled up at the big, bluff man. "Thank you."

Marle Damon's smile faded. "He's one of the strongest, most vulnerable men I've ever known. He deserves to be happy."

Deba was taken aback by his intensity. "I . . . I think most people wouldn't describe him as vulnerable."

"Most people don't know him." Marle's head lifted when he heard tinkling laughter, his features softening. "Only he can make her laugh that way . . . and I love him for that." Marle Damon took Deba's arm, ushering her down a dark hall. "The house seems pitch-black when one comes in from the sunshine, and I wouldn't like you to walk into a wall."

"Sounds uncomfortable." Deba smiled when she heard Marle chuckle.

"You are good for him. Come along. They're out in the solarium."

Deba didn't have time to drag her feet. Marle had a good grip on her arm and pulled her right along. In moments they entered a sun-drenched room, leafy trees cooling the glass walls. Deba expected heat. Instead it was cool and inviting, the indoor pool large and curving, surrounded by tile—much like a smaller version of the pool at Rancho Lobo.

When Deba paused to watch the tableau of Wolf holding someone in his arms as he leaned over a wheelchair, Marle smiled. "Darling, this is Aldebaran McCloud Beene."

The beautiful dark-haired woman held by Wolf stiffened, anger suffusing her face, before her eyes flew to Wolf's face. "And this does not infuriate you that she has written a book about you?"

"No."

Natasha looked puzzled. She started to rise, then fell back in her chair.

Deba noticed the palpable disappointment on the faces of both men. "You can walk, but don't choose to, is that it?" What had made her say such a thing?

The silence was solid, like a brick wall.

Natasha Sharansky urged Wolf back from her, staring at Deba for long hard moments. "Something like that."

"I think you should walk, no matter what the reason for not doing so. You were given a talent that few could ever imagine. If you can move those legs, even a little bit, you should do so." Deba had no idea why she was speaking so impertinently to a seemingly handicapped person and a stranger as well.

There were gasps from both Marle and Wolf.

Deba opened her mouth to apologize.

"Do not speak further, please." The voice lightly accented, as though English was not her first language. She inhaled deeply. "You cannot know why I sit in this chair."

"You're absolutely right." Deba's voice reverberated from the glass walls.

The fountain of water spurting into the pool sounded loud all at once.

"You look as though you're ashamed of what you said." There was a silky musical cadence to Natasha Sharansky's voice.

Deba stared into those very, very brown eyes, which glittered ebony for a moment. "I am. I don't know why I said it."

"Don't back down now, Aldebaran. You should hear the way she speaks to me, Natasha."

Natasha shot a look at Wolf when he spoke, her eyes crinkling in amusement. "I can't believe there is anyone who could put you in your place."

"Trust me. She does it all the time." Wolf leaned down and kissed the ballerina lightly on the cheek.

"I would like to see that." Natasha reached up and touched his mouth with one finger.

Deba smothered a gasp of pain at the sight of them together, her glance sliding toward Marle Damon. He was beaming!

Natasha stared up at Wolf for long moments, then she turned to look at Marle, her gaze softening, then she stared at Deba. Heavy moments passed. "Perhaps it is time to change my ways." Natasha's voice was painfully pensive. Though her gaze was on Deba, there was a faraway look to her as though she were gazing at an old, rather sad movie.

She inhaled and her eyes sharpened on Deba. "I've hugged the bitter past like a pacifier. How they've hated it." The dancer gestured to Wolf and Marle. There was a lacing of surprise in her voice. "They would never push me to do anything . . . yet it hurts them to see me like this." Natasha Sharansky frowned.

Still staring at Deba, the prima ballerina gripped the cushioned arms of the electronic wheelchair and pushed upward, beads of perspiration popping out on her face. "No, Wolf, do not help me. Miss Beene will catch me if I fall. Won't you?"

"Ah . . . what?" Deba was mesmerized.

"You look shocked, Miss Beene. Your . . . eyes . . . are starting from . . . your . . . head." Exertion made Natasha gasp and grit her teeth.

"Careful," Deba whispered, remorse wrenching her.

"No, I will not," Natasha said clearly. "I've been too careful. Now I will be venturesome like the great dancer I am." Natasha's chin lifted. "Have you been sent by the fates to prod me, Miss Beene?"

"I don't think so," Deba whispered, her hands going out instinctively when the other woman moved away from the chair in robotish movements that were shaky and out of balance.

"No, don't come closer, I will come to you."

"Lord." Deba felt helpless, angry with herself. When the woman after torturous forward motions was still yards away, she moved forward and took her hands. "How long since you've walked?"

"Almost a year," Marle Damon answered hoarsely, tears welling in his eyes.

"Do you think I'll dance again, Marle, darling?"

"If you want to, love, I'm sure you can." Marle Damon moved past Deba and took the dancer in his arms, all but lifting her from the floor. "You can do anything you choose."

Natasha's arms encircled him, her eyes closing. "Perhaps I'll try the barre."

"Don't take all your fences in one day, Tasha," Wolf said gently.

Deba was taken aback when she saw a tear on Wolf's face. How he must love Natasha Sharansky! Pain made her heart and mind constrict. She should walk away, leave. Why? She'd always known that Wolf wasn't hers to keep. Why let this drive her away any earlier than she would have to go? Could this pain be greater than the one she'd experience when she parted from him forever? When she'd left him in Mexico the first time, it had torn her apart.

From the shelter of Marle Damon's arms, Natasha smiled at Deba. "Perhaps you are good for him. When I read *Exclusive*

Rights I was very angry . . . but Wolf is not angry, so how can I be?"

"That's right, darling." Marle kissed the top of her head.

"And you like her, don't you?" Natasha looked up at her husband.

"Very much."

Natasha nodded and smiled.

"And I like her very much," Wolf drawled.

Natasha's tinkling laughter echoed in the room. "I guessed that. Shall we swim? No, no, Marle, I will walk to the steps."

"Fine, but I'll take your arm."

Again Natasha laughed. "Men can be such mules, Miss Beene."

"I couldn't agree more, and please call me Deba."

"No. Call her Aldebaran. That's her name. Stop scowling at me, darling."

"I'm not your darling." Deba spoke through her teeth, watching warily when he approached her.

Wolf swept her up, keeping her arms pinned to her sides. "Aren't you?"

"What are you doing? Put me down. Wolf!" Deba tried to struggle but she was manacled to him. She could hear Natasha's and Marle's laughter. "Don't you dare throw me in that pool."

"I wouldn't dream of it." Wolf walked out on the end of the diving board, smiling down at Deba. "Here we go." He jumped off with Deba in his arms.

Natasha shouted with laughter.

"Wolf, damn you," Marle called out, laughing.

Deba broke the surface, still held by Wolf. "My linen skirt! Cretin!" she sputtered, wet hair stringing down her face.

"Don't you feel cooler?" Wolf ducked when Deba took a swing at him, his head turning just a bit.

Deba saw her advantage and went over the top of him, pushing down on his head with all her might, sinking below the surface with Wolf.

"They are quite wonderful together," Natasha said in awe. "She is the child-woman he needs, the partner he craves. What can we do, Marle?"

"I don't know, love, but we'll come up with some answers. Look at you. Walking, maybe dancing soon. We'll figure out something. Won't we?"

"Yes." Natasha touched her husband's face. "He needs to be able to come out into the light, Marle. So shall we."

"Are you sure?"

"No. But I think it's right. Don't you?"

"Will you be strong enough, my love?"

"I think I'm getting stronger by the minute." A tear coursed down Natasha's cheek. "We are not the evil ones, Marle. We never were."

"I know that, my love . . . but there could be nasty repercussions."

"To hell with them, Marle. We've paid our dues."

"Yes, we have." He kissed her gently, then picked her up and carried her down into the water, smiling when she reproached him. "Don't take away all my perks, love. You know I love to carry you."

"I know."

Deba was stunned at the grace and power of the dancer in the water. Her legs moved fluidly and strongly, her arms carrying her through the water swiftly.

"Natasha was a great athlete, not just a dancer," Wolf whispered in her ear as he held her.

"Was that in Russia?"

"Actually, as you might know, Natasha was born here. Shortly after her birth she was taken to Russia with her mother and father and schooled there for several years. She began training with the Bolshoi from childhood. Her father brought her here to live when he was a diplomat in Washington."

"How long have you known her?" Deba didn't really want to know.

"Forever it seems," Wolf said easily.

Deba whirled to face him, having the distinct feeling that Wolf had been evasive. Before she could question him, he pulled her down under the water again, his mouth pressing to hers.

In moments the water was a cauldron of desire, burning them.

Wolf felt as though he would explode with want.

They burst from the depths like dolphins bound together.

Natasha swam to Marle's side. "They need to have time to explore those wild feelings, Marle. I want to be able to give them that time."

"Darling, don't . . ."

"I won't be impulsive."

Later in the day Deba was alone in her room, pondering the afternoon spent in the pool and alongside it, having fruit drinks with Natasha Sharansky and Marle Damon.

It was impossible to dislike Natasha Sharansky. She was electric, beautiful, warm, loving, generous.

Deba threw herself down on the bed, garbed only in panties. Pulling up the light summer quilt, she closed her eyes. She couldn't even dislike the woman who'd been a lover of many years to the man she loved.

She was dozing—half sleeping, half awake. When she felt the bed sag, she tried to make her eyes open.

"Hi."

"Wolf?"

"Who else?"

"Redford? Newman? Cruise?"

"Very funny." Wolf nipped her ear with his sharp teeth. "You didn't answer me."

"About what?" It felt so good to have him there, at her side, his body heating hers. She wished he wasn't so tangled in her life, so interwoven with her breathing, her pulse, her being.

"Are you going to stay with me?"

The logical answer was certainly not. There were too many gaps between them, too many unanswered questions. Neither was free to make choices, to have a healthy involvement with others. A resounding negative was the only response. "Of course."

"What?" Wolf reared up and lost his balance, falling with a resounding thud to the floor.

Deba scrambled over to the edge, peering down at him. "Break anything?"

"Nothing that would give us pleasure, my darling." Wolf reached up and pulled her by her upper arms.

"Stop. Fool." Then Deba was collapsing in a heap on him. "Didn't it hurt to have me land on you like that?"

"No. It felt wonderful. If you want to hurt me, walk away. You damn near did me in the last time you did it. Swear you won't do it again."

"Wolf . . ."

"Swear."

Deba shook her head. "It's so impossible to promise . . ."

"Swear."

"I swear."

Wolf kissed her deeply, edging her onto his chest so that she was lying supine atop him.

Deba could feel his body harden under her and it caused her pulse rate to skip and hop.

"I want you more now than I did when we were at the lagoon, darling."

"Me too."

Wolf let his hand whorl over her. "Your skin should be my only blanket."

"You could get cold in Alaska in January."

"Don't bet on it."

Her hand slid along the side of his body, then she hitched herself to one side. Never had she felt such a desire to give everything, herself, what she was, what she thought, give all to Wolf. The power of it shook her, made her body feel like a wet noodle, yet she'd never been so sure and strong.

"Ahhh, don't do that. Your velvet body . . ." Wolf's voice trailed thickly.

"I just want to . . ." Deba's throat closed in excitement when she gripped his aroused body.

Wolf's eyes popped open. "Darling?"

"I hope the door is locked."

"This is my suite. No one comes in here but the cleaning staff."

Deba was about to ask him how he had so much autonomy in his former mistress's home when his mouth closed over her nipple and she turned to fire. Blood rumbled through her veins, her hands closing convulsively around Wolf's head, keeping him tight to her, the rhythm of his loving going through her.

His eyes lit with a ferocious passion that titillated her as nothing had ever done. She groaned in awareness of his potency. Wolf Clinton was a man among men to most. To Deba he was the only man. That was a sad and happy acceptance in her life.

Wolf's hands curled into fists as he fought the sensual surge that hardened his body. Like an unfledged boy he was out of control with her. He'd come to terms with that when Deba left him, now it was a fatalistic, irrefutable knowledge that he had no wish to deny. "I want you, darling."

"I . . . I feel the same." Deba shivered with a need that

almost overwhelmed her. Wolf was all that was beautiful in her life. That was scary.

He smoothed his hand over her derriere. "I want to kiss your rounded body, sweetheart . . . all of it."

Deba nodded.

When the smile trembled across her face, Wolf thought he would burst. She was exquisite, ethereal, yet the earthiest creature he'd ever beheld. Wolf Clinton, most pragmatic, practical of men, wanted to compose a song, a lyric poem, an ode. Then he sat up with one powerful push, rising to his feet almost in the same motion, still holding tight to Deba.

Lifting her onto the bed, he followed her down, his hand going over her body, moving in slow whorls, lower and lower. Then his fingers intruded gently, beginning a wonderful slow, hypnotic rhythm within her. "Aldebaran, my love, you're very beautiful, the most beautiful woman I've ever known."

"Wolf." Harsh cries issued from her mouth as the sexual sensations crashed over her like an incoming tide flattening and dissipating any argument she might have against being in his arms. To hell with it! One day he might be out of her life, but he was here now. Natasha Sharansky was beautiful and she would draw any man. But for now her arms held him. It was her body he was kissing. That was enough. Let the future take care of itself.

His mouth moved down her body, blood igniting like phosphorus as her velvet body fired him. There had been women in every corner of the world who'd satisfied him. None had ever brought him to the white heat of giving that Aldebaran did and could any time she touched him, loved him.

She pressed her breasts against the lightly furred chest, feeling in that moment she'd given herself to Wolf and there was no turning back, that a major part of her clove to Wolf, melded to him.

Wolf touched her in all the secret places, just as she caressed him. Moment to moment the passion built to crescendo, until the rasping sounds of their breathing were the accompaniment to the joy. When he entered her, she took him deep inside, enclosing the man as he took the woman. The elemental explosion of love blew them apart, then rebuilt them as one.

It was a bittersweet delight that she loved him with an all-encompassing love and could love no other.

Harsh and beautiful was the acceptance that Aldebaran McCloud Beene had taken his life into her trembling hands, and she could keep it because it belonged to her. Wolf closed his eyes in wonder.

◇ 13 ◇

Marle Damon watched his wife from the open doorway. She'd been staring at the barre for long moments. When she gripped it with both hands and lifted her right leg, her groan was very pronounced. He moved, then caught himself and stayed still.

"Stay where you are, darling Marle. I know you're there. Don't you know that I can always feel your presence? Don't come near me. I'm fine." Natasha leaned over the barre and tried a few very simple moves. "It's going to take a while."

"And there's no rush," Marle told her hoarsely, tears in his eyes.

Natasha lowered her leg and turned, swiping at her perspiring brow. "I'm coming out of the closet, Marle."

Marle stiffened. "You mean you're going to try to bring your body back so that you can teach short sessions." His eyes went over her warily.

"I mean that I'm going to tell Aldebaran McCloud Beene about Willard Temple."

"Natasha! No!"

"Marle, you've turned so white. Don't look like that. Please, we have to free ourselves."

"We are free, here, together," he said huskily, his hands

opening and closing. "Temple is dead. There's no need to resurrect him. We're free."

"No, we're not, my love, we're prisoners, fugitives, and you know it."

Marle strode into the exercise room, his image in the wall mirror reproachful, looming. "I can't let you."

Natasha shook her head. "I've thought about it since Wolf arrived with Miss Beene. It's a cancer that must be excised, Marle. It's rotted all of us. We cower in corners like pitiful crooks."

"No," Marle whispered. "It's over, hidden, forgotten. Let it stay that way."

Natasha shook her head. "We pretend it's over, Marle. I wanted that, so did you. We've closed our eyes and minds to it, shunned it. But it's never been over. I've hidden away here and you with me. Just a convict and a keeper."

"It hasn't been like that."

"You're hurt."

"And afraid."

"I'm not. I'm tired of being afraid."

"I love you, I can't lose you. I almost did once and it nearly killed me." The first time he'd met her, her life had been in jeopardy and it had taken months to bring her back from the brink.

"I'll be strong, you'll see."

"There's Wolf."

"Yes, and he is the bottom line, the reason I've decided on this."

"Talk to him."

"You think he'll talk me out of it."

"I hope he will."

"I went through two years of therapy to help me deal with what happened, keep me from taking my own life, Marle. I found a great happiness with you, but I've still been in the closet, and what's unfair is that I've kept you there with me."

"I only want to be with you," he told her harshly.

"I know. I love you so, my darling, but I must do this. Now I think I should take out those black years and look at them, face them, air them, get it all out in the open, look the world in the eye." She inhaled deeply. There was such great pain in Marle's wonderful face. "All the soggy dread will dry up and blow away in the sunlight, Marle."

"Talk to Wolf," Marle said through his teeth.

"I will."

Wolf opened his eyes and knew at once he was in his suite at Natasha and Marle's. In milliseconds it registered that the heaviness on his arm was Aldebaran and that they had finally made love.

Contentment and serenity were mixed with the passion that lingered near the surface of his being. He sighed. All the pains and pangs that had assaulted him when he'd been apart from her were fading into insignificance. She was here, beside him! If only she could be his wife. He wanted that . . . so much! Children! Instinctively his arms tightened on her. Wolf pressed his mouth to her forehead. He needed her and he damn well would have her no matter what it took. He'd denied himself joy for too long.

When she wriggled restlessly, he let his mouth slide down her face, muttering love words. At once her motions ceased and she breathed easier.

Wolf looked down at her while she slept, noting the slight blue shadowing of her eyelids, the same coloration under her eyes. Her fears hadn't been assuaged, her terrors hadn't been expunged. There was still a core of deep loneliness in her that all his loving couldn't quite touch. He understood it, he'd been there. But it hurt him that he couldn't take all the tension from her life. It had been a hard road for her. Peace of mind was what she needed and he intended that she have it. She was still too slender. Worrying about her parents had given her stress, and playing a dangerous hopscotch with her life had added to it.

The cable car incident in San Francisco was never far from Wolf's mind. His imagination conjured up other bad moments that had caused Aldebaran to run and keep running. Damn it! He wouldn't stand for it.

He kissed Deba one more time, then eased himself free of her, padding into the bathroom and throwing cold water on his face. The image that stared back from the mirror was grim and hostile. If it took every resource he had, he would put peace back into Aldebaran's life.

Leaving the bathroom, he went into the sitting-room section of the suite, picked up the phone, and dialed. "Lazarus, it's

Wolf Clinton. No, I'm still in California. If all goes well we'll be leaving for the Orient next week."

"Something happen, Mr. Clinton?"

"Yes." Wolf explained about the cable car.

"Ummm. That's a little weird. I could have sworn we were on top of things with the Cosentinos, Mr. Clinton."

"Do you think they've bypassed all the usual sources and given it to a splinter group?"

"I don't know. I do know that there are some terrorist groups in this country that have been advertising in the gun magazines. Free-lance work. If the Cosentinos are dealing with them, it could be hard to nail."

"Damn! How the hell do they get away with it?"

"Freedom and license are sometimes interchangeable, sir."

"What is it? You sound pensive."

"I wish I had something more concrete for you, sir. We've covered things in New York and there are people dogging you in California. Mr. and Mrs. Brown are well and no one has approached the Winsomes . . ."

"But what?"

"Your friend Mr. Brown has read this new book that's to come out on you, sir, called EXPOSE: WOLF CLINTON. He says that he discussed it with you and you seem to think it was researched in great depth. But you insist you don't know the authors."

"I don't."

"Would the author have used pseudonyms, sir?"

"What? I don't know . . . but Chatsworth Brown might. I could call him."

"That might be a good idea. Maybe you should read the manuscript."

"I will. What do you plan to do about our plans to go to the Orient?"

"It's taken care of, same as the place you're staying. Two more men have been added to the three that have been on the ranch for some time now."

Wolf laughed harshly. "And Marle Damon doesn't know?"

"Nope. Hasn't spotted them yet. You said you'd like the mister and missus to feel . . . unthreatened, is how you put it, I recall."

"Right. But I think I'd better tell them what you're doing."

"Might be a good idea."

"Keep on this thing. I don't like the feeling that Miss Beene is being threatened by unknown forces."

"I don't like it either. We'll blanket the lady, sir."

"Do that." Wolf hung up the phone and dialed again. "Chatsworth? Fine. We're at Natasha Sharansky's. Tell me if you think that second book on me was ghostwritten."

"I don't think so, but I can check it out. My wife misses her friend, so do I."

"Maybe you could join us out here . . . for a vacation. You wanted to visit Maria's mother. We're in the hills above the Napa Valley." Wolf paused. "I'll send the plane for you and someone will guide you here."

Chatsworth whistled softly. "Something up?"

"Could be."

"I see. About that invitation. I think we might do that, but I'll get on this other thing right away and get back to you."

"Right. I won't say anything to Aldebaran until we talk again." Wolf hung up and went through to the dressing room, donning cotton jeans and a loose-hanging cotton shirt, both unbleached.

Then, shod in espadrilles, he looked in once more on a deeply sleeping Aldebaran, and left the suite.

Moving through the house with the ease of familiarity, he went down the front stairs and bypassed the kitchen.

Entering a tunnel-like corridor, he smiled when he heard voices coming from the room at the far end. So, Natasha was serious about what she'd said when she'd gotten out of her wheelchair and walked in the solarium. She had gone to the barre!

Wolf paused when he heard his name. Though he had no intention of eavesdropping, what Natasha said riveted his shoes to the floor.

"I tell you that Wolf will never have a life until I release him, and I will release him by coming out into the open with my story." Natasha pressed her hand to her husband's mouth. "Now, Marle, we've gone round and round on this. I won't change my mind."

"Natasha, darling, think what you're saying. All in one day, because a stranger prods you to get out of your wheelchair, you walk. Now you think you should bare your soul? Think, darling. You went through so much."

"Didn't we all, Marle? You suffered, so did Wolf, and all so needlessly."

Wolf heard the sadness in Natasha's voice, then he moved from the hall into the room. "I agree with Marle, Natasha. Don't be hasty. It took so long to heal the wounds, and . . ."

Natasha turned so fast she would have lost her balance if Marle hadn't steadied her. "Heal? You don't think that there's been healing any more than I do, Wolfgang." Natasha lifted her chin, her back straight and pressed against the barre. "Now is the time to attempt a healing . . . by exorcism." She smiled. "What a joke those books are, my dear. They didn't even touch the sewer of our lives, did they?"

"No," Wolf said softly.

"Don't," Marle whispered in tortured tones.

"Natasha, you can't do this." Wolf's voice was harsh.

"Would it hurt you so much, *mon cher*?"

"Forget about me. You mustn't do this."

"Who better?"

"Darling, listen to me. I . . ."

"I want children, Marle. I want to try to have them, and I will not have them with the black cloud that hangs over us."

"Children!" Both men spoke at once, their faces rigid with shock.

Natasha chuckled, the warm sound softening the faces of the two men. "And why shouldn't I try to have a child? I'm not forty yet."

"But . . . but, darling, we've never talked of . . . that is, I thought you didn't want . . . do you think we could?" Marle Damon looked disjointed, out of whack, a silly smile slipping on and off his face.

"Have you forgotten how it's done?" Natasha asked impishly, making Wolf laugh, his eyes widening as though he couldn't believe what he was seeing or hearing.

"No, I haven't." Marle smiled softly. "Don't forget I'm the man who puts you to bed at night and climbs in beside you."

"I thought you looked familiar." Natasha laughed out loud.

Wolf stared at her. "This is incredible. Have you regressed to childhood?"

"Maybe." Natasha cocked her head, arching her long, beautiful neck, her skin tight and unblemished, with a bluish cast to it making it seem too fragile, too fine.

Marle looked at Wolf sharply, then back at his wife. "I'm a little nonplussed myself."

Natasha put her arms akimbo and looked from one to the other. "I think I've been a mushroom long enough. I'm coming out of the dark. How does that sound?"

"Going to grace a table? Smothering a steak, maybe?" Wolf queried huskily, his strong mouth quivering, his eyes moistening.

"You can laugh if you want, Wolfgang, I'm going to do it." Wolf shook his head. "It's not mirth I'm feeling."

Marle half laughed, but his eyes stayed on his wife. "You might not like what she plans on doing. Wolf, do you think Natasha should open up about Willard Temple to Aldebaran?"

"What? Tasha? What does he mean?" Fear took a chokehold on Wolf.

"I'm going to tell her about Willard."

"No! I forbid it," Wolf roared, his body beading with cold moisture. Never! Damn it, never.

Marle stiffened, his hand going out automatically, though he knew his wife had nothing to fear from Wolf Clinton.

"You can't forbid me anything, Wolfie, you know that." Wolf looked helplessly at Marle. "Do something."

"What?"

"How do I know?" Wolf said brusquely. "But stop her."

"Wrap her in a rug and post her to Mongolia?"

"Not a bad first plan," Wolf muttered darkly, glaring at the dancer.

"Stop frowning, Wolf. You know I'm right. It's time. I hadn't realized how much I've vegetated until I read that book, *Exclusive Rights,* and realized that you are tantamount to being an expatriate, Wolf. That's wrong." Natasha shook her head. "Now this other book, from what you've told me, is less than kind, a nasty exposé on you. I hate it. It's all because of me."

"I have my life in order," Wolf shot back.

"Not really. I think you want to marry Aldebaran McCloud Beene, but I'll bet you you told her you couldn't marry her because you feared the notoriety might upset me."

The silence shot around the room, caroming thickly.

"I'm right, aren't I? You love her."

"I won't discuss that with you," Wolf said harshly.

Marle looked down at the floor. "I don't want her to open up that can of peas, Wolf, but it isn't fair that you . . ."

"I'm fine. And Natasha won't be doing anything. That's final."

Deba woke and rubbed her eyes, staring at the cream-hued grass-cloth wall covering. It took long moments to orient herself, then her hand went to one side. She was in Natasha's home, in Wolf's bed. "Wolf." He was gone! Had he left her? Had they made love? She noticed the pale bruise on her upper arm and felt her body blush. He had been kissing her arm, then she caressed his aroused body and his jaw had clamped over her arm. It hadn't hurt, but it had sent her libido into overdrive. Even now, seeing his mark on her made her blood hurtle through her veins, made her desire rise like a flood. She had never, ever imagined she could feel such an elemental, encompassing emotion. From the first moment she'd felt that way with Wolf. Wolf Clinton was her love!

Where was he?

Getting out of bed, she ambled barefoot to the bathroom, her hand trying to smother a yawn. Goodness! Where had the wonderful brand-new aches and pains come from anyway?

Faceup into the shower Deba laughed out loud, the sound having a new richness, a depth. "Wolf!"

"We can't talk you out of this?"

"No, Wolf, you can't. I'm going back to San Francisco. Either I stay in the house or I go to a hotel."

"House."

"Stop looking so desperate. You act like you're being threatened." Natasha smiled gently.

"That's the way I feel." Wolf stared at the new serenity in her stance, the relaxed way she moved her hands and arms along the barre. When was the last time he'd seen Natasha that way? Before Willard Temple! Wolf ground his teeth.

Marle Damon threw his hands up in the air, like a man out of control. Then he took a deep breath, his eyes still fixed to his spouse. "Do you want me to get tickets to the ballet?"

Natasha's head whipped around, her eyes widening on her husband. "Do you mean . . . ?"

"The Bolshoi is in San Francisco."

"Oh, Marle . . . Marle. Could we?"

"I'll get four tickets."

"Yes." Natasha blinked. "The Bolshoi. I think I'll go and lie down. I'm a little tired."

Wolf moved toward her.

Marle put his arm across the front of Wolf and shook his head, his eyes suspiciously bright. "I'll be along in a minute to see that you're all right, darling."

Natasha smiled and nodded, then she moved past the two men slowly.

Wolf watched her, his mouth tight. "I damn well will not let her be raked over the coals again."

Marle shook his head. "That's the way I felt when she first mentioned it . . . but . . . I'm starting to change my mind."

Wolf whirled to face Natasha's husband. "What the hell does that mean?"

"Have you heard her laugh like that in a long time?"

Wolf shook his head, slowly.

"Well, neither have I." Marle lifted his head, shrugging back his shoulders. "If she's going ahead with this . . . I'm not standing in her way. Her psychiatrist told me that we should have forced the issue years ago, but I couldn't do it. Now she's done it."

Wolf's teeth cracked together. "Are you out of your mind? You know what happened last time. I damn well won't let it happen again."

Marle inhaled heavily. "You'll stand by her, as I will."

"Marle, for Christ's sake, listen to reason."

"I haven't seen her stand in that proud way in so long." Tears sprang to his eyes. "Hell, if we go bust, we go together, but I'm not going to stand in her way."

"Man! Are you listening to yourself? Don't you remember how close we came to disaster last time? More than once we could have lost her." Wolf felt helpless; his body tremored with remembered pain. "She went through hell."

"Yes, I know. But you haven't been listening to Natasha, Wolf. She sounds so strong, so sure. And that hasn't happened since before . . ."

"*I* know when she was strong and sure," Wolf interrupted roughly. "Damn you, this is wrong." He spun on his heel and left the room.

He'd gotten onto the property, but something didn't feel right. Staying in place for ten minutes was arduous and nerve-punishing, but he needed to know more about his new environment . . . what threats there were. How he'd hated that rigid military school that his guardian had forced on him . . . but he had learned methods of survival that he'd used to great advantage these past ten years.

He hadn't been in place, in the tree, ten minutes when he saw the cordon of men moving toward him. They were combing the woods. Stilling himself, he tried to tamp down the flood of frustration and anger he felt at being stymied. Damn Wolf Clinton to hell. He'd even brought men to this remote place to protect that bitch and himself.

There was no way he could implement his plan here. He could get caught. And that wasn't going to happen. He'd come too far. Revenge could come another time.

Relaxing in his cover high in the tree, he leaned back and planned how he would accomplish vengeance. When he heard voices below him, he stilled even his breathing.

"I tell you, Petey, I feel someone's been here."

"Yeah, well, we'll keep looking. We'll head up the west side and come back this way, much more slowly. If anybody's here, we'll get 'em."

"You think it's more than one?"

"Hiring two specialists is always better. Backup."

"Yeah."

The moment the two moved away, he was out of the tree and moving fast toward the canyon, where he'd entered the property. He had no illusions about the thoroughness of the search on their return. They would check the trees. Moving more swiftly, he cursed silently. Damn Clinton and Beene. He would make them pay. He owed them more than one clean hit. He intended to hurt them.

Wolf was blind to everything around him when he stormed back into the suite. The silence told him that he was the only occupant. "Aldebaran, where are you?" His angry query ricocheted off the walls.

Fear replaced ire, taking him out of the suite on the run.

Once outside the ranch house he sprinted toward the stable, having no idea why he headed that way, fighting a panic that was taking hold of him.

"Hi." Deba had watched Wolf speed out of the house and

toward her. She realized he hadn't seen her sitting atop the corral fence in the shade afforded by a liquid amber tree.

Wolf skidded to a stop, whirling to face her. "Where the hell were you?"

"Here." Anger popped to the surface. "Don't yell at me, buster."

"Damn you, Aldebaran, I've got enough worries." Striding to the fence, he plucked her off as though she weighed ounces instead of pounds, hauling her close to his chest. "I'm damn well sick and tired of fretting about you." His mouth came down fast, fixing to hers with a fierce desperation.

Deba braced herself for impact and she got questing gentleness, tongue touching tongue, a beast just below the surface but held in check. Love bloomed in her like a rose after a June rain, and her whole being quaked in response to the assault. Her arms entwined around his neck, her body swaying into his, clinging. She felt irritation, angst, frustration, loving Wolf but feeling there were no longer choices. The questions of should she love him or should she back away no longer entered into it. Her heart had committed itself to him without her permission.

"Aldebaran, my darling, I need you."

The pain in his voice made her eyes fly open and she searched his face. "You have me." Irritation had vanished.

"Yes," he responded hoarsely. "At this moment I have you and I'm going to keep you. I can't lose you. Life is so damned dangerous."

"It is?"

"You know it is."

"Yes, I suppose I do," she responded slowly. "Not that I'm entirely sure I understand you."

"I know. There's a great deal you're in the dark about, that's for sure." Lifting his head a fraction, he studied her for a moment. "Will it bother you if Natasha and Marle accompany us back to San Francisco?"

"Certainly not. In that big house we'll all be rattling around. . . . Wait! Natasha? I didn't think she ever left here to stay elsewhere."

"She doesn't . . . hasn't since her arrival many years ago. Her trips away have been few, and she always returned at night."

Wolf's twisted smile touched her heart. "What is it?"

"I think you prodded her, cracked the shell she'd built around herself."

"What do you mean?" A shivery uncertainty assailed her.

"I mean I have never seen her as she was just a short time ago in the exercise room, at least not since . . ." His mouth tightened.

"Not since the murder."

Wolf reared back as though he'd taken a blow, then he nodded. "She's determined to go to the city. Today she not only walked, she was trying the barre."

"No!"

"You have tears in your eyes. Yet you barely know Natasha."

"I saw her dance once and she was incredible, an . . . angel."

"Yes, she was."

"You saw her dance many times."

"Many. But each time I was in awe of her great talent." Wolf looked down at her. "Why did you come out here alone? I didn't like it when I couldn't find you."

"I needed some air. I heard the birds sing and I couldn't resist."

"Why didn't you call me on the intercom? I would have come with you."

Deba pushed back from him. "I don't need a keeper, Wolf." For a moment she saw the raw, tortured look in his eyes, then it was gone. "Wolf, don't."

"I'm not going to let them hurt you."

"Wolf, we live in a no-man's-land of emotion. You know it, I know it." She shook her head. "How can there be hope for us?"

"That's damned foolish. I love you. You love me."

"But there's no future. Can't you see that?"

"No, I damn well can't. You're going to be with me, and I'm going to be with you. That's the present and future."

"Are the Cosentinos chopped liver?"

"I told you that was covered."

"Then why do you fly into a panic when you can't find me?"

"I didn't do that."

"Don't roar like a lion. You don't intimidate me."

"And you still have a scorpion's tongue."

Deba shoved at him with her hands. "I'd like to punch your lights out."

"Hey, there's a car coming up to the gate, Petey."

"I see it. Pick up the phone and call the house. I'll go out to the car." He gestured to some of the other men in the gatehouse with him. "Cover me."

The men nodded and melted out of the house.

Petey put his shoulders back and went out to the gate, speaking through it but not opening it. "What do you want?"

"We were given these directions by a man by the name of Lazarus. He was told to give me carte blanche by Wolfgang Clinton. My name is Chatsworth Brown and this is my wife, Maria."

"Wait there." Petey went back into the gatehouse and took the phone from a waiting henchman. "Chatsworth Brown and wife, sir. I'll describe them."

In minutes Petey was back at the gate activating the electronic release.

Chatsworth noted that as they entered, some men in Jeeps were ahead of and behind his car. "It looks like we're being escorted."

"Yes." Maria hitched closer to her husband on the bench seat. "Maybe we should have called first."

Chatsworth's mouth tightened. "No, darling. When I got the call from Aldebaran's parents, I felt I had to come here. It was not something easily explained on the phone. My message came in code, but I don't have anything like that with Aldebaran . . . and I didn't want to endanger them."

Maria stared at him. "Do you think our phone line was snapped?"

"Tapped, darling, and yes, it could have been. I've had it scanned periodically, and once someone had tied into it. Being cautious is being safe."

"I love you for taking care of Aldebaran and her family."

Chatsworth shot her a quick smile, blowing her a kiss. "I love you for everything." He frowned at the heavy undergrowth all along the narrow road they were traveling so slowly. "Fortunately, Wolf's kept us informed of his and Aldebaran's whereabouts. Had he not done that, we would never have found our way here."

"My mother was so curious."

Chatsworth stiffened.

"I didn't tell her anything, dear husband. I know how important it is to keep silent."

Chatsworth reached for her hand and brought it to his mouth.

"Isn't this some place?" Maria looked around her as they traversed the winding road. "It's so hidden away."

"Wolf left orders that I was to be given access to any place he inhabited, so . . ." Chatsworth's voice trailed. "What a nice house. And that must be the lady of the manor." Chatsworth parked on the turnaround driveway and turned off the ignition.

When the two of them got out of the car, Chatsworth frowned. "Excuse me for staring . . . but you look familiar."

"Thank you. My name is Natasha Sharansky. Perhaps you saw me dance at one time. I listened on the extension when you called from the gate, Mr. Brown."

Chatsworth didn't notice the outstretched hand until his wife prodded him. Then he closed his mouth, looking sheepish. "Sorry, it's just that I thought you were . . . that is, I . . ."

"You thought I was dead." Natasha smiled when Maria gasped and looked askance at her husband. "Most people do, but I'm actually just coming back to life."

Maria looked nonplussed.

Chatsworth stared at the dancer, then nodded slowly. "Did my friend Aldebaran McCloud Beene have anything to do with that?"

"Chatsworth!" Maria admonished.

Natasha chuckled. "I don't mind, Mrs. Brown. It's true. She did have a great influence on me."

Chatsworth smiled back. "Doesn't surprise me. Ah, Miss Sharansky, I saw you dance at Lincoln Center. You were magnificent . . . greater than anything I'd ever seen."

"Thank you. That was many years ago."

"I've seen your pictures," Maria ventured shyly.

"And you are Aldebaran's dear friend. She speaks of you so kindly."

"Yes." Maria stared at the other woman. Was she real? It was as though a slight breeze could blow her away, but the dancer still exuded an aura of strength and purpose. And she was incredibly beautiful, her dark hair pulled back in a bun, fine bone structure with high, wide, very pronounced cheekbones.

"Natasha!"

"Yes, Marle, I'm out here."

"I couldn't find you when I woke, and . . ." Marle Damon's eyes fixed on the other couple as though they were a vision. "Who are you? How did you get here?"

"They are friends of Aldebaran's and Wolf's, dear. Wolf gave permission for them to be on the property. I eavesdropped on the call and came out here to meet them."

"But . . ."

"It's all right," Natasha said airily. "I can handle these things."

Marle stared at her, his mouth opening and closing.

"Maria!" Deba had come from the back of the house, spotting the group in the inner courtyard, the dim coolness of the house camouflaging her. "Chatsworth! What is it? Is something wrong? My parents?"

"No, no." Chatsworth went past the others and enfolded Deba into his arms. "I did receive a message, that's why I'm here."

Maria moved forward, her arms enclosing her friend. "I have missed you, Aldebaran."

"And I have missed you." Deba kissed Maria, then Chatsworth.

"What the hell is going on? Why are you holding my woman?"

"Hello, Wolf." Chatsworth leaned back from Deba, chuckling. "Still like a bear with a sore paw where this lady is concerned, I see."

Marle Damon started to laugh, then pressed his hand to his mouth when Wolf glared.

"Wolfie, does everyone know that Aldebaran has a ring through your nose?" Natasha's tinkling laugh lifted in the air, pulling smiles from some of the others.

Maria rolled her eyes. "Why do people prod him so?"

Deba caught her whisper. "And you kowtow to him," she told her friend tartly.

"And you are always pulling his tail," Maria shot back pertly.

Wolf moved toward Maria and kissed her. "You are the only sensible one in this group. How are you?"

Maria chuckled. "You just say that because I don't tease you."

"Now you're catching on," Deba cut in sharply.

"They are battling, Marle," Natasha observed serenely. "Isn't it fun to watch them?"

Maria ignored her friend's glare and smiled at the dancer. "I thought that, too, at first, but it's a mating dance, my Chatsworth says."

"That's right, get them to train their guns on me." Chatsworth rolled his eyes.

"When they really get going you'll want to go up and nail the roof down. Won't they, Chatsworth?"

"Whatever you say, my love."

"Very funny," Deba muttered.

Chatsworth laughed. "She's right, and you know it."

Deba's face changed. "You have a message for me. Is it urgent?"

Chatsworth hesitated, his glance sliding over Marle Damon and his wife.

"It's all right, Chatsworth, you can speak in front of them. What's wrong?"

"Nothing, nothing. It's just that they're on their way home."

"Home?" Deba said stupidly.

"Why don't we go inside where it's cool and have something to drink?" Wolf had moved to Deba's side. Now he took her arm. He felt her body quiver. When she looked up at him, her eyes were shaded, remote.

"The side of your mouth is tremoring. Are you worried too, Wolf?" Deba asked him matter-of-factly.

"No." Tremor after tremor shook her body. She was forcing herself to be calm, but she was like a firecracker with a very short fuse. It wouldn't take much for an explosion. Wolf tightened his hold. "Stay calm, darling. Everything is all right. I have people on your parents."

Relief was a palpable slash across her features. "Thank you."

Wolf kept his arm around her when they entered the solarium at the back of the house.

When they were all seated with tall frosty drinks, Chatsworth looked at Deba. "They're coming home because the WPP thinks it's safe for them." He leaned forward and stared down into his drink. "They're homesick, Deba. They want to come back to the United States and see you on home soil."

One large tear coursed down Deba's cheek as she nodded. "I've missed them so much," she said hoarsely.

Wolf put his arm around her and kissed her cheek. "We'll be seeing them soon, love."

Natasha's glance touched her husband and he nodded almost imperceptibly. "They can stay at the house in San Francisco, Aldebaran."

Wolf frowned, and Deba shook her head. "No, they can't. As it is, I shouldn't be staying there if you're there. It would be too dangerous for you . . . and it could also imperil my family."

"She's right. I'll put them up at a hotel and . . ."

"I don't agree, Wolf," Marle interrupted. "I think Aldebaran's parents would be safer at the house. After a time we could move them out here to the ranch. No one could find them here."

"Oh, no, I couldn't . . ."

"I think Mr. Damon's right, Aldebaran," Chatsworth said firmly.

"So do I." Maria nodded firmly.

Wolf and Deba looked at each other.

"It's your call, darling."

"It would be so wonderful to be under the same roof as they, Wolf . . . but I don't know."

"Let me talk to Lazarus and see what he says, then we'll decide." He leaned down and kissed her, then rose to his feet. "I'll use the phone in the study."

When he left there was a silence.

"It was always like that," Natasha said gently. "He removes oxygen from the room and leaves a vacuum. It takes time to recover."

"That's the way I see him, too, but I like the way you said it," Maria observed.

Chatsworth smiled when Marle Damon laughed out loud. Then he looked at Deba, cocking his head to one side. "Don't you like us slicing, dicing, and mincing your man?"

Deba shot a look at Natasha, who stared at her serenely. "He . . . he isn't my man."

"He isn't anyone else's," Natasha said in a slightly reproving tone.

"That's for sure." Maria relaxed, not seeming to notice her

friend's sharp look. "Most of the time he eats Aldebaran alive with his eyes. It's kind of shivery and sexy."

"Maria," Deba said hoarsely.

"What? Are you getting a sore throat, Aldebaran? You sound funny."

"No."

"She thinks no one knows about her grand passion, darling." Chatsworth's smile widened when Deba glared at him and Marle and Natasha chuckled.

"Is that it? Don't be silly, Aldebaran. No need to be embarrassed. Everyone knows you and Wolf are mad for each other. It's like . . . like being in a volcano, being with the two of you," Maria told her kindly. "Now you're getting red in the face. Are you feverish, do you think?"

"No."

Maria looked alarmed. "She's choking, Chatsworth."

"Oh? Let me help." Chatsworth gave Deba a hearty smack on the back.

"Cretin," Deba croaked.

"Didn't it help?" Chatsworth smiled benignly.

"I think your friends want you to marry Wolfgang, Aldebaran," Natasha said sweetly.

"Out of the question," Deba said, coughing.

"I think I would be matron of honor," Maria announced grandly. "But you could be an attendant too."

"Maria . . ."

"Well, she could." Maria was slightly irritated with Deba. She turned back to Natasha. "I'd like her to have a shower. I didn't have one, and they are so useful. So many things Chatsworth and I have to buy now . . ."

"Maria," Deba said in a louder voice.

"I think that's a good idea," Marle interjected before Deba could say more. When Deba looked at him sharply, he smiled.

"True." Chatsworth added his touch.

"Stay out of this," Deba told him through her teeth.

"What did she say, Chatsworth?" Maria's eyes snapped in curiosity.

"She's beginning to agree with the consensus."

"Rat." Deba's whisper only touched Chatsworth.

"What consensus?" Wolf said, reentering the room.

"Nothing."

"It's more than nothing, Aldebaran," Natasha ventured

gently. "Maria Brown and I have decided to give Aldebaran a wedding shower."

"What!?"

"Easy does it, man, you damn near blew out my windows," Marle said easily.

"Sometimes Wolf is unruly," Natasha said, leaning toward Maria and Chatsworth.

"No, he isn't," Deba said swiftly. Then she sat back, her face slowly reddening.

"Aldebaran is always protecting something," Maria explained.

Chatsworth sat back, his glance touching Marle. "When they both let go, it should register on the Richter scale."

"Charming."

Deba jumped to her feet. "We are not getting married."

"You're not the only one involved in this. Don't speak for me, damn it." Wolf's face reddened, his stance bellicose.

The killing looks they exchanged rendered the others silent.

14

San Francisco was no different. It was the same city she'd left just a few short days ago. Why, then, did Deba feel as though she'd made a flying trip to Mars? That she was now on an alien planet? The world had tipped and she was slipping toward infinity. Earth was getting flat.

Wolf was out of sorts, at least that's the way Maria described him. Deba thought him manic, outrageous, insufferable.

On the second day after their return, when he walked into the vaulted ceilinged library where she was reading, Deba stiffened. Wolf glared at her, his hands clenching and unclenching. "Stop acting as though I'm going to commit mayhem."

"That's the way you look."

"I have a right to look that way. How dare you infer to our guests that we are not marrying?" His own ambivalence on the subject was forgotten in his ire.

"It wasn't an inference. We aren't marrying. And stop bellowing like all the bulls of Bashan."

"I should damn well paddle your backside."

"Try it and I'll punch your lights out."

Natasha had come down the stairs shortly before Marle.

As he was coming down the stairs he saw her standing in the large foyer, listening. "What in . . . ?"

"Shhh, they're at it again," Natasha said impishly, dimples flashing in her cheeks when she smiled.

Marle's heart turned over at the sight. He hadn't seen those dimples in many moons; now, in two days, he was seeing them all the time. "Eavesdropping? Shame on you."

"I can't help it. They're so funny, Marle. They are so much in love, they both want the same things and . . ."

"And because love has blinded them they can't see the obvious."

Natasha looked around at her husband and grinned. "I suppose it is cruel of me to enjoy it so much. But for so many years Wolf has been like a robot. Now Deba has stung him back to life." She shook her head. "He has carried the burden, Marle."

Marle frowned. "Darling, it was his choice."

"He was protecting me. I won't have it that way anymore. It's all going to come out in the open, where we can face it . . . beat it." Natasha's face twisted. "What good did it do any of us to hide?"

Marle put out his hand, then let it drop to his side. "Natasha, my darling, I'm afraid for you, but I'm with you all the way."

"I'll be strong, Marle. You'll see." Her face tightened for a moment, then it relaxed in a smile. "Let's go in there and referee."

Before they could do that, Deba stormed from the library, her face an angry mask. "He's impossible," she fumed.

"Oh, I know," Natasha murmured, her hand coming up to cover her smile when Deba glared at her before stomping up the stairs.

"You're baiting her," Marle said, surprised.

"Yes, I suppose I am."

"Wolf will explode," Marle said placidly.

"That's what I'm hoping."

"Little devil," Marle murmured, following her into the library.

"What are you grinning at?"

"Now, don't you pick on Marle just because you're making a jackass out of yourself with Aldebaran." Natasha smiled sweetly.

"Natasha . . . !"

"Pooh. You don't scare me, Wolfie."

"I'm not trying to."

Natasha went over to him and put her arms around his waist. "Tonight we go to the ballet, all six of us, and I want to enjoy it. Will you help me have a good time by being nice to Aldebaran?"

"I am nice to her." Wolf looked affronted. "Excuse me."

After he left the room, a smiling Marle looked at his wife, his smile disappearing when she gazed at him. "What are you thinking?"

"Tonight we go to the ballet. Tomorrow night at dinner, I will tell Aldebaran and her friends what really happened to Willard Temple. Marle, darling, you've turned positively ashen. Don't worry."

"God! Natasha, it frightens me to think of it."

"No more fears, Marle, no more."

"My darling, I trust you're right."

"I am."

Deba was pacing back and forth in the large suite that was part of the master suite, muttering to herself. "I'll kill him. He's insulting . . . and . . . and . . ."

"A first. You at a loss for words." Wolf propped his shoulder on the door jamb, scanning her from head to foot when she whirled to face him.

"Don't look at me like that."

"Like what?"

"Like I'm a pig on a platter with an apple in its mouth."

"You are definitely a delightful morsel to be savored, but I wouldn't describe you like that." His chest tightened, as it always did when he looked at her, his pulse hammering up into his throat.

Her body was melting like chocolate in the sun just because he was looking at her. "What do you want?"

"What I've wanted since we met. You." He pushed away from the jamb and approached her.

Deba held up her hands, palm outward. "No!"

Wolf stopped. "What do you mean?"

Deba swallowed. "You only want me periodically. I'm not a magazine to be delivered to your doorstep, Wolfgang Clinton."

"I want you all the time, even when I'm sleeping. And damn it, unless you order me out of here, I'm moving in here with you today, now." He stood with his hands hanging at his sides, staring down at her. "I want to love you and keep you, and I'm going to unless you send me away."

"How long can that last?"

"Forever. Are you willing?"

"We don't get along at times, we argue and get angry with each other." She stared at him. "And we have secrets."

"Yes, yes, I know all that, don't belabor it."

"I'm not belaboring it, I'm just . . ."

"Aldebaran! Damn it, do you want me?"

"Yes," she yelled back. "Stop bellowing."

"What did you say?" Wolf whispered.

"Cat got your tongue?" Deba's voice was shaking.

"I love you, damn you." Wolf scooped her into his arms, his mouth fixing to hers, easing her lips apart so that his tongue could enter, touching hers.

The kiss went on, magnetizing their two bodies, melding them together, making them one.

Wolf felt as though he was experiencing something brand-new. He was giddy, excited, feeling unfledged, as though going into alien, wonderful territory. Had he ever made love before? No! Aldebaran had taught him about love at the lagoon in Mexico . . . and he wanted to know more and more.

Deba pulled back out of breath—but so confident. Nothing had changed! It hadn't been a wonderful dream she'd had over and over. Lovemaking with Wolf was as perfect as her memory had told her. The golden moments at the lagoon were not a fantasy, but an earthy, heart-pounding fact.

All the passion that had erupted in Mexico was building in her now. She had the same need to give to Wolf, to take from him, to exchange the wonderful passion that had changed her life. It was as though all the doubts and irritations of the past years and the immediate past months when she'd been without him had dissipated in one flashing, sensuous moment. "You are one beautiful man, do you know that?" The words tumbled from her. She chuckled when color ran up his face. "Hasn't anyone called you beautiful before?"

"Maybe, but it never mattered until now." Wolf lifted his hand to her face, pushing back the heavy fall of hair. "I want you as my wife. Will you take a chance on me? I know it's a hell of a gamble . . . and maybe what we have will be damaged when I tell you what I must . . . but, damn it, I love you and I want to keep you happy and I promise I'll do everything I can to keep you that way all our lives." When he felt her knees buckle he pulled her up his body so that their faces were even, nose to nose, lips to lips. "Answer me, darling."

"Huh?"

"I have so much to tell you, some of it damned unpalatable, some that might even turn you away from me, but I know that it isn't enough for us to have a shaded relationship. It's all going to be out in the open."

"Did you ask me to marry you? What about the Cosentinos? I thought marriage was out."

"I did ask you. The Cosentinos are being handled. Marriage to you is definitely on . . . but I give you leeway to change your mind either way when I tell you what you must know and . . ."

"Don't get all involved in statistics. This isn't an application for employment, it's a proposal. Isn't it?"

"Yes."

"Then my answer is yes."

"What?" Wolf's arms slackened, Deba slipping down his body.

"Losing your grip?"

"You're going to marry me?"

"Yes." Could she hear her bridges crumbling? Were the barriers going up in smoke?

"God! I don't believe it!" Did they have a chance? Damn, they'd make their own luck. Wolf gripped her again, lifting her high on his chest and swinging her around and around.

"Stop, I'm getting dizzy."

"So am I. Oh, baby, I'll keep you safe." He kissed her hard, his hands going over her delicate body as though the touch of her was nourishment to him.

Deba reached up and scored a finger down his chest, her hand resting on his belt buckle.

Wolf lifted his head, staring at her, then he moved back a fraction and began unbuttoning her blouse. "Feel free to do the same."

"Thank you."

"Aldebaran, my love, I've dreamed of undressing you, kissing your wonderful skin."

"Strange, isn't it? I've had the same dreams about you."

Her husky voice aroused him to fever pitch. When he looked into her eyes and saw the hot desire he knew was mirrored in his own, his libido shot through the roof. Wolf's hand shook as he dropped a strap from her shoulder, his mouth following a path to her breast. "I love your body . . . I love everything about you . . . even when you insult me."

"I don't do that." Deba's words sighed from her mouth, her body pliant, willing, wanting. "This is so wonderful."

"Isn't it?" Wolf kissed her breast, teasing the nipple with his tongue. Her harsh breathing set him on fire.

When he eased the dress slacks down her body, he kissed the skin he bared.

His teeth nipped the inside of her thigh and Deba groaned out loud, holding his head close to her body.

Then he rose to his feet again, her clothes tossed to one side, near where Aldebaran had thrown his.

In seconds they were standing in front of each other, naked.

"What are you thinking, Wolf?"

"Do you remember when we went skinny-dipping in the lagoon?"

Deba lifted her hand and touched her index finger to his lips. "I recall a wonderful man who took me into a cave and stayed with me, to calm my fears, a man I could never forget, who lived in my heart when I wasn't near him." When she saw his eyes moisten, she felt tears in her own. She had the sudden, instinctive sureness that she had stepped inside Wolf, at that moment, beyond the wall he'd erected to protect himself.

"Touch me, darling."

Deba took hold of his aroused body, caressing him. His harsh, uneven breathing was a spur to her own passion.

Wolf bent and lifted her into his arms, his eyes fixed to hers as he walked the short distance to the bed. "I love you and I want you."

"Me too." Deba wound her arms around his neck, her mouth pressed to his ear. When he lowered her to the bed, she brought him down with her.

Side by side, they caressed each other fervently, but there was a slow, deliberate ease to it, as though they must savor every touch.

"Love me, Wolf."

"I've been loving you in my mind since that first day when I lifted you up behind me on Diablo and you were already in the throes of heat stroke."

"My gallant knight." Deba's hand lifted, coursing over his cheek, her fingers impressing along the way as though she would trace his bone structure.

Wolf's arms tightened on her, his mouth going over her hair and face. "I hunger for you all the time. You're food and drink to me, Aldebaran McCloud Beene, soon to be Clinton."

"When I was away from you, I felt lost." A sob shook her. Deba pressed herself to him, her body undulating gently against his, loving the satiny, hard-muscled body covering hers.

Wolf gasped when she pressed closer to him. "You're magic, Aldebaran."

Moving sinuously again, she kept her eyes on his face, noting his sensuous flinch, the flaring of his excitement in his eyes at once.

"Temptress." Wolf let his tongue rove her body, his mouth closing on one breast, taking the nipple into his mouth, and sucking gently.

"Wolf!" Her body was floating apart, clinging piece by piece to Wolf's, becoming part of him.

"I'm loving you."

Deba felt again that flare of need, the need to give and take that had happened the very first time Wolf had loved her. A familiar anticipation tumbled through her. Wolf was going to love her! How she needed that. Wolf was sexually insidious: he'd entered her, become a part of her, staying, clinging. Deba wanted him with an elemental, basic need that superseded all other sensations and emotions.

Nothing mattered at that moment. Whether it was safe or dangerous, she cared not a whit. She was with Wolf, she'd needed him so long.

When Deba touched the masculine nipples on that hard chest, Wolf gasped, his body arching. "What is it? Did I hurt you?"

"You stabbed me, darling, shot me, mugged me, took me. Damn, I have never had a charge like you give me." His hands convulsed on her, his mouth seeking hers. "I want a life with you, my sweet one."

Feelings exploded and imploded. Wolf didn't know if it was Deba groaning or himself. He was on fire, sliding through the heat so that it melted everything but his surety that Aldebaran was his life.

His feathering gentleness set Deba aflame, burning her with the cool, questing touch of true love.

His mouth moved slowly down her body, taking her pore by pore. When his teeth nipped the inside of her thigh, her legs parted for him, allowing his tongue to enter in the most intimate way. . . .

Love was peace, excitement, joy, fervor. All the elements were there.

Deba shook with need.

Wolf quivered with the core desire to be one with the woman he loved. He lifted himself up along her body when he felt her begin to quake, his own libido right on the edge, the taste of her on his lips permeating his being. She was more than a part of him, she'd become his essence. Everything now had new meaning, importance, a shine, a hue; every facet and nuance of being had luster. Interest in the smallest detail had been honed, all because of a waif who turned up on Rancho Lobo and took his heart.

Gently he entered her, want thudding through him, making a new pulse beat in his blood.

Deba took him deeply into herself, encompassing him, desiring him, needing him with a desperation she'd never known. Never had she felt such a want, or desired to give such pleasure. All the flowery beauty of classic poetry couldn't begin to touch the airy wonder, the pulsating joy, that filled her because Wolf was part of her now. She could extol him in sonnet, but that could never do him justice.

Wolf had never known such delight, hadn't even guessed that it was in the world or that he could ever experience it. Aldebaran had brought him to a volcanic wonder, filling him with driving passion; yet, first and foremost, all he wanted to do was pleasure her. All the joy of those days on the lagoon were with him again, the love pressure building in him like a lava ready to burst through its crust.

In slow, sweet remembered exploration, they touched each other, air rasping from their lungs as sexuality built to blinding force, closing out the world, encasing them in the special planet where lovers dwell.

In passion's spiral they rose to the heights, love sounds issuing from them as they held each other in the ultimate joining.

"I love you."

Deba was sure she said it.

Wolf knew he'd spoken the words that had coiled around his heart almost since their first meeting.

In panting heat, they came together and then subsided, arms around each other, their bodies beaded with love dew.

"Aldebaran."

"Yes." Deba couldn't open her eyes; a happy lethargy had glued them shut.

"Marry me."

"When?"

"Today."

Her eyes flew open. "Is that possible?"

"Oh, I think so, love."

"You look so lazy." Deba's finger scored down his chest.

"I feel replete and happier than I ever have."

"You're very sexy."

"And you're blushing."

"At times I'm silly."

"Does it bother you that I'm . . . Am I too sexual?" He grimaced. "I can't help it with you. You explode me like a bomb."

"It doesn't bother me because I'm the same with you."

"Don't sound so surprised."

"Well, I didn't think I could ever turn on like that . . . but I do . . . I did . . . every time . . ." Deba's voice trailed and she looked at him helplessly. "Is this the way it's supposed to be?"

"Yes. God, yes."

"I thought it might be."

"You sound sad."

"Well, it's not easy loving you."

Wolf felt as though he'd taken a punch in the solar plexus. Happiness shot through him like velvet spears searing him with the special moment. "Did I hear you right, my love?"

"Sure you did."

"A declaration of love shouldn't make you morose."

"I'd be so lonely now, if ever . . ."

"Never. Wherever you go, I'll be at your side." He watched the tears gather in her eyelashes. "I thought you knew that."

"It's so unfair to you." Deba sighed. "I should really

knock you on the head with a mallet, tie you up, and mail you back to Mexico, where you'll be safe."

Wolf looked at solemnly. "I'm too heavy for you to get me into a mailer."

"That's true." Deba ran her fingers over his face. "I want you to be safe."

"I will be safe with you."

"That's not true and you know it. It's so unfair."

"The only unfairness is to lose your love."

"You won't do that . . . but how can I protect you from the Cosentinos, Wolf?"

"You'll be protecting me by staying with me, darling. My senses are sharpened when you're with me, my instincts finely honed. I'll make fewer mistakes with you at my side." He grinned when he saw her reluctant smile. "Don't leave me. Promise."

"That's an easy covenant to make," she told him huskily.

"Make it."

"I won't leave you." Floodgates in her mind and heart let go, and such a joy filled her that she gasped.

Wolf had caught her close to him, but when he heard the sound, he pulled back. "Did I hurt you?"

"No, it just felt so good to commit myself to you."

Wolf blinked at her and swallowed. "That damned honesty of yours disarms me." He kissed her gently. "From the first you've challenged me, dared me, jousted with me, tossed many unpalatable things at my face, but I trust you more than anyone I've ever known . . . and I have from the start."

"Even when you found me in New York."

"I was furious with you, but even when I was in a deep rage about you, I never felt that I couldn't trust you."

"I feel like a German shepherd."

"Your ears are shorter." Wolf kissed her nose.

"Boor." Deba giggled, then stopped shortly. "That stupid giggle."

"You did that a few times when we were at the lagoon." He watched her eyes glint in memory. "It was good then, wasn't it?"

"It was wonderful."

Wolf kissed her lingeringly, his heart pounding when her fingers threaded through his hair. "We'd better get out of this bed. I have a wedding to plan."

"Oh, you have a few minutes," Deba said provocatively.

Wolf gasped when she touched his body with questing fingers. "Damn it, Aldebaran, I have to . . . God, don't stop, love, don't stop."

For a moment she experienced a flash of remorse, as though she'd been wrong to let her guard down, that it was foolish to lower all the barricades.

Then Wolf caressed her and all her misgivings evaporated.

It wasn't just by chance that Wolf found Natasha in the exercise room, sometime later.

"Darling Wolfie, you look . . . I don't know, I've never seen that look."

"I'm getting married in an hour, Tasha. Will you be a witness? No, no, don't cry, don't cry. You know I can't stand that." He hurried to her.

"These are tears of joy, Wolfie. I've waited a long time for your happiness . . . as well as my own."

He approached the barre and took her in his arms. "You mustn't overdo, you know."

Natasha pushed back from him. "I haven't felt this good since I danced with the Bolshoi." Natasha frowned. "If you are being married, maybe we shouldn't go to the theater."

"We can and will. First I'll get married." He hugged her tight. "We'll have four witnesses. You and Marle and Chatsworth and Maria."

Laughter bubbled out of her. "Storming full steam ahead as usual. Well, then, let's do it. Let me tell Marle. He'll be so pleased."

"Of course."

Natasha's eyes widened. "And I have just the dress. I haven't worn it in years, but Yves St. Laurent designed it for me. What is it? Why did you frown?"

"Aldebaran has nothing special . . . and I don't want to take the time to get her anything."

Natasha laughed. "Eager?"

"Very."

"Don't worry. I have a trunkful of things. Marle always drags everything along. We'll rummage and find something."

"You're shorter than she." Wolf laughed.

"Not by much . . . and she's very slender." Grabbing his hand, she led him from the room. "Let's find Marle."

When Deba came out of the shower sometime later, her mouth dropped at the array of clothing spread out across the bed, with Wolf looking down at them. "What's this?"

Wolf had been scanning the clothes. He turned at her query. "What do you think? These are Natasha's. I wanted to buy you something special . . . but there might not be time." Wolf studied her face. "I'm perfectly happy if you decide to wear a skirt and blouse."

Not taking her eyes from the luscious materials and colors, Deba moved toward the bed. "The colors and fabrics are wonderful. Let me look."

Wolf chuckled at the way she let the silks and satins run through her fingers, with small, happy sounds issuing from her throat. "When we go to Paris, you'll be able to choose your own wardrobe, darling." There was a crease of concern between her brows when she turned to look at him. "What's bothering you?"

"I don't want reams of clothing, closets of shoes. It's not my style."

"I know that. But you might enjoy a small foray. Right?"

"What woman wouldn't, but—"

"No buts, darling. A husband can shop with his wife. We won't be extravagant. What do you think of these? Should I return them to Natasha?"

"Yes . . . no. I'd like to try on a few." Deba looked at him ruefully. "They're beautiful."

"Do it."

Wolf paced the bedroom, more excited than he'd been at his last business takeover. "Hurry up."

"I can't get the zipper."

"That's what husbands are for, love. Come out here."

Deba had donned the apple-green chiffon silk that swathed around her body to end in a tiny kick ruffle. When she moved out of the bathroom, the gown seemed to flow out behind her.

"There. Turn around and let me . . . ." Wolf's voice trailed. "Wow. You do have a beautiful body, darling. And your eyes have turned a blue-green. I like that."

"I do too." Deba whirled away from him. "Is it too dressy for an afternoon wedding?"

"No. You're perfect."

Deba looked pensive. "When we go to the ballet tonight, we'll be—"

"Husband and wife."

"Yes."

"I like the sound of that."

Deba nodded, her throat full. "I'll try on the peach suit, I think. That's pretty and might be more appropriate."

"Whatever you say."

Deba finally decided on the peach suit.

"Wear the green tonight," Wolf said softly.

The civil ceremony didn't have the spiritual beauty of Chatsworth and Maria's but Deba was more deeply moved than if she'd been married in a cathedral.

The county clerk who married them shook their hands and wished them well.

"You're married, sister mine." Chatsworth had to pull Deba free of Wolf, who frowned at him. "Will you let her go for a minute?"

"No," Wolf muttered, glancing at Natasha when she pinched him on the arm and smiled.

"You are so happy, Wolf, but you cannot pen her up." Natasha kissed him.

"I'll bet he'll try," Maria said sagely. "You should have seen them in New York. Chatsworth said it was like tigers making a baby." Maria looked wide-eyed at Deba when she laughed. "But I don't know how he would know that," she labored to explain to a chuckling Natasha. "He has never watched tigers making babies. Have you, Chatsworth?"

"Caught you up, didn't she?" Deba whispered to her friend and father's agent.

"Brat." Chatsworth smiled at his wife when he answered Deba.

"Nope. Married lady."

"Right." Wolf took hold of his wife and kissed her hard.

"Told you," Maria whispered to Natasha.

"They are magic together," Natasha whispered back.

"Black magic at times."

Wolf heard Maria's answer and smiled at her. "You have that right, Maria love."

"He heard me. Oh, dear," Maria sighed, closing her eyes. "It might start a battle. Hang onto your hat, Natasha, which by the way is very charming. You look nice in that shade of coral."

"Thank you."

Marle moved to Wolf's side. "Congratulations, friend. You've made my wife very happy."

Wolf looked at Natasha, listened to her laugh. "She looks wonderful. I can't recall a time when she was more relaxed."

Marle looked around at everyone. "Listen up, bridal group. The party is moving to the Lalia. It's close to the theater, and after we have a leisurely dinner . . ."

"I was going to take them to the Scepter," Wolf interjected.

"Too dignified. We're going to celebrate."

Wolf looked at Natasha searchingly.

She nodded. "I chose the Lalia, Wolf."

Deba moved closer to her new husband. "Does the Lalia hold bad memories for her?"

"Yes." His arm tightened around his wife, smiling down at her. "Hello, Mrs. Clinton. Do you like your new name?"

"Very much."

"Shall we go?" Chatsworth came up on one side of Wolf.

"Bad timing," Wolf told him.

"You'd say that at any hour of the day if you were with Aldebaran."

"Damn you, Brown." Wolf's smile was lopsided.

"And you're worried about going to the Lalia." Chatsworth nodded. "I saw your face change when Marle mentioned the place."

Wolf glanced at Deba, who'd turned to speak to Maria. "Ah, Aldebaran was going to change into her green dress." Even to Chatsworth Brown, whom he trusted, the memories couldn't be verbalized easily.

"It's something about Natasha, isn't it, Wolf?" Chatsworth persisted.

"Yes, it was at the Lalia that someone, a very inebriated someone, called her a faithless bitch for letting her lover, me, kill her other lover," Wolf told him flatly.

"Jee-zus. Maybe we shouldn't go there. Did you kill the bastard?"

"I wasn't with her at the time . . . or I might have."

Chatsworth looked uncomfortable.

"What is it, Brown?"

"I have the feeling I might have killed the bastard myself. Natasha Sharansky is an exquisite female, pure, beautiful, kind. I can't blame Damon for adoring her."

"She is wonderful." Wolf's glance slid to his wife. "We have three wonderful women in our company this evening."

"Yes." Chatsworth scanned his wife, then his glance came back to Wolf. "It seems we're dining in tomorrow evening, that Natasha has a little surprise for us all."

"It would seem so," Wolf answered woodenly.

"And you know what it is."

"Let's say I suspect."

"And you're not happy about it?"

"No. Shall we join the others?"

Chatsworth eyed Wolf's progress as he crossed the room and took his wife in his arms.

"What is it, Chatsworth?" Maria moved closer to her husband.

Chatsworth smiled down at her. "Nothing, darling."

"But it is something. I can tell. You're worried. Is it because Aldebaran's parents will be arriving in the country soon?"

"No, that's good news," Chatworth murmured, kissing her gently. "I remember our wedding so vividly, my darling."

"You're putting me off," Maria said worriedly.

"It's all right. I'm sure it's making a mountain out of a molehill."

"Chatsworth, I'm frightened."

"No, darling, don't be. I love you."

◇ 15 ◇

"Wasn't the ballet wonderful last night?" Deba whispered to her husband, who'd woken her with a kiss.

"I've always liked the ballet. Last night it couldn't hold me, I had my wife on my mind too much."

"And what happened at intermission stayed on your mind, didn't it?"

Wolf hesitated. "The man had to be drunk," Wolf said tightly. He could tell her later that it had been Cosentino's nephew. First he would see all the Cosentinos imprisoned.

"That's why you pushed Maria, Natasha, and me into the cloakroom and closed the door?"

"And you didn't stay there." Wolf looked at her accusingly.

"My husband was in danger and you wanted me to cower in a closet?"

"I should know better. Ummm?" Wolf kissed the space between her breasts.

"Yes." Deba gripped his head between her hands, her body quaking momentarily as she visualized what could have happened if the security people hadn't been so quick. "He must have had the gun hidden on him, he wouldn't have gotten past the lobby if he'd been brandishing it."

"True. No doubt he was a crank." Wolf would keep her in the dark for the time being if it would give her peace of mind. If only he didn't have the skin-raising surety that he was missing something, a tiny infinitesimal piece of knowledge that would make the puzzle fit. What horrified him was that the puzzle included Aldebaran, yet all his sources had seemed to think that the Cosentinos had backed down, had been cowed.

Protecting Aldebaran had seemed so easy once he'd fixed on the Cosentinos . . . but now it was different. There seemed to be a new game plan, a new set of players. How were they planning to get to her? Were they using others to do it?

"Hello. Is anybody in there?" Deba tapped gently on his skull. "How soon they forget. The honeymoon over already."

Wolf turned to her and pulled her on top of him.

Deba could feel the thrill along her nerve ends as his aroused body pushed at her. "Well, maybe you haven't forgotten everything."

"I remember it all." He positioned her gently, undulating his lower body.

"Wolf!"

"Yes, darling. Are you remembering?"

"Yes, I'll never forget."

"What? This?" Wolf pulled her down tightly over his aroused body, his eyes fixed to her. Wanting her was like breathing, there was no control over it, it just was.

In a recalled ecstasy, Deba arched herself, her eyes drooping closed, caught in the wonderful sensation of taking and giving, loving and being loved. Each time he touched her was like the first time. No one had ever peeled her skin back to raw, loving flesh, no one could ever have plumbed the core of her as Wolf did. He excited her, wooed her, soothed her, cared for her, loved her, and made her whole.

"No! Too quick," Wolf said hoarsely, removing her despite her protests. "I'm still going to love you, wife of mine."

In heady acceptance she lay sprawled beside him, loving the way his eyes roved her body. They were like kisses, embraces, caresses. She needed that, desired it.

Slowly Wolf began the ritual, wanting her to be as torridly committed as he was.

All at once Deba was impatient. She wanted to love him, desperately. Pushing upward, she dislodged him.

"What? What is it, darling?" Wolf's slumbrous gaze went over her.

Deba maneuvered her body so that she was lying atop him. "Guess."

Wolf's eyes snapped clear, then narrowed, a smile twisting his lips. "Surprise me."

"Maybe I will." Reckless, in a fever, her blood tumbled through her like a cataract. Inhibitions formed by her nomadic life-style, the built-in wariness honed by being on the run, were shoved to the back closet of her being. Wolf Clinton was here, with her, in her arms. She was free, unfettered, and she needed to love him.

As though poised for a monumental moment, her hands sought him, eagerly exploring him, her libido climbing as her ministrations engendered groans and gasps from Wolf.

Deba became bolder. Leaning closer, she bit him in the neck, on the jaw, her tongue following her teeth, laving him, cooling the heat of her love bites.

In gentle ferocity she suckled the strong male nipples, moving down his body, hands and mouth caressing him wildly.

"Enough! I'm on fire."

"So am I," Deba breathed unevenly.

"Easy, my darling, this is going to last."

In sweet measured moves he scoured her body with his lips, lower, sweetly lower, until he could no longer tell whose body was tremoring, his or Aldebaran's.

At the moment he kissed her most intimately, her body arched and low, hoarse cries issued from her throat. The sound sent Wolf's libido through the roof, hot blood running through him like molten lava.

"Wolf!" In frenzied effort to control the simmering explosion in her body, she clutched him with fevered hands, bringing him back up her body.

It shocked and titillated Aldebaran when she tasted her own essence on his lips. Her hands moved convulsively over his shoulders and down his chest, running through the hair there, circling those hard masculine nipples. His body held a special erotica, a certain magic, for her. Though the memories of the lagoon had sustained her all those months when they'd been apart, the reality was so much more volatile than any mind could conjure that she gasped with its power. She loved him and needed to give to him.

Opening her eyes as he entered her, she looked straight into his, suddenly aware that at that moment in time, something changed; the golden, precious elements that were motes in the universe came to earth and clung to them, putting them among the stars. In milliseconds she was a nascent lover, rebuilt as a human being to be Wolf's love.

Hands laced with hands, they began a love motion that seized the vibrations of the ages and manacled them to each other.

"Wolf!"

"Darling!"

The words thrust from dry throats as the pulsations took them, melded them, and made them one.

In fierce culmination they gave to each other, their harsh breathing a symphony to the passion of the ages.

It took eons to come back to earth. Or was it seconds? Both clutched the ecstasy, wanting to sustain it as it had sustained them.

Wolf cuddled her close to him. "I wanted you so much."

"And I wanted you."

"All my life I'll want you, Aldebaran."

"Me too." Could they have a life together? Was there a chance?

Wolf hugged her close to him for long moments. Then he eased himself back from her, loving her languorous look, the satisfied curve of her body, the pliant lips. "You're very beautiful. Do you look like your mother?"

Aldebaran blinked. "What? Well, yes, in some ways I'm like her, but I'm like my father too."

"Brothers and sisters?"

"None. Starting a dossier on me?"

"No, boning up for my in-laws. I want to make a good impression."

Deba was going to laugh, then she noticed the tight look around his mouth. "You can't be nervous about meeting Mother and Dad."

"Why not? I haven't had too many in-laws, you know."

"They won't bite."

"I want them to like me," Wolf said harshly.

"And that's never happened to you, wanting someone to like you, is that it?"

"Right." Shaking his head, he held her tighter. "Let's face

it—nothing had ever mattered as much as it has since I lifted you onto the back of Diablo."

"And what a horse it was. I think I had to be a little light-headed to get on that creature."

"More than a little." Wolf's grip tightened a fraction. "You could have died in that damned heat. You weren't used to it." He buried his face in her neck. "I will never let anything happen to you. You're my life."

Apprehension rippled up and down her spine. Could they control the future? "I want to care for you too."

"Then stay with me. Swear it."

"I did that when I took vows with you," she told him softly. Rubbing her hand over the slightly bearded skin that required shaving twice daily, she let her fingers press the scar that ran from his left eye down to his chin.

"Does it disgust you, darling?"

"No . . . but I would like to know how it happened." She felt his whole body withdraw as though it had pulled in on itself, shrunk. "Wolf?"

"I heard you." Air rasped from his lungs. "I have to tell you sometime." He looked at her. "I don't want to lose you."

"There is no way that you can, unless you tell me to go."

"Aldebaran!" He buried his face on her breasts, his mouth suckling there as though he needed her sustenance. "Darling, I . . . I was involved with a killing."

"I know that."

"Did you know that the man was very close to me?"

Blood flowed out of her brain and down her body, congealing in her feet. "Yes, I guess I knew that too."

"I suppose you couldn't help but know that. The rags were full of it. It still jolts me to think of it."

"Can you tell me what happened?"

"Yes, I can . . . but unless you force me, I won't tell you until after tonight."

The harshness of his voice was an unknown quantity to her. Raising herself on one elbow she looked down at him. "Do you trust me?"

"Yes."

"And I trust you. So I won't ask any more of you than that."

"I love you more than I can ever say," he said simply.

Deba wanted to cry, so she hid her face against him. She

did trust him. Why had fear risen like a specter from the dead to hang over them? The unknown was a black threat that hovered just out of reach.

Wolf watched her while they dressed that evening. He'd seen the slight sheen of perspiration on Aldebaran's upper lip when they'd dried each other after their shower. She feared him! He'd seen fear in her eyes. Pain such as he'd never known took hold of him, a hole opening up in his soul at the thought of losing her.

"Shall we go?"

"Yes." Her voice had been tight, constrained. Was she already planning to leave him?

Dinner was a strange interlude. Only Natasha seemed animated and she seemed to direct all her conversation at Maria.

Marle watched his wife as he picked at his food.

Wolf looked at no one, his gaze seeming to fix on a portion of wainscoting.

Chatsworth looked concerned, puzzled, wary.

Deba seemed to chew each mouthful a thousand times, but if anyone had asked her what she'd eaten she couldn't have said.

"Shall we take our coffee and brandy in the library?" Natasha asked brightly, rising from her chair before Chatsworth, at her right, could move. Moving swiftly, she was out the door before any of the others could get out of their chairs.

Wolf cursed quietly and steadily as he threw down his napkin, not looking left or right. He rang the bell and a houseman appeared. "Put two bottles of cognac in the sitting room."

Deba found it hard to breathe as she rose and followed Maria, sensing that Wolf was right behind her. Wolf was strung tighter than a bow.

Natasha was already pouring demitasse when they entered, the thick rich coffee giving off a delightful aroma. "When everyone has their coffee and liqueur, I shall begin."

"Tasha . . ."

"No, Wolf, no more, I know what I'm going to do." There was an aura about her, as though a silvery shield had been cast as a barricade. Nothing could touch her.

Deba put down her cup, not having the strength to hold it. Foreboding shook her, apprehension shivered her body, filled her blood. Why should she be so fearful?

Natasha looked around at each one in turn, waited until

the houseman had left the room and closed the door, then she smiled. "This story has been in mothballs too long; it must be told." She reached over and patted her husband, who sat beside her.

Clearing her throat, her voice huskier than normal, she began. "My childhood was happy, my mother and father were loving people who doted on me." Natasha looked around the room, her back straightening. "Some of the biographies about me to the contrary, I was born here, to American parents, though my father had been born in Russia.

"When I began dancing, at a very young age, my father and mother decided to take me to Russia and let me train with the Bolshoi.

"Though times were very tight and hard in the Soviet Union then, my father, the well-known conductor Anton Sharansky, was able to pull a few strings with the State Department and the Kremlin. So we went. We lived in Russia for several years, and then we went to Paris to live. I was happier in Paris because I was able to see my older stepbrother more often, a step brother I dearly loved." Natasha took a deep breath. "My father was also very fond of his stepson and kept in close contact with him even though we lived in Europe and he lived in the United States. When I was eighteen and already on the stage, my . . . our dear parents were gone. Now there was only the brother and sister, who loved each other dearly."

Deba reached out to Wolf and he grasped her hand.

Maria put her hand to her mouth to stifle a sob.

Chatsworth kissed her hand.

"My career consumed me, nothing else mattered . . . but my brother. He was very wealthy and talented and was able to come to see me even when I danced with the Bolshoi. I was a star. It was then, when I came to America to dance, that I made up my mind to stay and be near my only blood relative. Dancing with the American Ballet was easier than dancing with the Bolshoi, but I was happy."

"Darling . . ."

"No, Marle, I will tell it all." Natasha smiled at him.

"All right."

Natasha folded her hands in her lap. "My brother was working in Los Angeles and I worked primarily in New York, except of course when I was on tour." Natasha put her hand to her lips to blot the moisture there. "While on tour I danced in

Los Angeles, so I saw my brother. At that time, on the first tour, I also met a man named Willard C. Temple."

"Tasha!"

"No, Wolf, do not interrupt me." Swallowing hard, Natasha looked into space and continued. "He pursued me. He was much older, but he was very fascinating . . . and kind, or so I thought. He showered me with gifts, he was always there. Little by little, he put a cloak around me, so that I was seeing no one but him most of the time." She inhaled raggedly. "He even managed it so that I fired the dresser who'd been with me for years. Anna contacted my brother when that happened. My brother called me and tried to dissuade me from limiting my social life. He told me I was too young not to be trying my wings with friends my own age. At that time he didn't know that Willard C. Temple was the man who was taking all my time. My brother knew Willard. Willard had backed a couple of his projects." Natasha paused and swallowed.

Deba leaned forward. "This is distressing you, Natasha. There's no need to . . ."

"But there is, dear Aldebaran, there is for all of us."

"Go on, Natasha," Chatsworth said softly.

"My brother called me and told me to come out to California and stay with him. I told Willard that I was going. He became incensed, very, very angry. He . . ." She inhaled deeply. "He struck me, many times, and then he raped me."

Concerted gasps were the only sounds in the room.

Marle Damon grasped his wife's hand and put his forehead in the palm.

"It seemed to please him so much to do this. When I told him I hated him, he struck me again and said that now I was his and he would do as he chose with me."

Deba saw the tears on Wolf's face and felt them on her own.

"I . . . I went to the hospital alone and was examined, but I didn't tell people who had done this to me. I was so ashamed, you see."

The murmurs from the women rose and died.

Natasha put her hand to her mouth, then she swallowed. "I was very frightened . . . but not intimidated. I knew that if I once got to my . . ." Her voice broke, but she shook her head when Marle would have said something. "I . . . I knew that my brother would protect me . . . and not even Russian wolves could penetrate the barriers he would put around me. The next day, though Willard Temple called me early to tell me he would be over that evening and that I was to wait for him, I packed my things. Though I was sick in heart and body and I flew out to my stepbrother. He met me at the airport and immediately wanted to know what was wrong." Natasha paused.

Marle handed her his cognac and she took a small sip.

"We were always *simpático*. My father used to laugh at how my brother and I would answer each other's questions before they were voiced." Natasha smiled shakily. "At first I said nothing . . . but he pressed me and I told him. Then I had to beg him not to do anything. I pleaded and cried, and finally he agreed to let things go. He took me to a specialist, who examined me and pronounced me fit, but my brother wouldn't stop there." Natasha inhaled. "I went through intensive psychotherapy. Though I kept on with my dancing and training in Los Angeles, I saw a psychiatrist and analyst at the same time. It took time but I began to deal with it." A tear rolled down her face.

Wolf leaped to his feet and went to her, kneeling in front of her. "Don't, Tasha, don't."

Natasha leaned over him. "Don't worry, dearest brother, I'm crying tears of joy. It feels so good to release the poison."

Deba sat transfixed, the world fading and receding before rushing in on her again. Natasha was Wolf's sister! She hadn't been his lover. It was too much to take in all at once.

Natasha smiled at Deba. "You, dear Aldebaran, needed to know this, as do your dear friends." Inhaling deeply, she gazed into the distance. "I thought I was through with Willard C. Temple."

"And he was your friend?" Maria blurted, then blushed to the roots of her hair when Wolf turned a hard glance her way. "Forgive me, I didn't mean to interrupt."

"There is nothing to forgive, Maria," Wolf told her hoarsely. "Though he was very well known to me, he was not my friend. After I heard my sister's story I hated him for what he'd done to Tasha." Wolf's mouth tightened. "I went to New York and confronted him. One of his many henchmen gave me this." Wolf fingered the scar on his cheek. "If I'd known he intended to follow Tasha to California, I would have moved heaven and earth to stop him."

Natasha waited for Wolf to return to Deba's side and take

her hands before continuing. "Willard Temple came to the house where I was staying in California, Wolf's house. Wolf was at work directing one of his great hits, *Witch Hazel*. Because he had been to Wolf's house on other occasions, the houseman let him enter before he left to go to the store. I was sitting by the pool and didn't know he was there until he loomed above me. I screamed but he put his hand over my mouth."

Maria moaned, turning her face into Chatsworth's shoulder.

Wolf couldn't unlock Aldebaran's hands. "Darling?" It shook him that she was so white.

"I will listen. It helps her," Deba said through cardboard lips.

"We struggled." Natasha said in a mechanical voice, her eyes glassy, as though her mind had carried her back to that moment. "Then we fell in the pool and I was free."

"He wasn't a good swimmer, Natasha was," Wolf said woodenly.

"I swam to the side and climbed out . . . frenzied, angry, fearful," Natasha continued. "I ran into the house like a wild woman, soaking wet, and into the library, where I locked the door, shaking as though my bones would fly apart."

"Don't say any more if it hurts you," Deba whispered.

"I must, because it has lacerated too many lives holding it inside. The price of freedom is pain," Natasha said simply. Then she inhaled, looking over their heads and continuing. "I hadn't reckoned on him coming in the French doors off the terrace. He knew the house so well, you see. When I saw him, I wrenched open the drawer of Wolf's desk, took the gun there, pointed it, and fired, over and over again. Wolf came in while I was shooting. He saw it all."

"And took the blame," Marle said softly, patting his brother-in-law's arm.

"She was right to kill him, I would have anyway if I'd come home sooner," Wolf said, his face twisted. "That son of a bitch deserved to die, but she couldn't take any more. As it was, she was in and out of hospitals for months afterwards. I couldn't let them kill her by their questions. I would do it again," Wolf said heavily.

Deba moved out of her chair, going down in front of him, lifting his hands to her face. "If I didn't already love you, I would love you for this, Wolfgang Clinton."

Wolf leaned forward and kissed her gently on the mouth.

"I'm not through," Natasha said in a strange, austere voice.

When Deba would have gone back to her chair, Wolf lifted her onto his lap, cuddling her close to him.

Natasha flashed them a tight smile and continued. "This was very hard for Wolfie. I tried to get him to change his story, but he took the blame for me. He would not even let me go to the trial. It was at this time that I met Marle. He had come to the hospital to see a friend and saw me and spoke to me. The doctors were pleased because they saw how I responded to his warmth." She smiled tenderly at her husband. "He came every day, and then, because I asked him to do it, he began going to Wolf's trial. They became friends."

"And that's the end of the story," Wolf interrupted brusquely.

Natasha's gaze went to her brother's and stayed there. "Except to tell you that I finally discovered what only Wolf and finally Marle knew . . ."

"Tasha!"

Deba could feel the erratic pounding of Wolf's heart and looked up at him inquiringly. His face was a mask of pain. "Wolf?"

"I must tell them, Wolf. Give me your permission," Natasha begged softly.

Wolf nodded once.

"Willard C. Temple was Wolf's father."

"God!" Chatsworth groaned, his eyes closing as he hugged his crying wife.

"Wolf," Deba cried, holding him tightly.

"Willard C. Temple was the man who was my biological father," Wolf said tautly. "A man who caused my mother great pain. Only by the great offices of Anton Sharansky was my mother able to divorce the man who'd tortured her and marry the man she truly loved, my stepfather. To me, Anton Sharansky was my father. From the time I was seven, he was the man who gave me love and guidance and whom I loved and respected dearly. He was Tasha's father as well."

"Hence the name Sharan, the name you used at the Winsomes' dinner party," Deba said softly.

"Yes, darling." Wolf looked down at her and kissed her

gently. "Now you know why I was so frightened and angry when I heard about *Exclusive Rights.*"

"Yes, yes. I'm so sorry."

"So am I," Maria said miserably.

"It all worked out fine," Wolf said softly, his grin twisting. "Not even the other book that's coming out was able to get these details."

"True," Chatsworth said grimly. "And I'm going to see that such a book will never be written." He looked at Marle Damon. "Are all her papers in a safe place?"

"In Switzerland, in a vault we have. Only Wolf or I can get them. They will become the property of Wolf's or our children," Marle said softly.

"Good. And I will scotch any and all rumors that move on the market, if any, if ever," Chatsworth said grimly, shaking his head when he looked at Wolf. "You are a brave man, my friend. If I'd had any idea . . ."

"It's all right. My sister seems fine . . . and she's come through this like a trooper," Wolf said, his gaze lightening as he looked at Natasha.

"It was a nightmare," Maria said accusingly. "That father of yours should have been drawn and quartered."

"I agree, Maria," Wolf told her.

"That was why Wolf and Marle have founded the Child Rescue Organization," Natasha said slowly, subsiding into a chair, leaning heavily on her husband. "So that children have a way out."

"I married a very special man," Deba murmured, the smile lighting her eyes. "I like that." Her eyebrows arched when the blood rose in Wolf's face. "Good. I can put you out of countenance now and then."

"She probably will be able to do that all the time," Maria said conversationally, her features less tense. "Aldebaran doesn't take any crepe from anyone."

When the others laughed, Maria looked at Chatsworth.

"I think you mean crap," he told her, biting back a smile.

"Oh. All right." She smiled at him, then at the others. "When we first arrived in New York a man tried to take our taxi and Aldebaran showed him who was boss." Maria smiled complacently.

"You've told that story," Deba reminded her.

"Are you sure?"

"Tell it again, darling." Chatsworth smiled at a narrow eyed Deba.

"I will. Aldebaran knocked the man into the gutter."

"That would not surprise anyone who knows her," Chatsworth muttered.

"Boor," Deba told her friend, though she couldn't stop smiling at him.

"Then there was the time the man pinched me on the train . . ."

"What?" Chatsworth didn't laugh, though his wife assured him it had been nothing.

"Maria!" Deba tried to interject.

Maria didn't seem to heed her. "Deba threatened to pick up her hot coffee and fling it at him. There was so much commotion that she scared him off." Maria smiled when everyone but Deba laughed.

"Are you groaning, darling?"

"Yes," Deba said limply. "Maria is so honest."

"You protected her. She knows that, and so do I. I love you for it, and so does she."

"And you love your sister."

"Yes. She was the baby in our lives." Wolf's gaze went to Natasha, held close by Marle. "You have no idea how much my mother, father, and I loved her. She was the brightest thing in our lives. Singing and dancing almost before she could walk. The servants in our house used to vie for the right to take care of her, but mother didn't often share her with anyone but father and me."

"And you were loved."

"Very much so. When I had holidays from school I would go to Paris. My father and I would go for long walks, pushing the baby in a stroller, and we would talk about everything. He was very learned and spoke about ten languages fluently."

Aldebaran became aware that the others were listening. "Go on."

"When our mother died, Tasha was only a teenager. Our father grieved mightily." Wolf looked into Aldebaran's eyes. "At times I thought we might lose him too." He sighed. "Then we did lose him, years later."

"He was a wonderful man," Natasha said softly. "He was so very proud of Wolf because he was so bright in school. Then when he came out of school he immediately began making a name for himself."

"Tasha," Wolf said mildly.

"Well, it's true, everyone knows how sweet and gentle you are."

"They do?" Chatsworth jumped when his wife pinched his arm.

Wolf and Marle laughed out loud.

Natasha frowned. "You do not believe that El Lobo foolishness, do you Aldebaran?"

"We-ell, now and then. Only a wolf could have found Maria and me in New York."

"Wolf loves you," Natasha said simply. "I was sure of that the moment I first saw you together."

Deba was interrupted by the houseman, who went to Natasha and whispered.

"At once. Right in here." Natasha wriggled free of Marle's arm and rose to her feet.

Marle rose as well. "What is it, love?"

The door opened wider and an older couple entered with one of Wolf's men at their back.

"Mother? Daddy?"

"Oh, my." Chatsworth jumped to his feet. "Professor and Mrs. Beene."

Deba didn't know how she crossed the room. Her knees had turned to soft rubber.

"My child."

Held by her parents, tears blinding her, Deba could say nothing.

"It's been too long, child, I know that," her father said in a breaking voice. "But thanks to your young man, we're back to stay."

Deba could only nod, not able to speak past the lump in her throat. When she felt a strong arm around her, she leaned against Wolf and let him make the introductions to the others.

"And I'm your son-in-law, sir. I hope you approve."

"It wouldn't make any difference, he would run off with her anyway," Maria said sotto voce to Natasha, who chuckled and nodded.

"I heard that," Wolf said, his voice amused when he turned to look at Maria. "How perceptive of you."

"Isn't she." Chatsworth kissed his wife. "Come, darling,

you too, Natasha, Marle, I want you to meet my second set of parents."

Deba was in a trance. She couldn't stop looking at her mother and father as they spoke to each one in turn. Often their glances would turn to her.

"They look well. Do they seem that way to you?" Wolf was at her side.

Deba nodded slowly. "I don't know what I expected. Scars, bullet holes, bruises, it's all been so frightening." She looked up at him. "Are they really in the clear? Can they live their lives now?"

"I have top men on them and the Cosentinos." Wolf had a distant look to him all at once. "The Cosentinos have a great deal to worry about at this point if they try anything, and they know that. I'm not averse to carrying out a threat. They know that too."

"The boy in prison?"

Wolf gazed down at her, his eyes flat, opaque. "Among others."

Deba held his gaze. "A crime against them could turn against us."

Wolf nodded. "Do you think I don't know you, my Aldebaran?" It would tear her apart to be a "participant" in a crime. Knowing about it would catapult her into it and that would damage her. "I will take steps reluctantly, but I will do it, if they try anything at all." It choked him to think of her pulling back from him, hating him.

Deba leaned against him. "I want us to have children."

Wolf lifted her chin as though they were alone in the room. "Do you, my darling?" She had voiced his biggest fear. Children tainted with Willard Temple's blood as he had been tainted. Despite wanting to raise children with her the last closed, locked door in his being would be very difficult to open even for Aldebaran.

"Oh, yes. Lots of them, and they're going to be happy and safe, until they're strong enough to wrestle their own bears."

"Making children calls for a strong commitment, making love the same." If it happened he would move heaven and earth to protect their progeny from the evil that was their grandfather. He would do all he could to see that nothing ever touched their children. They would have every chance to be productive citizens. Genes? What an awful word.

"What are you thinking?" What pain twisted at Wolf? Why had his eyes darkened that way?

◇ 16 ◇

"Are you out of your mind? You want me to go with you to Rancho Lobo? There's an army there."

"Don't you think I know that? I also know that Diego Da Silva is shooting another of his taco westerns there, those crappy flicks that are making him so much money at the box office. We'll walk right onto the place. You can be an extra, I'll . . . be elsewhere."

"You'd face Wolfgang Clinton? Because if you're on the ranch, he'll find out about it. He must know you hate him."

"He knows nothing."

"Okay, I'll do it. How will you get the explosives onto the ranch?"

"Let me handle that. You just keep in touch the way we planned."

"Don't forget my money."

"I forget nothing."

The other man shivered. No doubt a banshee had walked on his grave.

Wolf was nervous!

Marle handed him a coffee, which he refused.

Chatsworth offered him a cognac, which he accepted.

"Why the gloom? Man, you've been itching to have this second ceremony in front of her parents."

"Something's wrong, and I don't know what."

When Chatsworth would have scoffed, Marle touched his arm, drawing him away. "Don't laugh off his premonitions. He has an uncanny way of protecting his own."

"Are you serious? You think this is more than wedding nerves?"

"Yes. And that worries me."

"Cosentinos?"

"I don't know. Maybe. Wolf seems to think he has them tied in knots . . . but they haven't remained out of jail this long by being stupid."

Chatsworth nodded. He had a shivery certainty that whatever was building in Wolfgang Clinton's mind would spill over onto all of them at the rancho. "What should we do?"

"Wolf's done it."

The two men turned to look at the bride, who was dressed in cream-colored silky cotton; on her feet, handmade espadrilles of finest suede, the same hue as the dress.

"Wolf loves her so much. I think that's why he suggested this," Marle said softly.

Chatsworth nodded. "Professor Beene and his wife were so delighted with the idea." He sighed. "Aldebaran does look wonderful."

The ceremony was brief but beautiful, as was the blessing of the padre, who joined Wolf and Aldebaran in a second ceremony.

When they went into the dining room to eat, Deba pressed his arm. "What is it?"

It would have been easy to lie to her, prevaricate, but Wolf didn't want that. "I'm having the grounds screened."

"Something happened?" Deba's hand tightened on his arm.

An alarm sounding through the house cut through the light chatter and laughter of the dining room.

Silence. All eyes fixed on Wolf.

Keeping Deba at his side, Wolf went to a wall phone and lifted it. "What is it?"

Deba watched those hard, almost spatulate fingers tighten on the instrument before he replaced the receiver.

"Milo Crandall is here." He looked down at Deba.

"Maybe you remember the name. He was my assistant before you arrived at Rancho Lobo. He wouldn't know about the extra security systems. He tripped an alarm."

"I remember. I took his place." She felt his trepidation, his taut preparedness.

"Yes." What the hell was Milo doing here now? Hadn't he tendered his resignation? "I'll see him."

"May I come with you?"

"Yes." He'd get rid of him fast.

Wolf excused himself to his guests, explaining that someone was in the library. Holding his wife's hand, he led her down the wide corridor. "Did you ever think you'd marry twice?"

"No, but I'll bet it would be more of a shock for people to learn that you'd gone through two ceremonies."

Still chuckling at what Aldebaran had said, he pushed the library door open and spotted his former employee standing in front of his desk. Milo didn't look different, but there was an air about him. Cocksure? Wolf went around the desk and leaned toward the console.

"Don't bother, Wolf. I've already disconnected it."

Deba stared at the snub-nosed revolver in Crandall's hand. Wolf pushed her behind him. "This house is filled with my people, one sound out of whack and they'll be in here."

"You'd have to press the alarm first. Don't move." Crandall wanted to pull the trigger, but he had to be sure he hit his man with the first shot. Wolf wouldn't give him a second chance. Once he'd finished Clinton he would kill the woman. "I've been waiting a long time."

"It would seem." Wolf's brain tossed information around it like marbles in a drum, but nothing computed. "Complaining about your severance pay?"

"Don't give me that aloof crap, Wolf. I know all your tricks." Crandall smothered the shudder that threatened him. Wolf's eyes were murderous.

"Good, then there's no need to elaborate." Crandall was wild-eyed; like a tinder he could burst into flame. With Aldebaran behind him, Wolf couldn't take chances.

"You took away my big chance." Anger roiled through Crandall. It would be sweet to tear Clinton's heart out of his chest. "I spent two years researching that book."

Wolf could feel Aldebaran's gasp against his back. "So that's it. You wrote the second book."

"It should have been the only book." Crandall licked his lips to take the spittle from the corner of his mouth.

"You made money on it, Crandall." If he could maneuver Aldebaran away from the desk, if he could get his hand on the ivory statuette.

"Get her out from behind you. I want to see her." Crandall fully intended to savor every moment. They had taken away the chance for fame and fortune. They had to pay. Maybe killing the woman first would be best. That would tear up Clinton. No, too chancy. He saw the movement Clinton made and steadied the gun. "Stop. Move the woman out in front."

"Why?" Wolf needed time. It didn't take a clinical psychologist to read the mad glitter in Crandall's eyes. Had it always been there? Had he been too blind to see it? Or hadn't he cared?

"I wrote the book about you," Crandall blurted, a bubble at the corner of his mouth.

"You're . . ."

"Yes, yes, it's me. I'm Camper Rayton and Dall Dillon." Crandall centered the gun on Deba, though his eyes seemed focused elsewhere. "No one ever guessed that the two writers were one person."

Deba had moved slowly away from Wolf. It hadn't taken much effort to lift the small palm-sized steel exercise ball for hand strengthening that Wolf kept on a side table. Deba kept her hand in the folds of her wedding dress.

"It would have been made into a giant of a movie. I would've been rich beyond my wildest dreams. The book and movie would have made me more important than you."

"Aren't you rich now?" Wolf saw the shadows on the windows.

Crandall stared angrily. "It isn't enough. No one knows me, who I am. I'm going to blow up the rancho. That will give me my follow-up book."

"How's your mother?"

Crandall sneered. "The whore died when I was ten."

"I can see I let my guard down with you, Crandall," Wolf said easily. "Why did your credentials check out so well? I wonder."

"I took care of that. Two actors I knew took care of the family angle for me. I outsmarted you, Wolfgang Clinton."

"So you did." Keep him talking. People would soon be

checking. Damn! Why hadn't he run a backup check on him, he'd done it with the others. The time he'd hired Crandall had been just after the shooting of Willard Temple. How many other oversights and mistakes had he made then?

Deba swallowed, not able to smother the gulping sound. There was no way she was going to let Crandall kill Wolf. Because of the book put out by her, Crandall was going to kill Wolf. Damn him to hell, he wasn't going to get away with it.

"You." Crandall fixed on her again. "How did you dare write that book? You didn't know him as I did."

"No . . . but . . . but I like money too." Had she seen people moving beyond the windows? Would they come into the study? Please, let them come.

"And you damn well made a great deal of it. How much?"

"Ah, thousands." Had the book made that much money? Why hadn't she thought to ask Chatsworth? How much did a book make? Would Crandall believe her?

"More than that. You're lying."

"My . . . my agent handles the money end of it." Where were the guards? Didn't someone know Wolf was in danger?

Chatsworth opened the door behind them. "You two hiding out in—What the hell?"

Deba underhanded the steel ball right at Crandall in just the way she'd learned to throw a bowling ball, with a hook on it and everything on it she could muster. And she did it just milliseconds before Wolf leaped and the gun fired.

"Christ!" Chatsworth wheeled around, shouting into the hall. "Hurry. Damn it. Get in here. Trouble." Then he catapulted across the room to the two men lying on the floor.

Deba moved past Chatsworth, seeing only Wolf, who lay atop Crandall. "Wolf? Wolf?" Her voice rose by shaky degrees.

"I'm all right, darling." Wolf stood. "I pushed the gun back toward him and it fired into his chest." Embracing her tightly, he kissed her over and over again. "That was some toss, you caught him in the face and stunned him."

The room filled with people as though a magician had conjured them up from the nether regions.

"Wolf." Deba clasped him. "I can't lose you."

"You won't, love." Wolf's hands slipped on her. Breath still pumped in and out of him as though a lung had collapsed. Crandall had been aiming at Aldebaran, he'd wanted to kill her.

Had he instinctively known that the best way to kill him was to take away Aldebaran?

Lazarus came into the room on the run, his body crouched and ready, rising slowly when he saw the stranger on the floor. "Dead?"

"Yes. Sweep the grounds. He didn't come alone . . . and there are explosives somewhere."

"Christ!" Lazarus nodded, going to the console and dialing. "Alarm's out here."

"I know." Wolf cuddled Deba close to him. "See? It wasn't the Cosentinos."

"He was after you." Shiver after shiver assailed her. How stupid they'd been. Looking in all the wrong places while a killer stalked Wolf. Pressing her face to his shirtfront, she inhaled, held, exhaled, inhaled, held . . . using the breathing tricks that had been taught to her when she'd been in competitive swimming. It steadied her.

The room swelled with more people, but Aldebaran didn't move, didn't release Wolf.

"Darling." Her mother approached her. "It's all right."

"He had explosives." She turned her head a fraction. "He wanted to kill Wolf."

Wolf lifted her chin. "He was aiming at you, my love, because he knew that hurting you would kill me quicker than any bullet."

Aldebaran stared up at her husband, then her gaze slid to her mother. "I can't let anything happen to Wolf, you see."

"I understand, darling, but you can release him for a moment, can't you?"

"No!"

"She's hysterical, she's not crying or screaming, that's not her way," Maria said to Deba's mother as she and Natasha tried to pry Deba's hands from Wolf.

"Let her be. I can handle things from here." Wolf reached back and punched the console, then swore when it wouldn't work. "Chatsworth. Get on the one in the office. Remind them to go slowly and safely. Don't miss anything . . . pipes, wiring, stables trees . . ."

"Done."

"And Chatsworth, call the stables. Tell the men I want the engineer to ready the chopper. We're taking the women out of here."

"I won't leave you," Deba announced roughly.

"Darling, it won't be long."

"I won't leave you."

"We've got it, sir." A staccato voice came over the loud-speaker in the console. "We repaired the wires."

"Good. Did you get my instructions?"

"Yessir. Everybody's on it and . . . Wait, sir."

"What is it? Lazarus? Where the hell are you?"

"We found it. Diffusing it now. Could you get everyone out of the house, sir?"

"Right. Where are you? Where did you find it?"

Silence.

"Answer me. Where?" Wolf had a hard-rock certainty. His chest hurt with it.

"Mrs. Clinton's closet, sir."

"Goddamn, how the hell did they get so close?"

"I don't know, sir, but I'll find out."

"Let's get out of here." In short order Wolf shepherded his guests and employees to the outer courtyard.

Maria saw the cluster of men approaching first. "Juan? What are you doing here? Why . . ."

Chatsworth hugged his wife when he noticed her cousin in handcuffs.

"Oh, no, not you, Juan." Maria stared at the disheveled man between two grim-faced guards. "You would help that criminal in there to hurt my friends?"

Juan stared at her. "You have money, cousin. I don't. And I need it just like you."

"No, not just like me, Juan." Tears coursed down Maria's cheeks.

"No one can blame you for the actions of another, dearest friend," Deba whispered.

"I don't." Wolf leaned down and kissed Maria's cheek. "If it hadn't been Juan, Crandall would have found someone else."

"That's true." Natasha took Maria's hand.

Later, when the danger had been removed and they were able to return to the rancho, Dr. and Mrs. Beene took Maria aside and spoke to her for long minutes.

Maria was appreciably happier after that.

"What did they say to her, Chatsworth?"

"What you might expect, Aldebaran. They told her how

precious she was to them because of the wonderful friendship she had given you."

"That's true." Deba kissed her friend. "We've been through a lot."

"Too much, but a great deal of it was good."

Wolf assembled them all at table. "This is a celebration, in more ways than one."

"Yes, it is, dear brother. We are all out of the closet."

Somber faces smiled, then laughed as Natasha told anecdotes and stories about the people she met while touring with the ballet company.

"I do so like your friend Maria, Aldebaran."

"So do I, Mother." Deba held her parent's hand. "I can't tell you how good it is to have you here." Much of the heaviness that had been in her heart had lifted. Perhaps in time, she and her parents would be able to bridge the long separation they'd endured.

Deba fingered the pearls at her throat. Natasha had given them to her.

Natasha turned at that moment and caught the gesture. "There are so many pieces of jewelry for you, Aldebaran. Mama kept everything segregated." Natasha snapped her fingers. "I brought the old steamer trunk with me. Why don't we go through the papers Mama kept and see what we can find?" Natasha smiled. "Mama never threw anything away."

Mrs. Beene shook her head. "Those things belong to you and Wolf, dear, and should be gone through by you."

Natasha waved away all protests. "No, no, we're all family now, and it would be fun."

Mrs. Beene smiled and nodded. "I agree."

"Let's go." Natasha laughed out loud.

When the women left the room with two of the rancho workers, Wolf looked at his father-in-law. "My people will comb the grounds, sir. No stone will be left unturned."

"I know that. But I think it's over, don't you?"

"Yes. For the first time in many years, I believe it." If only he could put aside his last deep-seated worry. He couldn't.

Marle Damon nodded. "I hated what happened, but I'm glad it came to a head. He's dead and out of our lives. The Cosentinos are crippled." Marle smiled. "And my wife is alive again."

"When I think how that demon and my wife's cousin

could have blown us to pieces, I don't feel too charitable."
Chatsworth sipped cognac from his snifter. "Maria's mother
will take it hard. She raised Juan."

"Then do your best to put her mind at ease, Chatsworth.
We blame no one but the people involved."

"I'll make sure she knows that."

"Do you think the police will keep this under wraps,
Wolf?" Marle looked concerned.

"I don't know. But I'm not as upset about it as I once
would have been."

"I don't see you as getting too unraveled," Dr. Beene said
quietly.

"Only your daughter can do that to him, sir." Chatsworth
grinned.

"Very funny." Wolf didn't care what was said. He felt
buoyant with relief that it was over. He could handle anything
as long as Aldebaran wasn't being threatened. The dark fear in
his mind was his problem, no one else's. The police had taken
the body of Crandall. Juan had been arrested. "I hope you'll all
remain at the Rancho Lobo for extended stays."

"That's kind of you, my boy, and we will stay for a time,
but we need to get back to New York and manage some business we've been neglecting. My wife and I have notes for a book
that we would like to begin writing as soon as possible."

"As your agent, I can only applaud the move." Chatsworth smiled.

"Are you taking Aldebaran on a wedding trip, Wolf?"

"Yes. I think she could use the rest." He smiled at his
father-in-law. "And if you need it, sir, I have a place overlooking Central Park. Use it as your own, please." Wolf smiled.
"Aldebaran and I will be coming to New York often to see you,
as I hope you'll be joining us here."

"That would be a delight."

Chatsworth had to wonder about the tightness around
Wolf's mouth. Was it a hangover from what Crandall had tried
to do to them?

Maria watched Aldebaran's face soften and quiver as Na-
tasha emptied the trunk of its many mementos of her husband.
Was there a shadow in her eyes still? "It's over, Aldebaran.
Wolf will let nothing bother you now."

"I know. I love him."

"Why do you sound so tragic? That's a happy thought."

"I suppose it is."

"Tell me what bothers you, Aldebaran."

"It's nothing. I'm being foolish." Besides, Natasha might overhear if she told Maria that she thought her husband wouldn't want children. What would Wolf say if she told him how badly she wanted to get pregnant? He hadn't been able to hide his reticence with her when the subject of parenting had arisen.

Maria would have quizzed her more, but Natasha brought a length of turquoise silk out of the trunk, drawing her attention.

At length they decided to join the men, following the sound of voices coming from the library.

Mrs. Beene touched her daughter's arm. "You must have loved working here, child."

"Ah, yes I did, even though Julia had me worried a time or two."

"She's devoted to her jeffe," Mrs. Beene said absently. "What's wrong, Deba darling?" The mother used the love name she'd always had for her daughter.

"Nothing, Mother. I guess I haven't digested all that's happened in the past few days. Two weddings, your return, Crandall . . ." Smiling, Deba took her mother's arm, leading her into the big room.

The mother wasn't fooled. She'd seen the sadness in her daughter's eyes.

Wolf's eyes went right to his wife's, the conversation swirling around him as he studied the woman he loved.

The others talked loosely, mentioning Crandall, Juan, what could have been, rehashing the incredible day from a more objective standpoint now that it was well over.

"I hope everyone stays, relaxes, enjoys themselves. Dr. and Mrs. Beene, this house is yours for as long as you wish, but if you don't mind, I'm taking my wife away from here. Please stay at the Rancho, all of you, and enjoy." Wolf moved toward his wife, smiling down at a surprised Aldebaran.

"I thought we were staying here, Wolf." Deba liked the hot look in his eyes; her whole being reacted to it.

"We need to talk." Looking at her parents, his smile widened. "Aldebaran and I would like you to think of this as another home, though I understand why you'd want to locate in

New York if you're writing. And if there are other locales you might prefer from time to time, I have houses all over the country that you are welcome to use and keep as your own. But please stay until we return—I know my wife has much to say to you. It would please me to get to know you better." Then he looked at the others. "Stay, Tasha. I know you want to ride around the countryside with Maria, looking for rugs and artwork for your place."

"I understand you, my brother. We'll all stay, eat your food, drink your wine, and enjoy." Natasha grinned. "Hurry. I know you need to get your wife to yourself."

"Yes." Wolf kissed his sister, his mother-in-law, and Maria, then whisked his wife from the room.

Deba was rushed through changing her clothes. "But where are we going? Wolf, stop that, you can't dress me."

"I can try. You're too slow. You don't need any more things. There, that's it."

"But, but . . ."

"Trust me, Mrs. Clinton." Her slow smile melted him, weakened him even as it gave him strength. She was inside him, curled through him like a warm caress, making his blood run faster, his heart pump with renewed vigor. "You're like vitamins to me."

Forgotten were the clothes, the new wardrobe she'd planned on wearing. Wolf was the only important factor.

Milo Crandall had done Deba a favor. He's shown her how foolish everything in life was without Wolf. Nothing had value except his love. Her fears and uncertainties would be shelved, to be brought out in time and discussed. She would make sure that she didn't soon forget the pungent, painful lessons of Milo Crandall. "Let's go."

They ran down the stairs.

"No one's around."

"Good. Let's go."

"I wanted to throw my bouquet."

"Throw it at me."

Laughing, Deba followed him from the house.

The two of them stopped, stunned at the hail of birdseed and rice that came from the onlookers in the courtyard of the rancho.

"Oh, I love it." Rearing back, Deba flung the bouquet of

baby white roses and stephanotis into the group of laughing people.

"Chatsworth, darling, you caught it. Are you supposed to do that?" Maria stared at her husband, eyes rounded in wonder. "You do the funniest things sometimes."

Titters and guffaws rippled through the onlookers.

"What the hell?" Chatsworth glared at Deba as she doubled over in laughter. "Damn you, Aldebaran, you did that on purpose."

Deba couldn't stop laughing.

"Oh, darling, you shouldn't mind. That's a wonderful omen. I'll bet our baby will be a boy."

"Maria, don't give her anything more to crow . . . What? Maria what did you say?"

"We're going to have a baby."

"I think I'm going to cry." Chatsworth grabbed his wife's hand, lifting it to his mouth, his head bent toward her.

"Are you happy, Chatsworth?"

Chatsworth nodded, speechless.

Deba went up to them. "I'd say he was ecstatic." Deba put her arms around both her friends, smothering the raw questions that rose in her. Wolf was all-important. She would remember that.

"If it's a girl I'm going to call her Natasha Aldebaran Brown." Maria hugged her friend, tears slipping down her face. "I've been so happy since knowing you, Aldebaran."

"You call being dragged across the country by a lunatic being happy? I'm getting a shrink for you, darling wife."

Professor Beene and his wife chuckled.

Marle and Natasha hooted.

Deba punched Chatsworth in the arm amid all the laughter.

"Damn it, I'll never be alone with you. I'm not waiting any longer." Wolf scooped her up and ran to the waiting jeep. "Good-bye. See you soon."

Deba was thrown against him when he started the jeep with a jerk and roared away in a spray of stones and dust, good wishes ringing on the air. "Your driving hasn't improved."

"I'll get better. I just need . . . What the hell is this?"

A Jeep raced alongside of theirs, Marle at the wheel. "Catch. It's from Natasha. Good luck." The Jeep stopped, Marle crossing his arms on the wheel, grinning from ear to ear.

"What's this?" Deba had to shout over the roar of the engine.

"Who knows? Hang on, darling."

Laughter burst from Deba. "My mother and father must think I've married a madman."

Wolf laughed. "I like them."

"And I like your family. We're shouting like fishwives. I won't say another word until we're in the helicopter, which is where I assume you're taking me."

Wolf nodded, his face alight.

The helipad came into view. Wolf lifted her out of the Jeep and into the chopper in three powerful moves.

Aloft, he looked at her and grinned. "I love you."

"You'd better get used to seeing a great deal of me. I don't have that many changes of clothes. We'll be inside a great deal wherever we go."

"Where I'm taking you, you won't need that many articles of clothing."

"A nudist camp?"

"Almost."

Lights went off in her head, dazzling shards of joy. "The lagoon."

"Yes."

"Oh, Wolf, I've wanted to go back there. When I was heading back east I used to dream of our times there."

"Those dreams were mine as well and got me through some of the hard times." Wolf thought of the dreariness of his life when Aldebaran had left him, his hunger for more, how the rancho seemed more like a prison than a haven.

Deba closed her eyes, breathing evenly. They were married! Not once, but twice! And going to the lagoon. It seemed like a wonder, not a reality. Wolf had been in her reveries so much, she'd needed and wanted him so long. Now it was over, they were together, he was hers.

Glancing at the square box in her lap, Wolf smiled. "I hope Natasha didn't put snakes in there. She said she would pay me back one day."

"You did that to her, didn't you."

Wolf nodded.

"Monster."

"Brothers were made to plague their sisters."

Deba laughed comfortably. "You must have been awful."

"I think I was, but I loved her."

Deba turned her head to watch him. "I know that. What a wonderful man you are. No woman could ask for better." When she saw the blood run from his neck into his face, she asked, "Do I embarrass you?"

"You delight me as no woman ever could. Pleasing you has become a prime force in my life, my love."

The relatively short helicopter trip seemed shorter because of the warmth and contentment between them.

"Look, there it is." Eager, Deba strained forward. "It looks wonderful. Can we swim?"

"Right away, but no diving. We had a relatively heavy meal." Wolf shuddered.

"Someone walk on your grave?"

"I can't forget how terrified you were in the underwater cave." And the terror of Crandall threatening her was still a nightmare.

"You helped me through that."

Wolf landed the air taxi and helped her to the ground.

In minutes they'd taken in the things they needed, unpacked the food that had mysteriously been there when they'd taken off. Julia had again risen to the occasion, Deba was sure.

Then they went to the bedroom to change for swimming.

"No wonder you said I didn't need clothes. Who made all the sarongs?"

"A Mayan woman I know."

Standing on tiptoe, Deba kissed him, slanting her mouth across his.

"Ouch. Damn that package that Natasha gave you." Wolf pulled back when his wife giggled. "I suppose you want to open that before we go swimming."

"Hard choice."

"What if I want to make love first?"

"Another tough pick."

"Brat." He could see the sheen of perspiration on her upper lip. She needed the cooling swim. Lifting her into his arms, he carried her from the room. "We'll cool off, then we'll take things in order."

"Sounds good." Deba pushed her face into his neck.

At the side of the lagoon, Wolf grinned at her, then jumped off the side holding her.

"Monster, I wasn't ready." Deba placed her hands on top of his head and ducked him.

For almost an hour they played and cavorted in the blue water.

Cooled and refreshed, they went back to the cottage and changed.

Wrapped in a colorful peach sarong, Deba looked at the wrapped package on the bed.

"Go on, darling, open it."

Deba laughed. "Yes, I'm dying to know what's in it."

"Oh, my," Deba whispered when she'd removed the tissue. "Emeralds."

Wolf touched the gems, shaking his head. "I'd forgotten about these. They were my mother's. They were to go to me when I married. Natasha didn't forget."

"Oh, read the card, it's beautiful."

TO MY DEAREST BROTHER AND HIS DEAREST WIFE, WITH ALL MY LOVE. I'VE WAITED A LONG TIME TO GIVE YOU THESE. OUR MOTHER WANTED THAT. IT'S HER VERY SPECIAL NOTE THAT'S IN HERE. I HAVE A FEELING SHE'D WANTED TO GIVE YOU THIS WHEN YOU WERE MUCH YOUNGER. WHO WOULD HAVE GUESSED THAT WE WOULD HAVE LOST THEM SO QUICKLY. LOVE, N.

Deba held up the slightly yellowed sealed letter with Wolf's name on the front. "From your mother."

"Yes. I knew there were some papers that had come into Natasha's possession after our father's death. I never bothered with any of them, first because I was busy building a career. Then our lives became so hectic and cut up after that, I never bothered to look at any of it."

"You're nervous."

"A little. My mother and stepfather were very special people. They loved each other so much . . . it radiated off them." Wolf looked at her. "How they would have loved you."

"Would you like some privacy?"

"No, I want you here, beside me. I won't be separated from you."

Deba nodded, wanting to be with him, cuddling close to

him as he carefully slit the envelope and unfolded the two
sheets of parchment stationery.

> My darling son, I wanted to tell this myself. If
> you're reading this, it's because I didn't have time to
> tell you any of it before my death. I hope that's not
> the case. . . .

Wolf paused, shaking his head, tears in his eyes.

> It's only fair that you know that Willard C. Tem-
> ple was not your real father. Thank God. . . .

The papers fluttered to the floor.

Deba clutched Wolf. His face was paper-white. Could this
be real? Anger and shock tremored through her. Willard C.
Temple must have known. He'd tortured Wolf. How she hated
him.

Anxiety and joy warred in him. Could he believe what he
was reading? It would be too wonderful.

> I wanted to marry your father, Anton Sharansky,
> but he was in the Soviet Union and I'd been told he
> was dead . . . by Willard C. Temple. I married him
> when I was prostrate with grief and not thinking
> clearly. He hated me for loving Anton. He hated you
> on sight because he knew you were Anton's baby. You
> see, Willard C. Temple was sterile. What a blessing! I
> hope you stay clear of him. It took years to divorce
> him, and he swore vengeance. It has always been my
> feeling that he would revenge himself on you. Willard,
> I'm sure, is mentally ill, but he's also canny and dan-
> gerous. Stay out of his way. I hope you are happy with
> the news I give you, my beloved son.

> > Love,
> > Mother

> P.S. Anton doesn't know this either. I've had the
> strange feeling, right from the start of our marriage,
> that I had to protect him from Willard, any way I
> could. Not mentioning Willard's name helped. You
> see, if Anton discovers you're his son, he will move
> heaven and earth to make you his legally. He loves

you so . . . but then Willard could do something vile
and I can't chance it. Hopefully Anton and I will out-
live him. And anyway we've had darling Natasha, and
of course Anton loved you like a son from the start.
You see, Anton got out of the Soviet Union and tried
to find me. When he did, I began divorce proceedings.
How Willard hated that, but he couldn't fight the battery of lawyers Anton put against him. My darling
boy, I love you. If Willard is dead, tell your father
what I've told you, otherwise keep it a secret. It will
make Anton so happy to know you are his.

Wolf dropped the papers and turned to her, taking her in
his arms. "Darling, hold me."

"I'll never let you go."

"I feared for any children we might have, that they could
have his genes. Now we don't have to worry about that." Wolf
shuddered against her.

"I never did. I thought our child would be just like you. I
love you, Wolfgang Clinton."

"And I love you, Aldebaran McCloud Beene Clinton."

"Shall we change our name to Sharansky?"

Wolf shook his head. "I think Anton knows, wherever he
is."

"He's with your mother, Wolf."

"He didn't know, did he?"

Wolf shook his head. "He would have said something to
me." There was a sudden wrenching pain in his middle. Loss!
Knowledge that Anton was his father, lost to him all those
years. "He'd just gotten over a bout of pneumonia. It was his
first time back conducting. On the way to rehearsal there was
an accident . . ."

"What are you thinking?" The scar running from his left
eye to his chin whitened, puckering in on itself, his golden eyes
molten all at once.

"That maybe the accident to my father wasn't accidental."

"Temple?"

"Maybe."

Frost moved over his features, crystallizing the scar, stroking down into his being. The hard, crusty surface of Wolfgang
Clinton, who'd suffered under the hands of men but who'd protected himself, iced over once more. The old armor began coat-

ing his skin, putting a glitter in his eyes, slashing his mouth. Fear mounted in Deba as she watched the granite overlay deepen, the surface that would keep all out, fix and harden. "Darling?"

"Umm?" For a moment the hard mask slipped and the happy man looked through.

"You have a fine network of people working for you. Let's get them to chase down the facts on Willard C. Temple. Let's find out the truth."

Wolf blinked at her. "I was thinking that but it surprises me that you'd want that."

"I want anything that buries that macabre excuse for a man. Whatever it takes to put him in the back closet of our minds where he belongs, I would do. Hasn't he taken enough of your life, enough of your mother's, enough of Natasha's?"

"Yes."

"Then let's bury him, so he doesn't take you away from me."

Wolf reached for her, his mouth working over hers, his tongue twisting lovingly with hers. "No one could do that."

Deba placed her hands on each side of his face, forcing his eyes to look into hers. "Yes, yes, Willard C. Temple could, and he is now, unless we stop him. How he'd laugh. If he knew that he had crippled our love by making you doubt, hate, curse his existence, then he'd crow in hell, wouldn't he? Because he would win."

Wolf stared at her for long moment, his smile twisting. "How come you're so smart?"

"I'm like a wild animal who scents danger to my own, my darling. If coming out of my corner scratching, kicking, and biting will save us, I'll do that. That evil being, Willard C. Temple, will not destroy us from whatever home of Beelzebub he inhabits. He can't have you. You're mine."

"I am indeed." Blackness lifted from his soul. Clear vision made him buoyant. Joy in his woman made him far-seeing, strong. "We'll start the investigation when we get back, and we'll clean out every dark corner. For now, we'll put him in the garbage can . . ."

"Where he belongs."

". . . and have our honeymoon." Wolf touched her cheek. "I'm hungry for you."

"I'm half starved for you."

"Only half." Wolf pulled her to her feet. "Want to swim again?" He needed that exercise, that massaging of body and mind that the water could bring.

"Oh, yes, I would like that myself. In fact I can't wait to get in that water again." Scoring her fingernail lightly down the now softened scar, she looked into his eyes. "Just one among many things I can't wait to do."

"Sensuous woman, I love you." Wolf turned her around, lifted her hair, and kissed her nape. Then he reached around her and untied the sarong knot under her breasts. "This isn't suitable for swimming, Mrs. Clinton."

"I knew that." She looked over her shoulder. "Just think of the wonderful surprise you'll have for Natasha when we return."

Wolf grinned. "Maybe I shouldn't tell her. When she was little she always told me that since I was her big brother, I had to dance the ballet too."

"So you think she'll force your hand now?"

"You know Natasha. What do you think?"

"Oh, darling, I can wait to see you in a tutu."

"Leotard, lady, leotard."

"And you have such yummy legs that you'll have to shave. Ooo, I could do that. Oops! There goes that blush again."

"I told you what happens when you say sexy things to me. You arouse me."

"Everything arouses you."

"Everything about you, yes." He stood her on her feet, and the sarong slid to the floor. Turning her around, he gazed at her. Her breasts, bare and proud, caught his gaze, the nipples hardening. "Darling, are you getting aroused too?" Her body was a luscious pink pearl that beckoned him.

"Naughty, you shouldn't notice." Deba's hand went out to him and feathered over the front of his trousers. "Ummm."

"Yes." Wolf went down on his knees in front of her, easing her silky briefs down her legs. In slow, sweet strokes he kissed the flesh of her thighs.

Deba placed both her hands on his shoulders, kneading there, pressing the flesh and bones that were so precious to her.

Wolf took his time, his gaze roving her hotly. When he reached for her wedding shoes and slipped them on her bare feet, he inhaled shakily. "Fantasy time," he murmured, kissing the warm sweet juncture between her thighs with open mouth.

"What fantasy?"

"You standing front of me with nothing but satin high heels on. Lady, you destroy me." Wolf clamped his arms around her buttocks and lifted her as he stood.

"I'll hit my head on the ceiling," Deba said, laughing, loving the strength of her man.

"Duck."

"Wait, I have to get my suit."

"Nope."

The water was the same blue velvet of a short time past that feathered and massaged the skin like a careful lover, but there was an even greater luster of joy to it now.

Deba struck out strongly, knowing her husband was right at her heels. Wheeling over onto her back, she floated, her eyes on the blue sky, the slashes of powdery clouds, the wonder, the peace. Thank you for giving me Wolf.

"Did you just speak?" Wolf came up under her, cushioning her.

"Yes, I was giving thanks for you."

"Darling, I'm the one who's thankful. You gave me life." He turned her so that she floated atop him.

"All the gin joints in all the world and you hadda walk into mine."

"Your Bogie is awful, Aldebaran . . . and you walked into mine."

"I never did get a part in Diego's movie."

"I'll make movies of you every day of our life if you like."

"Just hold me and never leave me."

"Come live with me and be my love."

"I will, I will."

The months flew by. Deba had nothing but joy with Wolf. "Even when we argue, it's fun. I like making up." Deba yawned hugely. "Stop staring, I'm not going to explode tonight." She teased him constantly about his total concentration on her all during her pregnancy, but nothing wiped the concern from his eyes.

Wolf had even taken the prenatal exercises with her and had read every pamphlet he could find on the La Leche League.

But that night when she woke she knew before the spasm wrenched her that it was time for their child to be born. "Wolf?"

They'd elected to remain in New York for the birth, and Natasha and Marle had come East to stay with Chatsworth and Maria.

"Will you call them from the hospital?" Deba was sure he was going to get a ticket. Speeding through Manhattan? Insane!

"Who? Never mind. I want you to relax and pant, pant, pant. Stop laughing. This isn't funny. We're in labor."

"Yessir. Oooo."

"Damn that cab."

The flurry of getting into the hospital was overcome by the expedience of Wolf's carrying Deba and bellowing at everyone to get things prepared.

The labor was hard but not long.

"What do you think of your son and daughter, Wolfgang Clinton?" Twins! Even the doctors were surprised. One of the twins had been behind the other, so it had looked like one baby on the scan.

"Aldebaran, I love you." He bent over her, kissing her gently.

When the babies were a few months old, cosseted by their aunts Maria and Natasha, Wolf flew Deba to Mexico, not to Casa Lobo but to their private lagoon.

"Back to the scene of the crime, Aldebaran." Wolf kissed her shoulder as he lifted her out of the water. "Are you happy?"

"I never dreamed there could be such happiness, Wolf. You did that for me."

"As you did for me." He kissed her gently.

The passion, as it always had since the first time, erupted between them at once. Mouth locked to mouth, they sank down next to the lagoon.

The hot sun turned the water to diamond fire as they took each other in covenant and love for all time.

From the promise of passion to the peaks of desire...